About the Authors

USA Today bestselling, award-winning author **Lisa Childs** has written more than eighty-five novels. Published in twenty countries, she's also appeared on the *Publisher's Weekly*, Barnes & Nobles and Nielsen Top 100 bestseller lists. Lisa writes contemporary romance, romantic suspense, paranormal and women's fiction. She's a wife, mum, bonus mum, an avid reader and a less avid runner. Readers can reach her through Facebook or her website lisachilds.com

Cindi Myers became one of the most popular people in eighth grade when she and her best friend wrote a torrid historical romance and passed the manuscript around among friends. Fame was short-lived, alas; the English teacher confiscated the manuscript. Since then, Cindi has written more than fifty published novels. Her historical and contemporary romances and women's fiction have garnered praise from reviewers and readers alike.

New York Times and *USA Today* bestselling author **B.J. Daniels** lives in Montana with her husband, Parker, and two springer spaniels. When not writing, she quilts, boats and plays tennis. Contact her at bjdaniels.com, on Facebook at B.J. Daniels or through her reader group the B.J. Daniels' Big Sky Darlings, and on twitter at bjdanielsauthor

Indecent Proposals

Indecent Proposals:
The Shotgun Wedding

LISA CHILDS

CINDI MYERS

B.J. DANIELS

MILLS & BOON

First Published in Great Britain 2022
By Mills & Boon, an imprint of HarperCollins*Publishers,* Ltd
1 London Bridge Street, London, SE1 9GF

www.harpercollins.co.uk

HarperCollins*Publishers*
1st Floor, Watermarque Building,
Ringsend Road, Dublin 4, Ireland

INDECENT PROPOSALS: THE SHOTGUN WEDDING © 2022 Harlequin
Enterprises ULC

Explosive Engagement © 2014 Lisa Childs
Snowblind Justice © 2019 Cynthia Myers
Wedding at Cardwell Ranch © 2014 Barbara Heinlein

ISBN: 978-0-263-30570-8

MIX
Paper from
responsible sources
FSC™ C007454

This book is produced from independently certified FSC™ paper
to ensure responsible forest management.

For more information visit: www.harpercollins.co.uk/green

Printed and Bound in Spain using 100% Renewable electricity at
CPI Black Print, Barcelona

EXPLOSIVE ENGAGEMENT

LISA CHILDS

For my family—with great appreciation for all your love and support. Love you all!

Prologue

The bomb was set, so he carefully closed the door. When it opened again, the timer would activate—giving the victim mere minutes before the explosion. He exited the back door and breathed a sigh of relief that he was out of danger.

No. He wasn't out of danger yet—not until the bomb claimed its intended victim. He didn't enjoy killing, but he'd done it—more than once—out of necessity. He'd had to do it to protect himself.

That was all he was doing now—making sure that no one was left alive to link him to his crimes. Then, after all these years, he might finally have peace.

Chapter One

The sun shone brightly, setting the white bricks of the church aglow. It was a great day for a wedding. But Logan Payne couldn't forget that a funeral was also taking place today. He'd thought it might finally bring him some peace that his father's killer was dead. But it seemed more like an injustice that the man had lived for only fifteen years of his already too short sentence.

Maybe it was that sense of injustice that had made Logan uneasy. Or maybe it was the recent attempts on his life.

But he pushed aside that uneasiness and focused instead on the bride and groom. He lifted his hand, with birdseed stuck to his palm, and waved off his younger brother and his new bride. Nobody deserved happiness more than the two of them—especially after the hell they had endured to be together.

His sister, Nikki, glanced up at him through the tears glistening in her warm brown eyes. "Getting emotional, big bro?" she teased. Their family relentlessly teased each other.

The tears were all hers, but he played along. "Birdseed got in my eye," he said with an exaggerated blink. But then he squinted at a random glare and glanced toward the street where his brother's decorated SUV sat on the curb. Nikki had written Just Married across the back window and tied strings of pop cans to the rear bumper. A car slowly passed it, and as it did, a barrel protruded out of the dark tinted driver's window.

The SUV shielded the bride and groom, but Logan and his sister and his twin were exposed on the steps of the church. As the shots rang out, he knocked Nikki down and lunged at Parker, knocking him over the railing.

The shots weren't meant for any of his siblings. He knew that. But he had been standing too close to Nikki. And his twin was identical—same black hair, same blue eyes, same features. Today they were even both wearing black tuxedos. Logan covered Nikki's petite frame, shielding her with his body. And he tensed, waiting for the bullets to find their target in his flesh.

Tires squealed as the car rounded the corner and drove off. After a glance over his shoulder to make certain the shooter was gone, Logan helped his sister to her feet. She trembled with fear in his arms, but she was unhurt. Miraculously, Logan hadn't been hit, either.

The bride, Tanya, turned away from the SUV and ran back to the church. The groom, Cooper, was right beside her, yelling the name of his missing brother. "Parker!"

A hand rose above the shrubs on the side of the church's wide front steps. Cooper clasped it and pulled Parker from the branches and foliage.

"You okay?" Cooper asked him.

"Yeah, yeah," Parker replied as he brushed off his tux. "Logan knocked me over and pushed down Nikki." He waited—probably for Logan to make some smart-aleck comeback. That was the way the Paynes handled stuff— emotional stuff, dangerous stuff…with gallows humor.

But Logan couldn't find any humor in this situation. The grudge he'd been carrying, and how he'd acted on that grudge, was what had nearly killed his family. And these weren't the first attempts made on his life and Parker's, who must have been mistaken for him then, too.

"I'm sorry," he said.

His new sister-in-law's voice trembled with concern as she said, "I thought it was over. Mr. Gregory is dead."

Logan had been the one who'd taken the shot that had ended the life of her grandfather's lawyer. The man had been trying to kill her so that no one would discover that he'd embezzled her inheritance.

"This isn't about you," Logan assured the beautiful blonde bride. Guilt twisted his guts into knots. He hated that this shooting—that *his* problem—had marred what had finally been the perfect wedding for Tanya and Cooper. "This is about me. And revenge…"

Cooper's eyes, which were the same blue as his and Parker's, narrowed with suspicion, and he accused him, "You know who it is."

Anger, more intense and overwhelming than his guilt, surged through Logan. He knew who was behind all these cowardly shootings. He knew and he was damn well going to put a stop to it.

FOR THE FIRST time in fifteen years, Stacy Kozminski didn't have to go through prison security to see her father. All she had to do was walk up the aisle of the dimly lit church to where he lay in a casket before the altar. But that walk was the most difficult she had ever taken. Her knees trembled with each step she took, shaking more the closer she got to the altar.

To the casket…

The lid was open, but she needed to take a few more steps to see past the flower arrangements. Her knees shook even harder, threatening to give out beneath her. Maybe she would have crumpled right there, but a strong arm wrapped around her waist in support.

She uttered a sigh of relief that at least one of her brothers had showed up…because she had been the first and only family member to arrive at the church. With a smile on her lips, she turned her head, but the smile froze when her gaze collided with Logan Payne's.

His blue eyes icy hard with anger, he stared down at her.

He was mad at *her?* She was the one who should be angry—furious even because he had no right to show up at her father's funeral at all—let alone wearing a tuxedo. Her heart skipped a beat before the rate sped up. He looked damn good in the black tux with the pleated white shirt. The black bow tie had already been undone and the once-white silk shirt was a little smudged and rumpled. But still…

She hated him; she reminded herself of that as she jerked away from the unsettling warmth of his long, hard body. "What the hell are you doing here?"

And why had he put his arm around her? He was the last person from whom she would ever expect support—especially today.

"I think you know," he replied, his deep voice vibrating with anger.

She shook her head. "I have no idea…unless you want to make sure that he's really dead…"

With a trembling hand, she gestured toward the casket and toppled over one of the flower arrangements. The vase rolled across the tiled floor, leaving a trail of multicolored petals and water behind it. She gasped at what she'd done.

But Logan Payne didn't react. He was staring at the casket. Maybe she had been right about his reason for coming.

She followed his gaze to her father's corpse. She'd already seen it when he'd died. She had made it to the prison in time to say goodbye. Wasn't that supposed to have given her closure?

Stacy felt no calm acceptance. No gratefulness. She felt nothing but anger—all toward Logan Payne. So she turned back to him, and then she turned *on* him. Literally lashing out at him in her anger, she swung her hand toward his unfairly handsome face.

The man had some crazy reflexes, because he caught her wrist, stopping her palm just short of one of his chiseled cheekbones. Despite not slapping him, her skin tingled—maybe with the need to slap him yet. Maybe because he was touching her, his long fingers wrapped easily and tightly around her narrow wrist.

"I can't believe even you are such a heartless bastard that you'd show up at my father's funeral," she said, lashing out now with her words. "And in a tux, no less."

He glanced down at himself, as if he'd forgotten what he was wearing.

"But then I guess this is a celebration for you," she continued. "Do you intend to dance on his grave at the cemetery, too?"

She would make damn sure of it that he never got the chance—even if she had to throw him out herself since no other mourners had arrived yet. Where the hell were her brothers?

They had always been there for her when she needed them most. Until today...

"I've already been dancing," Logan replied.

She struggled against his grasp; she didn't want a man capable of such a hateful comment touching her.

"At my brother's wedding," he continued.

That explained the tux.

"But then somebody tried to kill me," he said. "Again."

That explained his white shirt being smudged and rumpled and his thick black hair disheveled, as if he'd been running his hands through it. What would it feel like? Coarse or soft? Not that she cared to ever find out. She didn't want to touch Logan Payne, and she sure as hell didn't want him touching her.

So she tried again to wriggle free of his hold. "Why are you telling me this?" she asked. "Do you think I care?"

"I think you're behind it," he said.

"Me?" She hadn't even been able to slap him. "How am I supposed to have tried to kill you?"

"You shot at me," he said.

"I don't own a gun." Her brothers had tried to give her one for protection, but she'd refused. Her protection had a threatening growl and a mouthful of sharp teeth to back up his threats. Too bad she hadn't been able to bring Cujo to the funeral.

He snorted derisively, as if he doubted her. Of course he doubted her; Logan Payne doubted *everyone*.

"You're doing it again," she said. "Accusing someone of a crime they didn't commit." She turned back to the casket. Her father was only in his early fifties but he looked much older. Prison had turned his brown hair white and etched deep lines in his tense face. Wasn't he supposed to look peaceful, like he was sleeping? But even in death, her father had found no peace—probably because of Logan Payne.

"I didn't accuse your father," he reminded her. "He was caught at the scene. He was tried and convicted."

"Of murder," she said. Shaking her head yet at the injustice, she added, "My father was not a murderer."

Patek Kozminski had been a lot of things—by his own admission—but he could have never taken a life. The judge and jury had come to the wrong conclusion.

"He killed my father," Logan said with all the rage and

anguish as if it had just happened yesterday instead of fifteen years ago.

She shook her head again.

"My father caught him in the commission of a felony…"

Logan Payne was no longer a police officer, but he still talked like one. His father had been a police officer, too, who'd caught her father robbing a jewelry store.

"He resisted arrest," he continued, "they struggled over the gun. And my father wound up dead."

"My father did not kill him." The man she'd known and loved wouldn't have resisted arrest; he wouldn't have fought with a police officer. He wouldn't have wrestled the gun away from him and shot him with it. There had to have been someone else there that horrible day, someone else who'd really committed the crime…

"My father is dead," Logan said.

"And now so is mine," she said, gesturing again to the casket, but this time she was careful not to knock over any flower arrangements. "Are you happy?"

Logan sighed. "No."

"No, of course not," she hotly agreed. "You would have rather he lived many, many more years and spent every one of them behind bars. That's why you showed up at every parole hearing to make sure he didn't get out."

"He killed a man!" Logan said.

Tears stung her eyes, and she shook her head. "No, no, he didn't…" There had to have been someone else…

"The judge and jury convicted him," he said it almost gently now, as if Logan Payne had any concern for her feelings.

He hadn't, or he would have stopped showing up at the parole hearings; he would have let her father get out of prison. If not for Logan fighting it, her father would have been granted parole. He had been a model prisoner.

He had been a model father, too—even from behind bars. Now she had no father at all. She could almost relate to Logan's rage, but hers was directed at him.

"He wasn't convicted of murder, though," he said, correcting her earlier comment. "It was manslaughter."

"Which is why he had been up for parole already four times." And why he would have been released...if not for Logan Payne.

"It should have been murder," he said. "The charge was too light. So was the sentence..."

"The sentence wound up being death," she said. "You gave him that sentence."

"I didn't—"

"If you hadn't showed up at those hearings, he would have been released. He wouldn't have been there for that crazy prisoner to stab. He wouldn't have been behind bars with animals like that!" She swung her other hand now. But his damn reflexes were so fast that he caught her wrist again. She struggled against his grasp and cursed him.

But Logan didn't even blink at her insults. His gaze remained steady and intense on her face. He was always so damn intense. Despite her rising temper, her flesh tingled and chilled, lifting goose bumps on her skin—even skin that was covered by her new black sweater dress.

"What the hell's going on?" a familiar voice demanded to know.

"Get your damn hands off her, Payne!" another voice chimed in.

Her brothers had finally arrived. She'd wanted them earlier—to be there for support over her father's funeral. But now she felt a rush of fear as they ran down the aisle toward her and Logan. She was actually afraid for Logan because her brothers were very protective of her—to the point that they had even killed for her.

Were they about to do that again?

Chapter Two

Logan released her—so abruptly that Stacy stumbled back. He would have reached for her again, just to steady her, but one of her brothers caught her. The other one reached for him. Garek or Milek—he didn't know who was whom. They weren't twins, but they looked nearly as much alike as he and Parker did. These guys were tall, too, but with blond hair and gray eyes.

Stacy had the same smoky-gray eyes—with thick lashes she kept blinking. Not to flirt with him—he was the last man she'd ever flirt with—but to fight back tears over her father's death. Her hair wasn't as blond as her brothers. It had streaks of brown and bronze and gold.

He jerked away from whichever brother was grabbing at him. Then he dodged the fist the man swung, even more easily than he had dodged Stacy's attempts to slap him. Maybe he should have just let her hit him. Maybe then she would have gotten the revenge she sought.

No. He doubted her quest for revenge would be satisfied until he was as dead as their fathers.

She might have been telling the truth about not owning a gun. But she didn't need to; she had brothers who would do anything she told them and that was the same as pulling the trigger.

He reached beneath the tuxedo jacket for *his* gun.

"Really?" Stacy asked, her voice shaking with anger. "You're going to pull a gun at my father's funeral?"

He paused with his hand on his holster. "Would you rather I just let them kill me?" He mentally smacked himself for the dumb comment. Of course she would rather he just let them. That was the whole point of trying to murder him.

"They're not going to kill you."

"Don't lie to him, Stace," one of them said.

"You're not going to kill him," she said with a meaningful glare at both of her brothers. "We are not going to ruin our father's funeral."

And that was the only reason that she wouldn't let them kill him *here*—in the dark church with its dingy stained-glass windows and scratched up tile floor. It wasn't as pretty and bright as the church he'd just left—the one his mother had bought and turned into a wedding chapel and reception hall.

"You don't think he's ruining it," one of the brothers asked, "by showing up here in a freaking tuxedo?"

Regret flashed through Logan, but he'd been so damn angry—and with damn good reason—that he hadn't considered how he was dressed before he'd rushed over from one church to another. "Sorry, I didn't have a chance to change between my brother's wedding and getting shot at."

"*If* you were shot at during your brother's wedding, maybe it had something to do with him or his bride," she said. "Why do you automatically assume it had anything to do with me or my family?"

"Because it did," he said with total certainty.

She shook her head. "We can't be the only enemies you've ever made."

Probably not, but he wasn't about to admit that to *her*. "Usually people appreciate what I do for them."

"You expect us to *appreciate* you keeping our father

in prison?" she asked, her gray eyes widening with shock and outrage.

"Let me kill him," one of the brothers pleaded with her.

She was younger than them, but she was definitely the one calling the shots, literally, in the Kozminski family. She stared at her father's body lying in the bronze casket and shook her head. "Not here, Garek."

Not "no," just "not here."

"And you wonder why I think it's you behind the attempts on my life…"

"Attempts?" she repeated.

The one she'd called Garek laughed. "And there's your proof that it's not us," he said. "We wouldn't have had to try more than once to kill you."

"I own a security firm," he reminded them. "I will not be easy to kill."

"I don't know…" the other brother, Milek, mused as he walked around Logan. "You showed up here alone."

"He's not alone," a deep voice very much like his own announced from the back of the church.

Of course Parker would have figured out where he'd gone. But he hadn't come alone, either. Their little sister had tagged along like she always had when they were kids. She hadn't outgrown that annoying habit yet. Fortunately, one of Payne Protection Agency's most loyal employees had come along, too. Candace Baker stood next to Parker, her hand beneath her jacket, probably on her holster.

Instead of being grateful for the backup, Logan was incredibly annoyed with the interference. And the doubt. He could take care of himself and them, and he had proven that again and again.

"What the hell are all of you doing here?" he demanded to know.

"Mom sent us," his twin replied.

"Of course she did." Their mother had a problem remembering that *he* ran Payne Protection—not her. Logan had overlooked her interference when it had involved her matchmaking his brother with his new bride. But he didn't want her interfering in his life. "She had no right…"

"That didn't stop *you*," Stacy bitterly remarked.

"I had no right to what, dear?" Penny Payne asked as she joined them in the church. Unlike him and Parker who wore the wedding tuxedos, she'd changed from her bronze-colored mother-of-the-bride gown into a black dress. She hadn't been on the steps to see off Cooper and Tanya. She must have been changing then—as if she'd always intended to attend the funeral of the man who'd murdered her husband.

"Why are you here, Mom?" he asked. He doubted he would ever understand her, but neither had his father. It hadn't stopped Nicholas Payne from loving her, though. And it wouldn't stop Logan, either, unless he wound up like his father: dead at the hands of a Kozminski.

Out of respect for Mrs. Payne, Stacy motioned her brothers back, but they were already stepping away from Logan. They wouldn't touch him now—not in front of his mother. She couldn't promise they wouldn't exact some revenge later.

Even now she wondered…

Could one of them have fired those shots at the wedding? Her heart pounded heavily with dread and fear. She couldn't lose one of them like she'd lost her father—to prison. They had both already spent too much time behind bars.

And she couldn't lose Logan Payne, either. Not for herself. She didn't care about him. But his mother loved him. And it would kill her to lose a child like she'd lost her husband.

Mrs. Payne swung her hand toward that child's face. His

reflexes weren't fast enough to stop her palm from connecting with his cheek. It wasn't quite a slap but a very forceful pat. "Why are *you* here?" she asked him.

"You must have heard the gunshots outside the church," he replied. "Somebody tried to kill me again."

Her hand trembled against his cheek, and she sucked in a shaky breath before asking, "Again?"

He groaned as if in regret at his slip or embarrassment of her concern. "Mom…"

Stacy's lips twitched at how close Logan Payne came to sounding like a petulant child. Even when he'd been a child of just seventeen at her father's trial, he had already seemed like a man. Strong. Intimidating. Independent.

"You don't need to be concerned," he assured his mother. "I'm putting a stop to it now. That's why I'm here."

"How is coming here putting a stop to anything?" Mrs. Payne asked, her usually smooth brow furrowed with confusion.

"You know how," he said.

"No, I don't." She shook her head.

"It's one of them," he insisted, but his gaze focused on Stacy.

"I don't understand," his mother continued. "Did you see one of them with the gun?"

Logan shook his head now.

"Then you have no business coming here today of all days," she said, "unless you've come to express your condolences and pay your respects."

"Is that why you're here?" he asked, his deep voice vibrating with betrayal. "Are you here to pay your respects to the man who killed your husband…who killed my father?"

Stacy's heart lurched with the pain in his voice. He was wrong about who'd taken his dad, but he'd still lost him, even sooner than she'd lost hers. At least she had been able to see her father the past fifteen years even though it had been behind bars.

"I am here for Stacy," Mrs. Payne replied, and her arm came around Stacy's shoulders.

She'd tried so hard to be strong—to be tough like her brothers and like Logan. But Mrs. Payne's warmth and affection crumbled the wall she'd built around herself so many years ago. Her shoulders began to shake like her knees had earlier.

"Is it okay with you that I'm here?" Mrs. Payne asked. "If it's too difficult, we'll all leave…"

"That would be best," a woman chimed in.

Stacy glanced up to see her aunt and uncle walking down the aisle toward them. Aunt Marta was tall and thin with frosted blond hair and a frosty personality. Uncle Iwan's hair had thinned while his body had widened. He was a big, imposing man, but he smiled at her. Aunt Marta glared. That look wasn't meant for Mrs. Payne but for Stacy. She'd been on the receiving end of it many times, but she was not yet immune to the coldness and shivered.

Mrs. Payne wrapped her arm more tightly around her, as if protecting her. She had done that in court fifteen years ago. A new widow then, she had still found sympathy for the daughter of the man convicted of killing her husband. Mrs. Payne had attended other court dates in Stacy's life—offering her support when Milek and Garek had faced their charges.

Stacy clutched at the older woman's waist. "Please," she murmured through the emotion choking her, "please stay…"

Mrs. Payne nodded. "Whatever you need, honey…"

Logan reached out a hand for his mother as if to tug her away from Stacy. He did not have Mrs. Payne's forgiving soul and warm heart. He was full of hatred and bitterness.

But then his fingers curled into his palm and he pulled back his hand.

"We'll discuss this later," he said.

Stacy knew he spoke to her, not his mother, and his words were a threat. He still considered her and her family responsible for the attempts on his life. And she wasn't entirely convinced he was wrong, especially with the way her brothers eyed him. He wasn't the only one in that church who was full of hatred and bitterness.

For the next hour those feelings were put aside, though, for grief and loss during the funeral mass and burial. While the others left for the funeral luncheon at what had been her father's favorite pub, she stayed behind at his grave site.

But she was not alone. She stared down at the fresh dirt covering her father's grave. A light breeze fluttered the leaves in the trees and tumbled the loose soil across the grave. She shivered at the cold, but it wasn't the breeze chilling her. It was the loss.

"I'm sorry," Mrs. Payne said. She hadn't gone with the others to the pub. She had stayed behind with Stacy, continuing to offer her support and sympathy. If only Stacy's own mother was as loving and affectionate…

But she was like Aunt Marta—she loved money and herself more than anyone else. Even her own children…

Stacy shook her head. "You have no reason to apologize."

"I am apologizing for my son," Mrs. Payne explained.

Knowing how much Logan would hate that, Stacy smiled and finally pulled her gaze away from the ground to face the older woman. "He's thirty-two years old. His mother should not be making apologies for him any longer."

Mrs. Payne smiled, too. "*She* has to when he's too stubborn to do it himself."

"He doesn't think he has a reason to apologize," Stacy

pointed out. "He thinks he's right." He always thought he was right.

"You are not responsible for those attempts on his life," Mrs. Payne defended her.

The woman's faith in Stacy warmed her heart. Not many other people in her life had trusted her so fully.

"No, I'm not," she said. Just like her father, she was not a killer.

Mrs. Payne's eyes were warm and brown but they had the same intensity of her son's blue eyes as her gaze focused on Stacy's face. "But you're not entirely certain someone in your family didn't fire those shots."

Stacy sucked in a breath of shock. Had Mrs. Payne really been offering her support, or had she been manipulating her into betraying her brothers?

"I can see your doubts."

Like her, they blamed Logan for their father's death. He hadn't put the shiv in him, but he had made certain that he stayed in prison long enough that someone else had. Her brothers had even suggested that Logan might have hired the other inmate to commit the murder. She didn't believe that; she knew Logan hadn't wanted her father dead. He'd just wanted him to suffer. And he hadn't cared that she'd suffered, too. Her brothers had cared, though—maybe too much.

But in reply to Mrs. Payne's remark, Stacy shook her head again in denial. She would not betray her brothers. She owed them too much: her life.

"I don't expect you to admit it," Mrs. Payne said. "You're too loyal for that—too protective of them."

She wasn't nearly as protective of them as her brothers were of her. They had sacrificed so much to keep her safe. She would do the same.

"And you're protective of your son," Stacy said. She'd

seen how shaken the woman had been that there had been attempts on his life. "Is that why you're here?"

"I'm here for you," Mrs. Payne insisted. "But if Logan is right…" She shuddered. "I can't lose him like I lost his father." She reached out again and took Stacy's hand in hers. "And I don't want you to lose your brothers, either."

Tears of frustration stung Stacy's eyes. "I can't…"

But as Mrs. Payne had seen, she already doubted them. Even if they weren't the ones attempting to kill him, they could be picked up on suspicion because they'd been so angry and so vocal about their hatred of Logan. She swallowed a lump of emotion. "I'll talk to them, make sure that they're not behind the shootings."

Mrs. Payne sighed. "It's too bad you have to have that conversation—that you have to show them you doubt them, that you think they could be responsible, that you think they could be killers."

After all they'd done for her, she didn't want to hurt them any more than they were already hurting. They had lost their father, too. "Then what do I do?"

Mrs. Payne squeezed her hand. "You marry him."

"What?" She couldn't have heard her right. It was like the words her father had uttered on his dying breath—incomprehensible.

"Your brothers would never do anything to hurt you," Mrs. Payne said. "So if they believe you're in love with Logan, they won't hurt him."

"I—I can't convince them of such a blatant lie…"

"You can if you marry him…"

Marry the man she despised more than any other? It just wasn't conceivable. She wasn't the only one shocked and appalled at such a terrible union.

A deep gasp drew her attention away from Mrs. Payne to her son. Logan stood near a monument behind her. His blue eyes were wide with shock and horror at his mother's outrageous suggestion. Then his lips began to move. But no words were uttered, or if they were, the shots drowned out his voice.

Gunshots reverberated throughout the cemetery, echoing around the monuments and trees. The sudden loud noise sent the birds flying from the tree limbs to form a dark cloud in the sky above them.

Not only had Logan Payne intruded on her father's funeral but so had his killer. Mrs. Payne's plan was never going to happen, because Stacy would probably wind up burying him before she could ever marry him.

Chapter Three

Pain gripped Logan's shoulder, but he ignored the hot streak down his arm as he reached for his holster and drew his weapon. "Get down!" he shouted.

His mother had instinctively ducked behind a cement monument. But Stacy stood still at her father's freshly dug grave, so when he knocked her down, she hit soft ground. Her breath left her lips in a gasp of warm air that caressed his neck.

And her soft curves cushioned his fall. She always acted so strong that he had expected her to be hard and cold. But she was soft and warm. She was also smaller than her big personality and more fragile than her tough attitude.

"Are you okay?" he asked as the shots continued to ring out, knocking leaves and twigs from the trees so they rained down on them like debris during a hurricane. For some reason he felt as though he were in the middle of a storm and not just of gunfire but of emotion.

Had his mother really suggested what he'd thought he heard? No. He must have misconstrued her words. Not even she was a big enough matchmaker to consider a marriage between him and Stacy Kozminski at all possible.

Stacy stared up at him through gray eyes wide with shock but hopefully not pain.

"Were you hit?" he asked. "Are you hurt?"

Eyes still wide, she finally moved as she shook her head. "Mom?" he called out. "Mom?"

"I—I'm okay," she replied, but her voice cracked with fear. As usual, it wasn't for herself as she anxiously asked, "Are you and Stacy okay?"

"Yeah…" He shifted, moving to roll off Stacy and return fire now that he knew she and his mother were safe. But Stacy gripped his shoulder, and he flinched in pain.

"You've been shot," she said, her voice breaking with urgency and concern. For him?

He shrugged his shoulders, but there was a twinge of pain. Maybe more than a twinge. He grimaced and lied, "I'm fine."

"You're bleeding," she said. Her palm smeared with his blood, she lifted it toward his face as if presenting him with evidence.

He didn't need to see it; he could feel it, sticking his sleeve to his skin. He glanced down then and noted the tear in the shoulder of his tuxedo jacket. *Oh, Mom was going to be annoyed that he'd ruined another one…*

"Are—are you hurt?" his mother asked, and unconcerned about her own safety, she began to rise from behind the monument.

"Stay down," he warned her.

"The shooting stopped," she pointed out.

But that didn't mean that the shooter was gone. He could have just been biding his time until he got a clear shot. And if someone really wanted to hurt Logan, he or she could do that most effectively by hurting his mother.

"Stay down," he told her again. "Don't move until we get backup." Maybe he shouldn't have convinced Parker and Nikki and Candace that he didn't need their protection. Maybe he should have let them stay with him like they'd wanted. Knowing them, they might have ignored his wishes—like his mother usually did.

Sirens wailed as police cars approached, lights flashing through the tree branches.

Stacy stiffened beneath him. Apparently, she had inherited her family's aversion to law enforcement. "Your backup has arrived."

To him, backup was his family and employees. But the police would do. He doubted they would apprehend the shooter, though. His mother was right; he was gone. He'd gotten away again.

He rolled off Stacy and stood up. Then he extended his uninjured arm to her. She stared at his hand before putting hers into it. Her hand was small and delicate inside his but not so delicate that she didn't have calluses.

"Maybe there will be an ambulance, too," she said.

"I don't need one."

"You were shot."

"You were shot?" his mother asked, her voice shrill with alarm as she rushed over to him.

"I was just grazed," he assured them. "There's no bullet in me." This time. But every attempt got a little closer, a little more successful. The shooter wasn't going to stop until Logan was dead.

STACY WAS FURIOUS and for once her anger wasn't directed at Logan Payne. Her heels clicking against the slate floor, she stomped across the crowded pub to the knotty pine-paneled back room where her family was drinking a farewell toast to her father.

Or was their farewell to Logan? Was one of them the shooter? Did he realize that he'd hit him? Maybe he thought he'd killed him.

He could have killed Mrs. Payne, too. Hell, with as

wildly as he'd been firing, he could have killed *her*. If Logan had ducked faster, the bullet that had hit him might have struck her instead. His reflexes had slowed at the wrong time for him, but the right time for her.

She shuddered but refused to give in to the fear that had paralyzed her at the cemetery. Anger was better; it made her stronger.

"Stacy!" Milek greeted her with a hug, his eyes bright with the sheen of inebriation. He was the lightweight of the family and could only handle a drink or two.

She slammed her palms into his chest, shoving him back with such force that he nearly fell over. But Garek, also standing at the bar, grabbed him and kept him upright.

"What the hell!" he protested.

"What the hell!" she yelled back at him. She didn't care if she hurt their feelings now. She was so pissed over getting shot at that she actually understood Logan Payne intruding on her father's funeral. "Which one of you idiots shot up the cemetery?"

"What?" Garek asked.

"I nearly got shot," she said.

"What! Are you okay?" Milek asked, grabbing for her again.

She jerked back. "I'm fine."

"It must have been Logan Payne," Milek murmured. "He must have shot at you…" A look passed between him and his brother—a look of rage and revenge.

"No," she said, in response to that look as much as her brother's statement. "Logan Payne is the one who got shot!" As if they didn't already know that…

"What's going on?" Aunt Marta asked. "This is inappropriate talk for a funeral…" She sniffed her disdain of her husband's niece and nephews. She had never approved of them because they were a convict's children. Her own husband was a criminal but since he had never been caught, he wasn't as unseemly as his brother and his offspring—mostly because of the lavish lifestyle his actions afforded her.

"Is Payne dead?" Milek asked.

Stacy's stomach pitched as she remembered the blood on his tuxedo. She shook her head. "No."

His mother had forced him to go to the hospital to make certain that the bullet had only grazed him as he'd claimed. Mrs. Payne had wanted Stacy to ride along—probably so that she could propose marriage between Stacy and her son again. Even if she talked Stacy into her outrageous plan, there was no way in hell that Logan would ever agree to become her husband—even if it were only pretend.

"That's too bad," Milek murmured with regret that Logan lived.

Had Milek been the shooter? Was that why he was drinking so heavily? Or was drinking his way of mourning their father?

Stacy wanted to mourn their father, too, but she'd hardly had the chance between Logan and the shooting. Before she could say anything else to her brothers, Aunt Marta grasped her arm and tugged her aside. Probably for another lecture on funereal etiquette.

"Why are you so angry with your brothers?" she asked.

Why was she so angry? Was it because if they were the shooters, they were risking prison again? Or was it because if they were the shooters, they were trying to kill Logan Payne?

She shook her head. "I'm not…"

"They are struggling with your father's loss," Aunt Marta said. "They didn't get the chance to say goodbye that you got."

"They could have stayed behind at the cemetery." She suspected at least one of them probably had...

"At the prison," Aunt Marta said. "The warden called you to see your father..."

She almost wished she had been spared seeing him like that, but he had asked for her. He had wanted to talk to her. She shuddered now as she remembered seeing him as she had, in so much pain, his life slipping away from him...

"What did he say to you?" her aunt asked.

Stacy tilted her head in confusion, uncertain that she'd heard the older woman correctly. They had never been close—at her aunt's choosing. She was hardly going to share any secrets with the woman now. "Why do you care?"

"I'm just curious..."

The woman was too self-absorbed to be curious about anyone but herself. She only wanted to know about things that might affect her. Why did she think Stacy's father's last words might concern her?

Stacy had no intention of satisfying the woman's morbid curiosity, so she turned away from her. But Aunt Marta grasped her arm in her talonlike fingers and asked again, "What did he say to you?"

The woman was persistent, or as Uncle Iwan would admit when he had too much to drink, a nag. She wasn't going to give up until Stacy gave her an answer. Any answer might do...

So she shook her head. "I couldn't understand him..."

Aunt Marta expelled a little breath—as if she were relieved. Had her brother-in-law taken one of her secrets to his grave?

Stacy had actually misled her aunt. She'd understood what her father had said, she just hadn't understood *why* he'd said it. When he'd spoken them, Stacy had put no credence in her father's last words. She'd blamed the strange statement on the painkillers they'd given him to make him comfortable because they hadn't been able to do anything else to treat his injury.

She still didn't understand why he'd said what he had…

"Son of a—!" Garek said as he turned toward the entrance to the pub's back room.

Logan Payne walked in as if he'd been invited. But Garek had been right to stop himself from finishing his curse. Mrs. Payne was the sweetest woman Stacy had ever met—the most forgiving and generous woman—and probably one of the smartest, as well.

"I thought you got shot," Milek drunkenly murmured. Had he thought that because of what Stacy had said or because he'd thought he'd hit him?

Logan probably wondered the same thing, because his eyes narrowed with suspicion. He gestured toward the tear in the shoulder of the tuxedo he still wore. It was even more rumpled and smudged with dirt and blood now. "The bullet barely grazed me," he replied. Then, with a sneer that was somehow both infuriating and sexy as hell, he added, "Somebody's a lousy shot."

Garek chuckled. "Then it can't be any one of us who's shooting at you. We would have hit you by now."

Despite her brother's bravado, neither he nor Milek were expert marksmen. They weren't killers, either, even though they had actually killed before. And if Logan kept goading them, they might kill again—right here.

Stacy had to do something to diffuse the potentially dangerous situation. It wouldn't be just dangerous for Logan, who was outnumbered, it would be dangerous for her brothers, too, because if they hurt him—or worse—they would go back to prison.

"Why the hell do you keep showing up where you're not wanted?" Aunt Marta demanded to know. This time her disdain was for the intruder. She usually considered her brother-in-law's children intruders, too, even though they were blood.

"He's wanted," Stacy said suddenly. She'd realized what she had to do back at the cemetery, maybe even before the gunshots had rang out. But in this moment, she made the quick decision that she was actually going to go through with it. "I want him here…"

Curving her lips into a big smile, she crossed the room to where he stood. His long body was tense. His face tight, he looked stunned, as if he'd been shot again—and that was just from what she'd said. She had no idea how he would react to what she was about to do. Maybe he would stop her before she could even act, like he had when she'd tried to slap him. But he just stood there when she wrapped her arms around his neck.

Why hadn't he stopped her? Why hadn't he caught her arms and pushed her away? He stared down at her, his blue eyes intense and watchful as he waited for her next move.

Could she…?

Bracing herself for what she had to do, she drew in a deep breath. Then she rose up on tiptoe and pressed a kiss to his hard-looking lips. But they weren't hard. They were surprisingly pliant and sensual and fuller than they looked in the tight line of disapproval into which they were usually drawn.

Now she was the one who was stunned—because he kissed her back. He clamped one arm, probably his uninjured one, around her back and pulled her tightly against him. Then he parted her lips and deepened the kiss.

Noise erupted in the room. Gasps. Shouts. Even a scream. But she could barely hear them for the blood rushing through her head, roaring in her ears. Her pulse pounded madly with adrenaline and attraction. Had it been so long since she'd been kissed that any man could affect her like this? It couldn't be just because it was Logan. She couldn't want a man that she hated as much as this one.

But no man had ever kissed her like he was kissing her—with so much passion and desire that her knees weakened and her head swam and she completely forgot why she'd kissed him in the first place.

When he pulled back, she was panting for breath. Against her lips, he murmured, "What the hell are you up to?"

For a moment she couldn't remember. Then it came back to her—the plan, his mother's outrageous plan.

She whispered back, "I'm saving your life." She turned toward her stunned family and announced, "Logan Payne is my fiancé. We're getting married."

Chapter Four

Logan's heart pounded so hard that it was the only sound in the sudden silence that had fallen after Stacy's insane announcement. He knew his mother had initially proposed this crazy engagement, but he hadn't expected that Stacy would ever agree to it. She hated him.

But he hadn't tasted that hatred on her lips when she'd kissed him so convincingly that even he had forgotten it wasn't real. He knew that she didn't really want him; she just didn't want her brothers going to prison for killing him. She was protecting Milek and Garek—not Logan.

So then she couldn't be behind the attempts on his life. Or maybe she had been, but his mother's idea had convinced Stacy to change her plan for revenge to one for marriage. But then marrying him might be more vengeful than killing him.

Not that he was going to fall in with his mother's crazy plan. He wasn't about to get coerced into marriage with a woman he couldn't...

Stand? More like resist. Why had he kissed her back? To punish her for the game she was playing? He'd like to think that but he had enjoyed it too damn much. Her mouth was so sweet and so damn sexy when it moved over his.

"What the hell is going on?" one of her brothers, his face flushed either with alcohol or temper, demanded to know.

"Just a couple of hours ago you were mad at him for crashing Dad's funeral and now you're engaged?"

Her other brother's eyes narrowed, he glared at Logan. "He must be threatening her."

"He saved my life at the cemetery," she said. "He took a bullet for me."

He was pretty sure that bullet had been meant for him and that one of her brothers had fired it. And that was the only reason he was refraining from calling her on her lie. As her fake fiancé, he had access to her family—hopefully enough access to gather evidence. Like the damn gun they kept firing at him...

She continued, "It was all very sudden."

"It's all B.S.," he whispered back at her.

She grabbed his hand and squeezed it. Hard. And he was surprised again that she had calluses on her small hands. What did she do for a living or for fun that had produced such calluses?

They were *engaged* and yet he hardly knew Stacy Kozminski.

"I'm surprised myself at the feelings I have for—" her throat moved, as if she were choking on his name or maybe just on her lie "—Logan."

Despite that kiss, he doubted her feelings had changed. She still hated him.

One of her brothers—Garek—voiced his sentiment. "You hate his guts, Stace."

She shook her head. "That's not true."

"You've said over and over that you hate his guts," Garek persisted. "Why are you lying about it now? What's he got on you?"

What did he think Logan could have on her? Proof that she and her brothers were responsible for the shootings?

He hoped like hell he had it, then he could call her on her lie and end this nonsense. Then he could call the police…

"My gratitude," she said. "He saved my life." She turned toward him and glanced up. Maybe her gaze was supposed to be adoring, but she just looked miserable. "He's my hero."

Garek snorted. "And that just erases everything else he's done to our father?"

Her snotty aunt added, "To our family? You're betraying your father. Your uncle. Your brothers…"

Ignoring her aunt, she replied to her brother only, "I understand why he's done what he has."

"I don't understand what you think you're doing," Logan murmured. Her family was never going to buy that she'd had such a drastic change of heart over *him*.

"If the situation was reversed," she continued as if he hadn't spoken, "we would have done the same. Or more…"

"He killed our father," Milek said, his words slurred. He had definitely been drinking. "And you're rewarding him for it."

"Logan did not kill Dad," Stacy defended him. "Some gang member did."

"He wouldn't have had the chance if your boyfriend—"

"Fiancé," she corrected her brother. "And stop. Just stop…all of it." She turned toward Logan. "It's been a long day. Please, take me home."

Did she mean his home? He wasn't about to bring her there. She would probably set it on fire. And he had no idea where she lived. But instead of asking any questions in front of her resentful family, he escorted her out of the pub.

"Have you been drinking with your brother?" he asked as he opened the passenger door for her.

"I'm not drunk," she said. Her gray eyes were clear as she glared at him.

"Then why on earth—"

"We can't talk about it here," she said. "There are cameras in the lot."

Her paranoia lifted his brows with surprise. "And you think your brothers would look at the footage?"

"I don't know about them," she said. "But I wouldn't put it past my aunt." She stepped on the running board of his SUV, but her heel slipped and she fell back against him. His arms closed around her, and he lifted her easily onto the seat. Maybe she was as exhausted as she'd claimed because she didn't fight him. Or maybe she was just worried about what her aunt might see on the security cameras.

"Okay, I'll drive you home," he said.

She waited until he rounded the front bumper and slid behind the wheel before she replied, "It's the least you can do since I'm saving your life."

"So you admit my life is in danger because of you?" His suspicions had obviously not been unfounded. He pushed aside the guilt he'd been feeling for interrupting her father's funeral to confront her. And it wasn't just his mother who'd made him feel guilty but Stacy had, too—with all the pain he'd seen in her gray eyes.

She was mourning. He understood that; he'd spent the past fifteen years mourning the loss of his father. Hers was to blame for that, but *she* wasn't. Maybe for the first time in fifteen years he realized that.

She emitted a soft, shaky sigh. "I'm not admitting anything, Detective Payne."

"I haven't been a detective for a few years." Not since he'd started Payne Protection Agency.

"I think you'll always be a detective," she replied.

"If I was, I wouldn't have to ask where you live," he pointed out. "I would already know."

She arched her brows in surprise. She must have assumed he knew. But Logan was just realizing how very little he actually knew about his fake fiancée. He had been so focused on what her father had done that he'd never paid attention to what she had done. Or what she was doing…

What was she doing? And not just with her life but with him? Why was she willing to pretend she was in love with him? What was her real agenda?

"I'll tell you where I live," she said. "But we have to stop somewhere else first."

Maybe her agreeing to his mother's plan was just a ruse for her to get him alone—somewhere that she would have no witnesses to her killing him.

WONDERING WHICH ONE would attack first, Stacy studied the two alpha males with which she shared the relatively small confines of the SUV. Cujo sat on the backseat, but the German shepherd's black-and-tan body was so long that his head reached over the console. She scratched him behind his droopy ear, and he whined and licked her face.

"I missed you, too," she murmured.

"Why'd you have him at the kennel?" Logan asked. He had obviously been surprised that was the place she'd had him stop before taking her home.

"Because I've been staying with a friend since my dad died," she said.

"And that friend didn't want *Cujo* staying, too?" he asked with a derisive snort.

The German shepherd whipped his big head toward Logan and nudged his shoulder with his nose. The SUV swerved a little before Logan gripped the wheel more tightly. "What he'd do that for?"

She chuckled. "That's his name."

"Cujo?"

The dog barked and then nudged him again. Logan held

his hand between them, letting the canine sniff him before petting his head. If Cujo had been a cat, he might have purred.

"Traitor," she teased him. The dog had apparently conceded which one of them was the true alpha male. She wasn't surprised it was Logan. Since he was the boss of the family business, his brothers and sister must have conceded he was the alpha male, too.

"That's probably what your family is saying about you now," Logan said. "That you're the traitor."

Her stomach churned with nerves. They were the only thing in it. She hadn't been able to eat since she'd seen her father in the prison infirmary. "Probably."

"So why did you claim to be my fiancée?" he asked. "Because you know your brothers have been trying to kill me?"

She shook her head. "I don't know any such thing."

"Liar," he softly accused her.

She should have been offended but *liar* was the least of his insults. He thought she was a killer, too. "You really think I put out a hit on you and hired my brothers to do it?"

"You wouldn't need to hire them," he replied. "They'll do whatever you tell them to."

That was what she was counting on—to keep them from killing Logan Payne. "If I wanted you dead, why would I tell them that I'm going to marry you?"

"You want to be able to collect my life insurance," he suggested, "as my widow."

"Hmm," she mock-mused, "I hadn't considered that." She nodded as if committing to the idea like she was going to try to make everyone believe she was going to commit to him. "At least then I'll get something out of this marriage."

He glanced at her, his blue gaze hot and intense. "If we

were actually going to get married, you'd definitely get something out of it."

Her heart flipped. "Are you flirting with me, Logan Payne?"

"Isn't that what a *fiancé* is supposed to do?"

She shrugged. "I have no idea. I've never been engaged." She didn't even date that often. That had to be why kissing him had affected her so much.

"Me, neither," he said.

"Why not?" she asked.

His mouth curved into a grin. "Do you think I'm way too handsome to still be single?"

Yes. But she would eat Cujo's kibble before she would ever admit that she found Logan Payne attractive. But she always had. Even during her father's trial, her brothers had accused her of having a crush on him because she hadn't been able to stop herself from staring at him.

But she replied with an insult, "I think you're pretty old to still be single."

He laughed. "You're only a few years younger than I am. Starting to feel like an old maid at twenty-nine? Is that why you jumped at my mother's crazy idea to marry me?"

"Your mother." Unable to help herself, she smiled with genuine affection for Mrs. Payne. "She's another reason I'm surprised you're still single. She's a *wedding* planner."

"And a matchmaker." He sighed. "She's the reason my brother just got married."

"She manipulated him into it?"

He nodded.

"I feel badly for the bride, then." She could commiserate with that whole manipulation thing.

"Why?" he asked. "You don't even know my brother Cooper. He enlisted in the marines out of high school and just came home a few days ago."

"Cooper? He's the one who was named after your father's partner?" She shivered at just the thought of implacable Officer Robert Cooper and how his testimony had helped seal her father's fate.

A muscle twitched along Logan's jaw and he nodded.

She shouldn't have brought up his father again. Even fifteen years later, he still felt the loss. So she had no hope of her grief ever lessening. But she would deal with that later—when she wasn't worried about losing her brothers, too.

"I don't know your brother," she agreed. "But I feel sorry for his bride because he doesn't love her."

"Oh, he loves her." Logan chuckled. "He's been in love with her since they were in high school together."

"So your mother really didn't manipulate him into marrying her, then." Maybe the woman wasn't some matchmaking mastermind.

"Oh, she did," he said. "Cooper's so stubborn he probably would have never admitted to his feelings."

"Stubborn or cowardly?" she asked.

Logan chuckled. "He's a highly decorated marine."

She shrugged. "Even a brave man can be a coward when it comes to love…"

"Sounds like you have a story about that," he mused. "Is it about your *friend?*" He'd said "friend" as if it meant something more than friendship and almost as if he was jealous that it might be.

"Why would you ask that?" And why would he sound jealous when he asked?

"I didn't see any friends at the funeral," he explained almost nonchalantly, "just your family."

"That's why my friend couldn't come," she said, "because of my family."

"He has a problem with your brothers, too?"

She nodded but didn't bother correcting his misconception about the gender of her *friend*. Maybe she had only imagined his jealousy, but if he actually was, she liked it—which was odd since she didn't like him. Sure, she found him attractive—maybe she was even attracted to him—but she still didn't like him.

"Even if I agreed to it, my mother's plan would never work," Logan warned her.

She was afraid of that, too, because she would have to convince her family that she loved a man she really couldn't stand. And she was no actress—she'd never even been very good at lying.

"And really, all you have to do to stop them from trying to kill me is to tell them to stop," he said, "because they'll do what you tell them to."

If only that were true…then she wouldn't have to fake an engagement, or heaven forbid, a marriage, if it actually came to that. And it might take marriage to convince her family that she was committed to Logan Payne.

"I'm not so sure about that," she reluctantly admitted.

"Then even you realize they're dangerously out of control," Logan said.

"I never said that!" she exclaimed, horrified that she might have inadvertently implicated her brothers. And, like Logan, she had no proof they were behind the attempts on his life. But thanks to Logan and the threats they'd previously made, she now had doubts.

"They've already tried to kill me. More than once," he insisted. "They need to be brought to justice."

"You have no evidence," she reminded him.

"I'll find it," he warned her.

"I buried my father today," she said, her voice cracking with the emotion that overwhelmed her. "Isn't that enough justice for you?"

Cujo whined and nudged her with his head, as if trying to comfort her. Surprisingly, he wasn't the only one because Logan's hand covered hers on the dog's fur.

"I'm sorry you're hurting," he said.

But he wasn't sorry that her father was dead and he was determined to arrest her brothers. He wasn't sorry about any of that…

She pulled her hand out from beneath his. If she couldn't stand his touch, how was she going to convince her family that she loved him? But then she'd had no problem with his touch earlier when he'd kissed her. Her lips still tingled from the electricity of that contact with his.

"We're here," she said with a sigh of relief as she just realized that he'd stopped the SUV outside her building. The street side of the ground floor held the storefront for her jewelry business, her workshop was in the back, and her apartment was above it. It wasn't the greatest neighborhood; that was why she needed Cujo. Even now a car alarm blared and police sirens whined in the distance.

Logan peered through the window and murmured, "This is really where you live?"

She'd never taken Logan Payne for a snob. "You mean because I'm the daughter of a jewelry thief and I live above a jewelry store?"

"I'm surprised you admit he was a thief," he said.

"He was a thief," she said. He'd always been honest about that. "But he wasn't a killer…"

Logan rubbed his temple and groaned as if sick of hearing it. But maybe if he heard it enough he would come to believe it. "I was actually referring to the dangerous neighborhood," he said as he continued to look around like a cop assessing the potential dangers of his beat. "Now I understand why you have the dog."

"Your mother is actually the one who brought me Cujo,"

she said. After the older woman had heard about her store being robbed, she'd talked an old friend of her deceased husband into giving the German shepherd to Stacy. "He was a K-9 cop."

"He doesn't look old enough to have been retired," Logan said as he scratched behind the dog's ear, which Cujo loved.

"He was shot," she said. "In the shoulder…" Like Logan had been shot. No wonder the two alpha males had come so quickly to an understanding. They were actually quite alike. Cujo wasn't always that nice or polite, either. That was why her friend hadn't wanted the dog staying with her, too—especially since he might have thought her Pomeranian was a squirrel. Cujo really hated squirrels.

Logan leaned his head against the dog and imitated the way Cujo nuzzled the few people he actually liked. "You're a hero," he praised the canine cop.

"He saved his partner," she said.

"That's what a partner is supposed to do," Logan murmured.

Somehow she suspected he wasn't talking about the partnership of their proposed marriage. "You're not going to do it, are you?"

"Marry you?" He shook his head. "It's a bad idea. And as I already pointed out, it would never work."

He was probably right. But she couldn't agree with him without a fight. She'd been fighting with Logan Payne too long to concede defeat. "That's your fault," she accused him.

His mouth curved into a sexy grin. "Are you saying that kiss wasn't convincing?"

If she said it wasn't, he might kiss her again—might try to prove how convincing he could be. She was tempted to lie because she was tempted…to kiss him again. But instead she shook her head and clarified, "It's your fault for being such a jerk all these years that they would never believe I could actually fall for you."

"And so they'll keep trying to kill me."

"Is that why you didn't give me up as a liar back at the pub?" she asked. "You were afraid you weren't going to get out of there alive?"

"I'm not afraid of your brothers," he said with a snort of disgust.

She was afraid of what they might do, of what they might have already done. They would do anything for her, and even though she hadn't asked them, she'd given them every reason to think she wanted Logan Payne dead. She needed to give them a reason to leave him alive—like their fake engagement.

She glanced around as Logan had, but she was looking for her brothers. They might have followed them from the pub. "You need to walk me to my door," she said.

"I thought you had the dog to keep you safe," he said. "Not that you're the one in danger…"

"I don't want you to keep me safe," she said. She wanted to keep him safe. Actually, she wanted to keep her brothers safe from themselves. "I want my fiancé to walk me to my door."

He uttered an exasperated-sounding sigh. "Stacy, I'm not playing along with my mother's plan."

"Do you want me to tell her—?"

"You can tell her—"

"—that her son is not enough of a gentleman to walk a lady to her door," she continued as if he hadn't interrupted her.

He groaned. But he opened his door and walked around to open hers.

Cujo jumped down with her and led the way to the back

stairwell. She fumbled in her purse before unlocking the door. Cujo's ears perked up, and a low growl emanated from his throat.

"He smells something," Logan said, and he was already pulling his gun from beneath his jacket, wincing only slightly at the strain on his wound. "Someone may have broken into your place."

"And locked the door behind himself?" she scoffed. "I doubt that."

The dog hurried ahead—with Logan in hot pursuit. "Stay outside," he ordered her.

But she didn't take orders from Logan Payne. He wasn't her boss. He had even refused to be her fake fiancé. So she followed. And then saw what Cujo had found: a pipe bomb sat on her kitchen table, red numbers blinking as the timer quickly counted down.

Chapter Five

The bomb went off with such force that it blew the lid off the bomb unit's transfer container. The stairwell rattled, boards giving away beneath the weight of the ATF agents and that container. The agents tumbled down to the concrete alley.

Logan's hand shook in reaction. He'd touched that damn thing. He'd defused it or at least he'd stopped the clock—a clock that hadn't begun its countdown until they'd stepped inside the apartment and activated it. After stopping the timer, he'd called ATF to dispose of the device since explosives often went off when moved. At least it hadn't blown up him and Stacy and her dog. The two of them crouched behind his SUV with him. Her arms wrapped tightly around the dog, Stacy held Cujo either to protect the canine or to thank him for protecting her.

He reached out and petted the dog's head. "You're a hero again, buddy."

"Are they all right?" Stacy asked after the welfare of the ATF agents.

He glanced back to where the agents scrambled to their feet. "Looks like nobody got hurt." Thank goodness for their protective gear and that container that had absorbed most of the explosion.

"What about my place?"

He hesitated until she grasped his arm. A twinge of pain shot through his wounded shoulder. He then realized maybe the bullet hadn't been intended for him at all. Maybe he hadn't been the intended target at the cemetery—just like he hadn't been the intended target of the bomb, either.

She jerked her hand away and said, "I'm sorry. I forgot you were hurt."

So had he.

She shuddered. "You could have been hurt so much worse," she said. "I can't believe you touched the bomb…"

He suppressed a shudder of his own revulsion. "Me, neither."

"It's a miracle you didn't get killed."

Especially given how easily the bomb had gone off in transport. "When my brother Cooper first got back home, I picked his brain for everything he'd learned in the service." Of course Cooper had thought that Logan was stalling giving him a real assignment or interviewing him to see if he was ready to take one. Cooper had already proven he was ready. And he'd even saved Logan's life after he'd left for his honeymoon. "He showed me and Parker how to defuse an improvised explosive device."

"He thought that was something you'd need to know?" she asked, her brow furrowing in confusion.

Actually Logan had thought that. "Payne Protection Agency promises to protect our clients from all dangers—even bombs."

"You protected me," she said, "and I'm not even your client."

"Maybe you should be," he said, "because someone just tried to blow you up. Who would do that and why?"

Her lips parted, and a ragged breath slipped out, but no words. And before she could form any, they were interrupted.

"Stacy!" a deep voice shouted as her brother Garek pushed through the police barricade set up around the perimeter of her building. An officer attempted to stop him, but he—with the help of Milek—pushed past him.

Logan held up a hand to the officer, verifying that it was okay to let them through. Okay for Stacy, anyway. He doubted that her brothers would ever hurt her. They loved her so much that they were distraught, their eyes wild with worry over finding the police barricade around her place. Maybe they'd heard the explosion, too.

"Are you all right?" Garek asked as he dragged her into his arms.

She clung to him, trembling. "Yes. Yes."

"This is your fault!" Milek told Logan. "This is your danger you've dragged her into with you!"

Logan shook his head, but before he could defend himself, Stacy pulled free of Garek and whirled toward Milek, who must have sobered up, because his eyes were clear now and his face pale. She poked his chest with a finger.

"You should be thanking him for saving my life again!" she shouted at her brother. "If Logan hadn't stopped that bomb from going off, it would have killed us!"

"Stopped the bomb?" Garek scoffed. "Your damn stairwell has been blown off the building! You could have been killed."

"The ATF agents set it off when they were moving it," Logan explained.

"My stairwell is gone?" Stacy glanced back at the building and shuddered. "That could have been us…"

"It was supposed to be you," Logan said. "The bomb was set inside your apartment." And it was impossible that the bomb was intended to harm Logan because no one—not even her brothers—could have guessed that he would have driven her home. Stacy hadn't announced their fake engagement until that afternoon. And even if they'd known he might step foot inside her apartment, he doubted that they would have risked her life even to take his.

So he wasn't the only one someone was trying to kill. Apparently, someone wanted Stacy Kozminski dead, as well.

STACY SHIVERED. SHE wasn't cold even though goose bumps lifted on her arms and the back of her neck beneath the heavy fall of her hair. Her skin was tingling because of Logan Payne's stare. He stood several feet away, deep in conversation with the ATF agents, but his gaze was on her, as if he was reluctant to let her out of his sight.

She had already spoken with them, answering all their questions the best that she could. Given that she hadn't been home since her dad died at the prison, she'd had no idea when or how someone had broken into her apartment to set the bomb. And she had absolutely no idea why.

Logan conversed with the agents now. He was probably the one asking the questions instead of answering them. But as he talked, he watched her. While his stare unsettled her, it also—oddly enough—reassured her. He had already saved her life once. Maybe twice if those shots at the cemetery had actually been intended for her.

But why would someone try to shoot at her? Or worse yet, blow her up? Unable to comprehend why anyone would want her dead, she murmured, "Why?"

"That's a damn good question," Garek replied as if she'd asked it of him.

Maybe still in shock over nearly being killed, she just shook her head. "I have no idea."

"Then why would you agree to it?" Garek asked.

Even further confused, she turned toward her brother and asked, "Agree to what?"

"You and Logan Payne," he said. "Why are you claiming you're engaged to the guy?"

She glanced to Logan again. At least he was too far away to hear her lie again and contradict it. Yet. He would eventually deny their engagement, but until then she intended to perpetuate the lie. "It's the truth."

Garek shook his head. "You hate the guy's guts."

"That was once true," she admitted. Even that morning it had been true. But she didn't hate Logan anymore—not after he'd saved her. That would have been ungrateful or, at the very least, stupid. She owed him her life. And maybe she could repay him with his. "But my feelings for him have changed."

Milek snorted. "Yeah, right…"

"Even if your feelings for him have changed," Garek allowed, "his feelings for you couldn't have. He's hated all of us for years because of what our father did to his."

"Our father didn't do anything to his," she insisted. Why was she the only one who believed in his innocence? How could his own sons doubt him?

Garek nodded sharply as if he was only humoring her. "Yeah, right, but Payne doesn't believe that."

That was definitely true. "But he doesn't hold us responsible," she insisted. Weakly. She really was a lousy liar.

"He always thinks the worst of us," Milek said. "He actually believes we've been shooting at him."

Despite Mrs. Payne's warning about hurting their feelings, Stacy had already accused them of shooting. But then they'd been drunk and she'd been angry. So now she kept her voice low and her gaze steady as she asked, "Have you?"

Garek sucked in a breath. "I guess your feelings for him really have changed," he said, "because you never would have listened to his suspicions before."

She might have listened, but she would have ignored them—even though she had never been able to ignore him. Even when she'd hated him...

Fully aware that her brother hadn't actually answered her question, she persisted, "Are they only suspicions?"

"Of course," Garek replied—as offended as she had been afraid he would be. His mouth pulled into a tight grimace of disgust, and he swallowed hard. "I can't believe you'd fall for Logan Payne..."

If she had, she would have been as disgusted with herself as her oldest brother was with her. But she couldn't let him see her true feelings, so she buried them deep and plastered on a dreamy smile.

"Why not?" she asked. "He's an amazing man."

"Amazing that he's still alive..." Milek murmured.

She shivered at her brother's ominous tone. Maybe he was just still drunk. He couldn't mean that he actually wanted Logan dead. But then maybe he did...

"Milek!" she admonished him. "That's a horrible thing to say."

He shrugged. "All I meant was that if someone has tried to kill him as many times as he claims, then it's amazing that they haven't succeeded."

Garek nodded. "It is amazing. But then we actually only have his word that these attempts were made on *his* life."

"I was there when he was shot at in the cemetery," she reminded them. And she had been so furious over it that she'd already accused them of being involved. They'd been drinking then and confused, so they probably hadn't realized that she'd already had her own suspicions.

"But was it really him they were shooting at?" Garek voiced her earlier fear. "Or was it you?"

She shrugged now. "I don't know about that, but I do

know that Logan wasn't the one shooting at me. He saved me at the cemetery like he saved me just now when we discovered the bomb in my apartment."

Her legs began to shake as she remembered that mess of wires and pipes sitting in the middle of her kitchen table where usually she displayed a crystal bowl of fruit or a vase of flowers.

"Has it occurred to you that he was able to stop it from going off so easily because he'd concocted the damn thing?" Garek voiced his own suspicions.

"He was able to dismantle it because his brother—the former marine—had shown him how to disarm improvised explosive devices."

"If his brother Cooper knows how to take the bombs apart, he must know how to put them together," Garek said.

"And Parker could have been the one shooting at the cemetery," Milek added.

Maybe her brothers hadn't sobered up yet. "Why?" she asked. "Why would they try to kill their own brother and risking hurting their mother, too?" The Payne family had already suffered too much loss, and that loss had brought them closer together, had made them more protective of each other. Not murderous.

"I can think of quite a few reasons," Milek murmured with a resentful glare in Logan's direction.

"They weren't trying to kill him," Garek explained to her. "They were trying to kill *you*."

"Why?" she asked.

"Maybe they actually think your crazy engagement story is the truth and they're trying to stop the wedding," Garek said.

Even though it had been Mrs. Payne's idea, nobody in

Logan's family knew about their fake engagement. And given Logan's opposition to it, they probably never would.

Garek continued, "But seriously, the Payne family would only act on the boss's orders."

"And Logan Payne is the boss," Milek added.

Maybe he was boss of Payne Protection, but Penny Payne was the boss of her family. And she would never allow any of her kids to hurt her. She knew how much Stacy had already been hurt. And so did her brothers.

They were only trying to protect her. And maybe they had reason to.

She really only had Logan's word that there had been other attempts on his life—attempts that hadn't involved her nearly getting shot or blown up, as well. She turned toward where he'd been standing with the ATF agents, but he was no longer there.

Then a strong arm curled around her shoulders and pulled her tight to his side. She didn't mistake him for one of her brothers this time. She recognized his touch now. Her body recognized it as her pulse quickened. But that might not have been with attraction; that might have only been with fear. She couldn't, and shouldn't, trust him. Because, as her brothers had pointed out, his feelings for her couldn't have changed. He still hated her.

But then why did he hold her so closely, nearly molding her body against his? Just to mess with her? Did he realize how much his nearness affected her?

"Payne, what the hell do you think you're doing?" Garek asked as he glared at Logan with hatred darkening his gray eyes.

She couldn't trust her brothers, either—because Logan might be telling the truth about the attempts on his life and he might be right about who was behind them.

Instead of ignoring Garek's impudent question, Logan—equally as impudent—replied, "I'm taking my fiancée home."

She barely managed to contain her shock. He'd been adamant that his mother's plan would never work, so why was he playing along now? Or was he only playing—just amusing himself by aggravating her brothers?

Garek tensed and bristled like Cujo when he saw a cat or a small dog or a squirrel. His upper lip curled, he barked back, "She is home."

With the stairwell blown off the side of the building, it didn't look much like home. But she could still access her second-story apartment through the inside stairwell.

"The ATF agents haven't cleared the building yet," Logan said. "Nobody's going to be allowed inside until they make sure it's safe."

"I—I should stay," she said, hoping to defuse the tense situation between Logan and her brothers, "while they do that."

"But even if the ATF agents declare your place safe," Logan said, "*you're* not."

She shivered.

"You would know," Milek bitterly muttered.

Logan nodded as if in agreement with her brother. Apparently, he hadn't picked up on the deeper meaning. "Neither of us is safe until we catch the person trying to kill us."

Was that why he was acting like her fiancé? Had he decided to use their fake engagement to try to find their would-be killers?

"Us?" Garek snarled the word. "You and Stacy are not an 'us.'" And her brother reached for her, clasping her arm to pull her from Logan's grasp.

Cujo growled in protest, echoing the sound Logan had

made low in his throat. His arm tightened around her shoulders, holding her against his side. And the dog stepped in front of him to protect them both from men he had never accepted as alpha males or friends.

"That damn dog likes you?" Milek asked, amused. "That dog doesn't like anybody but Stacy."

"That's not true…" But it absolutely was or at least had been.

Logan reached his free hand down and patted the dog's head. "It's obviously not true," he said. "But then not much of what you guys say is true."

"You self-righteous hypocrite!" Garek stepped closer, but the dog growled louder and bared his teeth completely. So the man stepped back.

"He's not," Stacy defended Logan. She believed that Logan thought he'd been doing the right thing, that he'd been getting justice for his father.

"This is ridiculous," Garek said. "I don't know what's going on between the two of you but it sure isn't love."

Milek studied them through narrowed eyes as if he was beginning to have some doubts that their engagement was fake. Maybe he'd remembered accusing her of having a crush on Logan during their father's trial. "Garek, you're not exactly an expert on love since you've never been in it."

But Milek had? She shrugged off thoughts of her brother's love life. She had enough problems with her own. Life. Not love life. She wasn't in love—no matter what she wanted her brothers to believe.

Garek shuddered. "And I never will be. That's one mistake *I* never intend to make." He turned back toward Stacy with an unspoken plea softening his gaze. "Don't make that mistake either, sis."

He only pulled out *sis* when he really wanted to get to

her. It brought her back to when they were kids. And what he and Milek had done to protect her...

"It's too late," she told him. She wasn't in love but she'd committed to Mrs. Payne's plan to protect Logan and to protect her brothers from themselves.

"It is too late," Logan said. "And it's been a long day for Stacy."

"Because of you!" Garek said. "Because *you* crashed our dad's funeral—because *you* put her in danger."

"He didn't put me in danger," Stacy said. But Garek had raised doubts in her mind...and she'd already had enough of those.

"It's been a long day," Logan repeated as if no one else had spoken. "So I'm taking my fiancée home with me."

Garek reached for her arm again until Cujo growled, and he pulled back. "Don't do this, Stace. Don't you dare go anywhere with him!"

But Logan was already leading her toward the SUV parked at the curb. Was her brother right? Was Logan actually the one who had put her in danger both at the cemetery and at her apartment?

What would happen when she was alone with him? Would he finally exact his revenge? Would he kill her?

Chapter Six

Stacy Kozminski was dead…to the world. She had fallen asleep in Logan's SUV on the way to his house. So after checking to make certain there was no bomb on his kitchen table, he returned to his vehicle, unlocked it and opened the passenger door.

Only Cujo lifted his head from the console. Stacy didn't stir. Her upper body slumped over the seat belt, and her hair had fallen over her face. Fear clutched his heart in a tight fist. Had someone gotten to her without his realizing it? No shot had penetrated the windshield or side glass, though.

And the doors had still been locked. No one had broken inside. They probably wouldn't have dared with Cujo guarding her.

Logan pushed her back against the seat and released the safety belt. Then he brushed her hair off her face and slid his fingers over her throat. Her pulse leaped beneath his fingertips as if she recognized his touch.

Or maybe she'd mistaken him for someone else. For the *friend* who didn't get along with Cujo. *Boyfriend?*

"Good dog," he praised the canine—for protecting her. Then he slid one arm underneath her knees and the other behind her back and lifted her from the seat. Just as she had against the safety belt, she slumped forward—against him. Her face settled into the crook of his neck and shoulder.

She murmured and sighed, her breath tickling his throat and causing his skin to heat.

And other parts of his body tensed…

How could this woman affect him like this? They had spent the past fifteen years hating each other…or at least he'd thought he'd hated her.

And not for the reason she and her brothers thought. He didn't blame them for what their father had done. He blamed them for not accepting it and for continuing to support a killer. And he resented her blaming him for her father's sentence and for making certain Patek Kozminski served it. Logan had only wanted justice for his father.

She'd thought he'd wanted vengeance. And she hated him even more than he'd thought he'd hated her. Then she shifted in his arms, burrowing even closer against him—almost into him. But she probably didn't know it was him.

She slept deeply, her heavy breaths steadily whispering against his throat. Even when he shifted her in his arms in order to shoulder open the door to his house, she didn't awaken. Or even murmur again.

Neither did his whistle awaken her when he called for Cujo to jump out of the SUV and join them inside the house. With the dog following closely behind them, Logan passed through the foyer and then the living room, sparing the couch only a glance before dismissing it. It was leather and cold. Even if he'd taken the time to put blankets on it, she deserved better than a couch after the hellish day she'd had.

But he didn't have any guest rooms. The second bedroom of the two-bedroom ranch house held his home office. So he carried her to his bed, which was soft and warm with plaid flannel sheets and a comforter. When he laid her onto the mattress, she hooked her arm around his neck, pulling him down with her.

After the long day he'd had, he should have been as exhausted as she was. He should have been willing to burrow into the blankets like she was and sleep. But if he laid down beside her gorgeous body, the last thing on his mind was going to be sleep. And some damn bodyguard he'd prove to be if he didn't stay awake to protect her from whoever meant her harm.

Harm? The bomb proved whoever was after her didn't want her just hurt; he wanted her dead.

Logan's arms tightened for a moment, holding her close. He didn't want her dead. He wanted her…which scared him more than someone shooting at him. He forced himself to release her and pull away. But he couldn't get far enough away to stop wanting her—not without compromising her safety.

He had to focus on protecting her. A cold shower might cool his reaction to having Stacy Kozminski in his house—in his bed. It might also stop his shoulder from throbbing and force him to think with his brain instead of another part of his body.

And it wasn't as if he was leaving her unprotected while he showered. She wasn't alone in the bed any longer. Cujo had climbed onto the mattress beside her. His furry body was tense and his ears up and alert for any sound of an intruder.

Eager to be rid of the tuxedo he hated wearing, he stripped off the jacket and then the shirt and left them in a trail that led to the master bathroom. But he held tight to the holster he'd removed with the shirt and placed his weapon on the granite counter within reach of the shower. He didn't drop his pants and boxers until he closed the pocket door and shut out the sight of Stacy sleeping in his bed.

He was too tempted to kick Cujo out of bed and take his place next to his mistress. His body throbbed, and it wasn't just his shoulder. A bandage covered the stitches, but he wasn't supposed to get it wet. He turned on the shower and stepped beneath the spray before the water had the chance to warm. It struck his skin like needles, nipping into his sensitive flesh. And he welcomed the pain.

Heck, maybe he was a masochist. Maybe that was why he had become attracted to a woman who hated him. And if he actually agreed to her and his mother's crazy plan to get married, it was destined to end badly. Painfully…

For him.

He glanced down at the bandage on his shoulder. Blood and water saturated the gauze and tape, and the wound beneath the bandage throbbed. But that pain was nothing in comparison to what she could do to him…

Was that why she proposed? To get close enough to him that she could hurt him herself? He should have told her brothers the truth since he doubted it mattered to them whether he was their sister's fiancé. They still wanted him dead. But maybe by posing as her fiancé, he could get close enough to them to find evidence like the gun or get them to confess to the attempts on his life.

A menacing growl emanated from the bedroom. The sound raised more goose bumps on Logan's flesh than the icy water had. He shut off the faucet and listened for whatever Cujo had heard. An engine rumbled in the driveway. And another…

A couple of vehicles had driven up to his house. How many people were after him and Stacy?

He grabbed a towel and hastily wrapped it around his hips before reaching for his holster and drawing his weapon. He slid open the pocket door to find Cujo standing on his bed, his hair bristling as he stood guard over his mistress. Curled up like a kitten, Stacy was still sleeping soundly.

"Good dog," Logan murmured before slipping from the

room to head to the front door and the driveway. Before he reached it, the door opened, so he cocked his gun.

"Don't shoot," his brother said with his hands lifted above his head.

"Then don't sneak up on a man who's been getting shot at," he cautioned Parker. Just in case he might be tempted to use it on his twin, he set his weapon on the butcher-block counter of the island situated between the open kitchen and living-room area. "What are you doing here?"

"It's that whole getting-shot-at thing," Parker said. "I'm checking up on you." He glanced back toward Logan's SUV—he must have closed the passenger door. "Making sure everything's all right…"

If he'd only been acting out of concern as a brother or even out of professional concern as a bodyguard, why hadn't he come alone? Their sister and their top security expert, Candace Baker, had come along with him in their own vehicles. As the women joined Parker inside his house, Logan asked, "What's really going on?"

"You tell us," Parker said.

"I wish I knew," he admitted. He had been so convinced Stacy was behind the attempts on his life. And maybe she was—maybe that was why she'd proposed. Or maybe she'd proposed to save him, as she'd said. But who was going to save her? Because that bomb was proof that he wasn't the only one someone wanted dead…

Parker expelled a ragged sigh of relief. "I knew Mom was messing with us."

"Mom doesn't *mess* with us," Nikki hotly defended her. She had no idea just how manipulative—albeit with good intentions—their mother could be.

Her face tense, Candace curtly explained, "She told us that you're marrying Stacy Kozminski."

He had thought news of the bomb at Stacy's apartment

might have brought them here as backup. But now he realized why they'd really shown up.

Parker shook his head. "She's gotta be messing with us. That's the craziest thing I've ever heard."

It was crazy. And Logan couldn't believe his mother's audacity in announcing his fake engagement to everyone. He really should call both her and Stacy liars. A marriage was out of the question. But an engagement…

He might be able to use that to his advantage. "What's so crazy about it?" he asked.

Nikki gasped. "I knew Mom wasn't lying, but I thought she was mistaken. You and Stacy Kozminski…"

"Would kill each other," Parker said. "You can't stand each other!"

"Is that why you guys are here?" he asked. "Is this some kind of intervention?" Maybe he needed one because he was afraid he'd lost his judgment where Stacy was concerned. He found her entirely too attractive…and damn near irresistible.

"Since the definition of an intervention is getting someone to stop doing harm to himself, that's exactly what this is," Candace replied.

"I'm not hurting myself," he said. It wasn't exactly a lie; the cold shower hadn't actually hurt him. That much…

"She will," Candace said. "She's been threatening you for years—every time her father came up for parole she threatened you to not show up."

She'd asked him not to speak at his hearings. She'd even begged once, and while he'd respected how hard that must have been for a woman as proud as she was, he hadn't granted her request. He'd spoken…and maybe his words had influenced the board to deny his parole.

"When her father died after the last hearing, I knew she would make good on her threats. I knew she would try to kill you," Candace said, her face reddening with outrage on his behalf.

She had protected him once from shots fired at him. But Logan had thought then that those shots had been intended for Cooper. Now he knew…

Candace reminded him, "You thought she was the one behind the shootings, too."

Parker's head bobbed in a sharp nod. "That's it. That's why you're doing this—to get evidence against her. It's that whole keep your friends close and your enemies closer…"

After that kiss, he had been tempted to get close to her. Real close.

"Stacy's not my enemy." She wasn't his friend, either, and given their families' histories, they were unlikely to ever become friends.

"Then what is she?" Candace asked, her usually even voice nearly shrill with emotion.

"My fiancée."

While Parker and Candace both sputtered at his announcement, Nikki remained oddly silent. She was usually the most gregarious of the Payne siblings—the most like their mother even though she vehemently denied the comparison. She wanted to be tough and cynical like her brothers. Logan preferred her as she was. Innocent and hopeful and maybe more romantic than she would ever admit. She studied him carefully, as if trying to find something that wasn't there: love.

"Did you let Mom talk you into this?" Parker asked. "Is this one of her matchmaking schemes?"

Probably. "You really think I would let Mom manipulate me into one of her plans?"

"If not, why are you marrying her?" Candace asked. Her voice was still shrill and now he recognized the anger behind it. Why was she so angry about his fake engagement?

Maybe if his siblings had come alone to see him, he would have admitted the truth. But all he really knew about Candace Baker was that she was ex-military and ex-police and now a damn good bodyguard.

He replied in the tone his siblings and employees alike knew brooked no arguments. "I have my reasons."

"Love," Nikki said, as if she'd found what she'd been looking for on his face.

Parker snorted. "Did you hit your head when Logan knocked you down on the church steps earlier? There's no love between him and Stacy. It's called hate."

"It's called passion," Nikki said. "That fine line between love and hate. Those two have been obsessed with each other for years. The way they've stared at each other during court and the parole hearings…"

Candace groaned as if she'd seen it, too.

What had they seen?

Nikki emitted a wistful sigh. "It's so Romeo and Juliet…"

"Yeah," Candace said. "Both of them wound up dead."

Parker chuckled. "Is that one of your reasons, Logan? Love?"

While Nikki continued to study his face, as if waiting for his confirmation, Parker and Candace looked beyond him to the woman who padded barefoot from his bedroom. Instead of her black funeral dress, she wore his tuxedo shirt now with the cuffs rolled up and the tear in the shoulder revealing more of her honey-toned skin. Despite the smudges and blood on the shirt, her black lace bra and panties were visible through the thin white silk.

"Okay," Parker said with an appreciative whistle. "I can see what those reasons are now."

What the hell was Stacy Kozminski up to now? Dressed

as she was, the woman was more dangerous than the bomb they'd found in her apartment.

WHAT HAD SHE been thinking? Stacy could have kicked herself for acting so impulsively as to take off her dress and pull on Logan's shirt. She wished that she'd brilliantly planned the action in order to prove the validity of their fake engagement.

But she'd really just acted on impulse. She'd heard that woman's voice—full of jealousy and disdain for her—and she had reacted. Childishly…

Heat flushed her face, but she refused to succumb to humiliation now—especially with that short-haired Amazon woman glaring at her with stark hatred. And jealousy…

Who was she exactly? Did she have a right to that jealousy? What was she to Logan? Stacy had seen her at the last couple of parole hearings, as if she'd come with him to offer her support. Or stick her nose in where it hadn't belonged. Logan had never been married, so she wasn't a current or even an ex-wife.

Girlfriend? Lover? Friend with benefits?

When the woman focused her gaze on him, the hatred left her eyes. Lust and adulation replaced it. "If you're doing this to stop the attempts on your life, it isn't necessary," she told him. "I can protect you—like I've protected you before."

"That won't be necessary," Logan said dismissively.

"You don't think you're in danger any longer?" Parker asked.

"I know that I can protect myself," Logan replied, "I am the CEO of Payne Protection."

With a chuckle of amusement, Parker assured him, "We definitely know you're the boss."

And that woman—that besotted woman—was apparently one of his employees since a family member wouldn't be looking at him like *that*. Like Stacy looked at him...

She couldn't *not* look at him. Except for the bandage on his shoulder, he wore only a towel slung low around his lean hips—his tight buttocks clearly defined, even through the thick terry cloth. His chest and back were bare and broad and all sculpted muscles.

Despite waking up thirsty, she was suddenly nearly drooling. Her skin heated and flushed with attraction. With need...

She had never needed anyone like this before. She had wanted a man before but she'd never *needed* one. Logan Payne was not just any good-looking man. He was the one who had kept her father from her when she'd needed him most. She looked away from Logan's brain-scramblingly sexy body, and her gaze collided with his sister's. Her dark eyes were so much like her mother's—so warm and affectionate. Stacy couldn't recall ever exchanging any words with the youngest Payne before.

Nikki spoke now. "Congratulations," she said as she closed the distance between them and pulled Stacy into a hug.

The woman even felt like her mother—like warmth and safety. But Stacy drew back. "Congratulations?"

"On your engagement," she said with a chuckle. Then she threw her arms around her brother and kissed his cheek. "Congratulations to you, too."

Logan's brows arched; he was apparently as confused as Stacy was over his sister's reaction. The others might have come to stage an intervention, as Stacy had overheard Logan remark, but not Nikki.

"You'll want to get together with Mom soon," Nikki spoke to her again. "Or she'll have your wedding all planned out without any input from you."

Parker and that woman were also looking at Nikki as if she'd lost her mind. But she just smiled and turned for the door. "We should leave them alone now," she said. "They've just gotten engaged."

The woman's face flushed again—with embarrassment and fury—and she turned that gaze of hatred on Stacy. "But Logan's still in danger—probably in even more danger now with her here."

Parker slid an arm around the woman's shoulders and turned her toward the door. "Nikki's right. We should leave them alone." He escorted the women out and then turned back and winked at his twin before he closed the front door behind them all.

Stacy wasn't so certain that leaving them alone was the best idea—especially when Logan turned toward her. His gaze was every bit as intense as his employee's. He was angry with her, but he wasn't just angry. There was passion burning in his bright blue eyes as he stared at her.

Despite the heat of that look, she shivered.

"Maybe you shouldn't have taken off your dress," he suggested. "Then you wouldn't be cold."

She wasn't cold. She was hot. So hot that she lifted trembling fingers to the collar of his shirt. But she hadn't done up that many buttons so she didn't dare undo any more. "I—I'm fine."

Logan shook his head. "You're lying to me again."

"I haven't lied to you," she said.

"You haven't told me the truth," he said. "Same difference."

"What haven't I told you?"

He shrugged. "If I knew, it wouldn't matter. But I can sense that you're holding something back."

More than he knew. And more than she would ever admit to...

She would touch a bomb before she'd confess to her attraction to him. The bomb was probably less likely to blow up in her face.

She shook her head. "You're paranoid."

"It would be foolish to trust you," he said, "and I'm no fool."

She wished she could say the same, but she had already made a fool out of herself by walking out of the bedroom wearing his shirt. Sure, she could have excused her action as proving their engagement real. But his family wasn't the one they needed to convince; it was hers.

"I know you're up to something," he said, and gestured toward his shirt. But then, his arm outstretched, he hooked a finger inside the collar and pulled her closer. "What are you up to?"

"About five-six," she quipped.

His mouth curved, a grin tugging up the corners of it. "Cute."

"I get that a lot," she said with a smile. God, she was flirting with the man. She was actually flirting. She *never* flirted.

"Your *remark* was cute," he clarified. "Not you."

She sucked in a breath—surprised that even he was insensitive enough to take back his compliment. "Okay, then…"

Since she had really come out wearing his shirt in order to stake her claim on her fake fiancé, she was definitely the fool. She turned back toward the bedroom—and her dress. But he caught her wrist and stopped her.

He stepped close to her so that she felt the heat of his nearly naked body through the thin silk of his shirt. "You're not cute," he repeated.

And she had begun to think that he wasn't as cruel as she'd always believed…

But then he leaned down, his mouth nearly touching her ear, and added, "You're beautiful."

She closed her eyes as pleasure at his compliment radiated throughout her. She wasn't used to compliments. In the past, either she or her brothers had scared off the men who might have been attracted to her. "Now who's up to something?"

"I'm just being honest," he replied. "You might want to try it sometime."

"Honest?" She snorted derisively at his claim of being honest and his insinuation that she wasn't. "You're just trying to flatter and disarm me."

He turned her around to face him. And seeing his handsome face and all that bare skin rattled her.

She couldn't think. She could barely breathe. Her pulse raced, and her heart beat frantically.

"You are beautiful," he said. "Even when I hated you, I couldn't help but notice that."

"You—you hated me?" She'd known it, but having him outright admit it…caused a twinge of pain in her heart.

Unabashed, he grinned. "You hated me, too. Hell, you still hate me—"

Stacy shook her head. "You saved my life," she said. "I can't hate you anymore." But she wished she could, because with the hatred gone, she couldn't fight the attraction she'd always felt for him.

"You could," he said. "But it would make our marriage a little intense."

Marriage?

Panic squeezed her lungs, stealing away her breath. She couldn't really marry Logan Payne. She opened her mouth to tell him that, but she couldn't get the words out.

Because his mouth covered hers, his lips sliding back and forth across her lips. The friction was sensual and delicious. She gasped at the rush of desire pulsing through her veins.

And he deepened the kiss, sliding his tongue through her parted lips. She pressed her palms to his chest, but she didn't push him away. Instead, she caressed his skin while she kissed him back.

Their pants for breath mingling, she could taste him. And feel him. His heart beat frantically beneath her palm, matching the crazy rhythm of her own madly pounding heart.

Her knees trembled, like they had earlier, and probably still because of her fear. She was afraid of all these feelings. Afraid that she felt this overwhelming desire—this intense need—for Logan Payne.

Maybe he was just playing games with her, manipulating her with compliments and his mouth and his touch. His hands slid over her back to the curve of her hips, which he clutched, as he dragged her up close to the evidence of his desire for her. He couldn't lie about that.

He wanted her, too. And as if he intended to take her, he swung her up in his arms and headed toward the bedroom. But a low growl stopped him, and his hard body tensed.

"Cujo," she murmured. "It's okay…"

But it really wasn't. Just hours ago Logan had accused her of trying to kill him and now he was kissing her? And worse yet, she was kissing him back. That wasn't okay. It was insanity. But she lied to Cujo because she didn't want the dog attacking Logan.

She didn't want him hurt.

Someone else had another opinion, though, because shots rang out in earsplitting, violent succession. Bullets shattered glass and splintered wood. Shelves and pictures fell from the walls.

Logan fell, too, taking her down with him. The near-dead weight of his long body pressed her into the carpeting of the living-room floor.

Had he been hit again? And this time more critically than his grazed shoulder?

Chapter Seven

Logan cursed himself as much as the shooter. How on earth was he supposed to protect Stacy when he allowed her to distract him so much that someone had been able to drive up to his house without his hearing the vehicle?

Cujo had heard it. But Logan hadn't reacted fast enough to the canine's low growl. And the shots had rung out…

His shoulder stung, but it was from the old wound. No bullets had grazed him this time. Flying glass hadn't even hit *him*.

But he stared down at Stacy. Like in the cemetery, her soft body cushioned his—having taken the brunt of the fall. "Are you all right?" he asked.

Her gray eyes wide with fear, she nodded but flinched as more shots rang out.

"Stay down," he told her even as he rose slightly to ease his weight off her. But he kept his head down as the firing continued.

She clutched at his arms, her fingers digging into his muscles as she held tightly to him. "You stay down, too." Her eyes widened with more fear. "And Cujo!"

The former K-9 barked at the door, digging at it in his urgency to escape and track down the shooter. But Logan heard the vehicle now, its tires squealing as it spun out of his driveway and back onto the street.

He jumped up and reached for the weapon he'd left on the island counter. But then he had to grab for his slipping towel. It didn't matter now. Even though he ran and threw open the door, he was too late to catch even a glimpse of the vehicle, let alone the shooter.

They'd gotten away. Again. Like every attempt before...

Cujo pushed past him and patrolled the drive, sniffing out probably every dropped shell. How many were they? How many shots had been fired?

It was a wonder neither of them had been hit. Stacy had said she was okay. But was she?

Logan hurried back inside the house. She hadn't moved yet. She was lying on the floor. Still. "Are you really all right?" he asked.

"Are they gone?" she asked.

"Yes," he assured her.

As if she'd been holding it the entire time, her breath shuddered out in a ragged sigh that drew his attention to her breasts. They nearly spilled over the top of her black bra. His shirt had fallen open across that decadent black bra and the matching panties. He groaned in frustration— of his attraction and that the shooter had interrupted them.

Then he tore his gaze from her and looked around his house, assessing the damage. The windows were broken, shattered glass scattered about the hardwood floor. Bullets had knocked pictures and shelves from the walls and penetrated the drywall.

"I should have known better..." he berated himself. Just days ago, Tanya's apartment had been shot up, but those bullets had missed Cooper and the woman who was now his wife. The shots had gone into the ceiling instead of them. Logan and Stacy almost hadn't been as lucky. If Cujo's bark hadn't made him take cover, they would have been hit for sure. "I shouldn't have brought you back here."

Stacy dragged his shirt back together, covering herself as best she could with the thin silk. "No, you shouldn't have," she agreed.

"And I damn well shouldn't have announced it in front of your brothers…" But he'd thought that doing that might actually keep them safe because her brothers wouldn't risk hurting her.

But maybe her family wasn't as close as he'd thought, especially given that someone had planted a bomb inside her apartment.

She vaulted to her feet and pressed her palms against his chest again. But she wasn't caressing his skin this time. She was shoving him back with such force for her delicate size that she nearly caused him to stumble.

But he held his ground and then he held her, sliding his arms around her trembling body. She struggled against him. "You're wrong! You're so wrong!"

He was. But he was referring to his feelings rather than his suspicions. Even now—even with his house in shambles around them—he wanted her.

He wanted to pick her up again and carry her to his bed, to ignore the damage and the continued threat to his life and hers. But he didn't want to just keep her safe.

He wanted her.

SHE WAS WRONG. She still hated him—because he was so quick to think the worst of the people she loved. And she hated that even though she hated him, she still wanted him. Her skin heated as she pressed her palms against his muscular chest. She intended to push him away, but she was tempted to clutch him close again—to finish what they'd started before the shooting had begun.

Had they actually been about to make love?

No, it would have been just sex; it wouldn't have been

making love. There had never been any love lost between them—except for the people they'd loved and lost. Their fathers...

And they would always blame each other for that.

So she forced herself to push back until she broke free of his arms. She stumbled a couple steps before regaining her balance. And, when she averted her gaze from his naked chest and lean hips, she regained her perspective.

"It can't be my brothers," she insisted.

"If you really believed that, you wouldn't have gone along with my mother's crazy plan to marry me," he said. "You know they've been trying to kill me."

"I don't know that," she said. And she'd been wrong, too—more wrong than he'd been—to so easily think the worst of the people she loved. It didn't matter how many times they'd wished him dead instead of their father; that had been just talk. Like the Amazon woman had said, Stacy had uttered her share of threats, too. Empty threats.

He snorted derisively. Maybe he still believed that she'd ordered her brothers to kill him. Or maybe he was just calling her out on the doubts she'd had over her brothers' involvement in those previous shootings.

"They are not the ones who've just shot up your house." She flinched as she took in the damage. She sure as hell hoped it wasn't them. "They know I'm here and they would never risk hurting me," she said. "Not even to hurt you."

"Maybe I'm not the only one they want to hurt," he said. "That bomb was planted in your apartment."

"My brothers had nothing to do with that bomb!" She had absolutely no doubts about that. They might kill *for* her—even if she hadn't asked—but they would never kill her.

"You can't be sure of that," Logan insisted.

"Your brother is the one who knows explosives." And he'd taught Logan enough to be able to stop one from going off. Had he taught him how to make it, too? Had her brothers been right to mistrust him? "And so do you..."

"Cooper shared only a little of his IED knowledge with me," he said. "I disarmed it more with luck than anything else."

She shook her head. "Nobody gets that lucky." At least no one she'd ever known.

"We did," he said. "Both of us. I was there with you."

"Only because I chided you into walking me to my door." She flinched with embarrassment over having done that.

"Chided me?" he asked, his mouth curving into a slight grin.

She clarified, "Threatened to tell your mother that you're not a gentleman."

"She's been told worse things about me," he assured her. "I walked you to your door because I wanted to. And I certainly wouldn't have wanted to if I'd known there was a bomb sitting on your kitchen table."

She believed him. Maybe she was a fool, like her brothers probably thought, to trust him. But she did. "Garek and Milek know nothing about explosives."

"You don't know that," he chided her now. Before she could protest, he added, "Anyone with internet access can learn about explosives."

"So anyone could have set that bomb," she agreed. "Except for my brothers." They weren't killers. *Anymore...* "They didn't shoot up your house, either, so they're not behind the other attempts." *Probably...*

His brow furrowed as if he struggled to follow her logic. He most likely couldn't accept that her brothers were innocent of anything. "Maybe whoever shot at us just now is who set the bomb in your apartment."

He had followed her logic. She breathed a sigh of relief. "And since we agree that's not Milek and Garek, we can break our fake engagement."

"I haven't agreed to anything," he pointed out.

"Logan!" she yelled with frustration at his stubbornness. "I know my brothers would never hurt me. Even *you* have to admit that." But she didn't really expect him to admit to anything—at least not to her.

"That doesn't mean that they haven't shot at *me* before," he said, stubbornly clinging to his suspicions. "I still think they could be behind the attempts on my life."

She shook her head in disbelief. "So you think that someone's trying to kill you—"

"Not someone. Your brothers."

She ignored his accusation and his interruption. "And someone else is trying to kill me? That's ridiculous."

He shrugged off her assessment of his theory. "Why would the same person want both of us dead? What enemy could we possibly share?"

She couldn't believe that she had ever made such an enemy. But she struggled even harder to believe that she shared anything with Logan Payne. She was trying to forget his kisses—but her lips tingled yet with the sensation of his lips sliding over hers.

"I don't know who it could be," she said. "But I know who it's not…"

He sighed in resignation. "Your brothers?"

"And since it's not my brothers," she continued, "there's no reason to continue our engagement, because it obviously didn't dissuade whoever just shot at us."

She waited for the surge of relief. She should be thrilled that her fake engagement was over—that she wouldn't have to pretend to be in love with the man she'd spent the past fifteen years hating. But that surge never came.

"I think it's more likely that there are two different people trying to kill us than that we would actually share an enemy," he said.

She sighed. "You still think my brothers are behind the attempts on your life."

"And you're not entirely sure that I'm not right," he said observantly.

She wasn't.

"So we're still engaged," he said.

"Why?" she asked. "The attempts are still getting made on our lives."

"The engagement gives us an excuse to be together," he said. "And keep each other alive."

"Or wind up killing each other and saving whoever's after us the trouble."

But that *whoever* apparently wasn't patient enough to wait until they killed each other. Cujo, who had never left his position near the front door, began to paw at it again and growl. The shooter or shooters might have returned— probably to find out if any of those bullets they'd fired had struck their target.

"Get in the bedroom," Logan told her.

Her heart pounded furiously but she couldn't stop a smart-aleck comment from coming to her lips—no doubt because of fear and nerves. "How can you think about sex at a time like this?"

He'd drawn his gun from his holster, his nearly naked body all tense and deadly but for the spark of humor her remark had brought to his bright blue eyes. He murmured, "You are going to kill me…"

"If you join me…" But he had a better chance of staying alive than facing the shooter or shooters alone.

He pointed her toward the bedroom. "Take Cujo with you. Go inside and lock the door."

"Cujo won't come with me." She didn't bother calling him, though, because she already knew he would ignore her commands. He was well trained but not strictly for obedience. Like Logan, the canine would always be a cop. The dog kept digging at the outside door, desperate to investigate whatever noise had drawn his attention.

Stacy suspected it was a car's engine but one that had been driven slowly enough that the noise was quiet. Whoever had driven up didn't want to be heard.

"I'm not going to take him outside with me." Logan shook his head. "The old boy's already gotten shot once. He's served his duty."

"You've already gotten shot, too," she reminded him. And she didn't want him getting shot again any more than she wanted Cujo getting shot again.

Logan shrugged his wounded shoulder. "The bullet barely grazed me." But blood had saturated the bandage, staining it bright red.

"Stay here with me and Cujo," she implored him. "Don't go out there." Because she was afraid that if he did, he might never come back.

But just as she'd known Cujo wouldn't listen to her, she knew that Logan wouldn't, either. Despite having gone into private protection, he was still a cop.

He touched her cheek. "Go into the bedroom and lock the door. And if I don't come back, there's a gun under the bed on the right side. Use it if you need to."

She shook her head. "I don't know how."

"Slide off the safety and shoot," he advised. Then he whistled low, commanding Cujo's attention. The dog turned his head toward them. "Guard her."

Cujo rushed to her side. He'd clearly chosen a new master—someone he would blindly obey.

Stacy didn't blindly obey anyone. "I'll get the gun," she agreed, "but I'm going outside with you. I'll be your backup."

He laughed. "You just admitted you don't know how to shoot a gun."

"And you told me how," she reminded him.

He shook his head. "You're not hired, Ms. Kozminski. You and Cujo need to go to the bedroom." He pointed, and the dog followed his command, nudging her with his big, furry head to push her toward the room. "And only touch that gun as a last resort to protect yourself."

Because he wouldn't be able to…

He was already heading—alone—toward the front door and whatever danger awaited him. He faced and survived danger all the time, so Stacy shouldn't be worried about him. Given their past, she shouldn't worry about him at all.

But she was worried. So worried that she crossed the room, rose up on tiptoe and pressed her lips to his cheek. "Be careful…"

Even as she said it, she knew he wouldn't heed her warning any more than she'd heeded his order. He didn't blindly obey, either.

But he hesitated for just a moment before he turned and opened the door. Then he slipped outside—to whatever danger awaited him….

Chapter Eight

Be careful...

She'd said it as if she cared, as if she was actually worried about him. But she couldn't have been. They weren't really engaged. They weren't really anything...but old enemies.

And almost lovers...

He forced thoughts of her kisses and her nearly naked body from his mind and focused on the vehicle idling in his driveway. Fortunately, he recognized the black Ford Explorer that was a twin to his.

"You plan on ever wearing pants again?" Parker asked from where he leaned against the side of his SUV.

Logan glanced down at the towel he'd forgotten he wore. The terry cloth was dry now.

"I understand why you might be distracted, though," his twin continued.

Logan glanced at his shot-up house. "Yeah..."

"I was talking about your fiancée," Parker said. "But I'm curious about this, too. That's why I came back when I heard the report of shots fired at your address on my police scanner."

Stacy had accused Logan of still being a cop, but he suspected his twin leaned more toward lawman than bodyguard. At least he'd come back alone…except for the whine of sirens in the distance.

"You should probably find some pants now," Parker remarked. Logan cursed and not just because his brother was always getting on his case, but because Parker wasn't the only one who'd returned. Candace Baker's pickup pulled into the driveway ahead of the police cars. Nikki and his mother would probably show up next. He stalked back into the house.

Just as he'd suspected, Stacy hadn't listened to him, either. She stood in the living room amid the glass and debris. But at least she'd put on her dress again. Without a word, he passed her and headed toward his bedroom and his clothes.

He dressed quickly, and the others were already inside when he walked back out. Cujo stood between them and Stacy, the hair raised on his neck as he uttered a warning growl.

"Good dog," he praised the canine.

"You gonna give him a treat if he bites us?" Parker asked.

"He probably is hungry," Stacy said. "I haven't had a chance to feed him since we picked him up from the kennel."

"Of course he would be *your* dog," Candace remarked.

His employee's scornful tone had Logan bristling, too. "My mom gave her the dog."

For protection. His mother had thought she needed it. Logan had assumed because of the neighborhood where Stacy lived. But what if his mother had suspected she was in danger for another reason?

He needed to speak to his mom.

"I need to talk to you," Candace said.

The sirens screeched as the police cars pulled into his driveway. "You're not the only one…"

Logan wasn't thrilled about having to take part in another police report. He hadn't liked that part of being a lawman, and he hadn't anticipated taking and giving police reports in his private protection business. And after all the attempts on the lives of his brother Cooper and his bride, Logan had overloaded on police reports.

But now it had gotten even more personal; now he had become a killer's target. But *he* wasn't the only one.

"The police are going to want to talk to you both," Parker said. "I can take Stacy out." He reached out as if to take her arm, but Cujo growled through bared teeth and Parker jerked his arm back. "Damn dog." He turned toward Logan. "Does he go after you like this?"

Logan chuckled. "No."

"We're twins," Parker said. "You'd think that would fool him."

But clearly the dog knew which of them was which, and he only approved of Logan touching his mistress. Logan was going to have to get the former K-9 officer some special treats.

"I'll go with you," Stacy told his brother as she took his arm.

Logan's stomach muscles clenched with dread. And, he hated to admit, jealousy…

His brother was a notorious playboy. Parker never dated a woman for very long before he moved on to the next conquest. And there was always another conquest. Women were never able to resist Parker.

"I'll go, too," Logan said.

His brother turned back to him, his brows raised in question while his eyes twinkled as if he was fully aware and amused by Logan's jealousy.

"They're going to want to talk to me, too," he explained.

But Candace clutched at his arm, which elicited another

growl from Cujo and a warning snarl. She didn't jerk back like Parker had, though.

And Logan had to put his hand on the dog's head to settle him down. "It's okay," he assured his canine protector. But it wasn't…not with his employee holding him back as Parker and Stacy walked outside together—Stacy's small hand on Parker's strong arm.

"Why do you have to talk to me so badly?" he asked Candace. "I'm kind of otherwise occupied…"

"With Stacy Kozminski," she clarified with a snort of disgust. The female bodyguard obviously didn't appreciate his fiancée's attributes as much as Parker did.

He glanced out the shattered window to where his twin stood close to Stacy, his arm actually around her shoulders as she spoke to the police officers. Maybe he was only offering support. But knowing Parker, Logan doubted it and gritted his teeth so that he didn't shout out a protest.

"She's my fiancée," he said through those gritted teeth. Parker probably couldn't hear him, but the words were meant for his twin more than his employee. She shook her head as if in denial of his words.

"You're acting like this engagement is real."

"Why would you think it isn't?" he asked.

"It's like when Cooper married Tanya the first time, as part of the job," she replied. "Just to protect you…or her…"

Cooper had only married Tanya because her real groom had been abducted and she'd needed to marry in order to collect her inheritance. The former marine had said it was for her—for her protection—but he'd also married her because he'd loved her. Always had and always would…

"Cooper and Tanya are definitely real," he reminded her.

She nodded in agreement. "Cooper and Tanya are different. They're in love."

"I'm not talking to you about my love life," he said, and tugged free of her hold on his arm.

"I want to talk about your life," she said. "Being with her is going to put you in danger."

"I was already in danger," he said.

"And you thought she was behind it," she said. "That she told her brothers to try to kill you."

Hearing Candace say his theory aloud made Logan realize how paranoid he'd sounded when he'd accused Stacy of such a horrendous crime. Pushing aside the last of his little, niggling doubts, he admitted, "I thought wrong…"

"No," she said. "You're right. She's done it before. They've killed for her before."

"You don't know the whole story about that…"

"Do you?"

He should have. His mother had tried to tell him, but he'd resented her sympathy for the daughter of his father's killer and had refused to listen. He shook his head in reply to Candace's question, but most of all in disgust at his own single-mindedness. He should have listened to his mother.

He should have learned more about Stacy Kozminski. But he'd hung on so stubbornly to his resentment.

"I know that one man is dead because of her," Candace said. "I don't want you to be the next." Ignoring Cujo's warning growl, she stepped closer to Logan. "Let *me* protect you…"

Her strange tone and urgency had his skin chilling. He'd already told her he could protect himself. Why was she so insistent?

LOGAN'S EMPLOYEE WAS in love with her boss. It was obvious to Stacy. It was obvious to Parker, who watched as Logan and Candace walked out of the shot-up house to talk to the police officers. Logan's twin stared at the female bodyguard with pity. The officers were done questioning Stacy now, but she loathed stepping back inside that house…for all the things that had nearly happened inside it.

They had nearly been shot. And they had nearly made love. Stacy wasn't sure which would have wound up hurting her more.

"How long has she been in love with him?" she asked his twin.

Parker shrugged. "She left the police department to work for him."

"A long time…" She'd even tagged along to those last two parole hearings. Stacy shivered now as she remembered the woman glaring at her—probably because of the things Stacy had said to Logan. Some not so very pleasant things.

"Yes." Parker sighed now with that pity. "He doesn't know, though."

"What would he do if he knew?" Stacy wondered aloud. Would he act on the woman's feelings? Would he return them?

"He would probably fire her," Parker said. "Which is why none of us has pointed it out to him. She's a damn good bodyguard, and her firing would be a huge loss to Payne Protection."

She nodded in understanding. Parker didn't want her to tell Logan, either. "Why would he fire her, then?"

"Because he would worry that she might lose her perspective." Parker's mouth curved into a slight grin. "He's always adamant about never letting emotions interfere with an assignment."

She laughed.

"Seriously," Parker said. "Logan is a very unemotional guy. Keeps everything inside—never shows his thoughts or feelings."

"Logan?" she repeated, totally shocked at his twin's

assessment of the hotheaded, openly judgmental man she knew. "Do you have a triplet? Because you haven't described the man I know."

"You bring out another side of him," Parker said. "You bring out his emotions." He chuckled now. "That's probably why he's always…" He trailed off, his face flushing with embarrassment over what he'd nearly revealed.

But she knew. "Hated me? Resented me?"

Parker shrugged but didn't deny her comments. "I always thought that it was just about your dad…"

So had she.

"But obviously it was more personal than that. Now I know why he stared at you all the time—he was attracted to you. That probably made him resent you even more." Parker grinned. "I'm glad he finally stopped fighting his feelings."

Hers was the family they needed to fool. Not his. So she opened her mouth to set Parker straight. "It's not what you think," she said. "It's really not…" *Real.*

But before she could finish her confession, a strong arm slid around her shoulders, and Logan pulled her tight against his side. "It's really not what?" he asked. His blue eyes held a warning for her to not admit the truth.

And with the Amazon bodyguard standing behind him, Stacy had no intention of doing any such thing…but sliding her arm around his waist. She felt a twinge of regret that he'd replaced the towel with jeans and a cotton shirt. "Sweetheart," she asked, "are the police done with their report?"

Candace snorted derisively. Over the endearment? Had Logan told her the truth? Stacy doubted that or he wouldn't have stopped her from telling his brother. "It'll take the crime scene techs a while to finish processing…"

She would know since she had once been a cop like Parker and Logan. Before Parker's admission, Stacy had assumed she might have been ex-military like Cooper Payne. She certainly looked the part of a G.I. Jane.

"And it's gonna take a contractor even longer to repair the damage," Parker added. "You're going to need someplace else to stay."

"Maybe the ATF is done with my place," she said. She would like to go home. Alone. But she doubted that Logan was about to leave her side until they figured out who was trying to kill them—since that was the only reason he'd agreed to their fake engagement.

Logan's hand skimmed down her arm to her hip, and he suggestively offered, "We can check into a hotel…"

She shivered in anticipation of what they could do in that hotel. Bad things…

To each other. But mostly bad things for her.

"A hotel won't take Cujo," she reminded him.

As if he'd heard them discussing him, the German shepherd leaped through the opening of the shattered window. They could probably bring him back to the kennel. He would be safer there. But before she could suggest it, the dog rushed to Logan's side.

He patted his head. "Hey, old boy, you've saved our lives a couple of times already. We need him."

"You have other protection," Candace said.

"He'd go crazy in the kennel now," Logan said. "Because he knows we're in danger."

"He's a dog," she murmured disparagingly.

"He's a cop," Logan said in the dog's defense. "He was K-9 before he got shot."

The woman turned toward the dog with new respect. "You're a good boy…"

Her praise didn't woo Cujo any more than it must have Logan. Neither of them paid her any attention as a jangle of metal had them turning to Parker.

He held up a ring of keys. "My place has a fenced yard. The dog would love it."

Logan grabbed the proffered keys and asked, "Where are you going to stay?"

Parker's mouth curved into another grin. "I'm not welcome in my own house?"

"The dog is all I need for backup…"

"The dog can't shoot a gun," Candace said. Obviously she could. She had one holstered beneath her arm like the guys. Could she set a bomb?

Like Logan, she'd thought Stacy was behind the attempts on his life, so she may have decided to get rid of any threat to the man she loved. And if Nikki and Parker were right and Logan had looked at her the way they claimed, maybe the woman had decided to remove the threat to his heart, as well.

Not that Stacy believed she could ever really claim Logan's heart. He would never get over his resentment of her.

"Logan wants to be alone with his fiancée," Parker said, which probably added unnecessary fuel to the woman's already burning resentment. As he had earlier, he hooked his arm around Candace's shoulders and led her toward their vehicles. But then he turned back and said, "Don't worry about me. I'll stay with Mom."

"Sure you wanna risk it?" Logan teased. "Mom's on a roll right now…"

Parker's laugh rang out as he walked away. He stopped at the woman's vehicle first and opened her door for her. The woman didn't appear to appreciate his gentlemanly gesture. She glared at him before sliding beneath the wheel. He slammed the door shut and patted it as if it were a horse he was urging to giddy up. After a few tense moments of staring back at Logan, the woman finally started the engine.

"What is he risking?" Stacy asked. She felt as if she were

the one risking everything—alienating her family, making an enemy in the woman who had a crush on Logan and falling for her fake fiancé herself. If it were up to her, she would have preferred to stay with Mrs. Payne than alone with her oldest son.

"He's risking his playboy status." Logan waved at his brother's SUV as the man drove away. Then he pressed his hand to the small of Stacy's back and guided her toward his own vehicle. As his brother had for the bodyguard, Logan opened the door for Stacy.

She climbed into the passenger's seat and asked, "Do you think your mom will talk Parker into a fake engagement, too?"

Logan laughed now. "I don't think even Mom could ever maneuver Parker to the altar." He closed her door and walked around to the driver's side.

Stacy felt as if *she* was the one who'd been maneuvered…into once again being alone with Logan Payne. After he and Cujo jumped inside the SUV, she remarked, "We could have stayed with her."

His handsome face pulled into a tight mask of disapproval. "And put her in the cross fire—again—of whoever's shooting at us?"

"No. Of course not," she said. "I would never want her getting hurt because of me. But you probably think that I have already hurt her…"

He tensed with obvious concern for his mother's safety. "How?"

Stacy paused, surprised that he hadn't immediately agreed with her. "Because of what you think my dad did."

"I *know* that your dad did it," he said, his tension easing only slightly. He turned the key in the ignition, starting up the SUV. "*You* didn't do it. I don't blame you."

Maybe she hadn't heard him correctly over the rumble

of the engine. "Yeah, right. You have definitely blamed me and my brothers."

He groaned. "I haven't blamed you for what your dad did. I've blamed you for refusing to admit what he did."

She still refused. "That's because he didn't do it," she insisted. "He never would have pulled the trigger."

"They struggled over the gun."

"He wouldn't have reached for it," she insisted. "My father hates—" a twinge of pain struck her heart as she realized she had to correct herself and use past tense "—hated guns. He never would have touched it."

"It was just the two of them in that room," Logan said. "What do you think happened? How did my father wind up dead and yours not?"

She pointed out what had always been so obvious to her. "There was someone else in that room."

"Officer Cooper didn't see anyone else leaving it," Logan said.

"He wasn't there yet," she said. She had memorized the officer's testimony, and despite fifteen years having passed since the trial, she hadn't forgotten a word. "Your father got to the room first. His partner was slower—too slow to see who really shot your father."

A muscle twitched in Logan's cheek as he turned away from her, his focus on his driving as he steered around the crime scene and police vehicles parked in his driveway. "Your father never said that there was someone else in the room."

Her father had never said anything about what had happened that horrible night. He had chosen to not even testify at his own trial. "I know he wouldn't have done it."

"Then why not tell the police who did?" Logan asked. "He had to have witnessed it."

"I don't know why he wouldn't tell…" Tension throbbed

behind her eyes, so she squeezed them shut to relieve some pressure of trying to convince Logan her father was innocent. Why was she even wasting her time? She'd had fifteen years to convince him and had failed. She knew she would never really get through to him. "I don't know…"

Instead of laughing at her or calling her naive as she'd suspected he would, Logan offered an explanation. "Maybe he was protecting someone."

Hope rushed through her, and she opened her eyes to stare at him in shock. "You believe me? You believe my father was innocent?"

He shook his head and dashed her hopes.

If he kept blaming her dad for his father's death, there was no future for them. That anger and resentment would always remain between them.

Her breath caught with more shock that she had actually hoped there might be a future for them. Had she become such a good actress that she'd convinced herself their engagement could be real?

"I don't know what to believe," he admitted.

"About my father?" He had given her doubts about her brothers; it was only fair that she gave him doubts, too.

"About you," he said. "I thought you were responsible for the attempts on my life, that you'd put your brothers up to it…"

His suspicions chilling her, she shivered. She had been a fool to think there would ever be a future between them. He didn't think the worst of just her family; he thought it of her, too. He always had and that hadn't changed.

Only her feelings had begun to change…

But maybe it was just gratitude that she felt for him since he had saved her life. Twice. But even before that she'd begun to think a little differently about Logan Payne… because of her father's cryptic last words.

"I've been told you've done it before," Logan said. "That you've had your brothers kill for you."

Given the way he'd phrased it, she had a pretty good idea who had told him. The jealous female bodyguard might have bent the truth, but she hadn't outright lied.

So Stacy admitted it. "They have killed for me."

Chapter Nine

Logan hadn't expected her to freely admit it—not when she clung so stubbornly to the illusion of her father's innocence. Stunned by her admission, he'd driven in silence to his brother's house.

"Is this it?" she asked doubtfully as he pulled up to the traditional two-story brick Colonial. "This doesn't look like a place your brother would live…"

"He claims he won it in a poker game," Logan said with a slight chuckle. He suspected his brother used the four-bedroom house to lure women into thinking that he might secretly want a wife and kids someday. But he doubted the playboy Payne would ever wed—no matter how much Mom tried to coerce him into getting married.

She shrugged. "Sometimes I wonder how well we really know our families…"

If she hadn't had doubts about her brothers, she wouldn't have acted on his mother's marriage suggestion. But hearing her actually admit it had disappointment causing a twinge of pain in his chest. Even while her blind devotion to her father had frustrated him, he'd also admired her loyalty to her family.

"No," she said, as if realizing he'd misconstrued her comments. "That's not what I meant."

"You weren't talking about your brothers?"

Silence was her telling reply.

"You told me earlier that they killed for you before," he reminded her. And he'd been so stunned that he hadn't uttered a single word the entire drive to Parker's house.

Her body bristling with defensiveness, she replied, "I didn't tell them to—"

"But they killed for you."

"To protect me," she said.

He tensed now. "Protect you? Has someone tried to kill you before?"

Her teeth sank so deeply into her bottom lip that she probably almost drew blood, and she shook her head.

So they hadn't killed in order to save her life. What other excuse was there for taking a life? "What were they protecting you from, then?"

She shuddered with such revulsion and horror that he regretted ever bringing up what had obviously been a painful experience for her. As if sensing her pain and feeling it, too, the dog whined and rubbed his head against hers, tousling her streaky blond-brown hair.

"Stacy…" He was going to tell her that she didn't have to tell him, that he didn't need to know. But he realized that he did—that he suddenly needed to know everything there was to know about his fake fiancée.

She drew in a shuddery breath, as if bracing herself, before she continued. "When my father went to prison, we had to go live with my mother again and my—my stepfather."

Outrage coursed through Logan as realization dawned. "Did he…"

She shook her head. "He was trying to…but my brothers broke down the bedroom door. They saved me…but our stepfather died."

If Logan had been the one to break down that door, the

bastard wouldn't have survived his wrath, either. For once he respected her brothers. "Which one did it?"

"I don't know," she said. "I blacked out. And when I woke up, they were both hurt badly and he was dead."

"They never told you?"

She shook her head. "It doesn't matter which one of them did it. They both saved me, and they both went to jail for it."

And knowing that cemented Logan's certainty that they would never risk hurting her—not even to protect themselves. They might be trying to kill him, but someone else was trying to kill her. "But if they were both badly beaten, they shouldn't have been charged with anything. It was self-defense."

It had at least been defense—of their sister.

She nodded. "It should have been, but my mother testified otherwise."

"She testified against her own children?" Now he was the one horrified. His mother would have killed the man herself if he'd ever tried to touch one of her children.

"She said that I told them to do it." Her voice cracked with emotion. "Because I was mad that he rejected my advances."

That must have been the twisted story that Candace had learned.

"The jury convicted them of manslaughter," she said, "but the judge believed me over her and gave them light sentences. Milek went to juvenile detention and Garek a minimum security prison for six months."

Neither of those were easy stints. But the jury had convicted them and the judge had probably sentenced them because they'd had previous offenses for stealing, like their father. Could either of them have been with him that night?

But Logan wasn't thinking about that night now. He was

thinking about Stacy. "And what about you?" he asked. "Where did you go?"

"I wasn't charged with anything," she said.

"But where did you go?" he asked. "You couldn't have kept living with your mother."

She shuddered again. "No. She signed off her parental rights the day my stepfather died."

"Were you still just fourteen, like you'd been during your father's trial?"

She nodded.

"So you went into the system?"

Her lips curved into a wistful smile. "That might have been better. Because my father asked him, Uncle Iwan let me live with him. But his wife wasn't very gracious about it."

Logan shivered as he remembered the older woman's icy demeanor. "She doesn't seem like the motherly type."

"No. But until I met your mother, I really had no idea what motherly is supposed to be."

She'd obviously had a horrible example of motherhood.

"Your mother is great," she said with more of that wistfulness.

He sighed and agreed, "Yes, she is."

She drove him crazy much of the time—because of her generosity and forgiveness and, most of all, her meddling. But her heart was always in the right place; sometimes it was just too damn big.

Except this time.

He finally understood why his mother had taken such an interest in the daughter of her husband's killer. And he loved her even more for it. His mother. Not Stacy. He didn't love her. But he didn't hate her anymore, either.

"She's great," Stacy repeated. "But she's wrong about the two of us."

Remembering the taste and sensation of Stacy's lips beneath his, Logan's pulse quickened with awareness and attraction and he wasn't so certain that his mother wasn't right about them.

"Her plan isn't working," Stacy continued. "Since our *engagement,* we've nearly been blown up and shot. You really should just take me home. ATF must have cleared my place by now. The building isn't even that big."

The building. "Could the bomb have been meant for the landlord? Maybe someone mistook him for living above the store?"

"The landlord does live above the store," she replied.

He tensed. "You don't live alone?"

"No. I don't."

He'd really misunderstood the situation with her. He'd thought she was as single as he was. But he wasn't just confused. He was disappointed. "Why didn't you say something earlier? The bomb could have been meant for your... *roommate.*"

"My roommate has no enemies." She patted the dog's head. "Cujo is my roommate."

What kind of game was she playing with him? "He's damn well not your landlord, though."

She giggled.

The realization dawned on him. "You own the building," he said.

She nodded. "Me and the bank. Given the property values in that neighborhood, I'm not sure which of us owns more, though."

"And the jewelry store? A tenant?"

She shook her head. "No, it's mine. I design and sell my own jewelry."

That explained the calluses on her hands since she worked with metal and tools and stones. He could have

said something about the irony she'd brought up earlier—
not only did the daughter of a jewelry thief live above a
jewelry store, she owned the jewelry store. But he saw more
significance than irony in the situation. "So the bomb could
only have been meant for you."

She shook her head again. "I don't know why. I have
even fewer enemies than Cujo."

"What about your mother?" Any woman who would
testify against her own children...

"She wouldn't have waited fifteen years to exact her revenge," she said with a dismissive shrug. "And she moved
on a long time ago and has been married twice since my
stepfather died." Her face flushed as if she was embarrassed over her mother's behavior. But she'd felt no shame
over her father...

"Now you know why I'm still single," she said.

He wasn't sure if it was because of what had happened
with her stepfather or because of her mother's multimar-
riages. But he nodded.

"You know all my secrets," she said.

"I doubt that."

"You know there's no reason for anyone to want me
dead."

"Maybe there's no reason," he allowed. "But someone
still wants you dead. Or they damn well wouldn't have
planted a bomb in your apartment." He got out the driver's side and walked around the hood to open her door. "So
we're staying here tonight."

The sun had dropped low in the sky, the last rays of it
shimmering across the asphalt of Parker's street.

"Do you want me to carry you inside again?" he asked.
Part of him hoped she did. He liked carrying her, liked the
slight weight of her curvy body in his arms, her head on
his shoulder...

"No." She sighed and stepped down from the SUV. "It is getting kind of late to go back to my place."

"And yours isn't the safest neighborhood in the daylight," he said. But he didn't intend to let her go home in the morning, either. He didn't intend to let her out of his sight until he figured out who was trying to kill her.

Cujo jumped down from the SUV and followed closely behind his mistress. The dog knew that she was in danger. If only Stacy realized it, too…

SHE WAS IN DANGER. More danger than she'd ever been in before, and she'd had some close calls both in the past and recently. But then her life had been in danger.

Now she was worried about her heart. Why had she told Logan so much about herself? Why had she shared more with him than she ever had with anyone else?

It wasn't as if he was really her fiancé.

He was actually the only enemy she had. But if he was trying to kill her, why did he keep saving her?

In the dim light from the street, he fumbled with Parker's keys before unlocking the door. Cujo pushed past him and crossed the threshold, sniffing his way across the hardwood floor of the living room. Then he bounded up the stairs.

His behavior reminded Stacy of the way he'd acted at her apartment. Her pulse quickened with another kind of fear. "What's he doing?"

The dog's footsteps scratched across the hardwood floors overhead. Logan sighed. "Probably tracking a woman to Parker's bed."

"I'm guessing there've been several," she mused. Was he just following the old scents?

"And several have come back to wait for him."

The dog barked.

"There's a woman in his bed now?" she asked.

"Probably…" But Logan reached for his gun, as if concerned that it might be another kind of threat.

"But the door was locked."

"I'm not the only one he's given his key to," Logan replied. "Usually he gets them back, but sometimes someone makes a copy."

The barking intensified and so did Stacy's fear. "Then he should change his damn locks."

Logan grunted in agreement as he headed toward the stairs. Stacy followed, but he shook his head. "Stay here."

She shook hers in response. She wanted to see what kind of woman would let herself into a man's house and crawl into his bed. And why did an image of herself lying naked in Logan's bed flash through her mind?

Could she be that kind of woman? For him, she was afraid that she could become that desperate, that needy…

She shuddered in apprehension.

"I'm sure it's nothing," Logan said. "Nobody knows we're staying here tonight."

That wasn't true. Parker knew. And more perilously, that jealous Amazon knew.

Could that be who waited in Parker's bed…but for Logan?

She paused midstep, not certain she wanted to see this. But then Cujo growled.

Logan could probably call him off; the dog had recognized him as the alpha male and his master. But Cujo had belonged to Stacy longer. So she continued up the stairs behind Logan.

He moved stealthily down the hall. Stacy tried but, despite being smaller and lighter, she couldn't make her footsteps as quiet as his. The man could have been a jewel thief himself. But he was all about law and order.

And security.

As her father and her brothers had discovered, there was no security in stealing. While her brothers crimes had led to jail time, her father's had led to his death. But then Logan's dad, who'd been all about law and order, too, had also died.

Panic clutched her heart as he stepped through a doorway. His shadow fell back into the hall—dark and foreboding. Had he stepped into a trap?

"Get out of here!" he yelled.

And he wasn't talking to some naked woman in Parker's bed. He was talking to her as she joined him inside the room. While the traditional-looking family home had been misleading about Parker's personality, the bedroom was not. The four-poster king-sized bed and its black satin sheets dominated the space. A black-framed mirror adorned the wall across from the bed and another mirror adorned the ceiling above it.

Maybe that was why Cujo had been barking. Like cats and squirrels and rabbits, he didn't like other dogs, either. Probably because he considered himself a cop instead of a canine.

But Cujo wasn't looking into the mirrors. He was crouched under the bed, growling.

Was the woman under there? Because there was no one in the perfectly made bed.

Logan was crouched down beside the dog, his attention divided between whatever was under there and her. "Get out of here!" he said.

But curiosity overwhelmed her and she leaned down to look, too. Like the bomb on the kitchen table, this one was a tangle of wires and canisters and a clock with flashing numbers. There was time left on this one, though.

Several minutes.

"I can't believe this," she murmured.

"And I can't disarm this one," Logan said with a groan of frustration.

"But you did the other one…"

He shook his head. "This isn't like Cooper described. I don't dare touch it."

She'd rather he didn't try. "We have to leave," she said.

"You go." He slid his gun back into his holster and pulled out a cell phone. "I'm going to call the bomb squad."

She remembered how long they'd taken to get to her apartment. If Logan hadn't disarmed it, it would have exploded for sure. Like this one would…

"Come with me," she pleaded.

"Go," he told Cujo.

But she hadn't been talking to her dog. She'd been talking to her man. Well, he wasn't her man. And if he blew up, he would never be.

The dog refused to leave Logan's side. And so did she.

"You're only going to distract me," he said. "And I need to pay attention to what the bomb squad is telling me."

She hoped they'd tell him to leave.

"Get out of here," he told her again. "Or all of us will die."

She didn't want any of them to die, him least of all.

"Stacy…" He'd dropped the demanding tone and turned his attention from the bomb to her, his gaze intent and imploring.

She could ignore his orders. But she couldn't deny his wish. Hopefully he couldn't deny hers, either. "Please leave with me," she said. "The house doesn't matter."

"I don't know how much damage this bomb can do," he said. "It could take out more than this house. It could take out the whole neighborhood."

The suburban neighborhood with all those houses full

of families who were probably just finishing up dinner and getting ready for bed.

He handed her his keys. "Take my SUV and drive as far away as you can…"

Before the bomb explodes?

If it did, it wouldn't just take out all those families. It would take out Logan, too.

She didn't want to distract him. But she pressed her lips to his, kissing him deeply. Kissing him as if it were the last time…

SHE WAS GONE, but not so long that his lips weren't still tingling from her kiss. So Logan struggled to concentrate on the instructions coming through the telephone. What if she hadn't gotten far enough away to be out of the danger zone? According to the size of the bomb, that danger zone could encompass multiple blocks.

"Are you sure about this?" a man's voice, sharp with impatience, emanated from the cell phone pressed to Logan's ear. He must have misinterpreted Logan's hesitation for fear. "You can leave and let us handle it when we arrive."

He would like to do nothing better, but he'd found the timer on the device and the numbers were flashing fast. Too fast…

"The minutes are ticking away on this thing," Logan said. And to prove his point of how little time was left he used his cell phone to snap a picture and send it to the ATF number to which dispatch had forwarded his call. He was talking to the captain of the bomb squad, something O'Doyle. "You would never get here in time." Not if the clock was right. He hoped like hell the clock wasn't right. "I'm your only chance."

And that chance was getting slimmer by the second.

"You're taking the biggest chance here, Payne. If this thing blows up in your face…"

He would have no face or anything else left to worry about. But he was more worried about Stacy and her safety. Maybe he should have let her stay. But he hadn't seriously thought she would leave. She hadn't done anything else he'd told her to do.

And maybe she shouldn't have listened to him this time, either. Maybe this was all a ploy to distract him—to get him to not only let her out of his sight but to actually make her leave him.

"How can I be sure this thing is even real?" Logan asked. If he'd been tricked into letting his protective subject out of his sight, Parker would never let him live it down. And if something happened to Stacy, he wasn't sure how he would live…without her.

Even when he'd hated her, she'd constantly been in his thoughts, on his mind.

"I'm studying that picture you snapped me," Captain O'Doyle said, his voice gruff with concern and frustration. "And that thing is not only real but it's incredibly hard to dismantle."

Logan's stomach lurched and he groaned. "Maybe I should just try to evacuate the neighborhood instead." If he drove through the area and blew the horn on his SUV…

No, Stacy had taken his vehicle. Hopefully she'd taken the SUV and was still driving it far, far away.

"There's no time," the captain repeated what Logan had already said. What he already knew.

He drew in a deep breath to steady his nerves and his hands. "Okay, I can do this." Without exhaling, he drew in another breath, swelling his lungs with air and courage. "I can do this…"

Maybe if he said it enough times, he would convince himself and the captain.

"I need you to be completely focused on my instructions, Payne," O'Doyle said, "or you're going to blow yourself up and take most of that neighborhood with you."

Innocent people would lose their lives. And, if she hadn't driven far enough outside the danger zone, Stacy would lose her life, too. So he had to focus, like the captain had warned him. Or he wouldn't be able to protect Stacy or himself.

"Okay," he said. "Tell me what to do. I'm ready…"

To defuse a bomb. Not to die. He wouldn't give whoever was trying to kill him the satisfaction of succeeding. And he didn't want to die before he'd indulged his curiosity—and his inconvenient attraction—to his fake fiancée.

STACY'S HEART BEAT fast and furiously. And her hands trembled so badly that she dropped Logan's keys onto the curb beside the SUV. He wanted her to leave.

He needed her to leave so that he could focus. Knowing that, she picked up the keys and used the fob to unlock the driver's door. Then she slid behind the wheel and fumbled the keys into the ignition. But she didn't have the strength to turn the key.

She couldn't leave Logan to face that kind of danger alone. She would let herself quietly back inside the house; Cujo was so focused on the bomb that he wouldn't give away her presence. She would be quiet. Logan would never know she was there. But she would be there. For him…

Leaving the keys dangling from the ignition, she opened the driver's door to step back onto the curb. But before she could close the door behind herself, strong hands wrapped around her arms.

"You can't make me go," she said. "I'm not leaving you!"

But those weren't Logan's hands on her arms. If they

were, her skin would be hot, her pulse racing. Instead, she felt only fear. Fear for him and that bomb he would probably die trying to defuse.

And now she felt fear for herself.

Chapter Ten

Lights flashed—on emergency vehicles and on news crews' cameras. Logan squinted against the flashes and peered around, but he couldn't find Stacy. She was gone. He couldn't really blame her. After all, there had been a bomb about to explode that would have, as he'd suspected, taken out most of the neighborhood. His hands shook slightly now, in reaction, but thankfully they'd been steady when he'd needed them to be. Or no one would have been able to identify what might have been left of his body.

"You should consider joining the ATF," the bomb squad captain told him. "You have a knack for this."

"I wouldn't call it a knack," he said. "I'd call it really bad luck."

Clothed all in black with a shaved head, Captain O'Doyle looked like a humorless, no-nonsense kind of man, but he chuckled. "The bad luck would have been if you hadn't disarmed the bombs."

"The bad luck was finding two in one day."

"That is bad luck," the captain agreed. "What's going on with you?"

"I wish I knew…" He'd thought it had been about him—all those shots fired at him. But how could someone have known he would be at his brother's house tonight?

Only Parker and Candace knew…

And whoever might have been milling around the crime scene at his house. Could someone else have blended in with the techs and officers and eavesdropped on their conversation? Maybe they had even seen Parker toss him his house keys?

"What the— What happened here?" Parker asked as he ran up the street from the blockade at the end of it. "My whole neighborhood's been evacuated!"

"This is his house," Logan explained to the captain.

"We have to finish clearing it before we can let your neighbors go back to their homes."

"There are no other explosives," Logan said, and he reached down to pet Cujo's head. The German shepherd leaned heavily against his leg, totally exhausted from his day of saving lives. "This former K-9 cop would have found them. He really has a knack for this."

Captain O'Doyle narrowed his eyes and studied the dog. "We could use him with ATF. You could bring him with you when you join us." One of the other agents called out to him and he headed off.

"ATF?" Parker asked.

"I have a job," Logan reminded him.

"Since you seem to have this whole other calling, I wouldn't mind stepping in as CEO of Payne Protection," Parker said. "It would be a sacrifice, of course…"

"Of course." Logan watched as the bomb squad carried off the undetonated bomb. He held his breath, but it didn't go off in the container as the one at Stacy's apartment had. This had been an entirely different kind of bomb. So, as ATF had told him, it was either a different bomber or a bomber with different signatures. Or two brothers who'd each constructed one of the bombs?

He focused on his own brother again. "But it's a sacrifice you won't need to make."

"I will if you get yourself killed," Parker said. "And right now I'd say my chances of taking over as CEO are pretty good. What's going on?"

Logan shrugged, but his muscles were tense and he grunted at a flash of pain in his wounded shoulder.

"You've been shot at more than once and nearly blown up twice," Parker said.

That wasn't why he was tense.

"Where is she?" he asked, his heart pounding even harder than it had when he'd been disarming the bomb. But then he'd needed to be calm. That was why he'd told her to leave, so worrying about her safety wouldn't distract him. So her closeness wouldn't have his heart pounding as hard and fast as it always did in her presence. "She took my SUV and left. Where is she?"

Parker didn't ask who, he just asked, "She took off?"

"I told her to," Logan explained. "I didn't want her getting hurt. I gave her my keys…"

And he thought she'd taken his SUV and left. But the bomb squad van, which was really the size of a city bus, backed out of the driveway now and revealed the SUV still at the curb where he'd parked it.

"That's not mine," his brother said. "I wasn't allowed onto my own street—let alone anywhere near my driveway."

Logan hurried over to the SUV and reached for the driver's door. It was already open, the dome light shining onto the empty front seats and reflecting off the keys dangling from the ignition.

She had intended to follow his order to drive off, but something—or somebody—had stopped her. He shouted her name, "Stacy!"

"She's not here," Parker stated the obvious. "But she wouldn't have left the SUV and walked off. The way you two are acting—" he narrowed his eyes on Logan's face, as if he questioned if they were only acting "—I doubt she would leave you alone with the bomb. I doubt she'd leave you of her own free will at all."

Apparently Stacy was a better actress than Logan was… because she definitely would have left him. She hadn't wanted to be here with him at all. She'd wanted to go home. But then after they'd discovered the bomb, she had protested leaving him—until he'd insisted—and before she'd left, she'd given him that kiss.

She could have meant that kiss as goodbye forever or as incentive for another hello…

Logan had taken it as incentive.

"Talk to the officer at the barricade," Logan directed his brother. "See if they saw her leaving when they drove up to secure the area."

Parker nodded and hurried back down the street to where the officers and several reporters and other onlookers stood by the barricade. Bulbs flashed and people shouted to him—wanting answers about the evacuation and the presence of the bomb squad. Parker couldn't give anyone answers; he didn't have any himself.

Neither did Logan. Who had set the bomb inside the house? It had been very real, but maybe the person who'd set it hadn't considered it foolproof. And so he'd waited outside to finish off whoever might have escaped the explosion.

Stacy had escaped the bomb, but she hadn't escaped whoever had taken her right from his vehicle. Had they dragged her off to theirs or was she somewhere in the area?

"Track her," he ordered Cujo. The dog cocked his head as if trying to understand. "Your mistress. Track her." Stacy's scent—her sweet, flowery scent—should be easy for the dog to pick up, Logan figured. He could still smell it— he could smell her—on his clothes and on his skin. The

German shepherd lowered his head and sniffed around Logan's truck, and the black-and-tan fur rose and bristled on his neck and back. He hadn't picked up just Stacy's scent; he'd picked up the scent of a stranger, too. The dog followed his nose along the curb and stopped and growled.

Stacy and the stranger's short trail had disappeared—undoubtedly into the back of another vehicle. Logan had been so careful to make certain that nobody had followed them from his house. But then the bomb proved that someone had beaten him there. They must have parked along the street, waiting to make sure the bomb left no survivors.

But Stacy had survived. The bomb.

But was she alive now?

WAS HE ALIVE?

Had he survived the bomb?

Stacy trembled with fear and rage. She leaned forward from the backseat to slam her hand into her brother's shoulder. The car swerved off the winding drive. "How dare you kidnap me!"

"Don't do that!" Garek protested. "Aunt Marta will kill me if I put ruts in her lawn."

Not that Aunt Marta had ever done her own landscaping. She had a grounds crew for that and a house crew to clean the three-story brick mansion to which Garek was driving up.

"And we didn't kidnap you," Milek said, adding his two cents from the shotgun seat.

"You grabbed me off the street like a couple thugs!" she reminded them.

"You were going to run back into a house that you told us had a bomb in it," Milek argued. And they actually hadn't pushed her into their backseat until she'd told them about the bomb. "We couldn't let you risk your life."

"What about Logan?" she asked.

"We don't care about his life," Garek replied. "And for the past fifteen years, neither did you."

"I care," she said. It was no longer a lie. "Take me back there."

Garek shook his head as he turned off the car. "Even if I wanted to, I couldn't," he said. "The police were evacuating the neighborhood as we were leaving."

"Why were you there?" she asked. She would have asked them earlier, but she'd been too furious with them, too furious that they were taking her away from Logan and leaving him alone to face peril.

"We were there to protect you," Milek said.

"Logan is protecting me," she said. Hopefully doing so hadn't cost him his life. Her stomach pitched at the thought—the horror—of Logan dying. Part of that horror was guilt that she had once wished him dead aloud when his statement to the parole board had kept her father in prison.

"He's not doing a very good job of protecting you," Garek complained as he opened the back door for her. He'd locked it earlier so that she hadn't been able to escape the car and run back to Logan and the bomb. "He brought you back to his place which got all shot up. You could've been killed."

"You were there?" she asked.

Had they done the shooting? She hadn't thought they would put her life in danger—not even to take Logan's. That was why she'd proposed to the man she'd always considered an enemy—to keep her brothers from doing something they would regret. Or that she, at least, would regret.

Garek narrowed his eyes and stared at her disapprovingly, like the overprotective big brother he'd always been. "We followed you from your place to *his*."

Logan had told them where he was bringing her. Had they doubted him? Did they doubt their engagement?

"And then you followed us to his brother's?" She hoped they'd followed and not gone ahead to set that bomb. But these were her brothers. They wouldn't risk her life. Would they?

"You didn't ask us if we saw who shot at you at his house," Milek mused. "Why? Did Logan Payne convince you it was us?"

She couldn't deny that he'd tried, but she shook her head. "Did you see anything? At Logan's house? Or at Parker's? Did you see anything suspicious?"

"After we followed you back to Logan's, we left for a while," Milek said with a glance toward the house and the woman who stood in the open doorway.

Following his gaze, she gasped in shock that it wasn't Aunt Marta who stood in the doorway but Mrs. Payne. Aunt Marta and Uncle Iwan stood behind her. Marta looked ready to throw her out while Uncle Iwan just looked as confused as Stacy was.

"I thought you brought me here for an intervention," Stacy said.

Garek laughed. "That would have been a better idea. You must be on something if you're really considering marrying Logan Payne. We should've brought you to rehab instead of bringing you here."

"Why did you bring me here?" she asked...if it hadn't been to talk her out of marrying Logan Payne. But her stomach pitched again as she realized they might not need to talk her out of anything. She might have already lost her fake fiancé—not to the truth but to a bomb.

Garek gritted his teeth so hard that his words were barely audible as he replied, "We brought you here to plan your wedding."

"Not because we think you should marry this creep," Milek said, his voice low so only she and their brother could hear. "We don't think you should. We don't think you actually will."

"We think you're teaching us a lesson," Garek said. "Or maybe you're teaching him a lesson. Or maybe you're just messing with everyone's heads. But you're not marrying him." He shook his head as if he was trying to convince her—or himself.

"Then why bring me here to plan my wedding?" she asked. Here, of all places. She'd hated living with her aunt and uncle so much that she would have accepted the woman's offer to send her off to boarding school if it wouldn't have been too hard for Stacy to visit her brothers and father in jail.

With a sigh of resignation, Milek replied, "Because she asked us to."

Not Aunt Marta. She would want even less to do with her niece's wedding than Milek and Garek did. Mrs. Payne had asked them, and because Mrs. Payne had asked them, they had obliged her.

Mrs. Payne must not have known about the bomb, or she would have been at Parker's house despite the evacuation order. She would have been there making sure she wouldn't have to plan a funeral rather than a wedding.

Stacy dragged her feet as she approached that open doorway. She didn't want to be the one to tell his mother about the bomb. She didn't want to break a heart that had already been shattered when the woman had lost her husband. But then tires squealed as another car pulled through the gates of the estate, and she turned back toward the black SUV.

Before the vehicle came to a complete stop, Logan threw

open the door and jumped out. He was alive! Relief flooded her, weakening her knees as she trembled from the surge.

Garek cursed. "How did he know where to find us?"

The bigger question was how had he survived a bomb? According to him, Cooper had only given him a crash course in improvised explosive devices and he'd gotten lucky last time.

"I told Logan where to meet us, of course," Mrs. Payne said as she joined them on the front steps. Maybe Aunt Marta had thrown her out of her house. "He needs to help plan his wedding."

He wanted nothing to do with a wedding—at least not with a wedding to her. He was going to expose her for the liar that she was. But Stacy didn't care. She didn't care about anything except that he was alive.

STRUCK WITH SUCH FORCE, Logan stumbled back. It was nothing in comparison to what the blast of the bomb might have been had the bomb gone off. But Stacy had nearly exploded off the front steps of her uncle's house as she'd vaulted into his arms. He caught her, his arms closing around her as if they knew she belonged in them. With him...

God, Mom was getting to him with all her brainwashing romance nonsense. Over Stacy's head, he glared at his mother. Why had she come here of all places? And had Garek and Milek bring Stacy here, as well?

One of these people was a killer. Heck, maybe all of these people were killers. Or they would be if one of the bullets had struck, if one of the bombs had exploded.

He held Stacy close to protect her. But he needed to protect his mother, too—from her own optimism. "Mom, it's late. You shouldn't have called this meeting tonight."

She clapped her hands together, and everyone jumped as

if another shot had been fired. "There is no time to waste to plan your wedding."

Planning a wedding would be a waste—because the wedding would never take place. She knew that, and that was probably why she was pushing him.

"There's a three-day waiting period for licenses in Michigan," the wedding planner reminded everyone. "But I know a certain judge who might waive that given the circumstances. He did it for your brother."

"Because someone was trying to kill him and his bride," Logan said.

His mother arched a brow. But he didn't need a reminder. He knew someone was trying to kill him and Stacy, too. He could understand one of them trying to murder him—to avenge Patek Kozminski's death.

But her…?

Why would anyone want Stacy dead?

She'd been a pain in his ass, but he didn't want her gone. He just wanted her. Now.

But not as his bride.

"We can't get a license tonight," he said. "It's too late."

"But the judge would meet us down at the courthouse. All he needs is your birth certificate and social security card." She held up an envelope. "I brought yours. And Mrs. Kozminski has Stacy's."

Maybe that was why she'd come here—for that paperwork. Or maybe she wanted to prove to Logan that none of these people wanted him dead. But with the way all the Kozminskis were looking at him, he was lucky that looks couldn't kill. The only Kozminski not looking at him had her face in his chest, her body trembling in his arms. Had she really been that worried about him?

Or was she only trying to sell their fake engagement in order to keep her family from committing murder?

"You—you cannot plan a wedding in three days," Marta Kozminski protested. "That would be impossible."

"I can do it," the wedding planner assured her. "In twenty-four hours…if the judge will waive the waiting period."

"He doesn't need to do that," Logan said.

Stacy tensed in his arms. Maybe she worried that he was going to expose her lie. Her brothers shared a significant look, one almost of triumph.

"I knew it!" Garek said. "I knew it was all bull. You two hate each other's guts. There's no way that you're actually engaged!"

"I don't hate your sister," Logan said.

"Do you love her?" Milek asked.

"Of course he loves her," his mother answered for him. "All these attempts on their lives have forced them to confront their feelings for each other—their love for each other."

Either she was delusional or she really wanted to plan another wedding.

"We realize you're all shocked," Logan said. "We're shocked, too. So we need some time alone to work everything out." He wanted to get Stacy and his mother out of there, far away from all the possible threats.

"So you're not engaged?" the aunt asked hopefully.

Stacy looked at him now, tipping her face up to his. He wanted to kiss her. He *needed* to kiss her. She waited like the others—waited for him to tell the truth and expose their fake engagement.

Chapter Eleven

So Logan lied. "We're engaged."

He wasn't sure it would stop the attempts on their lives, but it would put him in proximity to the suspects to find out which one might be behind the attempts. Of course the Kozminskis hadn't let him or his mother inside their house yet. But as their niece's fiancé, they would eventually have to let him into their family circle. More important, the engagement would also put him in proximity to Stacy. Close proximity. To protect her...

"If you're really engaged, then where's the ring?" Marta challenged them.

Logan spared his mother a glance. She should have known her plan would never work; these people would not be easily fooled. They were used to running the con, not falling for it.

"I—I will design my own, of course," Stacy replied.

"So he's telling the truth?" Marta asked, still skeptical.

Stacy stared at him, surprised that he had actually lied, and nodded.

"Were *you?*" her aunt asked.

Stacy's brow furrowed with confusion and she turned back to the older woman. "What?"

"When you told me that you didn't understand your

father's last words?" she asked. "Were you telling the truth then?"

"Dad's last words?" Milek repeated. "What's Aunt Marta talking about?"

Logan was wondering the same. But his mother remained silent, as if she already knew. How close was she to Stacy?

"The warden called her to go to the prison," Garek answered for her. "Dad was asking for her." Was that bitterness or resentment in her brother's voice?

Maybe he and Stacy had been completely wrong about them; maybe they didn't love her as much as either had thought. Maybe that was why the engagement hadn't stopped the shooting or the bombs...

"But he must have died before you got there," Milek said as he reached out to squeeze her shoulder in sympathy. "He was mortally wounded."

She swayed on her legs and leaned heavily against Logan's side. This wasn't easy for her—talking about what must have been a horrific last encounter between her and her dying father. How had Logan not known that she'd been there, that she'd seen the man she'd loved above everyone else die?

"He was alive," she admitted. "But he was barely lucid."

"But he said something to you," Marta Kozminski insisted.

Her brow furrowed again—in irritation as much as confusion. "Whatever my father said to me was between him and me," she said, her voice sharp with anger. "It had nothing to do with *you.*"

"It has nothing to do with her," Garek agreed. "But he was our father, too. If he told you something, Milek and I should know what it was."

She shook her head. "It was nothing..."

Marta sneered derisively. "Then you would just say what it was."

Maybe the icy blonde woman was right. If it had been nothing, why wouldn't Stacy just share it? Was whatever her father had told her the reason she was so convinced that he hadn't been alone when his father died? That someone else had been involved?

He wanted to know the truth, too, but he didn't want to press her. She was already trembling with either shock or exhaustion from the eventful day she'd had.

Stacy shook her head. "He was drugged—for the pain. What he said made no sense."

The aunt nodded, as if in acceptance. But then she sighed. "It is late and my husband and I have no interest in planning a wedding—not so soon after a funeral. It would be in extremely poor taste." She grabbed her husband's arm and tugged him back inside the house and closed the door on them all.

Yet slamming the door on family wasn't poor taste?

Stacy uttered a shaky little sigh of relief. Because they were gone? Or because they'd stopped hounding her about her father's last words?

Her brothers had fallen silent, too. Logan wasn't sure if it was because of the engagement or because of the talk of their father's last moments. The horrific last moments that Stacy alone had witnessed. He tightened his arm around her as her brothers stepped away.

Were they angry with her over the engagement or over her not sharing her father's last words? Logan suspected she was only protecting them.

"We can go back to the chapel," his mother suggested. "And continue the planning."

He shook his head. "We're exhausted, Mom."

"Is that all it is?" she asked, her eyes wide and wet with tears. "Are you mad at me?"

He sighed and eased his arm from around Stacy to put it around his mother. Then he guided her toward her car. Fortunately, the gates were still open; she could drive away. "You shouldn't have come here."

"But I thought it might help…"

His voice low, he said, "It could have gotten you killed."

"None of the Kozminskis would hurt me."

Because they knew she'd already been hurt enough.

"I can't say the same," he said. They all wanted to hurt him. He still wasn't sure that he could trust Stacy. But even if he couldn't trust her, he had to protect her. He was a bodyguard—it wasn't just what he did…it was who he was.

She lifted a slightly trembling hand to pat his cheek as she so often did. "You're my only child that gets mad at me."

A twinge of guilt struck his heart, but he grinned at her words. "I'm the only one who calls you on your crap."

She chuckled. "Yes, you are, my eldest." She pressed a kiss to his cheek and whispered in his ear. "You're going to find out that I'm right about you and Stacy. You're finally going to be happy. That's all I've wanted for you and your brothers and sister."

That was how she justified her meddling—with love. But she was wrong if she thought his and Stacy's engagement had anything to do with love. It had to do with blackmail. Threats. Attraction. Desire…

He closed her door and patted the roof of the car, urging her to start her engine. He held his breath, not releasing it until her car drove through the gates and away from danger. Then he turned back to the remaining Kozminskis. He wasn't sure who posed the greatest threat to him:

the brothers who clearly wanted to kill him or the woman who distracted and attracted him.

Somehow he suspected it was she who would be his downfall.

THE SILENCE WAS even more chilling than the cool night breeze. Stacy shivered. But she didn't break the silence as she and her brothers stared at Logan Payne.

She'd hated him for so long. That hate had kept her strong while she'd worried about her incarcerated dad and her brothers. But the hate was gone now. And she felt weaker and more vulnerable than she'd ever had.

"Tell us the truth," Garek urged her.

"I told you Dad was out of it," she replied. "His last words made no sense." Or so she'd thought at the time. But now she wondered if he might have been right...

"Not about Dad," Garek clarified. "Tell us the truth about this engagement."

"It's not real," Milek said as if trying to convince himself.

After all those years of her very vocal hatred of Logan Payne, she didn't blame them for doubting that her feelings could have so drastically changed. But when she'd seen him step out of that SUV, she'd felt more than relief and something very far from hatred.

"It's real," Logan answered for her. He wrapped his arm around her, and the warmth of his long, muscular body chased away the chill.

Despite his words, she knew he was lying. It was only real to her. She wasn't sure what it was to him. A joke? A cover to get him close to her family?

"If it's real, why didn't you have your mom rush the marriage license like she wanted?" Milek asked.

"A day or three isn't going to make a difference," he said. "Stacy and I *will* be getting married."

Garek cursed, making his opinion of their union clear. Then he shook his head. "It ain't going to happen."

"Why's that?" Logan asked. "Don't think I'll live to make it to the altar?"

Garek shrugged. "I don't know. But I'd think that eventually your luck'll run out, Payne."

That was Stacy's fear, too. She'd been so scared that he hadn't survived the last bomb. "No," she protested. "It won't run out. We will be getting married."

"Well, until you are, you need to stay with us," Milek said.

Garek nodded in agreement.

She laughed. "When did you two get so old-fashioned?"

"Maybe we've always been," Milek replied. "You just never gave us reason to worry about you before."

"Why are you worried?" she asked. "Because someone's trying to kill me or because I'm engaged to Logan Payne?"

Garek grunted as if he were in physical pain. "Both reasons."

"Then you should be glad she's engaged to me," Logan said. "I'll protect her."

Garek scoffed. "You put her in more danger. She needs to stay far away from you!" He reached out for Stacy's arm.

Cujo wasn't with them, but Logan took his place, snarling, "Don't touch her!"

"She's my sister," Garek said with a snarl of his own.

"She's my fiancée."

"She has a mind and a mouth of her own," Stacy interjected.

"Then tell him," Milek said, "that you're leaving here with us."

She shook her head. Earlier she'd wanted to go home—

alone. That was what she'd told Logan when he'd brought her to his brother's house. But after finding that bomb, everything had changed for her.

She was too scared to be alone now. But she wasn't afraid for herself. She was scared—she was terrified—for Logan. She couldn't shoot or defuse bombs, but she wanted to protect Logan. And maybe her presence alone would do that…if her brothers were responsible for the attempts on his life. If they believed she really cared about him, and she stayed close to him, they would stop. They wouldn't risk hurting her.

"I'm leaving here with my fiancé," she told her brothers.

"And don't try to follow us this time," Logan warned them.

"We can't trust you to protect her," Milek said. "You've nearly gotten her shot and blown up."

"He did protect me," Stacy said. "I'm not hurt." But she worried that she would get hurt. Not physically—because Logan wasn't just lucky. He was a talented bodyguard. But she worried that she would get hurt emotionally…because she was starting to believe their engagement was real and that Logan Payne might actually care about her. And that belief would only lead to disappointment. She'd stopped hating him, but she wasn't sure he could stop hating her or her family.

As LOGAN HELPED her into the passenger's side of his SUV, he glanced over his shoulder. He couldn't believe that her brothers hadn't tried to stop them again—that they had just let them walk away. But Stacy had made it clear that she was leaving with him.

Why?

He stared into her face and noticed how her gray eyes darkened with fear. She was afraid. "Don't worry," he reassured her. "I'm taking you to one of the safe houses I use for clients in danger."

Which was where he should have taken her when he'd first found that bomb in her apartment—instead of to his place and then to Parker's. But he'd been so certain that her brothers were responsible that he'd been convinced the attempts would stop when she was near him.

Either he was wrong about them or she was. Maybe they didn't care as much about her as either of them had thought.

She tensed as if something had just occurred to her and asked, "Where's Cujo? I thought you'd left him in your car. He didn't get hurt—"

"No," Logan told her. "I brought him back to the kennel where we picked him up. I thought he'd had enough excitement for one day."

She nodded. "Of course. But we can pick him up now."

He wasn't convinced the excitement was over. "It's late," he reminded her. "We'll have to wait until morning."

Which was probably only a few hours from now. He closed her door and walked around the front to the driver's side.

Like thugs on a street corner eyeing a potential victim, her brothers watched him. The weight of the gun in the holster beneath his arm reassured him. But he didn't want to shoot one of Stacy's brothers. She would already probably never forgive him for her father dying in prison, but if he had to kill one of her brothers, too…

He had been so positive that they were responsible for the attempts on his life. But now he hoped they weren't. He hoped it was anyone else.

But who? And why would that person be after both him and Stacy?

He opened the driver's door and slid beneath the wheel. The dome light illuminated Stacy's pale face. The only color to her blanched skin was the dark circles beneath her eyes. She was exhausted. It hadn't just been one long emotional day but a few days for her.

"I'll keep you safe," he promised in case her brothers had put any doubts in her mind. But then the bomb had probably done that.

"I know."

Did she really? Did she trust him?

He felt the weight of that trust more heavily than his weapon. He would keep her safe, or he would die trying.

She must have really trusted him because she lay back and closed her eyes. So she didn't see the lights behind them.

But he saw them and cursed.

Her body tensed, and her eyes opened. She hadn't been asleep at all. "What?"

"Your brothers must be following us again." At least this time he'd noticed them. How had he missed their tail before?

"They want to protect me," she said.

He wasn't so certain that was their real purpose in following them. But then he didn't blame them for not trusting him with her safety. But because he suspected them, he sped up to lose them.

"I'll protect you," he said.

"Why?" she asked.

"I'm a bodyguard," he reminded her. "It's what I do." He made a couple quick turns, and the road darkened behind them. He'd lost the tail. That easily?

Too easily…

He pressed harder on the accelerator and squealed around a few more sharp turns.

Stacy braced her hands on the dashboard. "But why protect me?" she asked. "I didn't hire you."

"You didn't need to," he said. On some level he felt as if he owed her. Keeping her father in prison had been the right thing—the just thing—but it had also hurt her. The road remained dark behind them. At this hour, theirs was the only car on the road.

"Why did you lie to my family about the engagement?" she asked.

He shrugged. Maybe his mother had gotten to him—not with her matchmaking, but with her suggestion that a marriage between him and Stacy would stop the attempts on his life. The engagement hadn't. But that might have made her brothers even more determined to kill him before he could marry their sister. The engagement might have put him in even more danger.

"Maybe I wasn't lying," he said. "Maybe we should make it real."

The lights flashed behind him again—the beams on bright—as the car roared up behind them. "Your brothers..."

She turned toward the lights and then jerked forward, her head dangerously close to the dashboard, as the car slammed into the back bumper of his SUV.

"That's not my brothers," she protested, her voice cracking with fear. "That's someone trying to kill us."

The car must have been bigger than it looked, because as it slammed into them again, the SUV swerved, nearly sliding off the road.

Stacy screamed, and Logan cursed. He'd promised to protect her. And he intended to keep that promise. But that driver wasn't just trying to kill them; he was *determined* to kill them.

Chapter Twelve

Maybe we should make it real…

Stacy had never gotten the chance to ask Logan what he'd meant before all hell had broken loose. She braced her hands on the dashboard as the car struck them again with such force that the SUV swerved off the road. It spun around, and her head struck the post next to her seat between the passenger side doors.

She screamed again as fear overwhelmed her.

Spots danced before her eyes, her vision blurring. She blinked to clear her mind—to focus—but her ears rang from the impact of hitting her head.

Gravel flew up behind them, pinging off the metal. Logan steered between trees. Metal crunched now as the side mirror twisted off and broke. Then he was back on the road, behind the car—his lights shining into the vehicle and illuminating two shadows.

"Are you okay?" he asked her, his voice gruff with concern. "Stacy!"

The urgency in his voice jolted her. "I'm okay," she said, even as her head throbbed with pain and her heart with fear. "Are you?"

"Oh, yeah," he said. Excitement replaced his concern as he sped up. The pursued had become the pursuer. He struck the rear bumper of the car.

The gunfire hadn't killed them, neither had those two bombs, but his driving might. He cursed, then sighed. "I can't…"

Was the car faster?

"Why not?" she asked. She wanted this person stopped—wanted this all to be over.

"They probably have guns."

So he braked and spun the SUV around, going the other direction. Stacy braced her hands against the dashboard as he careened around corners, taking an on-ramp well over the posted speed. They were on the freeway only moments before he crossed four lanes to an off-ramp. The car tires squealed as he careened around that sharp turn.

Feeling sick, she turned toward him and noticed a slight grin on his lips. "You're enjoying this," she accused him.

How was that possible when she had never been so scared? Except maybe when they'd found the bomb or been shot at…

"The driving, yes," he admitted.

He was quite the expert driver. He'd handled the other car slamming into them, and he'd certainly lost that car now. There were no headlights behind them. Not even any taillights ahead of them.

"I haven't enjoyed getting shot at or defusing bombs." The grin left his face, replaced by a tension that had a muscle twitching in his cheek. "I haven't enjoyed any of that."

"I haven't," she said. "But I thought you would be used to getting shot at and nearly blown up…what with being a bodyguard now and a cop before that."

He sighed. "Just because I'm used to it doesn't mean I enjoy it."

"Then why do you do it?" she asked. "Why would you go into private security?"

"To keep people safe," he said.

"Then why didn't you stay a police officer?" she wondered. "They keep people safe."

He shook his head. "No. They don't."

Was he thinking again of Robert Cooper, of the cop who hadn't protected his partner, Logan's father?

"The police show up *after* the fact," he said. "*After* someone's violated the restraining order or after a stalker crosses the line to violence."

"You saw a lot of horrible things while you were with the River City Police Department," she realized. And because he had been too late to help those victims and probably because he'd been unable to save his father, too, he'd gone into private protection.

"What you saw would have been worse," he said. He reached across the console for her hand, intertwining their fingers. "When you went to the prison infirmary."

She shuddered at the memory of her father in so much pain and the awful helplessness she'd felt. "I wish I'd been able to do something for him…"

"The doctors weren't able to save him," he said. "There was nothing you could do. I'm surprised he would even want you to see him like that."

Apparently even Logan had known that her father had always tried to protect her. And maybe that was what his last words had been about…

"Whatever he'd wanted to tell you must have been really important," he said, his deep voice rising slightly as if in a question.

It hadn't seemed that important at the time he'd said it. In fact, she hadn't understood him at all. Until now…until she'd become Logan Payne's fake fiancée.

Maybe we should make it real…

Did he actually want to marry her?

"What did he say to you?" Logan persisted.

She uttered a weary sigh. "Like I told my family, I don't want to talk about it. I'm exhausted…"

He squeezed her fingers. "I'm sorry."

Guilt flashed through her. She had lied to put him off as she had everyone else. But then she realized she wasn't lying. She was completely exhausted, so exhausted that she settled against the seat and closed her eyes. She didn't notice his driving or the danger anymore. With his hand holding hers, she felt safe—truly protected for perhaps the first time in her life, and sleep claimed her.

EVEN THOUGH HE'D driven like a madman, Logan had been careful. No one could have followed him this time. But then he hadn't thought he'd been followed before…until the Kozminskis had. Had her brothers been in the vehicle that had tried to force them off the road? Or was she right? Had it been someone else?

Just like he'd steered it between trees, he steered the SUV through a narrow garage door built into the basement of the safe house where he'd brought his fiancée. Was it fake anymore? Or should she become his bride?

She murmured in her sleep, drawing his attention. Not that she'd ever *not* had it. Even when he'd been watching the rearview mirror for any sign of someone following them again, he had been aware of her sleeping in the seat next to him. She hadn't been lying about being exhausted.

Even now she barely stirred as he reached over and unbuckled her belt. Like he had earlier that day—or yesterday, actually—he carried her into the house. But this wasn't his house.

He'd brought her to a lakefront condo that a grateful client let Logan use when he, the owner, was in Florida. The town house was one of several in a converted piano factory. He had to shift Stacy in his arms so that he could operate the wooden elevator to carry them to the upper floors from the basement garage.

Her head slid into the cradle of his neck and shoulder, and her lips brushed across his throat. His heart raced.

He should have been exhausted, too. It hadn't just been a long day. Because of the danger his brother and his bride had been in, it had been a long week with little sleep and too many rushes of adrenaline.

But this—holding Stacy in his arms and, earlier, kissing her—was a bigger rush than defusing bombs or dodging bullets or evading vehicles. But she wasn't awake...

"Sorry," she murmured sleepily, her breath warm against his ear.

He cleared his throat. "Sorry?"

"Sorry you have to keep carrying me." She wriggled in his arms until he loosened his grasp enough that she slid down his body.

"I don't mind," he said. He actually enjoyed it, enjoyed taking care of a woman who was usually so fiercely independent and strong. "I know you're exhausted."

"You must be, too."

He shook his head. "No, not so tired anymore."

The elevator ground to a halt on the top floor—the bedroom loft. Now he wasn't tired at all. He slid open the wooden accordion door. She started across and stumbled on the uneven threshold and fell back against him. He caught her up in his arms again and carried her to the bed.

"You don't need to do this," she protested.

"Maybe I want to do this," he said as he lowered her to the mattress, which was on a bamboo platform with pillows piled up against the exposed brick wall.

He wanted to join her in the bed. But he forced himself to release her and step back.

"You do?" she asked.

"I want to keep you safe," he said. And if he intended to do that, he needed to control his urges. He wanted her—badly—so badly that he wouldn't be tender and gentle. And she was too tired—physically and emotionally—and too vulnerable to deal with his desires.

"Where are we?" she asked as she peered around at the brick and exposed ductwork and beams and the scarred hardwood floors.

"A safe place."

"You're not going to tell me where," she surmised. "I wouldn't tell anyone where we are, you know."

"I know," he said. "You're good at keeping secrets." He doubted she would tell him what her father's last words had been, but there might be another way he could find out. "This condo belongs to a friend…"

She glanced around again at all the dark woods and fabrics. "It's not a female friend, right? It doesn't belong to that Amazon who works for you?"

He shook his head, confused by the sharpness of her tone. "No."

"You didn't tell her where we are?"

"I didn't tell anyone," he assured her. "We're safe. But we would've been safe if Candace knew where we are, too."

She chuckled. "You would be. But not me."

"What do you mean?"

"How can you be so observant and not realize how she feels about you?" she asked.

"What do you mean?"

"She's in love with you," Stacy said. "She's obsessed with you. And she must've considered me a threat—even before our fake engagement. She went to the last couple of parole hearings with you."

Maybe he was more tired than he'd thought because she

wasn't making any sense to him. Candace was in love with him? "What are you saying?"

"It could have been her shooting at us earlier," she suggested. "It could have been her who set the bomb. She was one of the few who knew we were going to Parker's."

That was true. But in love with him?

Then he remembered how she'd acted about the engagement announcement. She hadn't just been concerned. She'd acted almost jealous. But even if she had feelings for him, she wouldn't have tried to kill Stacy. Or him.

Candace had been a cop, too; she had sworn to protect and serve. She would never endanger anyone. "No."

Or would she? She had been acting strangely.

"You would rather think it was my family," Stacy accused him.

"I would," he admitted. Because if it wasn't, then he had been wrong about everyone, and he had always prided himself on being a good judge of character.

Her weariness was back and her shoulders slumped as if she was defeated. "At least you're being honest with me."

"You're tired," he said. "Go back to sleep."

She stood up next to the bed and turned to look at it as if considering. "Is there only one bed?"

"Don't worry," he said. "It's yours." Then he chuckled. "Apparently, your brothers aren't the only old-fashioned ones in your family."

Her eyes flashed at him with annoyance. "I'm not old-fashioned." And as if to prove it, she reached for the zipper at the back of her dress.

She was going to undress in front of him?

His heart slammed into his ribs. But the dress didn't come off. The zipper didn't even come down.

She bit her lip as she continued to tug. "It's stuck."

"Let me help you," he said. Gripping her shoulders, he

turned her back to him. Then he pushed aside the heavy tangle of her tawny-colored hair and fumbled with the zipper of her black dress.

"It's stuck," she said.

Fabric was caught in it. She would have dressed quickly back at his house—after the shooting and before the police arrived—so quickly that she'd caught the fabric. He pulled it loose. Then he swallowed hard before pulling down the tab. Metal zipped as the teeth separated, baring a strip of skin that looked silky. That strip revealed the curve of her spine and the dimples at the base of it—on the rise of her butt.

His heart beat erratically—as if it were stopping and starting. He drew in an unsteady breath as the dress fell, sliding down her body.

He'd seen her in the black bra and panties earlier when she'd worn his shirt over them to flaunt their fake engagement. They were engaged. But they weren't really together despite what they'd nearly done earlier, before someone had shot up his house.

But the two of them probably would have stopped—even without the gunfire. Too much history and pain separated them. He wanted to close the distance between them. But he forced himself to step back again.

"I'm…uh…I'm going to shower," he said. And hopefully the water would be icy enough to cool the heat of his desire for her.

She turned toward him and stood there in just that black bra and panties. Maybe she was so tired she was befuddled, because she looked confused. And vulnerable.

The vulnerability steeled his control. He could not take advantage of that vulnerability.

He backed away until he stepped through the doorway to the master bath. Then he closed that door between them.

Like the rest of the town house, it was all brick, dark wood and shiny steel. He set his steel—his holstered gun—onto the counter along with his cell phone. Then he shucked off his jeans and the cotton shirt, which fortunately bore no bullet holes. He dropped it onto the floor along with his boxers.

Then he turned on the shower and stepped beneath the blast of cold water. The water pressure was forceful and loud—but not so loud that he didn't hear the telltale creak of the door opening.

He had been so certain that he'd lost that car that had tried driving them off the road. He'd been so certain that they would be safe here...

But Stacy wouldn't have followed him into the bathroom. She had looked so exhausted that she'd probably dropped onto the bed and fallen immediately back to sleep. So someone else must have gotten inside the town house.

His heart beat heavy with dread and fear. They would have gotten to Stacy already.

Could he get to his gun before they got to him?

Chapter Thirteen

Strong, wet arms wrapped tightly around Stacy, lifting her off her feet and whirling her around to face a naked, mad Logan Payne.

"What are you doing?" he asked.

That was a damn good question—one she should have asked herself before she'd followed him into the bathroom. But that look on his face—that look she'd mistaken for longing and desire—had drawn her after him.

That look was replaced with anger now. "You shouldn't sneak up on me. I could have hurt you."

He would hurt her. Eventually. She was certain of it because she was beginning to have feelings for her fake fiancé. And he obviously didn't return those feelings.

"Why'd you come in here?" he asked. "Did you need to use the bathroom?"

"I—I…I needed…" Him. She'd needed her fiancé. Her face heated with embarrassment over that need, but she couldn't admit it now, not in the face of his anger.

"What do you need?" he asked her. He stood before her gloriously naked, and she couldn't help but stare, her gaze skimming hungrily over every slick, muscular inch of him. As she watched, his body grew hard and tense. His voice gruff with desire, he asked again, "What do you want?"

She'd been keeping secrets from him. But she couldn't

lie about her feelings anymore. "You," she replied. "I want you. I need you."

He carried her again, but this time she didn't protest. Her skin heated everywhere his skin touched. And then instead of just laying her down on the bed, he followed her down— his body covering hers while his mouth covered hers.

He kissed her passionately, as if he was as hungry for her as she was for him. His lips pressed against hers and his tongue delved inside her mouth, making love to it, like she wanted him to make love to her body.

She'd never felt such passion. Such need. Her arms clasped his back, her fingers skimming down his spine to his tight butt. She pulled him against her arching hips. His erection hardened and pulsed against her.

He groaned. "Stacy, slow down…"

She nearly giggled. That was something she'd never been told before. Usually she was told that she went too slow, that she was too cautious. Even he had accused her of being old-fashioned and the comment had stung because it was true. That was why there had been so few men in her life and even fewer in her bed.

He leaned his forehead against hers and drew in deep breaths. But she could feel his heart racing against hers. He wanted her as much as she wanted him.

"Why?" she asked. "Why do I have to slow down?"

He kissed her lips again but it was a light, gentle kiss. "So we can make it last. So I can last…"

"It's okay if you don't," she assured him.

He shook his head. "No, it's not. I want you to enjoy this," he said, "every bit as much as I intend to."

She was enjoying it—every soft kiss. He moved from her lips to her chin and then down her throat. He flicked his tongue across her leaping pulse point. Then he nibbled on her collarbone.

While he'd told her to slow down, the man moved fast, removing her bra and panties before she even realized they were gone. She realized when he touched her there—first with his fingers tracing over the curves of her breasts before teasing the nipples. One hand moved lower, over her stomach to the small mound between her legs.

She squirmed beneath him as pressure built inside her. While his hands stroked her breasts and lower, his lips moved back to hers. The gentle kisses were gone as he kissed her more forcefully now.

Her hold on reality began to slip as he drove her crazy with those kisses and caresses. And she wanted him to descend to madness with her, so she touched him, too. She skimmed her palms over his muscular chest and down his stomach until she could encircle him with her hands. It took both and still he protruded over the top.

He groaned into her mouth. "Stacy…"

"I'm not slowing down now," she protested. Not when the pressure building inside her was about to snap her in two. He stroked her again—deep—and she peaked. Panting for breath, she arched against him. But she wanted more than his touch. She wanted all of him, so she guided his erection inside her.

He thrust, sliding in and out of her, driving her to the brink of madness again as passion overwhelmed her. She'd never felt anything like this—such an intensity of desire and pleasure.

And such intimacy…

With him inside her, she felt so close to him—closer than she'd ever felt to another human being. He kept his mouth on hers, kissing her as deeply as he was driving inside her. And he kept touching her, running his hands all over her body as if he were trying to memorize every inch of her flesh.

She kept touching him, too, unable to stop touching him, unable to stop moving beneath him. She squirmed and arched. Then he reached between them and rubbed his thumb against the most sensitive part of her, and pleasure overwhelmed her again. She screamed his name as her body shook and shuddered with an orgasm more intense than any she'd ever felt before.

With a guttural groan of pleasure, he joined her, his orgasm filling her. He settled his forehead against hers and stared deeply into her eyes.

And she hoped that he didn't see what that had meant to her. *Everything.*

She had just made love to the man she'd spent the past fifteen years hating. If lying about being engaged to him was a betrayal of her family, this was worse. Making love with him was a betrayal of herself...

"This was a mistake," she murmured.

He sucked in a breath as if she'd struck him. "I thought you wanted it."

"I did," she said. And she did again—even though he was still inside her. She wanted him. "But it complicates everything."

"Everything wasn't already complicated?" he asked. "With people trying to kill us?"

"I was thinking more of our history," she said. Their complicated history of hating each other.

And finally he pulled out of her.

She felt empty—more empty and alone than she'd ever felt, even when her father and brothers had been *away.*

He uttered a ragged sigh. "That's right. You hate me."

"Ah, hell," she murmured as she pushed him back onto the mattress. "I don't hate you. I wish I hated you..." But she was afraid that she was falling for him instead. She swung one leg across his lean hips to straddle him. "I want you…"

His hands caught her hips, his fingers digging into the flesh of her butt as he stilled her. Had she reminded him that he hated her?

"I'm going to need a minute to recover."

He lied. It didn't take him a full minute to recover. It took him much longer to reach his pleasure breaking point, though. So she was able to enjoy herself—setting her own pace as she slid up and down him and rocked back and forth.

Sweat beaded on his upper lip and the muscles in his arms and neck corded and pulsed. He waited until she peaked again, and then he thrust up, hard, and joined her in ecstasy.

She dropped onto his chest, so exhausted that she was boneless with sexual satisfaction. She'd never been so fulfilled or so exhausted. Feeling safe and secure in his arms, she easily fell asleep.

LOGAN SHOULD HAVE been tired. Exhausted now. But he couldn't close his eyes. He could not take his gaze off her. He watched as the bright sunshine of midmorning streaked through the bedroom blinds and fell across Stacy's face, illuminating her already luminous beauty.

He would like to blame his inability to sleep on his having to stand watch and protect her. But he had made certain that no one had followed them here. And nobody knew where he'd brought her. He hadn't even told Parker.

Not that he told Parker everything. Despite being twins, they didn't have that intuitive connection that twins were rumored to have. They didn't tell each other everything. Parker had his secrets—about women. Logan suspected he'd slept with a few of their female clients, which was an offense that merited termination from the Payne Protection Agency. So of course he wouldn't have admitted to the boss what or whom he'd done.

But Logan kept his secrets, too—about women. He wouldn't admit to his feelings for his fiancée to his twin. He wasn't even ready to admit to those feelings to himself. For so long he'd thought he'd hated Stacy Kozminski. When they'd made love, his feelings had been intense—more intense than anything he'd felt before. He definitely didn't hate her.

But he didn't want to love her, either…because nobody kept more secrets than Stacy Kozminski. And he couldn't love someone he couldn't trust.

A phone rang, shattering the silence of the town house and scattering Logan's thoughts. Beside him, Stacy tensed and jerked awake. In a fearful whisper she asked, "Who knows we're here?"

"Nobody," he soothed her. And that was probably why someone was calling—to find out where the hell he was. "That's not the landline. It's my cell."

He'd left it on the bathroom counter with his gun. So he had to leave her to answer it. He had to unwrap his arms from around her warm, nude body. Then he had to slide across the bed. Cold air rushed over him, chilling his naked skin as he padded into the bathroom and grabbed his phone.

If it was Parker…

But it wasn't Parker's number on the caller ID. He answered, "Logan Payne."

"Payne, Captain O'Doyle here."

He'd recognized the number; it wasn't one he was ever likely to forget, but one he hoped he would never have to use again. "Captain, I didn't think you were serious about that job offer—at least not serious enough to call so soon."

"It's nearly noon, Payne," the captain replied with a chuckle. "I didn't think I'd be waking you up at noon."

"You didn't wake me." And it was noon? How had he stayed awake all night?

"Too much adrenaline to sleep," the captain replied. "That usually happens after defusing a monster like that bomb."

It wasn't the bomb that had had adrenaline rushing through his body. It was Stacy.

"And I was serious about that job offer," O'Doyle continued. "But that's not why I called. I got back the initial report on the bomb."

"The monster?"

"No, that one's pretty professional."

"The first one wasn't?"

"No. It was crude and amateurish. If it's the same bomber, he's a fast learner and vastly improved for his second attempt."

"When I was back on the force, whenever we were chasing a serial killer, we wanted to find his first kill because that was the one he would have made his mistakes on..."

The captain chuckled. "You are good, Payne. You're wasted on private security."

He glanced through the open door to where Stacy had fallen back to sleep in the bed—her beautiful face and naked body completely bathed in sunshine now. "No. Not wasted at all."

Not as long as he could keep her safe.

"So what did you find on the first bomb?" he asked.

"We learned that the components to buy it were stolen from a hardware store just down the block from the jewelry store."

"Were there cameras? Witnesses?"

"No cameras, and it happened after the place closed. No one sees anything in that neighborhood, you know."

"Of course not."

"But we know what day the store was broken into."

And when the captain named the day, Logan's blood chilled. It was the same day that Stacy's father had died in prison. Why had someone chosen that day to make the bomb and set it in Stacy's apartment?

Because of her father's last words? The words she'd refused to share with anyone else—even with her family?

"I thought you'd be more excited about the news," O'Doyle said.

"I'd be more excited if we knew who actually made the bomb."

The ATF agent chuckled. "Thought you'd want me to leave some work for you to do. Let me know if you figure it out…"

"When," Logan corrected him. "I'll let you know *when* I figure it out." Because it had just occurred to him how he might do that.

He hung up on the ATF agent and returned to the bed where Stacy slept. But he didn't join her on the soft mattress and the silk sheets. He just stood over her, watching her sleep as he must have most of the morning.

He wanted to keep her here—in this private town house where nobody knew where they were. He wanted to keep her safe. But she would only be truly safe when the threat against them was eliminated.

"Stacy…"

She didn't stir.

"Stacy!"

She jerked awake like she had when the phone rang. "What? What's wrong?"

Everything.

"You have to get up," he said. "You have to get dressed."

"Why?" she asked. "Why are we leaving? Does someone know we're here?"

"Nobody does," he assured her.

"Then why can't we stay?"

He wished they could. He wished they could just pretend the outside world didn't exist. But they didn't have that choice. They had families. Businesses. Responsibilities. And they couldn't take care of any of those if they were dead.

And while nobody knew where they were now, somebody might figure it out. So they needed to figure out who that somebody was first.

"We can't," he said. "We need to leave."

"Where are you taking me?" she asked as she sat up and the sheet slipped lower, revealing all her sexy curves.

He just wanted to take her over and over again. But if they made love, he wouldn't be able to do what he had to. He would want to stay forever in this place where they'd made love.

"Are you taking me to another safe house?" she asked.

He shook his head and reluctantly replied, "I'm taking you to prison."

Chapter Fourteen

I'm taking you to prison.

His words rattled her. After that horrific day she'd watched her father die, Stacy had never intended to return to River City Maximum Security Penitentiary. Yet here she was, walking through the high fence—with armed guards standing watch in high towers.

Her stomach knotted with nerves and grief. As much as she had loved seeing her father, she'd hated coming to the prison. But since it was the only way she could spend time with him, she'd overcome her fears and reluctance. But she wouldn't be able to see him today.

She wouldn't be able to see him ever again. Because of this place, she'd had to bury him. And she used to blame this man for his death. But this man was now her fiancé.

As they went through security, he watched her carefully—his blue eyes intense. He acted concerned and regretful. But if he were either of those things, he wouldn't have forced her to come back to this place. After they cleared security, a heavily armed guard escorted them to another part of the prison—away from the visiting areas and cells.

She had been there once—after her father died—to collect his last effects. The guard opened the door to the reception area for the warden's office. A young secretary glanced up from her desk. She flashed Logan a big smile and then spared Stacy a sympathetic glance. "You can have a seat. It'll be a few minutes before Warden Borgess can see you."

Logan nodded at the woman before steering Stacy toward chairs at the other end of the reception area as if he didn't want the secretary to overhear the conversation he anticipated them having.

"I don't understand why you think we had to come here," she said for the umpteenth time. But he had yet to answer her. So they actually hadn't had much of a conversation yet. "If it's to find out what my father's last words were, you're wasting your time."

"And keeping that secret is probably how you've endangered your life," he said.

"I've endangered *my* life?" she repeated, anger replacing her sadness at being back at the prison. "You're blaming *me* for the bombs and the shootings?"

He glanced toward the secretary, who was either fascinated with their argument or probably just with him. Then he lowered his voice, as if that might make Stacy do the same. "That isn't what I meant."

"It wouldn't be the first time you've blamed me," she said. "When you confronted me at my father's funeral, you thought I was the one shooting at you." And that same day they'd become engaged and then hours later they'd made love. Maybe grief over her father's death had addled her mind so that she'd acted more impulsively than she ever had in her life. But making love with him had actually been the most impulsive thing she'd ever done.

"I didn't think you were personally shooting at me," he said.

"You thought I put my brothers up to it."

"That was before I learned you really don't have that much control over them."

She felt as though she no longer had any control over any aspect of her life. Hopefully the ATF had cleared her building so that she could go back to the store and the workshop behind it. She needed to design something. She needed to control something—even if it were only metal and stones. But even if her building was reopened, it still wouldn't be safe—not until she and Logan caught whoever was trying to hurt them.

That was why she had put aside her fears and anguish and agreed to return to the place where her father had suffered and died. "I don't understand what you think we're going to find out here."

"Neither do I." Warden Borgess stood in the open doorway to his office. But he held out his hand to Logan and shook it heartily. Then he awkwardly patted Stacy's shoulder just as he had the day her father had died. That day he'd been full of guilt and regrets. "I still can't understand what happened to Mr. Kozminski. None of the other prisoners had *ever* showed any ill will toward him…" He shook his head.

Logan's brow furrowed. "So that attack on him was not provoked?"

Stacy gasped that he could still think so little of her father. But then he still believed that he had killed his father.

"Absolutely not," the warden said, as astonished by the comment as Stacy was. "Nobody had bothered Patek until that day."

"Is it possible to speak to the prisoner who attacked him?" Logan asked.

Fear clutched Stacy's heart, squeezing it tightly. She didn't know how Logan had confronted the man he believed had killed his father; she didn't want to ever see the monster who'd taken hers. She'd already had enough nightmares about him.

Borgess shook his head.

"If you asked, he might be willing to speak with us," Logan said.

The warden shook his head again. "No, it's not possible. The man died that very same day."

Stacy gasped again. "What?"

"I tried to let you know," the warden said, "but you didn't return the messages I left for you."

She hadn't wanted to hear from the warden again—or from anyone else associated with the prison that had taken away her dad.

He continued, "I figured you were busy planning services for your father."

She nodded. She had been busy planning the services. But Logan Payne had forced those plans to go awry. Instead of mourning her father, she'd gotten engaged.

"Who killed him?" Logan asked.

Borgess shrugged. "I don't know."

"You must have seen something on security cameras."

"The camera in that area had malfunctioned that day."

"So it was premeditated. Someone had messed with the camera before they attacked him. That someone must have had easy access to that area."

"All the prisoners do," the warden replied a bit defensively. Had he thought Logan was implying that a guard had killed the man?

Was that what Logan was implying?

"I'd like to see the visitor logs for that prisoner," he said.

Warden Borgess narrowed his eyes. "As I understand it, Mr. Payne, you're no longer with the River City Police Department. Aren't you private security now?"

"Yes, that's why I'm here. Stacy's life is in danger and I'm trying to find out why someone set a bomb in her apartment on the day her father died."

The warden's eyes opened wide with alarm. "Are you all right, Miss Kozminski?"

She nodded. "Logan defused it."

The warden turned back to her bodyguard/soon-to-be husband. "You must be very good at your job, Mr. Payne."

"That's why I'm here," Logan repeated. "That's why I need to see who'd been visiting the prisoner who killed Mr. Kozminski."

"From your years with the River City Police Department, you must remember the law and the privacy rules that prevent me from giving you that information without a warrant," he replied almost regretfully.

"What about Stacy's father? Will we need a warrant to see his logs?"

"All you need is Ms. Kozminski's permission. She was his power of attorney and legal representative."

Both men turned to her, but Stacy hesitated. She wasn't certain what Logan hoped to gain by looking over visitor logs for either prisoner.

"If we're going to find out who's after us, we need to get as much information as we can," Logan said.

It was true. It was why they were there. She nodded her agreement. "Yes, I'd like to see the logs."

Borgess turned back toward his office. "I will personally pull those from my computer and print them out. It will only take a moment."

A moment for fifteen years of visits? Was that how few people had visited her father?

Regret and loss pulled heavily on Stacy, and she dropped back into the chair she'd been sitting in before the warden had stepped out of his office.

"Are you okay?" Logan asked, his deep voice vibrating with concern.

"Can I get you anything?" the secretary inquired.

Her father. That was all she wanted back. But he was gone forever.

Maybe that was why she had become engaged to Logan, why she'd left her family to be with him. So she wouldn't feel so alone. But she knew that he wasn't going to stay her fiancé, let alone ever become her husband. As soon as they were safe again, they would break up.

WARDEN BORGESS WAS only gone a few minutes. But it felt much longer, and with each second that ticked past, Stacy had grown more pale and shaky. If she hadn't already thought Logan was an uncaring jerk, she certainly would have after today.

He never should have brought her back here. Forcing her to do so had been heartless and insensitive. But the warden wouldn't have handed over the visitor logs, as he was now, without Stacy's permission.

"If there's anything else I can do for you, please let me know," the warden said, but he spoke to Stacy, his gaze warm with concern and maybe attraction. He was a young warden, and his ring finger was bare.

But then so was Stacy's and she was engaged now. He really should have gotten her a ring…

"We'd also like her father's personal effects," Logan added.

"I already gave those to Ms. Kozminski," Borgess said. "The day her father died."

The day the bomb had been set to blow up her apartment and anyone and anything inside it. The minute they'd stepped through the door, the timer had been tripped so that it had begun counting down the less than a minute they would have had to get out of the place. Was that why it had been set—to destroy whatever Patek Kozminski might have left behind?

He couldn't share his suspicions with Stacy in front of the warden, though. He didn't entirely trust the man. The prisoner who'd killed her father had turned up dead a bit too conveniently and easily for Logan's peace of mind. Because he didn't want to reveal any of his theories, he even waited until they'd exited the prison gates and climbed back inside the damaged black SUV before looking at the logs.

Stacy sat quietly in the passenger's seat as if the prison visit had physically drained her. But then she hadn't gotten much rest—because they had been too busy making love to sleep.

"What do you see?" she asked.

"A woman who loved her father very much," he replied honestly as he brushed a strand of hair back from her face and tucked it behind her ear.

She shivered, but it wasn't from cold. Maybe his touch had given her chills. She sighed and said, "I meant in the logs."

He'd perused them quickly but one name had kept jumping out at him. "I saw that in the log," he said. "In how many times you visited him."

She shrugged. "It wasn't enough."

"Once a week?"

She uttered another shaky sigh. "That was all that was allowed, but I wish it had been more."

"At least you came as often as you could," he said. "I still feel guilty for all those times I blew off watching a game or going to the restaurant with my old man so that I could hang out with my friends instead."

"You were a teenager," she excused him. "Teenagers think they and everyone around them are immortal."

Her visits hadn't been any less frequent when she'd been younger. She'd always made time for her father. But then she'd already known there was no such thing as immortality or her dad wouldn't have been in prison for taking a life.

But had he taken it?

Maybe Stacy was getting to him, but he was beginning to have his doubts. He was beginning to wonder if she was right. That her father and his hadn't been alone that night that one of them had died and the other had been arrested for it.

"Nobody's immortal," he murmured as he started the SUV. "That's why we need to figure out who's after us. Because eventually we're not going to survive the bombs or the gunshots."

She shuddered.

"That's why I brought you here," he said as he drove out of the prison lot. "I wouldn't have put you through coming back here for any other reason."

"You weren't just torturing me?"

"I don't want to hurt you." That was why he'd tried to resist her last night; he hadn't wanted to take advantage of her vulnerability. But she'd wanted him. Last night. Today she would barely even look at him.

"Not anymore," she said of his statement.

"I never wanted to hurt you," he said. "That's not why I showed up at your father's parole hearings. I just wanted justice for my father." But now he wondered if in that quest for justice a horrible injustice had taken place.

"Then you should find out who really killed him," she suggested.

He nodded in agreement. "I intend to look into it more," he said. "I want to know the truth."

She grasped his arm. "Thank you. Thank you for listening to me."

It wasn't just her certainty that had given him doubts but also what he'd found in the visitor logs. Instead of taking the turn toward the city, he turned toward the rural outskirts. "That's why we're going to talk to someone else who was there that night."

"Your father's old partner? You're not going to learn the truth from him. For fifteen years, he's been blaming my father."

"Then why has he been visiting him nearly as often as you have?"

She sucked in a breath. Of shock.

Logan had felt the same way when he'd seen the name on the visitors logs. Shocked. And confused. He probably would have felt the same way over his mother's name appearing frequently in the logs—if she hadn't already admitted to visiting the man. But his mother's visits made more sense; she was the forgiving sort. Robert Cooper wasn't.

"I don't like the man," she admitted.

Neither did Logan. When he had been with the police department, he'd never lost a partner. And since he'd gone into private protection, he had never lost a client. He couldn't understand how Robert Cooper had lost his partner.

"But you're right," she continued, "that we need to talk to him. He must know more about that night than he admitted—like who else was there."

"But why would he have let that person get away with murder?" Robert Cooper might not have been a good cop, but he'd still been a cop. And to let a criminal get away with murder...

She shrugged. "I don't know. Nothing about that night ever made any sense to me."

"But you were fourteen then and convinced that your father was the greatest man in the world." At seventeen, he hadn't been much older but he'd believed the same thing about his father. "What if we find out it really was your father who killed mine?" Would she be able to handle her father's guilt?

Her face grew pale again and her eyes widened with horror. "It wasn't my dad. It couldn't have been…"

Chapter Fifteen

But what if it had been?

Would Stacy be able to deal with her father not being the man she had always believed him to be? She'd known he was a thief. He had never hidden that from his family.

But a killer?

She couldn't accept that.

"Are you okay?" Logan asked again.

She nodded. Even if it was true, she would be okay. But *they* would never be okay. She wouldn't be able to be with him again knowing that her father took his father from him. She would never be able to make up for what he'd lost, never be able to give him enough love to make up for the love he'd lost.

Love?

Did she love Logan Payne?

Panic clutched her heart. *Damn it. Damn him...*

She had fallen for her fake fiancé. But those feelings would never be reciprocated—probably not even if they learned that someone else had killed his father. If she hadn't forced herself on him, would he have made love to her?

She doubted it.

"How much farther?" she asked. They'd been driving for a while on what had seemed like a rather circuitous route.

But then through the trees sunshine glimmered off water. They'd been traveling around lakes.

"Not much," he replied. But despite the curvy roads, Logan had had more attention on the rearview mirror than the windshield.

"Is someone following us again?" she asked. Panic pressed on her lungs, stealing her breath. He'd saved them last night because whoever had been following them hadn't just wanted to know where they were going, they'd wanted them dead.

He shrugged. "Maybe..."

So that meant yes.

"Did you lose them?" she asked.

He shrugged again. "Maybe..."

But when he stopped the SUV, he kept his hand on his holster when he stepped out of it. He leaned back inside. "You can stay here," he suggested.

For her protection from whoever had followed them or from whatever his father's older partner might say about that night?

"I want to hear this, too," she said. "I want to know why he visited my dad." She'd looked at the logs and couldn't believe that the man who'd arrested her father had visited him more than his own brother had.

And even more than his sons had.

But then part of that time, they had been busy serving their own sentences behind bars. Because of her...

And Aunt Marta had never visited her brother-in-law. Which was odd given that before she'd married Uncle Iwan, she had dated Stacy's dad. But then he'd fallen for her mother or at least for her beauty. There wasn't much more to her mom than her looks, which she constantly used to find a richer, more successful man. That was why Stacy's dad had started stealing—to provide for the woman. But it had never been enough.

Too bad the woman hadn't realized that nothing was more valuable than love. True love.

If only Stacy could find that for herself...with Logan. But he was barely aware of her now, his hand on his weapon and his gaze scanning the trees surrounding the little log cabin where his father's old partner must have retired. With rough-sawn logs and a wraparound porch, it was rustic but charming.

Birds chirped, and brush and branches rustled from the feet of scurrying squirrels and chipmunks. She'd been a city girl her whole life, but she could see the appeal of such a remote area. The peace...

But then shots rang out, shattering the peace.

"Damn it!" Logan shouted as he crouched behind the driver's door he'd left open.

"Duck down!" he yelled at Stacy. But she'd already lain across the front seat as much as the seat belt she still wore allowed her to move.

Had they been followed from the prison as he'd suspected? Or were the shots coming from the house? When he looked back at the cabin, he noticed a gun barrel protruding from an open window.

"It's me, Cooper!" he yelled. "Don't shoot!"

"You've gotta be kidding me!" the older man said as he hurried out the front door, the shotgun slung over his shoulder. "I thought you were those damn kids..."

"Kids?" Logan asked, wondering why the retired cop would have been shooting at kids, either.

Robert Cooper shoved a shaking hand through gray hair that was standing on end. "They've been breaking into the summer cottages around here."

"So you were going to shoot them?" Logan asked. Had the retired cop lost it? He was older than Logan's dad would have been; Robert had been the senior officer of their doomed partnership.

"I was shooting up in the air, so I wouldn't hit anyone. I just wanted to scare 'em," Robert said.

"Mission accomplished." Logan glanced at Stacy, who was still crouched below the dash. "It's okay," he assured her. But he wasn't certain of that—if the old man had lost it…

"I wouldn't have fired if I'd realized it was you," Cooper said. "But you've never been here before—not like your brothers have."

His brothers were more forgiving than he was; Stacy could vouch to that.

"They've come up to fish on the lake with me," Robert continued. "Have you come up to fish, Logan?"

He had, but for information instead of actual fish. He replied, "I'm not the sportsmen my brothers are." He walked around the car and opened the passenger's door for Stacy.

"You didn't come alone?" Robert asked.

Stacy stepped out, and the older man uttered a loud gasp. "Is that the Kozminski girl?"

"Yes," she answered for herself.

The older man chuckled gruffly, awkwardly. "I never thought I would see the two of you together. Since you were kids, you've been sniping at each other."

But they weren't sniping at each other anymore. "Someone else is sniping at us," Logan said. "With guns—"

"I wouldn't have shot if I'd known it was you," the older man said again.

"I'm not talking about today," Logan explained. "We've been getting shot at the past couple of days and someone even set a bomb in Stacy's apartment."

The retired cop turned to her. "But you're all right? It didn't go off?"

She shook her head. "Logan defused it."

"He was with you then, too?"

"We're together now," Logan said. "We're actually engaged." Whether the engagement was real or not didn't matter…because the feelings between them—the complicated, messy feelings—were real.

The older man gasped again and pushed his knuckles against his chest, as if the news had shocked him so much he was having chest pains.

Logan started toward him. "Are you all right?"

He nodded. "I—I just can't believe you two could ever overcome your differences."

Logan wasn't certain how that had happened, either—except that he had finally stopped blaming Stacy for supporting her father and had begun to admire her fierce loyalty. "I'm not sure we're all that different," he admitted. "We both love our families. Our fathers…"

She turned toward him, her gray eyes showing her surprise and appreciation.

But the retired cop expressed his surprise with a coarse curse before adding, "Her father killed yours. I didn't think that was something you'd ever get over, Logan."

"My father didn't pull the trigger," she said.

"He told you that?" Robert asked. "He told you that he didn't do it?"

She shook her head. "He would never talk to me about that night. But I know he didn't do it—that he couldn't take another man's life."

"What did he tell you?" Logan asked the former officer.

The older man glared in annoyance. "You know what he told me. You read the report. You were in court for my testimony. Your father caught him stealing and they struggled over the gun."

"I'm not talking about what he told you that night," Logan clarified. "I'm talking about what he told you all the times you visited him in prison."

The retired cop's already ruddy face flushed deep red. "What are you talking about?"

Stacy held up the visitor logs that the warden had printed out for her. "It's on here—all your visits to my father."

"Several over the years," Logan said. "Almost regular visits. If you knew everything you needed to about the night my father died, why did you keep going back to talk to his killer—unless you knew that he wasn't the killer."

His face flushed an even deeper shade of red until he was nearly purple. But his voice was gruff with disappointment when he replied, "You let her get to you, Logan."

"She's convinced that her father didn't pull the trigger," Logan said, "that someone else was there that night."

"There was," Stacy insisted.

Logan stepped closer to the porch, careful to stay between the loaded shotgun and Stacy. The ex-cop might not have been as forgiving as Logan had found himself to be regarding the daughter of the man convicted of killing his father.

"Did you see someone else?" Logan asked Robert. "Is that why you kept going to see Kozminski? To find out who was with him that night?"

The older man sighed. "There could have been someone else…"

"Why didn't that get into your report?" Logan asked. "Or your testimony?"

"There *may* have been someone else," he said. "But there was *definitely* Kozminski. He was there robbing the place.

I wasn't going to let him get away with murder because of reasonable doubt."

Logan had it now. Reasonable doubt. And Robert Cooper must have, too, because he'd kept visiting Kozminski.

"Who was it?" Stacy asked. "Who did you see?"

The older man shook his head. "Just a shadow—fleeing the building. I would have given chase, but I wanted to make sure my partner was all right. I'd already fallen too far behind him during pursuit, and he wasn't answering his radio call."

Logan shuddered as he realized why: because his father had been lying dead on the jewelry store floor with Patek Kozminski standing over him. That was the image he'd always had in his head—the image Robert Cooper had put there with his report and his testimony. And that was why Logan had stayed so angry at Stacy's father.

"So you just decided to pin a murder on my father that he didn't commit?" Stacy asked, her voice rising with anger.

"He never denied it," Robert pointed out. "He never proclaimed his innocence."

No. He hadn't. And there was only one reason for that. "He was protecting someone," Logan said. "You must have suspected that, too."

Robert nodded. "That is why I kept visiting him. I wanted him to tell me. But he never admitted anything to me." The retired cop turned toward Stacy. "Did he ever tell you anything?"

She shook her head. "I already told you that he refused to talk to me about that night."

"Even the last time you saw him?" Robert asked. "He didn't even tell you on his deathbed?"

"No," she said. "He still wouldn't talk about what happened."

"He didn't say anything about my father at all?" Logan

asked. If Patek Kozminski really had killed a man and was about to die himself, wouldn't he want to make amends? Penance? Beg for forgiveness? But an innocent man had no reason to ask for forgiveness...

Could Stacy have been right all this time? Her father had been stuck in prison for a crime he hadn't committed. Logan had wondered before if he could forgive her for what her father had done. But could she forgive him for helping keep an innocent man in prison?

"He didn't talk about your father," she said.

And he was grateful that she'd at least revealed that much about the words over which she had been so secretive.

"So he didn't say anything about who else was there that night?" the ex-cop persisted.

"No."

"He died protecting whoever else had been there," Logan said. So it had to have been someone close to him. Someone he'd loved...

Stacy must have come to the same realization because the color left her face, leaving her skin translucent except for the dark circles beneath her smoky-gray eyes. Because if her father had loved that person enough to protect him, she probably loved that person, too.

"He didn't say anything. But did he leave you anything?" Robert asked. The cop had retired a few years ago, but apparently he had not forgotten how to interrogate a suspect.

But Stacy wasn't a suspect. There was no way that she had been there that night. She would not have let her father go to prison for something she'd done.

"Was there anything in his personal effects?" Robert probed. "A letter? A journal?"

She shrugged. "I don't know. I haven't gone through his stuff."

"Did the bomb destroy his things?" Robert asked.

She shook her head. "No. I didn't bring his effects home with me."

She hadn't gone home from the prison. She'd gone straight to a friend. And she must have brought her father's stuff with her.

Her eyes widened again, as if she'd followed Logan's train of thought, too. If there was something in her father's stuff, some kind of confession or evidence, then whoever had that stuff was in danger. She grasped Logan's arm and murmured, "We need to leave."

"Where are his things?" Robert asked.

Logan covered Stacy's hand with his and squeezed. He didn't want her to say anything else in front of the old cop. "It's okay," he told the man. "We've got it from here."

The retired cop stepped forward so abruptly that he nearly stumbled down the porch stairs. "No. You can't cut me out of this investigation. I've been working this case for fifteen years."

"No, you haven't," Logan said.

Robert pointed toward the log printouts in Stacy's hand. "You saw my visits. You know I have been trying to get to the truth."

"No," Logan repeated. "A real cop would have included everything he'd seen in his report and his testimony."

"And then Patek Kozminski wouldn't have gone to prison."

Stacy gasped.

"No," Logan said. "He'd still been caught in the commission of a felony. A man had died during that felony. He would have gone to prison for those charges, but the real killer wouldn't have been free the past fifteen years."

"You think Kozminski would have given him up in some kind of plea deal?" Robert asked.

Logan shook his head. "No. But I would have been looking for the killer. And I wouldn't have stopped until he was brought to justice." And he wouldn't stop now.

He opened the passenger's door for Stacy. But she hadn't yet slid into the seat when the shots rang out. Logan reached for his weapon and turned toward the older man. But Robert Cooper wasn't firing. His shotgun was still slung over his shoulder.

The shots came from behind the already battered SUV— from the street. They had been followed from the prison. Logan pushed Stacy into the vehicle and drew his gun. But the window of the passenger's door shattered as the shots nearly struck him. He had no protection. No time to return fire.

No time left…

Chapter Sixteen

Stacy couldn't stop shaking. Those shots had been so close, but not to her. Like always, Logan had protected her. But he wouldn't have been able to protect himself. He'd had no time to take cover. No time to draw his weapon.

Fortunately, the old cop had fired his shotgun. Tires had squealed as whoever had followed them sped off. Tires squealed now as Logan rounded one of the curves around the lakes.

She braced one hand on the dashboard and clutched the armrest with her other hand. "You're not going to catch them." Not with all the hairpin turns and two-track roads running off the main street. "They could have gone anywhere."

"I knew we were followed from the prison," he said, berating himself.

The only people who'd been able to follow him so easily were her brothers and whoever had driven them off the road the night before. As Logan had pointed out, her father had been protecting someone the past fifteen years—someone he'd loved. His brother or his sons?

She shook her head. It couldn't be any of them. Her family wouldn't have let her father spend fifteen years in prison for something he hadn't done. It had to have been someone else—someone who'd killed once and would have willingly killed again if any of the shots had struck Logan or her or if either bomb had exploded...

Bomb? What if one had been set at her friend's house? Hopefully the bomber hadn't figured out where she'd been staying since her father's death. But what if she'd been followed...

She reached for Logan's arm again, grasping it tightly as she gave him the address. "You have to take me there."

"Why?"

"It's where I left my father's things—the things the warden gave me that Dad had had at the prison."

"The letter or journal?"

"I don't know what was in the box," she said. "I didn't look through it." There could have been evidence in it—a deathbed confession. But she cared less about that and more about her friend's safety.

"Whoever's trying to kill you doesn't know that," Logan said. "They think your father told you something or gave you something."

"Right now the important thing is making sure my friend is safe." She reached inside her purse for her cell phone. The screen was black, the battery completely dead. "Damn it."

"You left your charger at your friend's," he surmised.

It wasn't the only thing she'd carelessly left there. "I thought I'd be going back there after the funeral."

Logan fell silent, but he kept driving just as fast as he had earlier—as if he were pursuing someone. Or running from someone. He was ignoring her now, but he hadn't ignored her last night.

Heat flashed through her at the memories of their lovemaking. She had no regrets about making love with him. Her only regret was putting her friend in danger.

"Please hurry," she said.

But he shook off her grasp. Then he handed her his cell phone. "Mine's charged. Call your friend."

She punched in the number she'd memorized long ago. But nobody answered. "It went to voice mail."

What if there was a reason for that? What if there had been another bomb? Tears of fear and concern stung her eyes. "I will never forgive myself if something's happened…"

Amber Talsma was more like a sister than a friend. They would have been sisters—if she and Milek hadn't broken up instead of getting married.

Panic clutched her stomach as Logan turned onto the suburban street. What if the house was gone? Obliterated?

But then there would have been a police barricade and reporters. And there was nothing like that. The house stood in the middle of the well-maintained green lawn. With its fieldstone and shake siding, it had an open floor plan and several big bedrooms. That was how Amber had convinced Stacy to stay with her—because she had so much room.

Stacy hoped that Amber wouldn't regret having her stay. She hoped that she hadn't endangered her and the other person who lived with Amber and her little dog. The minute Logan pulled the car into the driveway, Stacy threw open her car door and ran for the house.

The front door opened and a child greeted her, propelling his small body into her arms. There was no man in Amber's life; just a boy.

"Are you okay?" she asked him, love warming her heart as she pulled him close. "Is your mother okay?"

"She's in the shower," the four-year-old replied. "I'm 'kay, Aunt Stacy."

"No, you're not," his mother said as she crossed the foyer. "You're in trouble for opening that door, mister."

Amber's smile froze and she reached for the towel she'd wrapped around herself as she stared behind Stacy.

She turned back toward a clearly shocked Logan. She probably should have corrected his misassumption earlier about her friend being male. And she probably should have warned him about her nephew. He looked nearly as shocked as if she'd opened the door to a bomb.

AFTER A THOROUGH search, they concluded there was no bomb. Logan had cleared the house of explosives before they'd left Amber Talsma and her son. And now, as they drove away, Stacy was clearing the box of belongings Warden Borgess had given her.

"Is there anything in there?" he asked, glancing over at her. But then he returned his attention to the rearview mirror and the road ahead of them.

She uttered a broken sigh. "Nothing about your father's death."

He glanced over again to the stack of photos and cards through which she was thumbing. "He saved them all?"

"Yes, all of them," she replied, her voice shaky with tears. "Every card and picture I ever gave him."

"Did you give him pictures of his grandchild?" Logan asked. "That boy is your nephew, right?" Not only had he called her "aunt" but he was a gray-eyed blond-haired miniature of her brothers while the child's mom had red hair and green eyes.

She hesitated as if considering lying to him. "He might just call me that because his mother and I are such good friends."

Before he'd learned Amber was a woman, he had thought they were more than friends, and he'd been ridiculously jealous. Because of the boy, they actually were more than friends; they were family. "Is he Garek's or Milek's son?"

She sighed and held up a picture of a pudgy baby. She had given her father photos of the child. "Milek, but he doesn't know."

"That's one hell of a secret to keep."

"Amber has her reasons."

"What are yours?" he asked, appalled that she would keep such a secret. Maybe she wasn't as loyal to her family as he'd thought she was. "He's your brother. You should tell him. I would tell Parker if he had a kid."

She chuckled. "If Parker's reputation is to be believed, he probably does."

He nearly chuckled at the thought of his twin with a kid. "There's no way. He would never be that careless."

But then it suddenly occurred to him that *he* had been that careless. He hadn't protected her when they'd made love. And if they had made a child together, he wondered if she would tell him. Or would she keep that secret as she had kept so many other secrets?

"Milek was careless," she said, "with Amber's heart. He broke it when he broke off their engagement. She didn't want to use her pregnancy to keep him. She didn't want to trap him into marriage."

He knew Stacy really didn't want to marry him at all. If she were pregnant, she was as unlikely to share that information as her friend. He would have to make certain that no matter what happened between them that they stayed in touch.

"They wouldn't have had to marry for Milek to be part of the boy's life," Logan said. "He could still spend time with him—still support him."

"Amber's a lawyer," she informed him. "The assistant district attorney, actually. She supports herself."

"Is she really going to get a warrant for the visitor logs of the prisoner who killed your father?" he asked.

Stacy nodded. "Definitely. She knows how important it is that we find out why my father was killed."

"Because someone had wanted him silenced." Someone had been afraid that he might finally reveal who'd really killed his father. And if that someone was willing to have one relative killed, they were definitely willing to kill another. He shouldn't have brought her with him.

He should have asked Parker or one of the other bodyguards of the Payne Protection Agency—besides Candace—to keep her safe. But Stacy had insisted on coming along. She had even refused to give him the address he'd needed unless he brought her along.

"We're here," she said as he pulled onto a city street.

This wasn't a residential area of River City. It was the warehouse district, and none of these warehouses had been converted to condos as far as he knew.

"They really live in one of these?" he asked.

She pointed toward one. It was brick instead of the cold-looking metal of the other buildings. But it still looked more industrial than residential.

He pulled the SUV to the curb and parked. But before he could slide out from behind the wheel, Stacy grasped his arm. "You can't tell Milek that he has a son," she said.

"It's not my secret to tell," he told her.

"It's not mine, either," she said.

"Do you think Milek is going to be okay with that when he learns the truth?" he asked. "And he will someday. He's going to be furious with you."

She sighed. "He's going to be furious with me anyway." She glanced toward the warehouse. "I'm not sure I can do this."

"Then let me," he offered. But he wasn't eager to face her brothers, either—at least not Milek. It wasn't his secret to keep or expose, but he wished to hell that he'd never found out.

Stacy followed him to the front door, though. Or at least he assumed the electric overhead door was the front. It rolled up when Stacy pushed a button. There was a foyer of corrugated metal and brick and off that interior foyer was another door that opened as they approached it.

Garek filled the doorway. "Why did you bring *him* here?"

"Why shouldn't she have brought me?" Logan wondered. "Afraid I might check serial numbers and find some stolen property?"

Garek uttered a particularly crude curse.

"Hey, I'm going to be your brother-in-law," Logan goaded him.

"She might have fallen in love with you, but I haven't," Garek said.

Stacy's face flushed with bright color, but instead of addressing her brother's comment, she ignored it to ask, "Is Milek here, too?"

Logan hoped he wasn't. But the other man appeared behind Garek.

"I'm here," he said. "What's going on? Did you set a date for this farce of a wedding?"

Logan would rather plan a honeymoon than a wedding. The thought of a honeymoon—of several nights of making love like they had—filled Logan with need. If only they had been able to go away—just the two of them…

But it would never be just the two of them. There would always be their past and the secrets between them.

"We're still not safe," Stacy answered her brother.

"There have been more attempts on your life?" Garek asked with a glare at Logan. "I thought you would keep her safe!"

"Obviously he has or I wouldn't be here," Stacy defended him.

"But it has to end," Logan said with a pointed glare of his own at Garek. He still couldn't look at Milek. "It has to end now."

"You really think we would hurt our sister?" Milek asked, his voice gruff with disappointment and hurt.

How would he feel when he learned he had lost three or four years of his son's life? Logan hated secrets; he'd had to keep clients' secrets before but Stacy wasn't *paying* him to protect her. She wasn't his client.

She was his fiancée, though. And after last night that felt more real than fake. And fiancée probably trumped client. So he had to keep her secret, too.

But she grabbed his hand and squeezed it in warning— as if she suspected he was tempted to tell the truth.

"People will take desperate measures to protect themselves," he said. "So maybe you would hurt your sister to protect yourself."

"Protect myself?" Milek repeated. "Nobody's trying to kill *me.*"

"Protect yourself from going back to jail," Logan clarified.

Garek stepped back. "Check all the serial numbers you want. We're not criminals."

Logan wasn't so sure about that but he begrudgingly gave them the benefit of the doubt. "Maybe not anymore…"

"You just can't let go of the past, can you?" Garek said. "I don't know how you ever fell for Stacy. Our dad was hers, too."

Panic clutched his heart as he realized that her brother was right. He had fallen for Stacy. But he wasn't sure how, especially when he knew that he couldn't trust her.

"I'm not so sure that your father was the one who killed my father," Logan conceded.

Milek chuckled. "She really has gotten to you."

More than she knew...

"I kept telling you that Dad wasn't alone that night," she said.

"And he listened to you?" Garek asked, his gaze returning to Logan. His eyes narrowed in consideration.

"Did you think no one ever would?"

"I'm not sure anyone should have," Garek said with an apologetic glance at his sister. "When it comes to our father, Stacy is still a little girl idolizing her daddy."

And instead of understanding that like her brothers did, Logan had resented her love for her father.

"That might be the case," he said, agreeing with Garek to a degree. "But my father's partner just admitted he saw someone else that night."

Garek's tall body tensed. "Who did he see?"

"Just a shadow," Stacy said, almost as if reassuring her oldest brother. "But it proves there was someone else there that night. Someone else who shot Officer Payne."

Milek wistfully sighed. "I wanted to believe you, Stacy. I wanted to believe that Dad was innocent, but he would never talk about that night."

And that was ultimately what had convinced Logan. A guilty man would have begged for forgiveness at the end, may have written a letter of apology to the family he'd deprived of a father. "He probably wouldn't talk about that night because he was protecting someone."

"Someone?" Garek repeated, one of his blond brows arching with the question.

"I suspect one of you," Logan said. "Who else would he have willingly gone to prison to protect?"

Milek chuckled. "We were kids. We wouldn't have gone to prison."

"You were teenagers," Logan said. "You may have been tried as adults. Garek was—"

"When we killed a man in defense of Stacy," Garek finished for him. He turned to his sister. "How could you let him turn you against us?"

She flinched as if he'd slapped her. "All I want is the truth."

"Dad didn't tell you on his deathbed?" Garek asked.

"Your father didn't tell her which one of you was with him that night—which one of you really pulled the trigger and killed my father," Logan assured him. "So you didn't have to try to hurt her."

"I would never hurt *her*," Garek said. "But I can't say the same about *you*."

"Garek!" Stacy yelled. But it was too late. Her oldest brother was already swinging.

Logan dodged the first punch. But Milek swung, too, and his first connected with Logan's jaw, knocking him back. Then, enraged, they both jumped on him. Two on one wasn't fair.

But Parker and Cooper had teamed up to fight Logan before, when they were kids, and he'd prevailed then. But his brothers hadn't actually been trying to kill him.

The Kozminski brothers wanted him dead. And this wasn't a fight that Logan was sure he could win.

Chapter Seventeen

Curses and grunts filled the air in which fists flew and blood spattered. Logan could have pulled his gun—could have fired at them to stop the assault. But apparently he didn't want to kill her brothers.

Stacy couldn't say the same of Garek and Milek. They piled on Logan, pounding. Panic and fear burning in her lungs, she screamed at them to stop. And then she pounded, too, hitting and kicking her brothers. She grabbed their hair and tugged, pulling them back. Pulling them off the man she loved.

"Stop it! Stop it!" she screamed, in such a panic that she hadn't realized they'd already stopped.

Garek rubbed his head. "Damn it, Stace, you pulled out a handful of hair."

"He's my fiancé," she declared. "I want to marry him." And that was the truth.

"That's the last thing *we* want," Garek said, and he fisted his hands and turned back to Logan.

Milek had already climbed back onto her wounded fiancé, his arms raised to swing again. Logan wasn't fighting them off; he had to be hurt. Maybe badly.

"It's what Dad wanted!" she yelled. "Dad wanted me to marry Logan. Those were his last words to me."

"What?" Milek asked, but he stopped fighting midswing.

"Why?" Logan asked that question. "Why would your father want you to marry me?"

She'd wondered that, too. She hadn't understood what he'd been telling her.

"He admired you," she said, and she dropped onto her knees next to her fiancé. He was bruised and his lip was oozing blood. But he sat up easily as if nothing was broken.

"He said you were a man of conviction. A man of integrity and honesty. That you fought for those you loved," she continued. "He didn't think I would be able to find a better man than you to marry."

"Dad really said that?" Milek asked, doubtfully. "His last words were about Logan Payne?"

She nodded.

"Why didn't you tell us this before?" Garek asked.

"Because it was personal," she said. And she'd been embarrassed that her father had spent his last living moments matchmaking. Maybe that was why she loved Penny Payne so much; she reminded Stacy of her father. "And it had nothing to do with either of you."

Garek snorted. "That was the usual for Dad. He was all about his little princess."

She winced at her brother's resentment. She had never heard it before. Could Logan be right about her brothers actually wanting to hurt her?

"He loved you both, too."

Garek laughed. "Then why was he training us to be thieves? He brought us along with him on jobs."

Oh, God, Logan had been right. "You were with him that night? That was why he never said anything? Why he served the sentence—to protect one of you?"

Garek laughed again—bitterly. "You didn't know our father at all, Stacy. He started bringing me and Milek out on jobs when we were twelve so that if we got caught, we'd only go to juvie. If one of us had been with him that night, he wouldn't have taken the rap for us. One of us would have taken it for him."

Pain and disillusionment overwhelmed her and she gasped. Logan's arm slid around her shoulders, and he pulled her tight to his side as if to protect her. He could save her from physical harm, as he had already so many times. But he couldn't protect her from emotional harm.

"I knew you were willing to hurt her," Logan said. "And you found the most painful way to do that."

Despite his swelling eyes, Milek glared at his brother. "That was harsh," he admonished him. "She didn't need to know any of that."

"But was it true?" she asked.

"It wasn't so much that he forced us to steal," Milek said. "It's just what was expected of us as Kozminskis. Our traditional profession is jewelry thief—like Payne's is law enforcement."

"And because of that," Garek said, "a Payne and a Kozminski should never marry. Dad was wrong about that, too."

She had asked them before, but since they were actually being honest now—brutally honest—with her, she asked again, "Is that why you've been trying to kill him?"

Garek cursed. "We haven't been trying to kill him."

Logan grunted in protest.

"Beating the crap out of you is different than shooting at you," Garek pointed out. "Besides, we don't even own a gun."

"Neither did Dad," Milek said. "The only Kozminski who ever owned one is Uncle Iwan."

"Iwan?" Logan asked.

"He wouldn't try to kill you," Stacy said. But her uncle had always been an enigma to her. Unlike her charming father, Uncle Iwan had always been quiet and withdrawn—as if fearful to speak up in front of his overbearing wife.

Garek moved and grunted. "I wouldn't be too sure about that."

"But why?" Stacy asked. "To avenge our father?"

But according to the logs, he hadn't even visited his brother that often. How close had they really been?

Milek shrugged. "That's what I thought. That it must have been him shooting at Logan since we knew it wasn't us." But he spared his brother a glance as if he wondered.

Hadn't Garek and Milek been together every time the shootings had happened?

"Maybe it wasn't Logan he was shooting at or trying to blow up," Garek said.

Stacy gasped. She and Uncle Iwan had never been close but… "Why would he want to hurt me?"

Garek mused, "Aunt Marta is really damn concerned about what our father told you on his deathbed. That's because she doesn't want to lose her meal ticket. She doesn't want Uncle Iwan going to jail."

Logan tensed. "You think your uncle was there that night? You think he's the one who killed my father?"

"But why would Dad take the rap for him?" Milek asked.

Garek pointed at her. "So she would have a legal guardian. He'd been caught stealing. He was going to jail no matter what, and he didn't want our mother getting custody. He wanted Uncle Iwan to take her. To protect her."

Tears stung her eyes. "Do you hate me?" she asked her brother.

Garek leaned forward and cupped her face in his palm. "I love you. You're my little princess, too, Stace. I would do anything to protect you. That was why I never told you about Dad. I wanted to leave you that fantasy you had of him being such a good man."

"But he wasn't?" Logan asked the question.

"He was a thief," Garek said, and a trace of self-loathing replaced his earlier bitterness.

"But he wasn't a killer," Milek said. "Stacy has been right about that. He taught us how to bypass security systems and break into safes and vaults. He taught us how to use tools, not guns. He never wanted us to carry a weapon. He wouldn't have had the gun that night."

"But your uncle has a gun?" Logan asked. "You've seen it?"

Stacy nodded. "He showed it to me when I first came to live with him and Aunt Marta."

Logan's brows rose in surprise. "He showed a teenage girl a gun? To scare you?"

"To make me feel safe," she said. "I had nightmares—because of what happened…"

"With our stepfather," Milek said, as if wondering if she'd told Logan.

"The pervert," he said—the bitterness all his now.

Garek nodded heartily in agreement. "He sure was."

Logan's arm tightened around her.

Garek added, "You're safe now, Stace."

But Logan shook his head. "She won't be safe until we figure out who's been trying to kill her."

"And you," Milek added, as if he cared.

How could men pound on each other one minute and bond the next? Even though she'd been raised with them, she would never understand them.

"I'm more concerned about Stacy," Logan said, but even as he said it, he was easing away from her. "Can you guys keep her safe?" He stood up as if he was leaving.

She stood up, too—so quickly that she was dizzy for a moment. He grabbed her shoulders and steadied her. "Where are you going?" she asked. But she knew.

"I have to do this…"

"I know," she said. "But I'll go with you."

"We can all go," Milek offered.

Logan shook his head. "I have to do this alone."

"That makes no sense," Stacy said. "You don't have to—"

"It was his father who died," Garek said. "So he has to do this alone."

For vengeance? Was he going to kill her uncle?

LOGAN WAS MAD enough to kill. But he was madder at himself than anyone else. Why hadn't he more thoroughly investigated his father's death? Sure, he'd been a kid when it had happened fifteen years ago. But since then he'd gotten a degree in criminal justice and then had become a cop before his quick promotion to detective.

He should have looked into it more—should have gone over the reports and the testimony with more scrutiny. He should have listened to Stacy.

Sure, her brothers were right that she had idolized—or rather idealized—her father. But even they had had to admit that he wasn't a killer. He'd never even carried a weapon on him. So where had that gun come from? The gun with which Logan's father had been killed?

Had it been one of Iwan Kozminski's? If so, he must have replaced it with the gun that he'd showed Stacy. To reassure her and stop the nightmares? Or to scare her?

Her uncle wasn't the loving male figure her father had been. Even from behind bars, her father had tried to protect her—so much so that he'd been willing to take the rap for another man's murder. Sure, he hadn't been the completely innocent man Stacy had believed him to be, but neither had he been the monster Logan had considered him all these years.

Did Stacy consider *him* a monster? And not just for keeping her father in prison but for what she was afraid he might do to her uncle? He wouldn't kill anyone except in self-defense. He could have pulled his gun on her brothers and saved himself the split lip and bruised ribs that throbbed with pain. But Stacy loved her brothers so much that she would never forgive him taking one of their lives.

And she'd saved him. She'd fought at Logan's side instead of against him. She'd acted like his partner, like his wife. Maybe he should have let her come along today. But he trusted her aunt and uncle even less than he trusted her brothers.

As they'd been the night before, the gates to the Kozminskis' estate stood open, as if they were expecting him again.

Had Garek or Milek called ahead to warn their uncle?

He reached for his holster to make sure his gun was easily accessible. Then he parked the SUV and approached the three-story brick mansion.

Suddenly the front door opened and Iwan stepped outside with narrowed eyes. "What are you doing here?" he asked nervously.

"Were you expecting someone else?" A long black car pulled through the open gates. And Logan noticed the suitcase Iwan Kozminski pulled behind him. "You're leaving town?"

"I—I need to make a business trip," he replied.

"What exactly is your business, Mr. Kozminski? I've never been told what you do for a living." He assessed the impressive house. "But you must do it very well." He hadn't been caught like his brother had been. Or maybe he'd just run faster...

"Who's here?" a female voice asked. Marta Kozminski stepped out of the foyer, a drink in her hand. "Oh, *you*..."

She swirled the ice cubes and stared down into the liquid as if unable to meet his gaze.

He had no warrant. No legal way to keep Iwan from leaving the country, which was what he was certain he was doing, so Logan asked, "Can you take a later flight? I'd really like to talk to you."

"I can't imagine what we have to talk about," Iwan replied. "We barely know each other."

"And yet we're going to be family," Logan reminded him.

"I don't understand why his niece would ever marry you," Marta said. "That girl has always been strange, though."

Because she'd been self-sufficient? Because she cared more about people than money? He bit his tongue to keep from uttering those questions. But he couldn't stay silent. "She's an amazing woman."

Iwan sighed and waved off the car. "I'll take a later flight."

Marta shook her head. "You don't have to talk to him. He's not a police officer anymore. He's not really even family."

"I will be," he promised her.

She flounced back into the house. Probably to pour another drink. Iwan stepped back to escort Logan inside. He wondered if he should have brought backup. Not Stacy or her brothers but maybe his brother. His family deserved the truth about their father's death, too.

But that was why he hadn't called any of them. He didn't want to say anything until he knew the entire story. He didn't want to bring up all that pain and all those bad memories until he'd found the person who was really responsible for their father's death.

"What do you want to discuss with me?" Iwan asked as

he led the way through a marble-floored foyer to a darkly paneled den. "Stacy's brothers?"

"Those hooligans," Marta snarkily remarked from where she stood at the bar, pouring herself another drink just as he suspected. She glanced up and pointed toward his face. "Did they do that to you?"

"Yes," he answered.

"Animals…"

He wasn't so sure about that anymore. Maybe their pounding on him had addled his brain, but he had actually begun to trust them—or he never would have left Stacy in their protection. But what if that had been a mistake? An even bigger one than coming here without backup?

"They love their sister, though," he said. He had to convince himself of that or he would rush back to make sure she was all right with them, that they hadn't hurt her.

"Maybe too much," Marta said. "Since they went to prison for her."

They had been willing to do time to keep her safe; they wouldn't have let their father do time for their crime. Robert Cooper had to have seen someone else that night.

"Their father went to prison for her, too," Logan said.

"He went to prison for killing your father," Marta heartlessly reiterated. "How could you have forgotten that?" Obviously she didn't want him forgetting.

"That's the crime he was convicted of," Logan agreed. "But it wasn't the one he committed."

Iwan studied him. "I didn't believe my brother could ever take a life, especially the life of a policeman. But I thought *you* were convinced of his guilt."

"He was guilty," Marta anxiously insisted. "Did he say something else to his daughter? Did he make some crazy claims on his deathbed?"

That Logan was the man for her—that had been a crazy

claim. How had Patek Kozminski ever thought that a relationship between them would work?

"The arresting officer is actually the one who made the claim—that there was someone else there that night," Logan said. "He saw that someone…"

Iwan shrugged. "Then why didn't he testify to that? Why didn't it even get into his report?"

"He wanted to make sure that your brother was convicted. But he never stopped looking for the man he saw that night, the one that I believe actually pulled the trigger." He focused on the older man, studying his face for any sign of guilt. But the guy was so controlled, probably from all those years of being a jewelry thief. "Was it you?"

"Drop it!" Marta screamed. "Just drop it!"

"I can't," Logan said. "I need to know the truth. I need to know who really killed my father." But from the corner of his eye, he caught the glint of metal.

Marta brandished a gun. "Drop it!" she yelled again.

But instead of giving up his weapon, Logan pulled it and pressed it to her husband's chest. "I don't care if she shoots me, I want the truth before I go. I need to know. Was it you that night?"

"I told the officer that Iwan was with me that night," she said, hysteria making her voice shrill. "He was with me!"

"And you wouldn't lie for your husband?" he scoffed. "I don't believe you." He turned back to Iwan, but even with the gun pressed against his chest, the man betrayed no emotion—not guilt or even fear. "You and your brother were thieves together."

"He was teaching his sons, too," Marta said.

"But it wasn't them."

"It wasn't me," Iwan said, and finally he nervously glanced down at the gun pressed to his chest. "I wasn't with him that night."

Marta sucked in a breath as if she was surprised by the news.

"He wasn't with you, either," Logan surmised and he eased back with the gun. The safety was on; he wouldn't have actually pulled the trigger. He wasn't so sure about Marta Kozminski. "So *where* were you?"

The older man sighed. "You don't need to know that— you just need to know that I wasn't with my brother."

"Neither were his sons. So who could it have been? Was there someone else he worked with?"

"A cop," Iwan replied. "He had a cop in his pocket. That was how he'd gotten away with so many heists."

"Which cop?"

"I thought it was your father," Iwan said. "I thought that's what happened that night—that they had a disagreement over the percentage each would keep, and your father wound up dead."

Logan shook his head. "That's not possible. My father was not a dirty cop."

Iwan shrugged. "I don't know. I could have sworn it was him."

Was it possible that Logan hadn't really known his father? That like Stacy had hers, he had idealized his dad, too?

"I want to know," Marta said, and now she swung the gun toward her husband. "I want to know where you were that night. All these years I thought you were with him. I thought you pulled the trigger, too. I know Patek wouldn't have had the nerve."

"It wasn't me," Iwan insisted. "I wasn't there."

"Then where were you?" she screamed. She was drunk and now she was hysterical.

The situation had quickly gotten out of hand. Logan

turned toward her and estimated if he could reach for the gun before she could fire it.

"Where were you?" she screamed again. And then her gaze grew wilder. "You were with her? That whore you've been seeing? The one you were probably going to meet today?"

Before Logan could grab the gun, she pulled the trigger. The bodyguard in him reacted, and he put himself in front of the bullet.

Chapter Eighteen

The shot reverberated outside Uncle Iwan and Aunt Marta's house. And a scream tore from Stacy's throat. She ran toward the house, but Garek caught her arms, trying to hold her back. She wriggled free of his grasp and ran inside. Her feet pounded across the marble floor of the foyer. "Logan!"

Hysterical cries emanated from the back of the house, from the area of the den. Stacy ran. But her brothers had caught up with her and beat her to the doorway.

"Damn it, Aunt Marta!" Garek exclaimed. "You killed him!"

Pain clutched Stacy's heart, and tears burned her eyes. "No! No!"

She pushed past Milek so she could see. Two men lay on the floor in a pool of blood. Logan and her uncle.

Aunt Marta stood over them, her hand shaking with the gun that Garek quickly wrestled from her grasp. "Give me the gun, Marta!"

Stacy dropped to her knees beside her fiancé. "Logan! Logan!"

His eyes—those brilliant blue eyes—opened and focused on her face. And relief flooded her.

"She has a gun," he warned her, clasping her close as if to protect her. Blood from his shirt stuck to hers, staining it.

"Garek got it away from her," she reassured him.

And in the distance sirens whined. Police were on the way.

"Where are you hurt?" she asked, her fear and panic rushing back over her. "Where did you get shot?"

He touched his side. "I tried to stop her. Tried to step in front of it…"

He hadn't been her intended target?

"How's Iwan?" Logan asked, and with only a slight grimace, he rolled toward the older man. "Did he get hit?"

Uncle Iwan's eyes were closed and blood oozed from a wound in his chest. Logan touched his neck. "He has a pulse. Call an ambulance."

"Cheating swine," Marta cursed her husband. "He better not make it."

"If he doesn't, you'll spend the rest of your life in prison," Logan warned her. He might have been wounded, but not so badly that he was weak from the injury.

And a short while later, officers led her off in handcuffs while paramedics loaded Uncle Iwan into the back of an ambulance. Logan refused to ride in one, so Milek drove him and Stacy in his car while Garek followed in the battered SUV.

Parker and Nikki and Mrs. Payne met them at the hospital. "I'm okay," he told his family as they rallied around him. "It was a through and through. How's Iwan?"

"They took him to surgery," Garek replied. "His condition is serious, but not critical."

Parker slammed his fist into Garek's jaw. "You did this. You shot my brother."

Milek grabbed Parker and shoved him back. "Get off my brother!"

"Stop," Logan yelled, then grimaced and grabbed his side. "They didn't do this. Marta was trying to shoot her husband and I stepped in front."

"You've been shot again," Mrs. Payne exclaimed, her eyes glistening with tears. Her slight body began to tremble. Stacy reached out to her, putting her arm around the older woman.

"It's a through and through," he repeated. "I'm fine." And a short while later, a doctor agreed with him when he pronounced it okay for a bandaged Logan to leave the hospital.

"Uncle Iwan's still in surgery," Garek told her. "And Aunt Marta's getting booked."

Stacy was more concerned with her new family than her old family. She had stayed with Mrs. Payne and Nikki while Logan had been getting examined and x-rayed. Parker had paced and talked on his cell phone. He pocketed the phone now and told his twin, "They're going to run ballistics on that gun and find out if Marta was the one shooting at you and Stacy."

Logan nodded. "That's good. I'm not sure she would have known how to make those bombs, though…" His voice trailed off on a slur. He was completely exhausted.

Because of her family…because of her…

"Let me take you home," she said.

He shook his head.

And her pride stung and pain squeezed her heart. He was rejecting her.

"Not home. To *our* place," he said. "Where we went last night…"

Where they had made love. She wasn't sure how to get there since she'd slept during the ride. But she didn't admit that until they had said goodbye to everyone and were alone in the car.

As exhausted as he was, he insisted on driving to make sure that they weren't followed. But he winced and grimaced every time he turned the steering wheel.

"You shouldn't be driving."

"I'm fine," he insisted. And he proved it by making it safely to the town house. But as soon as they were in the elevator, he leaned heavily against one of the walls. So Stacy slid beneath his arm and wrapped her arm around his uninjured side to keep him on his feet.

"You're not fine," she said.

"If we get married, you're going to have to promise to stick by me in sickness and health," he threatened.

"If we get married…" It wasn't likely to ever happen. Their engagement hadn't stopped the attempts on their lives. How would a wedding?

"I'll also have it put in the vows that you always have to be honest with me," he added.

Obviously it was still bothering him that she was keeping a secret—a big, almost four-year-old secret—from her brother. "I have been honest with you," she said.

"Always?"

"I haven't lied to you," she said.

"But there's more to being honest than just telling the truth," he stubbornly persisted. "There's being open and forthcoming. Being honest means no secrets."

The elevator stopped on the top floor and saved her from replying. Because if she agreed, she would have to tell him how she felt about him—that she loved him.

But maybe she didn't have to tell him to be honest about her feelings. Maybe she could just show him. So she unbuttoned his bloody shirt and pushed it from his shoulders. Then she unsnapped his jeans and lowered his zipper and helped him take off his pants. Then she gently pushed him back onto the bed and joined him.

He groaned.

"Are you in pain?" she asked, concern stilling the fingers she'd run over his chest. He had a bloodstained bandage on his shoulder and another on his side. And his skin was bruised and swollen in places. But other parts of him were swelling, too, in reaction to her touch.

"You can ease my pain," he said.

She kissed his chest, gently touching her lips to each bruise. Then she moved to each nipple and then to each ripple of muscle as she moved over his washboard abs to his hips.

He groaned as her lips closed over him, and she drew him into her mouth. But he pulled her up before she could give him pleasure.

His hands shook as he removed her clothes. He cupped her breasts and teased her nipples with his thumbs and then with his lips. And his hand moved lower, between her thighs.

She squirmed as pleasure shuddered through her. He'd barely had to touch her to make her feel gratification. He lifted her thigh so that she straddled him, and he thrust inside her.

The pressure built again, winding tightly inside her. With his fingers skimming along her jaw, he tilted her head down and kissed her. His tongue moved between her lips, teasing and tasting her.

Her heart pounded heavily with excitement and desire. She had never wanted anyone as much as she wanted her fiancé. And as she climaxed again, she cried out with pleasure and nearly declared her love.

But then he was clutching her hips and thrusting deep as he joined her in release. With slightly shaking arms, he held her close—as if he never intended to let her go.

"I'm too heavy," she sleepily protested. "I don't want to hurt you." Blood was already seeping through the bandage on his side.

"Then stay where you are," he groggily replied. "Stay with me…"

Exhaustion finally claimed him, and he fell asleep. As he breathed evenly and deeply, his chest moved against her breasts. And she wanted him again. Still. Always…

She must have fallen asleep, though, because she didn't awaken until an alarm…or a phone…jingled. Her phone had died. So it must have been Logan's. She dragged herself from his arms and fumbled around in the dark, looking for his jeans that she'd discarded on the floor.

The phone rang again, the screen illuminating the pocket, so she finally found it. Because she recognized the number on the screen, she answered it.

"Stacy?" Amber asked.

"Yes."

"Are you all right?" her friend asked. "I heard about your aunt and uncle."

"Is he okay?" She should have called her brothers and followed up. But she'd been more concerned about her fiancé.

"He made it through surgery," Amber said, "and his prognosis is good. But I'm not actually calling about that. I got the warrant."

Stacy's breath caught with momentary fear. She'd wanted the warrant, but she didn't want to have to go back to the prison. "Okay, I'll see when Logan can drive back out to the penitentiary."

"He's not with the River City P.D.," Amber said. "He can't serve it, so I did it myself. I got the visitor log. I also looked at your father's. And there was one name in common."

Stacy's stomach knotted. But she had to know. "Who was it?"

"I need to report this to a detective with the P.D., too,"

Amber said. "But honestly, I'm not sure who to trust. This is bad, Stacy."

"Who?"

When she heard the name, she gasped. But it shouldn't have been that much of a shock; it should have been obvious to her. Her father had spent fifteen years in prison for this man's crime, but that sentence hadn't been bad enough, he'd ordered her father's death, too.

She clicked off the phone and sat on the side of the bed. The numbness of her father's loss began to wear off, leaving only crippling pain. It hurt. It hurt so much to have lost him. Maybe he wasn't the perfect daddy the little girl in her remembered. But he hadn't deserved to die like he had. He hadn't deserved fifteen years locked up like an animal.

The bed shifted as Logan rolled over and stretched. Then he groaned, probably in pain from his injuries.

"Are you all right?" she asked, and her voice cracked with her grief.

"I'm fine," he said. "But you're not. Who was on the phone?"

She didn't want to tell him because she knew he'd want to go off alone again. But he'd asked her to always be honest with him, to keep no secrets from him. "Amber."

"She got the warrant," he said.

She nodded.

"She gave you a name. You know who it is," he said. "You know who killed my father."

"And mine," she said. "There was only one person who visited both my father—frequently—and his killer."

"Cooper," he uttered the name like a curse. He was already climbing out of bed, already reaching for his clothes. She grabbed his arm, trying to stop him. Or at least slow him down.

"I don't want you to go alone, though."

"You're not going with me," he said. "I promised to keep you safe. I want you to stay here."

She wanted to believe he was so concerned about her safety because he loved her, too. But it was just who he was—a bodyguard.

"Call the police," she urged him. "I don't want you to put your life at risk again." He had already had many lucky escapes; his luck was bound to have run out by now.

HIS LUCK HAD run out. Robert Cooper realized it the moment that Logan Payne drove back into his driveway. The shotgun was loaded and sitting next to his chair. But he didn't reach for it. Yet.

He'd do what he had to do, though. He waited for the knock at the door, but Logan just walked right in, his gun drawn. Maybe he should let the boy have this—justice. It was long overdue.

Logan stared down the slightly unsteady barrel at the man he'd resented for the past fifteen years. He'd resented that his father's partner hadn't protected him that night. Now he knew that he should have hated the man because he hadn't just not protected him—he had killed him.

"Why?" he asked.

"You know why," the retired cop replied. He looked older than his sixty-some years now. His sparse gray hair stood up, disheveled, and gray stubble clung to his sagging jowls.

Disgust overwhelmed Logan and he bitterly surmised, "Money."

"I had a deal with Kozminski," Robert said. "He cut me in for looking the other way."

"And my father?" Had he been a dirty cop like Iwan had implied?

Robert Cooper sighed. "He wouldn't look the other way. When he caught us that night, he was going to arrest us both, so I pulled my drop gun and killed him."

"And Kozminski went along with it?" Logan asked. "I don't understand why he wouldn't have told the truth."

"Because he loved his kids."

He tightened his grip on his gun. "You threatened them?" They'd just been kids then—younger even than he'd been.

"Yes," Robert replied. "And I would have followed through on the threat. I would have killed them. And he knew it. That's why he kept quiet all these years."

"Then why did you hire the other inmate to kill him?"

Robert shifted forward in his chair, but only to point a finger at Logan—not a gun. "That was your fault."

"Mine?"

He nodded. "You kept getting his parole denied. And he wanted out. He was going to talk."

A pang of regret struck Logan's heart. If only he had let Kozminski's parole get granted, Stacy's father might still be alive. Might've been able to walk her down the aisle...

To him?

She would never marry him. She would never forgive him for getting her father killed. She had been right about that.

Logan was the one who'd been wrong. About everything...

"Is that when you started shooting at me?" Logan asked.

The older man shook his head. "I never shot at you."

"You did the day I drove up here," Logan reminded him.

"I thought you were coming to arrest me," he said. "That you'd figured it out already."

"There were other shots fired that day," he said. "You must be working with someone else."

Cooper shook his head. "I haven't worked with anyone since Kozminski."

"There was the prisoner you had kill him…"

The older man shrugged. "Some people have owed me favors."

Logan's stomach churned with self-disgust that it had taken him so long to figure out what should have been so obvious. "So if it hasn't been you shooting at me, it must have been someone who owed you a favor—because I've been shot at a lot over the past few days," he said. "Once at a safe house and then again at the church the day my brother Cooper got married."

"That wasn't me or anyone working for me," Robert insisted. "I made a promise to your father."

"After you shot him?"

The older man nodded. "I respected your father. He was a good man. I promised him that I would never hurt his wife or kids."

"But you promised Kozminski the exact opposite."

"They're Kozminskis," he said, as if that justified his actions. "They're all criminals."

"Stacy isn't. She's my fiancée."

"She wasn't when I set the bomb in her place or when I shot at her at the cemetery. I was sure the old man would have told her the truth, that he wouldn't have wanted to die with his baby girl believing he was a killer."

She was more loyal than that. "She never believed it," Logan said. And he should have trusted her instincts sooner.

"She's a stubborn woman," Robert remarked. "She's going to be a challenge as a wife."

Getting her to be his wife would be the challenge. But

Logan had a bigger challenge at the moment—getting the loaded shotgun out of Robert Cooper's reach before he used it. But before he could move toward it, the old man grabbed it, aimed and fired.

Chapter Nineteen

Stacy's scream echoed the gunshot.

But this time Milek and Garek held her back from rushing toward the house—toward Robert Cooper's cabin. Garek reminded her, "He warned us that Cooper could have rigged his place with a bomb."

That was why they'd picked up Cujo from the kennel and brought him along. Parker had snuck him in the back door while Logan had calmly walked in the front to confront his father's killer.

Had he become the man's most recent victim?

Her heart pounded frantically. And she trembled. She couldn't lose Logan. He wasn't just her fake fiancé. He was the love of her life. When he finally stepped out onto the porch, she wanted to run to him, wanted to throw her arms around him and never let go.

But she couldn't move. Her legs kept shaking. She had to wait until he walked down to her and her brothers. Her breath caught as she noticed that blood spattered his handsome face. "Are you—" she stammered. "Are you all right?"

He ran his hand over his face and smeared the blood. "Yeah, it's all over now. He killed himself."

"Is it all over now?" Parker asked as he brought Cujo around from the back of the house.

"Did that damn dog find another bomb?" Garek asked.

Parker shook his head. "No, but the old cop denied ever trying to kill Logan."

Logan snorted. "And you believe him?"

"He admitted to everything else," Parker said. "Why lie about that?"

"Because he's the person who killed our father and framed another man for it," Logan replied.

"Why didn't our dad tell the truth?" Garek asked.

Logan glanced at Stacy. "Because he was threatened."

"What more could Cooper do to him?" Milek wondered.

"Take away his family," Logan said. "He threatened to kill all of you if your father didn't keep his secret."

The color fled from Garek's face, leaving him pale and shaky. "He really did love us."

She squeezed his arm. "All of us," she said. "He loved all of us."

"Why'd the crazy cop kill him now?" Milek asked.

Logan grimaced. And she worried that he'd re-injured himself. But then he said, "It was my fault. If I hadn't fought his parole…"

He blamed himself…like she had been blaming him for years. But she couldn't do that anymore. Her brothers, however, didn't love Logan like she did.

"You got him killed," Garek accused him. "It's all your fault!"

Parker stepped forward with a snarling Cujo. "Take that back. Logan has risked his life over and over to save Stacy's. He loves her."

If only that were true…

But apparently Logan didn't share that infamous psychic connection with his twin.

"It's okay," Logan said with a reassuring pat on Cujo's head. "I understand…"

"I think you were right," Parker said. "I think these guys are behind the attempts on your life."

Was that true? Had Robert Cooper really not shot at Logan? Had that been one of her brothers?

"It could have been Aunt Marta," she offered.

Parker nodded. "Could have been. The forensics haven't come back on her gun yet."

But Marta really had no reason to avenge her brother-in-law's death. She hadn't cared about him; she'd only cared about keeping her husband and her lifestyle. It could have been her brothers. "Or it could have been that Candace woman," Stacy suggested—a bit desperately. She couldn't lose another member of her family. "She's been desperate to protect you…"

"She was with me the first time I was shot at," Logan remarked. "It wasn't her."

And it probably wasn't. She would have tried to kill Stacy but not the man she loved.

"So what you're saying is that there's someone out there still—someone who wants to kill you?" Stacy asked as she realized that she was bound to lose Logan.

SOMEONE WANTED HIM DEAD.

His future brothers-in-law or someone else?

It wasn't Candace. She stood before him now, her letter of resignation on his desk between them. He had no idea when she'd left it there. This was his first time back in the office—the afternoon after his father's killer had killed himself.

"Is this what you want?" he asked.

"I can't have what I want." Her face flushed as she must have realized how her remark sounded.

"I'm sorry."

She shook her head. "No. I should have known that you only saw me as an employee."

"And a friend," he corrected her.

"You never looked at me the way you look at Stacy, the way you looked at her even before your engagement," she said with a wistful sigh. "You love her."

He did love her. "Is that why you're giving me this?" He pointed at the letter.

She shook her head. "I figured she told you and that neither of you would want me working for you anymore."

"I don't want to lose one of the best damn guards I've ever had." He ripped up the resignation. "Will you stay on?"

She nodded. "I've heard you still need protection yourself. Your father's old partner claims he wasn't the one taking the shots at you." Parker must have filled her in.

"O'Doyle from the ATF doesn't think he set the second bomb, either."

"The one at Parker's?"

He nodded.

"Do you think her brothers are behind it?" she asked.

He hoped not. But he'd called them to his office, too. They passed Candace on her way out. Garek whistled at her, which elicited a glare.

"You must have a death wish," Logan remarked. "She could easily kill you."

"It might be fun to go out that way," he murmured appreciatively.

Milek grabbed his brother's arm and tugged him fully into Logan's office. "We're not here for fun."

"No, we're here for an interrogation," Garek surmised. "Let me spare you the inquisition. It's not us. We're not trying to kill you."

"Someone is," Logan said.

"You proved it wasn't the dirty cop?"

He nodded.

"Then you know what you have to do," Garek said.

"Of course," Logan replied. "I have to find out who-ever's after me."

"You have to let Stacy go," Garek corrected him. "As long as you're still in danger, so is she."

Milek sighed and ruefully agreed. "He's right. Someone could accidentally shoot her while they're trying to hit you."

Logan flinched as he realized that they made sense. He was putting her in danger.

"You promised to keep her safe," Garek reminded him.

"And if you love her as much as I think you do," Milek said, "I think you know what you have to do."

Let her go...

The words were ringing in his head when he rang the bell at the front of her store. The gate was down yet, cover-ing the door and windows. But she opened up the door, then unlocked and lifted the gate with his help. Metal screeched as it rose high enough for him to duck through the open door with her and Cujo, who stayed by her side. Like Logan wished he could.

Her shop was as vibrant and vivacious as she was— filled with sparkling stones and gleaming metals. Neck-laces and earrings and bracelets dangled from displays on the counter. And inside the display cases, smaller pieces glittered and shone, drawing his attention.

"You made all these?" he asked, awed by her talent.

She nodded.

"They're beautiful." One piece in particular piqued his interest. A diamond sparkled between two rubies in a band of braided yellow gold. He would have liked to have slid that ring on her finger someday—when he proposed for real.

But he couldn't give her a ring now. Not when he had to end their engagement.

"That's my favorite," she said, her breath soft on his cheek as she leaned close to him to stare into the display with him.

He wanted to turn his head. He wanted to kiss her. Heck, he wanted to do more than kiss her. He wanted to carry her upstairs to her apartment and make love to her.

But if he touched her again, he wouldn't have the strength to do what needed to be done for her protection. He closed his eyes and held his breath, unable to look at her or breathe in her sweet, flowery scent.

She moved away from him, and the loss of the heat of her closeness chilled him. She shivered, too, as she walked away. "I know why you're here," she said.

"You do?"

Had her brothers warned her?

She nodded. "You're pretty obvious."

Could she see how much he wanted her? How much he needed her?

"I am?"

"You're breaking our engagement," she said.

Then he wasn't obvious at all. But he had to admit, "I think it's for the best."

Her head jerked in a sharp nod. "It's not like it was real anyway."

Pain jabbed his chest—his heart specifically—and he gasped at the intensity of it. It may not have been real to her, but it had felt real to him.

"So it's what you want, too…"

"It was never supposed to be real," she said. "It was just supposed to stop the attempts on your life."

While there hadn't been one since Robert Cooper had killed himself, Logan was certain he was still being followed. Stalked. He couldn't risk her safety until he knew for sure that no one would try to kill him again and, as her brothers had pointed out, maybe inadvertently hit Stacy instead.

But he couldn't say goodbye completely. He couldn't just walk away…with nothing. "That ring in there." He pointed toward the case. "I want to buy that from you."

"It's not for sale," she said.

"Your business must not do that well if you refuse to part with the merchandise," he teased.

She stared wistfully at the ring. "I told you that's my favorite piece."

And that was why he wanted it—to remember her and how much he'd wanted to put that ring on her finger. But having it would probably just prove a painful reminder of what he'd lost. Even if he wasn't still in danger, they wouldn't have a future—if she couldn't forgive him for his part in her father's death. "Never mind then."

Reluctant to leave, he reached down to pet Cujo. The dog flopped onto his side, encouraging Logan to rub his belly, too. He obliged. "You were the best backup I ever had," he said, "you saved my life more than once."

"And mine," Stacy said.

He'd stalled long enough, so Logan headed toward the door. But he hadn't made it very far before she called out, "Wait!"

He tensed, uncertain what he would do if she wanted him to stay. He couldn't put her at risk. But he would never be able to resist her, either.

He heard the jingling of keys as she opened the display case. Then she was beside him, pressing something into his hand. His skin heated from the tantalizing contact with hers. But before he could grab her hand and hold on to her, she pulled free and stepped away from him. He opened his palm and stared down at the diamond-and-ruby ring.

"I thought it wasn't for sale," he said.

"It's not," she said. "I don't want you to pay me for it. I just want you to have it."

He stared down at it and now the longing was all his. He wanted it, but he wanted it on her finger.

She uttered a shaky chuckle. "I don't know what you're going to do with it. Give it to your mom?"

She wasn't the woman he wanted to wear it. He could only imagine it on one woman's hand. He offered it back. "It's your favorite piece. You should keep it."

She shook her head. "I want you to have it—in appreciation."

"Appreciation?"

"Cujo wasn't the only one who saved my life more than once," she said. "You did, too."

"I was the one who put you in danger," he said. "It was my fault." And that was why he couldn't put that ring on her finger. But he would keep it. He closed his fingers around the metal and stones and headed for the door.

She murmured, "It was easier to hate you."

He turned back to ask her, "Easier than what?" and he noticed the tears glistening in her smoky-gray eyes. Cujo moved closer to her, as if offering comfort. And as if realizing that it was Logan's fault that she was upset, he uttered a low growl at him.

She shook her head, refusing to answer him.

"Hate me again, then," he said, hoping that hating him would stop her tears. "Remember that it's my fault you lost your father. It was because of my need for justice." He shook his head. "It wasn't justice. You were right. I wanted revenge."

But now the revenge was on him—because he was the one who'd lost everything. And if he didn't find out soon who was after him, he might even lose his life.

Chapter Twenty

It had been so much easier to hate him than to love him like she did. Through the tears stinging her eyes, she could barely see Amber standing on the other side of the display case. She'd immediately called her after Logan left. Her friend's beautiful face was now twisted into a grimace of sympathy. And Stacy began to cry again.

"Why didn't you tell him how you feel about him?" Amber asked. "It's obvious how much you love him."

Stacy shook her head, refusing to admit to feelings that weren't reciprocated. "Ignore this," she said, gesturing toward her wet face. "I'm just on emotional overload. It's been so crazy that I never had the chance to mourn my father."

"So your tears are for him?"

They should have been. He hadn't been the perfect man she'd thought he had been, but he'd been a better man than many had believed. An innocent man. Relatively…

A pang of guilt struck her already aching heart, and she shook her head. "I'm just an emotional mess."

"Are you…"

She tried to focus on her friend again. "What?"

Amber arched a brow. "Could you be…?"

She froze in shock as she realized that her friend thought she could be pregnant. And it dawned on Stacy that she very well could be. They hadn't used protection any time they'd made love.

"You could be," Amber answered her own question. "What will you do if you are?"

She loved Amber, but she wouldn't do what she had. She wouldn't keep her child from his father. "I promised Logan no more secrets."

"So then you've already told him that you love him," Amber said.

And another pang of guilt struck Stacy. She was still keeping one secret from him.

Amber chuckled. "So you've not been entirely honest with him."

Stacy shrugged. "I am not going to tell him that I love him when I know that he doesn't love me."

"Are you sure about that?"

She nodded. "Definitely."

"Because I saw the way he protected you—"

"That's just his job," Stacy said. "That's who he is—a bodyguard. A lawman."

"I think you should tell him how you feel," Amber persisted.

"I haven't always agreed with your decisions, either," Stacy reminded her. "But I've supported you."

Amber sighed. "I hope you don't regret your decision."

Did Amber regret hers?

Before she could ask, the door to the shop opened. Her pulse quickened as she glanced up, hoping it was Logan, hoping that he'd changed his mind and had come back to propose for real.

But it was her brothers.

Amber's face turned a mottled shade of red and she averted her gaze from Milek. But he spared her only a glance. His focus was on Stacy. So was Garek's, his gray eyes dark with concern and fear.

She shuddered. They had never looked at her like that before, not even when she'd told them that their father had died. Her stomach dropped with dread, and she lifted a hand to her mouth to hold back a sob.

"No, no…" Then she forced herself to drag in a deep breath, forced herself to calm down, because she wanted them to tell her the truth. She had to know. "Is he dead? Is Logan dead?"

Amber gasped and grabbed her arm, silently offering her support. But Garek stepped closer and pulled her into his arms. Stacy slammed her hands into his chest, pushing him back.

"Tell me! Tell me!"

"You didn't see the news?" Milek asked.

It played out on a small screen in the corner of the store, but she had muted the volume. She glanced up at it and saw that the news had broken into regular programming. Crews filmed outside a familiar-looking brick building, smoke rising up from an SUV burning at the curb nearly obliterated the sign on the building. But she discerned that the words on the sign spelled out Payne Protection Agency.

The volume was off but the report streamed on the bottom. "Explosion believed to be car bomb. Two confirmed casualties. One injured en route to the hospital."

Two confirmed casualties…

She screamed and clutched at Garek. But then she pushed him back again. "We have to go to the hospital."

"He would have been in the SUV," Garek said. "He would have been one of the dead. The other was probably his twin or his sister…"

She wanted to deny it, but her brother was probably right.

"We have to be there," she said. "Mrs. Payne was there for us so many times."

Milek spoke up. "She's right. We need to go."

Garek cupped her face in his hands and stared down at her, studying her. "Can you handle this?" he asked.

No. If her brothers were right, she had just lost the man she loved. Her worst fears were confirmed at the hospital. The injured man lying in the hospital bed wasn't Logan; he had to have been one of the casualties.

But instead of needing comfort, his mother was offering comfort to some other women in the waiting room, and Garek and Milek had gone to interrogate doctors and nurses for more information. So Stacy walked up to the bed alone, tears streaming down her face as she focused on Logan's twin.

"Is—is he…?"

Parker's face—so handsome and so like Logan's—was scratched and bruised. And his blue eyes were nearly vacant as he stared up at her as if he had no idea who she was. Or who he was…

But she knew: he wasn't Logan. The man she loved was gone.

IT WAS WORSE. So much worse than Logan could have imagined. How on earth had he not put it all together before this—before lives had been lost? Two of his employees had died because they'd jumped into a Payne Protection Agency company SUV and it had been wired to explode.

One of those casualties could have been Stacy. Her brothers ran up to him in the hall. He braced himself, expecting Garek to throw a punch. "You were right," he said. "You were absolutely right about my putting her in danger. I'm glad I listened to you."

He was so grateful that he'd listened to them.

Garek grabbed him as he'd suspected he would. But instead of slugging or shoving him, he pulled him close and... *embraced* him. "Thank God you're all right," his longtime enemy said. "It would have devastated her if you'd died."

His heart clutched. "She's here?"

Milek nodded and then pointed toward his brother's room. "She's in there."

He turned toward the room, but he could see only a shadow through the door. "Does she think Parker is me?"

"No, she thinks you're dead."

Pain at the thought of leaving her clutched his heart. "What? Why?"

"The news reported two casualties," Milek said.

"Damn it!" Logan pushed past Garek and headed toward his brother's room.

Stacy was sitting on his bed, holding his hand. In sickness and health, but what about love? Maybe she did think Parker was him...

But then she turned, as if she felt his presence, and saw him. And she jumped up from the bed and vaulted at him. "You're alive!" She threw her arms around his neck, clutching him close. Tears from her face streaked down his neck and dampened his shirt.

He pulled her back so he could see her face—her beautiful face. Her eyes glistened with more tears. Happy tears.

"I'm sorry," she said. "I'm sorry for crying all over you. But I'm just so happy you're alive."

"Your brother did the same thing when he saw me in the hall," he said. "Got all emotional over me."

"Milek?" She laughed.

"Garek."

She laughed harder. "No!"

"Seems he's kind of sweet on me," he said, and ignored

the good-natured curse from the hall. "What about you? Are you sweet on me?"

She drew in a deep breath and then murmured, as if to remind herself, "No more secrets."

"You've been keeping one from me?" God, was she pregnant? He'd worried that she might not tell him if she was.

"I'm in love with you," she said, and then she was in his arms again.

But he was the one who'd pulled her close this time. "I thought you hated me again. That you blamed me for causing your father's death," he said. "It was my fault he didn't get parole…"

"Robert Cooper might have had him killed anyway," she said. "You can't blame yourself for that. I don't." She pulled back to look at his face again. "Is that why you broke our engagement?"

"I didn't want to," he confessed. "But I didn't want you in danger." He forced himself to release her and to step back. "I didn't want to lose you forever the way we've lost two employees. Like we nearly lost Parker."

His twin groaned. "I'm coming back. Damn explosion addled my brain."

Logan didn't know what *his* excuse was. While he'd been in his office when the bomb went off, his walls had only shook a little. But maybe it had shaken him up enough to come to his senses and put it all together.

"The bomb was in your SUV," he told his twin. Their employees had unfortunately asked to borrow it for a fast-food run. "And the bomb was in your house…"

Stacy's eyes widened as she realized what he had when he'd rushed outside to find Parker's SUV burning. "Whoever was trying to kill you wasn't trying to kill *you*," she said. "He was trying to kill Parker."

"I'm still in danger, though," he said, "because someone keeps mistaking me for him. And me being in danger puts you in danger, too."

"I have a thought about that," Parker said, and as he sat up, he nearly toppled out of the bed.

Logan's heart clutched with concern for his brother. "You're lucky you can think at all with that concussion." But the doctors had already assured them that it wasn't life threatening.

"It's nothing," he said. And compared to what had happened to two of their employees, it was. "I can handle it. And I can handle whoever's after me. Take your fiancée and elope. Get the hell out of here."

Logan shook his head. "I can't leave you alone—not to face this kind of danger."

"You just said you don't want to lose her," Parker argued. "So don't put her in danger."

"We can help," Garek Kozminski offered as he stepped into the room with Milek. "We want to help."

"What are you saying?" Logan asked. "You want me to hire you?"

Garek outright laughed but then he shrugged. "I don't know. Maybe you should. It took me just a couple of calls to learn what you guys have yet to figure out."

"What?"

"Someone put out a hit on Parker Payne."

Logan stared at him in shock. That explained all the different attempts on their lives—different assassins. It was much worse than he'd thought.

Garek continued, "I'm sorry, man, sorry that I thought it was you putting our sister in danger. I shouldn't have interfered. I can see that you love her."

"Do you?" she asked hopefully.

How did she not know?

Because he was an idiot...

He dropped to his knees and pulled out the ring she'd given him—her favorite piece. "I love you with all my heart, Stacy Kozminski. Will you marry me, really marry me? Will you become my wife—my partner—for the rest of our lives?"

She nodded. "Yes, of course, I'll marry you." She held her hand steady as he slid the ring on to her finger.

"And we'll all work together to make sure those lives are very long," Garek assured them.

Penny Payne clapped her hands together, drawing their attention to where she stood in the doorway. "See, I told you they're good boys."

Logan laughed. "I don't know about that," he said. "But they're family now." Just like the Paynes, the Kozminskis protected the ones they loved. With their help, he believed they could keep Stacy and Parker safe.

"One big dysfunctional family," Garek added.

Her gesture was small, just her palm sliding over her stomach, but Logan caught it. And hope burgeoned inside him like a baby might be burgeoning inside his fiancée.

Their family was probably going to be getting even bigger. But first they had to make certain that they didn't lose one. That no one carried out that hit on his twin.

"Together we can handle anything," Stacy declared, as if she sensed his concern. "My father was right. You are the man for me."

"And you're the woman for me." He hoped his mother still had her connection to rush the marriage license. He didn't want to wait another moment before making Stacy his bride.

He had no doubt their lives would be full of danger and craziness, but, more than that, it would be full of love.

* * * * *

SNOWBLIND JUSTICE

CINDI MYERS

For Gay and Reed.

Chapter One

Snow sifted down over the town like a downy blanket, turning trash piles into pristine drifts, transforming mine ruins into nostalgic works of art, hiding ugliness and danger beneath a dusting of wedding-cake white.

The murderer lurked behind a veil of snow, fresh flakes hiding his tracks, muffling the sound of his approach, covering up the evidence of his crimes. Deep cold and furious blizzards kept others indoors, but the killer reveled in his mastery over the landscape. His pursuers thought he was soft, like them. They couldn't find him because they assumed conditions were too harsh for him to survive in the wilderness.

And all the while he was waiting, striking when the right opportunity presented itself, his intellect as much of a weapon as his muscles. The woman who lay before him now was a prime example. She hadn't hesitated to stop when he had flagged her down on the highway. He was merely a stranded motorist who needed help. He was good-looking and charming—what woman wouldn't want to help him?

By the time she realized his purpose, it was too late. Like the officials who tracked him, she had underestimated him. The lawmen doubted his ability to instill trust in his victims, and were awed by his talent for killing quickly and efficiently while leaving no trace.

He lifted the woman's inert body into the car, arranging it into an artful tableau across the seat. There was very little blood—none in the vehicle— and no fingerprints or other evidence for the sheriff and his deputies to trace. They would search and examine and photograph and question—and they would find nothing.

He shut the door to the car and trudged away as the snow began to fall harder, a sifting of sugar over the bloodstains on the side of the road, and over his footprints, and over the signs of a struggle in the older snow beside the highway. The killer ducked behind a wall of ice, and disappeared out of sight of the empty road. Wind blew the snow sideways, the flakes sticking to the knit mask he had pulled up over his face, but he scarcely felt the cold, too absorbed in the details of his latest killing, reveling in his skill at pulling it off—again.

There were no witnesses to his crime, and none to his getaway. The lawmen thought they were closing in on him because they had linked his name to his crimes. But they didn't realize he was the one drawing nearer and nearer to his goal. Soon he would claim his final victim—the woman who had brought him to Eagle Mountain in the first place. After he had taken her, he would disappear, leaving his pursuers to wonder at his daring. They would hate him more than ever, but some part of them would have to admire his genius.

"I FEEL LIKE I should apologize for seventeen-year-old Emily's poor taste in prom dresses." Emily Walker looked down at the dress she had unearthed from the back of her closet that morning—too short in the front, too long in the back, entirely too many ruffles and a very bright shade of pink.

"It will be fine as soon as we straighten out the hem and maybe take off a few ruffles." Lacy Milligan looked up from her position kneeling on the floor beside the chair Emily stood on, and tucked a lock of her sleek brown hair behind one ear. "You'll look great."

"Everyone is supposed to be looking at you when you walk down the aisle in that gorgeous bridal gown—not at the clashing train wreck of attendants at the front of the room," Emily said. Watching Lacy wouldn't be a hardship—she was gorgeous, and so was her dress. The same couldn't be said for the bridesmaids' makeshift ensembles. "Let's hope the highway reopens and the dresses you chose for your wedding can be delivered."

"Not just the dresses," Lacy said. "The wedding favors and some of the decorations are waiting to be delivered, as well. Not to mention some of the guests." She returned to pinning the dress. "With less than a week to go, I can't risk waiting much longer to figure out how to use what we have here—including this dress." She inserted a pin in the hem of the skirt and sat back on her heels to study the results. "As it is, I may be going through the wedding shy one bridesmaid if the highway doesn't open soon."

"The road is going to open soon," Emily said. "The weather reports look favorable." Since the New Year, the southwest corner of Colorado had been hammered by a wave of snowstorms that had dumped more than six feet of snow in the mountains. The snow, and the avalanches that inevitably followed, had blocked the only road leading in and out of the small town of Eagle Mountain for most of the past month.

"Travis tried to talk me into delaying the wedding." Lacy sighed. "Not just because of the weather, but because of this serial killer business."

A serial murderer who had been dubbed the Ice Cold Killer had murdered six women in the area in the past few weeks. Lacy's fiancé—Emily's brother Sheriff Travis Walker—had been working practically 'round the clock to try to stop the elusive serial killer. Emily thought postponing the wedding until the killer was caught and the weather improved wasn't such a bad idea, but she wasn't a bride who had spent the past six months planning the ceremony and reception. "What did you tell him?" Emily asked.

"I told him I'm willing to postpone my honeymoon. I understand that being a sheriff's wife means putting my needs behind those of the town. And I've been patient—I really have. I haven't seen him in two days and I haven't complained at all. But Sunday is my wedding day. All I ask is that he be here for a few hours. The case will wait that long."

"It's not just Travis," Emily said. "Half the wedding party is law enforcement. There's Gage." Emily and Travis's brother was a sheriff's deputy. "Cody Rankin—he's technically on leave from the US Marshals office, but he's still working on the case. And Nate Harris—he's supposed to be off work from his job with the Department of Wildlife to recover from his ankle injury, but he's as busy as ever, from what I can tell. Oh, and Ryder Stewart—he's had plenty of time to help Travis, since most of his highway patrol territory is closed due to snow."

"Then they can be here for a few hours, too," Lacy said. "That may sound terribly selfish of me, but I put so much of my life on hold for the three years I was in prison. I don't want to wait any longer." Lacy had been wrongfully convicted of murdering her boss. She and Travis had fallen in love after he had worked to clear her name.

"Then you deserve the wedding you want, when you want it," Emily said. "I hope my brother was understanding."

"He was, after I whined and moaned a little bit." Lacy stood and walked around the chair to take in the dress from all sides. "I didn't tell him this, but another reason I want to go ahead with the wedding is that I'm beginning to be afraid the killer won't be caught. Travis and every other lawman in the area has been hunting this guy for weeks. It's like he's a ghost. Travis and Gage and the rest of them work so hard and the murderer just thumbs his nose at them."

"It's crazy." Emily climbed down off the chair and began helping Lacy gather up the sewing supplies. "At first I was terrified. Well, I guess I'm still terrified, but honestly, I'm also angry." She patted Lacy's shoulder. "Anyway, I'm not going to let the killer or the weather get me down. The weather is going to hold, the road will open and you'll have a beautiful wedding, without my fashion faux pas spoiling the day."

"I hope you're right and everyone I invited can be here," Lacy said.

"Who in the wedding party is still missing?" Emily asked.

"Paige Riddell. She recently moved to Denver with her boyfriend, Rob Allerton."

"Of course." Paige had run a bed-and-breakfast in town prior to moving away. "I never knew her well, but she seemed really nice."

"She is nice. And I really want her here for my wedding. But you can't fight nature, I guess, so we're going to make do no matter what." She turned to Emily. "Thank you so much for everything you've done to help," she said. "Not just with the wedding preparations, but all the work you've put into entertaining the wedding guests who are already here. I forget that the weather has forced you to put your own life on hold, too."

Like everyone else who had been in town when the first blizzard struck, Emily had been stuck in Eagle Mountain for most of the past month. "The first few weeks I was on my winter break," she said. She was working on her master's at Colorado State University and was employed by the university as a teaching assistant and researcher. "It's just the last ten days that I've missed. Fortunately, the university has been very understanding, letting me complete some of my coursework and research online, delaying some other work and arranging for another researcher to teach my undergrad class until I get back."

"I'm glad," Lacy said. "Can you imagine having to delay your master's degree because of snow?"

"Snow has its upsides, too," Emily said. "That sleigh ride last week was a blast, and I'm looking forward to the bonfire Wednesday."

"Every party you've thrown has been a big success," Lacy said. "I'm sure most brides don't entertain their guests so lavishly."

"Well, everything has gone well except the scavenger hunt," Emily said. "I wouldn't call that a success."

"It's not your fault Fiona was murdered during the party." Lacy hugged herself and shuddered. "I thought for sure Travis would catch the killer after that—he was so close, right here on the ranch."

Just like that, the conversation turned back to the Ice Cold Killer as the two friends remembered each of his victims—some of them locals they had known, a few tourists or newcomers they had never had a chance to meet. But every person who had fallen victim to the killer had been young and female, like Emily and Lacy. They didn't have to say it, but they were both keenly aware that they might have been one of the killer's victims—or they still might be.

Emily was relieved when the door to the sunroom, where they were working, opened and Bette Fuller, one of Lacy's best friends and the caterer for the wedding, breezed in. Blonde and curvy, Bette always lit up the room, and today she was all smiles. "Rainey just got back from town and she says the highway is open." Bette hugged Lacy. "I know this is what you've been waiting for."

"Is Rainey sure?" Lacy asked.

"Rainey isn't one for spreading rumors or telling lies," Emily said. The ranch cook was even more stone-faced and tight-lipped than Travis. Emily looked down at the dress she was wearing, now bristling with pins and marks made with tailor's chalk. "Maybe I won't have to wear this old thing after all."

"Rainey said there was a line of delivery trucks coming into town," Bette said. "Which is a good thing, since the stores are low on everything."

"I'm going to call Paige and tell her and Rob to drop everything and drive over right now—before another avalanche closes the road," Lacy said. "And I need to check with the florist and look at the tracking for the bridesmaids' dresses and the wedding favors and the guest book I ordered, too."

"I can help you with some of that," Bette said.

"You two go on," Emily said. "I'll finish cleaning up in here." The prom dress—pins and all—could go back in the closet. If she was lucky, she'd never have to put it on again.

As she gathered up the clutter from around the room, she thought of all the work that went into weddings. This was only her second time serving as a bridesmaid, and she was looking forward to the ceremony, though she was a little nervous, too. Mostly, she hoped she wouldn't get too emotional. Weddings were supposed to be hopeful occasions, but they always made her a little melancholy, wondering what her own wedding would have been like—and how different her life might have turned out if she had accepted the one proposal she had had.

Who was she kidding? If she had agreed to marry that man, it would have been a disaster. She had been far too young for marriage, and he certainly hadn't been ready to settle down, no matter what he said. At least she had had sense enough to see that.

She was stowing the last of the sewing supplies and looking forward to changing back into jeans and a sweater when the door to the sunroom opened again and a man entered, obscured from the waist up by a tower of brown boxes. "I met the UPS driver on the way in and he asked me to drop these off," said a deep, velvety voice that sent a hot tremor up Emily's spine and made her wonder if she was hallucinating. "Whoever answered the door told me to bring them back here."

"Thanks." Emily hurried to relieve the man of his burdens, then almost dropped the boxes as she came face-to-face with Brodie Langtry.

The man who had once proposed to her. She felt unsteady on her feet, seeing him here in this house again after so long. And if she was upset, her family was going to be furious.

"Hello, Emily." He grinned, his full lips curving over even, white teeth, eyes sparking with a blatant sex appeal that sent a bolt of remembered heat straight through her. "You're looking well." A single furrow creased his brow. "Though I have to ask—what is that you're wearing?"

She looked down at the prom dress, the hem lopped off and bristling with pins, one ruffle hanging loose where Lacy had started to detach it. She looked back up at Brodie, feeling a little like she had been hit on the head and was still reeling from the blow. "What are you doing here?" she asked.

"As it happens, the Colorado Bureau of Investigation sent me here to help your brother with a case," he said. "I hear you've got a serial murderer problem."

"Does Travis know you're coming?" Her brother hadn't said anything to her. Then again, he was probably trying to spare her feelings.

"He requested assistance from the CBI, though he doesn't know it's me. Is that going to be a problem?"

She bit her lower lip. "I don't know."

"It's been five years, Emily," he said.

Right. But it might have been five minutes for all the pain that was twisting her stomach. She hadn't expected to react like this. She was supposed to be over Brodie. "You never answered my letter," she said.

The crease across his brow deepened. "You sent me a letter?"

"You mean you don't even remember?" The words came out louder than she had intended, and she forced herself to lower her voice. "I tried calling, but your number had been changed. Travis found out you'd been transferred to Pueblo, so I wrote to you there."

He shook his head. "I never received your letter. Why did you write?"

Did he really not know? She pressed her hand to her stomach, hoping she wasn't going to be sick. This was too awful. "It doesn't matter now." She turned away and tried to make her voice light. "Like you said, it was five years ago. I'm sure Travis will appreciate your help with the case." Her brother was nothing if not a professional.

Brodie was silent, though she could feel his eyes boring into her. She began looking through the stack of packages. "I'll ask again," he said after a moment. "What is that you're wearing?"

"It's a prom dress," she managed.

"Isn't it the wrong time of year for prom? And aren't you in graduate school?"

Her eyes widened and she froze in the act of reaching for a package. "How did you know I'm in graduate school?"

"I might have checked up on you a time or two. They don't have proms in graduate school, do they?"

He'd *checked up* on her. Should she be flattered, or

creeped out? "It's the new thing. Haven't you heard?" She continued scanning the labels on the boxes. She picked up the one that surely held her bridesmaid's dress. Maybe instead of stuffing the prom dress back into her closet, she'd burn it at Wednesday night's bonfire. That would be appropriate, wouldn't it?

"What is all this?" Brodie swept his hand to indicate the piles of boxes, bits of tulle, sewing supplies, silk flowers and other flotsam piled around the room. "Are you getting ready for a big party?"

"Travis is getting married on Sunday," Emily said. "I guess you didn't know." Then again, why would he? He and Travis had stopped being friends five years ago.

"No, I didn't know. Good for him. Who's the lucky woman?"

"Her name is Lacy Milligan. I'm sure you don't know her."

"No, but I know of her. Now it's coming back to me." He grinned. "Lacy is the woman Travis arrested for murder—then after new evidence came to light, he worked to clear her name. I remember the story now, though I didn't know a wedding was in the offing."

It hadn't taken long for the media to latch onto the story of a wrongly accused woman falling in love with the law enforcement officer who had sent her to prison in the first place, then worked to clear her name. Most of the state was probably familiar with the story by now, but Emily didn't want to discuss it with Brodie. "Travis is at his office in town," she said, deciding it was past time to send Brodie on his way. "It's on Main. You can't miss it."

Before he could answer, her cell phone buzzed and she grabbed it off a nearby table. "Hello?"

"Hey." Travis's greeting was casual, but his voice carried the tension that never left him these days. "I was trying to get hold of Lacy, but I can't get through on her phone."

"I think she's talking to Paige, letting her know the highway is open."

"She's terrible about checking her messages, so do me a favor and tell her I'm not going to be able to take her to dinner today. I'm sorry, but we've had a break in the case."

Emily's heart leaped. "Have you made an arrest?"

"Not exactly, but we know who the killers are. One of them is dead, but the other is still on the loose."

"A second murderer?" Travis had long suspected the Ice Cold Killer might be more than one man. If he had caught one of the killers, surely that meant he was closing in on the second. Maybe the case would be solved before the wedding after all. "Lacy will be glad to hear it," Emily said.

"Maybe not so glad when you tell her I have to miss dinner. I need to focus on tracking down the second man."

Which meant he probably wouldn't be home to sleep, either. "Travis, you can't keep working around the clock like this."

"We're going to get some help. The Colorado Bureau of Investigation has agreed to loan us one of their investigators. Now that the road is open, he—or she—should be showing up anytime."

She glanced over her shoulder at Brodie, who was looking out the window. The past five years had been kind to him, filling out his shoulders, adding a few fine lines around his eyes. He wore his hair a little longer than when she'd last seen him, and sunlight through the window picked out the gold streaks in the brown. Add in chiseled cheekbones, a dimpled chin and a straight nose and it was no wonder he could be mistaken for a model or a movie star.

As if sensing her staring at him, he turned and met her gaze, then cocked one eyebrow, lips half-curved in a mocking smile.

"Emily? Are you still there?" Travis asked.

"Um, your help from the CBI is here," she said. "It's Brodie Langtry." Not waiting to hear Travis's reaction, she thrust the phone at Brodie. *It's Travis*, she mouthed.

Brodie took the phone. "Travis! It's been a long time. I'm looking forward to working with you on this case... Yes, I volunteered for the job. To tell you the truth, I thought it was past time we mended fences. I know we didn't part under the best of circumstances five years ago and I'd like to clear the air. I've been catching up with Emily."

She cringed at the words. She and Brodie didn't need to "catch up." They had had a fun time together once, and if it had ended badly, she took most of the blame for that. She'd been young and naive and had expected things from him that he had never promised to give. She wouldn't make that mistake again.

While he and Travis continued to talk about the case, she turned away and began opening the boxes, enjoying the way the scissors ripped through the tape, letting the sound drown out their conversation. As an investigator with the Colorado Bureau of Investigation, Brodie would no doubt bring a welcome extra pair of eyes to the hunt for the Ice Cold Killer. She needed to remember that he was here to help Travis and probably didn't have the least interest in her. So there was no need for her to feel awkward around him.

Brodie tapped her on the shoulder and held out her phone. "Travis didn't sound very happy to hear from me. Why is that, do you think?"

"You'll have to ask him." But she would make sure Travis didn't tell Brodie anything he didn't need to know. Best to leave the past in the past.

"I'm going to meet him in town and get caught up on this case," he said. "But I'm hoping to see more of you later."

Before she could think of an answer to this, he leaned forward and kissed her cheek. "It's great to see you again, Emily," he murmured, and she cursed the way her knees wobbled in response.

Then he strode from the room, the door shutting firmly behind him.

Emily groaned and snatched a pillow off the sofa. She hurled it at the door, half wishing Brodie was still standing there and she was aiming at his head. Brodie Langtry was the last person in the world she wanted to see right now. This next week with him was going to be her own version of hell.

Chapter Two

Brodie drove through a world so blindingly white it hurt even with sunglasses shading his eyes. Only the scarred trunks of aspen and the bottle-brush silhouettes of pine trees broke the expanse of glittering porcelain. If not for the walls of plowed snow on either side of the road, it would be difficult in places to distinguish the road from the surrounding fields. After five hours of similar landscape between here and Denver, Emily, in her crazy ruffled pink dress, had stood out like a bird of paradise, a welcome shock to the senses.

Shocking also was how much Travis's little sister had matured. She'd been pretty before—or maybe *cute* was the better word—vivacious and sweet and attractive in a lithe, youthful way. She had filled out since then, her curves more pronounced, her features sharpened into real beauty.

She seemed more serious, but then so was he. Life—and especially a life spent working in law enforcement—did that to people. He'd seen a dark side to people he couldn't forget. It was the kind of thing that left a mark. He couldn't say what had marked Emily, but he saw a new depth and gravity in her expression that hadn't been there before.

He had been such a rascal when they were together five years ago. He had thought Emily was just another fling. He had felt a little guilty about seducing one of his best friend's sisters, but she had been more than willing. And then he had fallen for her—hard. He hadn't been able to imagine a future without her, so he had laid his heart on the line and asked her to spend the rest of her life with him. And she had stomped his heart flat. The memory still hurt. He had offered her everything he had, but that hadn't been enough.

So yeah, that was in the past. He wasn't here to re-hash any of it, though he hoped he was man enough to treat her with the respect and kindness she deserved. He owed that to her because she was Travis's sister, and because she had given him some good memories, even if things hadn't worked out.

And now there was this case—a serial killer in Eagle Mountain, of all places. Remote tourist towns weren't the usual hunting grounds for serial killers. They tended to favor big cities, where it was easy to hide and they had a wide choice of prey, or else they moved around a lot, making it tougher for law enforcement to find them. Yet this guy—this Ice Cold Killer—had targeted women in a limited population, during a time when the weather kept him trapped in a small geographic area.

Then again, maybe the killer had taken advantage of the road reopening today and was even now headed out of town.

Brodie steered his Toyota Tundra around an S-curve in the road and had to hit the brakes to avoid rear-ending a vehicle that was half-buried in the plowed snow-bank on the right-hand side of the county road. Skid marks on the snow-packed surface of the road told the tale of the driver losing control while rounding the curve and sliding into the drift.

Brodie set his emergency brake, turned on his flashers and hurried out of his vehicle. The car in the snow was a white Jeep Wrangler with Colorado plates. Brodie couldn't see a driver from this angle. Maybe whoever this was had already flagged down another driver and was on the way into town. Boots crunching in the snow, Brodie climbed over a churned-up pile of ice and peered down into the driver's seat.

The woman didn't look like a woman anymore, sprawled across the seat, arms pinned beneath her, blood from the wound at her throat staining the front of her white fur coat. Brodie was reminded of going trapping with an uncle when he was a teenager. They'd come upon a trapped weasel in the snow, its winter-white coat splashed with crimson. Brodie hadn't had the stomach for trapping after that, and he hadn't thought of that moment in twenty years.

Taking a deep, steadying breath, he stepped away from the vehicle and marshaled his composure, then called Travis. "I'm on County Road Seven," he said. "On the way from the ranch into town. I pulled over to check on a car in a ditch. The driver is a woman, her throat's cut. I think we've got another victim."

BRODIE KNEW BETTER than to tell Travis that he looked ten years older since the two had last seen each other. Working a long case would do that to a man, and Travis was the kind who took things to heart more than most. Brodie was here to lift some of that burden. Not everyone liked the CBI interfering with local cases, but Travis had a small department and needed all the help he could get. "It's good to see you again," Brodie said, offering his hand.

Travis ignored the hand and focused on the vehicle in the ditch, avoiding Brodie's gaze. A chill settled somewhere in the pit of Brodie's stomach. So this really was going to be tougher than he had imagined. His old friend resented the way things had ended five years ago. They'd have to clear that up sooner or later, but for now, he'd take his cue from the sheriff and focus on the case.

"I called in the plate number," Brodie said as Travis approached the stranded Jeep. "It's registered to a Jonathan Radford."

Travis nodded. "I know the vehicle. It was stolen two days ago. It was driven by the killers."

"Killers? As in more than one?"

"We've learned the Ice Cold Killer isn't one man, but two. One of them, Tim Dawson, died last night, after kidnapping one of my deputies and her sister. The other—most likely Alex Woodruff—is still at large."

"And still killing." Brodie glanced toward the Jeep. "Most of that blood is still bright red. I think she wasn't killed that long ago."

Travis walked around the Jeep, studying it closely. "Before, Alex and Tim—the killers—always left the victims in their own vehicles."

"Except Fiona Winslow, who was killed at the scavenger hunt on your family's ranch." Brodie had familiarized himself with all the information Travis had sent to the CBI.

"They broke their pattern with Fiona because they were sending a message," Travis said. "Taunting me.

I think Alex is doing the same thing with this Jeep. He knows that we know it's the vehicle he was driving until recently."

"Do you think he's driving this woman's car now?" Brodie asked.

Travis shook his head. "That seems too obvious to me, but maybe, if he hasn't found another vehicle. He thinks he's smarter than we are, always one step ahead, but we know who he is now. It won't be as easy to hide. And it will be harder for him to kill alone, too. He's going to make mistakes. I can see it with this woman."

"What do you see?" Reading the case files Travis had emailed was no substitute for eyewitness experience.

"The woman's feet aren't bound. The others were. Maybe that's because he didn't have time, or without Tim's help he couldn't manage it." He moved closer to look into the car once more. "The collar of her fur coat is torn. I think she struggled and tried to fight him off. Maybe she marked him."

"The others didn't have time to put up a fight," Brodie said, recalling the case notes.

Travis opened the door and leaned into the car, being careful not to touch anything. With gloved hands, he felt gingerly around the edge of the seat and along the dash. When he withdrew and straightened, he held a small rectangle of card stock in his hand, the words *ICE COLD* printed across the front. "He's following his pattern of leaving the card," Brodie said.

"He doesn't want there to be any doubt about who's responsible," Travis said. He pulled out an evidence envelope and sealed the card inside. "It's another way to thumb his nose at us."

They turned at the sound of an approaching vehicle, or rather, a caravan of two sheriff's department SUVs and a black Jeep, traveling slowly up the snow-packed road. The vehicles parked on the opposite side of the road and two deputies and an older man bundled in a heavy coat got out.

"Hello, Gage," Brodie greeted one of the deputies, Travis's brother, Gage Walker.

"You're about the last person I expected to see here," Gage said. He seemed puzzled, but not unfriendly, and, unlike his brother, was willing to shake Brodie's hand. "Typical of CBI to show up when we have the case half-solved."

"Dwight Prentice." The second deputy, a tall, rangy blond, offered his hand and Brodie shook it.

"And this is Butch Collins, the county medical examiner." Travis introduced the older man, who nodded and moved on to the car. His face paled when he looked into the vehicle.

"Something wrong?" Travis asked, hurrying to the older man's side.

Collins shook his head. "I know her, that's all." He cleared his throat. "Lynn Wallace. She sings in the choir at my church."

"Do you know what kind of car she drives?" Brodie asked, joining them.

Collins stared at him, then back at the Jeep. "This isn't her car?"

"It was stolen from a local vacation home two days ago," Travis said. "We think the killer might have been driving it."

"I don't know what kind of car Lynn drove," Collins said. "Only that she was a lovely woman with a beautiful soprano voice. She didn't deserve this. But then, none of them did." He straightened his shoulders. "Are you ready for me to look at her?"

"Give us a few seconds to process the outside of the car, then you can have a look." Travis motioned to Gage and Dwight, who moved forward.

Travis indicated Brodie should follow him. "I need you to get to work on identifying Lynn Wallace's vehicle," he said. "I think Alex will ditch it as soon as he can, but he might not have had a chance yet. You can use my office."

"Tell me what you know about Alex," Brodie said.

"Alex Woodruff. A college student at the Colorado State University—or he was until recently. He doesn't have any priors, at least under that name, and that's the only name I've found for him."

"Emily goes to the Colorado State University, doesn't she?" Brodie asked. Knowing he was coming to Eagle Mountain, he'd checked her Facebook page. "Do they know each other?"

The lines around Travis's mouth tightened. "She says he participated in a research study she and her colleagues conducted, but they weren't friends, just acquaintances."

"What brought him to Eagle Mountain?"

"He and Tim supposedly came here to ice climb over their winter break and got stuck here when blizzards closed the highway. They were staying at an aunt's vacation cabin until recently."

"I'll get right on the search for the car," Brodie said. As he walked to his SUV, he considered the connection between Alex Woodruff and Emily Walker. His work investigating crimes had taught him to be skeptical of coincidence, but until he had further proof, he wasn't going to add to Travis's concerns by voicing the worry that now filled his mind. What if the thing that had brought Alex and Tim to Eagle Mountain wasn't ice climbing—but Emily?

Chapter Three

"Thank you, Professor. That would be so helpful. I'll review everything and be ready to discuss it when I see you next week after the wedding." Emily hung up the phone and mentally checked off one more item on her Tuesday to-do list. All her professors had agreed to excuse her for another week so that she could help with the preparations for Travis and Lacy's wedding. Though she could have made the six-hour drive back to Fort Collins to attend a few classes and try to catch up on all she had missed while stranded by the snow, the last thing she wanted was for the road to close again, forcing her to miss the wedding.

Instead, someone in her department had volunteered to make the drive out here to deliver files for Emily to review. She had protested that it was ridiculous to make such a long drive, but apparently more than one person had been eager for the excuse to get off campus for a while. The risk of getting stranded in Eagle Mountain if another storm system rolled in had only heightened the appeal.

She moved on to the next item on her list. She needed to check on her horse, Witchy. The mare had developed inflammation in one leg shortly after the

first of the year and veterinarian Darcy Marsh had pre-
scribed a course of treatment that appeared to be working, but Emily was supposed to exercise her lightly
each day and check that there was no new swelling.
Slipping on her barn coat—the same one she had worn
as a teenager—she headed out the door and down the
drive to the horse barn. Sunlight shimmered on the
snow that covered everything like a starched white
sheet. Every breath stung her nose, reminding her that
temperatures hovered in the twenties. She still mar-
veled that it could be so cold when the sun shone so
brightly overhead, giving the air a clean, lemony light.

The barn's interior presented a sharp contrast to the
outside world, its atmosphere warm from the breath of
animals and smelling of a not-unpleasant mixture of
molasses, hay and manure. A plaintive *meow!* greeted
Emily, and a gray-striped cat trotted toward her, the
cat's belly swollen with kittens soon to be born. "Aww,
Tawny." Emily bent and gently stroked the cat, who
started up a rumbling purr and leaned against Emily's
legs. "It won't be long now, will it?" Emily crooned,
feeling the kittens shift beneath her hand. She'd have
to make sure Tawny had a warm, comfortable place
to give birth.

She straightened and several of the family's horses
poked their heads over the tops of their stalls. Witchy,
in an end stall on the left-hand side, whinnied softly
and stamped against the concrete floor of her stall.

Emily slipped into the stall and greeted Witchy, patting her neck, then bent to examine the bandaged front
pastern. It no longer felt hot or swollen, though Darcy
had recommended wrapping it for a few weeks longer to provide extra support. Emily breathed a sigh

of relief. For a brief period during her childhood, she had considered studying to be a veterinarian, but had quickly ruled out any job that required dealing with animals' suffering.

"Are you contemplating climbing down out of your ivory tower and hiring on as the newest ranch hand?"

Emily froze as Brodie's oh-so-familiar teasing tone and velvety voice flowed around her like salted caramel—both sweet and biting. She was aware of her position, bent over with her backside facing the stall door, where she sensed him standing. She turned her head, and sure enough, Brodie had leaned over the top half of the stall door, grinning, the cat cradled in his arms.

With as much dignity as she could muster, she released her hold on the horse's leg and straightened. "Brodie, what are you doing here?" she asked.

He stroked the cat under the chin. Tawny closed her eyes and purred even louder. Emily had an uncomfortable memory of Brodie stroking *her*—eliciting a response not unlike that of the cat. "I was looking for you," he said. "Someone told me you're in charge of a bonfire and barbecue here Wednesday."

"Yes." She took a lead rope from a peg just outside the stall door and clipped it onto Witchy's halter. The mare regarded her with big gold-brown eyes like warm honey. "What about it?"

"I was hoping to wrangle an invite, since I'm staying on the ranch. It would be awkward if I felt the need to lock myself in my cabin for the evening."

She slid back the latch on the door and pushed it open, forcing Brodie to stand aside, then led the mare out. "I have to exercise Witchy," she said.

He gave the cat a last pat, then set her gently aside

and fell into step beside Emily, matching his long strides to her own shorter ones. "I didn't realize you were staying at the ranch," she said. He hadn't been at dinner last night, but then, neither had Travis. The two men had been working on the case. Frankly, she was shocked her parents had invited Brodie to stay. They certainly had no love lost for him, after what had happened between him and Emily.

"When the CBI agreed to send an investigator to help with the Ice Cold Killer case, Travis asked your parents if they could provide a place for the officer to stay. They were kind enough to offer up one of their guest cabins."

"Wouldn't it be more convenient for you in town?" she asked.

"There aren't any rooms in town," Brodie said. "They're all full of people stranded here by the road closure. I imagine that will change now that the avalanches have been cleared and it's safe to travel again, but in the meantime, your folks were gracious enough to let me stay." He fell silent, but she could feel his eyes on her, heating her neck and sending prickles of awareness along her arms. "Does it bother you, having me here?" he asked.

"Of course not."

She led Witchy out of the barn, along a fenced passage to a covered arena. Brodie moved forward to open the gate for her. "Are you going to ride her?" he asked.

Emily shook her head. "She's still recovering from an injury. But I need to walk her around the arena for a few laps."

"I'll walk with you." He didn't bother asking permission—men like Brodie didn't ask. He wasn't cruel or demanding or even particularly arrogant. He just accepted what people—women—had always given him—attention, time, sex. All he had to do was smile and flash those sea-blue eyes and most women would give him anything he wanted.

She had been like that, too, so she understood the magnetism of the man. But she wasn't that adoring girl anymore, and she knew to be wary. "Of course you can come to the bonfire," she said. "It's really no big deal."

She began leading the mare around the arena, watching the horse for any sign of pain or weakness, but very aware of the man beside her. "Tell me about Alex Woodruff," he said.

The question startled her, so much that she stumbled. She caught herself and continued on as if nothing had happened. "Why are you asking me about Alex?"

"I've been reviewing all the case notes. He was here, at the scavenger hunt the day Fiona Winslow was killed."

"Yes. He and his friend Tim were here. I invited them."

"Why did you do that?"

"I knew the road closure had stranded them here and I felt sorry for them, stuck in a small town where they didn't know many people. I figured the party would be something fun for them to do, and a way to meet some local people near their age." She cut her gaze over to him. "Why are you asking me about Alex?"

He did that annoying thing Travis sometimes did, answering a question with a question. "You knew Alex and Tim from the university?"

"I didn't really know them." She stopped and bent to run her hand down Witchy's leg, feeling for any warmth or swelling or sign of inflammation. "They both signed up as volunteers for research we were doing. Lots of students do. Most of the studies only pay five to ten dollars, but the work isn't hard and cash is cash to a broke student."

"What kind of research?" Brodie asked.

She straightened and looked him in the eye. She loved her work and could talk about it with almost anyone. If she talked long enough, maybe he'd get bored and leave. "I'm studying behavioral economics. It's sort of a melding of traditional psychology and economics. We look at how people make the buying decisions they make and why. Almost every choice has a price attached to it, and it can be interesting what motivates people to act one way versus another."

"How did Alex and Tim hear about your experiments?"

"We have flyers all over campus, and on social media." She shrugged. "They were both psychology majors, so I think the research appealed to them. I ran into Alex in a coffee shop on campus two days later and he had a lot of intelligent questions about what we were doing."

"Maybe he had studied so he'd have questions prepared so he could keep you talking," Brodie said. "Maybe he was flirting with you."

"Oh, please." She didn't hide her scorn for this idea. "He was not flirting. If anything, he was showing off."

One eyebrow rose a scant quarter inch—enough to make him look even cockier than usual. "Showing off is some men's idea of flirting."

"You would know about that, wouldn't you?"

His wicked grin sent a current of heat through her. "When you're good, it's not showing off," he said.

She wished she was the kind of woman who had a snappy comeback for a line like that, but it was taking all her concentration to avoid letting him see he was getting to her. So instead of continuing to flirt, she started forward with the horse once more and changed the subject. "Are you going to be able to help Travis catch the Ice Cold Killer?" she asked.

Brodie's expression sobered. Yes, nothing like a serial murderer to dampen the libido. "I'm going to do my best," he said. "We know who we're looking for now—we just have to find him."

She managed not to stumble this time, but she did turn to look at him. "You know who the killer is?"

He frowned. "Travis didn't tell you?"

"I haven't seen Travis in several days. He's either working or spending time with Lacy. He told me on the phone that one of the men he thought was involved is dead, but that there was another one he was after."

Brodie said nothing.

She stopped and faced him. "Tell me who it is," she said. "You know I won't go talking to the press."

"The man who died was Tim Dawson," Brodie said.

All the breath went out of her as this news registered. "Then the other man is Alex Woodruff." She grabbed his arm. "That's why you were asking me about him. But he and Tim left town when the road opened briefly a couple of weeks ago. Travis said so."

"They moved out of the cabin where they were staying, but now Travis believes they stayed in the area. If you have any idea where Alex might be hiding, or what he's likely to do next, you need to tell me." She

released her hold on him and stepped back, the mare's
warm bulk reassuring. If her suddenly weak legs gave
out, she'd have the animal to grab on to. "I hardly know
him," she said. "But a serial killer? Why would a smart,
good-looking guy from a well-off family want to murder a bunch of women he doesn't even know?" And
how could she have spent time with Alex and Tim and
not seen that kind of evil in them?

"You're more likely to have an answer for that than
I do," Brodie said. "You're conducting a lot of research
on human behavior and motivation. Didn't you do one
study on what motivates people to break rules or to
cheat?"

"What did you do—run a background check on me?
That's creepy."

"All I did was look at your public Facebook page,"
he said. "And there's nothing creepy about it. I knew
I was coming here and I wanted to see how you were
doing—as a friend. I guess you never did the same
for me."

She couldn't keep color from flooding her cheeks.
She had, in fact, perused Brodie's Facebook page more
than once, as well as Googling his name for tidbits of
information. Not because she still felt anything for him,
simply because she was curious. "All right," she said.
"As long as you're not being a creep."

"Such technical language from a psychologist."

"Behavioral economics is different," she said.
"There's psychology involved, of course, but nothing
that would give me insight into the mind of a serial
killer."

"I think you're wrong," he said. "I think you probably can tell us things we don't know about Alex Woodruff. You've always been smart about people."

I wasn't smart about you. She bit her lip to hold back the words. "I'm sure the CBI has profilers who specialize in this kind of thing," she said.

"Yes, but they don't know Alex, and they don't know Eagle Mountain. You do."

She searched his face, trying to read his expression. He was focused on her in that intense way he had—a way that made her feel like she was the only person in the world he wanted to be with right this second. "What do you want from me?" she asked.

"I want you to think about Alex, and about this area, and see if you can come up with any ideas that might help us."

She shook her head. "I think you're grasping at straws. You need to consult a professional."

"We will. You're just another avenue for us to explore. You never know in a case like this what might be the key to a solution."

"Does Travis know you're asking me to help?"

"No, but I can't see why he'd object. I'm not asking you to do anything dangerous."

She nodded. "All right. I don't think it will do any good, but I'll think about it and see what I can come up with."

He clapped her on the shoulder. "Thanks. I knew I could count on you."

How had he known he could count on her? But she couldn't ask the question. He was already striding out of the arena, his boots making neat prints in the raked dirt.

Brodie had to know she would do anything to help

her brother. If Travis had asked her for help with the case, she wouldn't have hesitated. That she was less willing to cooperate with Brodie probably said more about her feelings for him than she cared to admit.

Never mind. She would try to come up with some ideas about Alex and—with her help or not—Travis and Brodie would catch him and put him in jail for a long time.

Then she could go back to her normal life, with no serial killers—and no former lovers—to unsettle her.

"YOUR SISTER HAS agreed to serve as a consultant on the case."

Travis was so even-keeled and unemotional that Brodie considered it a personal challenge to attempt to get a reaction from him. He'd scored a hit with this announcement.

Travis looked up from the file he'd been studying, eyes sparking with annoyance. "What could Emily possibly contribute to the case?" he asked.

Brodie moved out of the doorway where he'd been standing and dropped into one of the two chairs in front of Travis's desk. The small office was spartan in appearance, with only a laptop and an inch-high stack of papers on Travis's desk, and a few family photographs and citations on the walls. Brodie's own desk at CBI headquarters in Denver was crammed with so many books, files and photographs his coworkers had hinted that it might be a fire hazard. But hey, the clutter worked for him. "Emily knows Alex Woodruff and she's studied psychology," he said. "She can give us insights into his character and what he's likely to do next."

"She's an economics major—not a profiler."

"We'll still consult the CBI profiler," Brodie said. "But I think Emily will come to this with fresh eyes. Besides, she knows this county almost as well as you do. She might be able to give us some new ideas about places to look for him."

Travis shook his head. "He's probably left the county by now. The highway is open, and he has to know we're on his trail. A smart man would be half-way to Mexico by now."

"You and I both know criminals rarely behave the way most people would. Alex may be smart, but he's arrogant, too. He's been taunting you, leaving those business cards, killing a woman on your family ranch, going after one of your deputies. He still thinks he can beat you."

"Maybe." Travis fixed Brodie with a stare that had probably caused more than one felon to shake in his shoes. "This isn't some scheme you've come up with in order for you to spend more time with Emily, is it?" he asked. "Because I'm not going to stand by and let that happen again."

"Let what happen?" Brodie had a strong sense of déjà vu. He recalled another conversation with Travis that had begun like this, five years ago, when his friend—only a deputy then—had accused him of trying to seduce Emily.

"Emily really hurt when the two of you broke things off," Travis said. "It took a long time for her to get over you. I don't want her to have to go through that again."

Brodie bristled. "She's the one who ended it, not me."

"You must have had something to do with it."

Brodie ground his teeth together. He did not want to argue about this with Travis. "I didn't come here to get back together with your sister," he said. "I came to help with this case. I asked Emily to consult because I think she's another resource we can draw on."

Travis uncrossed his arms, and the tension around his mouth eased. "Fair enough. I won't rule out anything that might help us catch Alex Woodruff. Speaking of that, have you had any luck tracking down Lynn Wallace's car?"

"Not yet. She drove a white Volvo." Brodie opened his phone and read the license plate number from his notes. "Nothing flashy. Fairly common. Easy to hide."

"Right. I'll put my deputies on the lookout." He turned to a map pinned to the wall of his office. Pins showed the locations where each of the Ice Cold Killer's seven victims had been found. "Alex and Tim working together concentrated the murders in three areas," he said. "Christy O'Brien and Anita Allbritton were killed within Eagle Mountain town limits. Kelly Farrow and Michaela Underwood were both murdered in the area around Dixon Pass and the national forest service land near there. Fiona Winslow, Lauren Grenado and Lynn Wallace were all killed within a couple of miles of the Walking W ranch." Travis indicated a third grouping of pins on the map.

"Does that tell us anything about where Alex might be hiding now?" Brodie asked.

Travis pointed to a red pin on County Road Five. "We know Tim and Alex were staying at Tim's aunt's cabin, here, when the first three murders took place. They spent some time in a vacation home here." He indicated another pin. "And they may have been at this summer cabin in the national forest, here, for the other murders. Now—who knows?"

A tapping on the door frame interrupted them. Both men turned to see office manager Adelaide Kinkaid, a sixtysomething woman who wore what looked like red monkeys dangling from her earlobes, and a flowing red-and-purple tunic over black slacks. "We just got word that a fresh slide on Dixon Pass sent one vehicle over the edge and buried two others," she said. "Fortunately, they were able to dig everyone out pretty quickly, but the road is closed until they can clear up the mess."

Brodie groaned. "How many delivery trucks do you suppose got caught on the wrong side of this one?" he asked.

"Probably about as many as were able to leave town when the road opened," Adelaide said. "Everyone is just trading places."

"I'll take your word for it," Brodie said. "You do seem to know everything." He leaned toward her. "Are those monkey earrings?"

"Yes." She tapped one earring with a red-painted fingernail. "Do you like them?"

"Only you could pull off a look like that, Adelaide," Brodie said, grinning.

She swatted his shoulder. "You're the kind of man I always warned my daughters about."

"What kind is that?"

"Too smart and good-looking for your own good. The kind of man who's oblivious to the broken hearts he leaves behind."

"Adelaide, Brodie is here as a fellow law enforcement officer," Travis said. "He deserves our respect."

"I'm sure he's a sterling officer," Adelaide said. "And a fine man all around. Just not marriage material—which is probably okay with him." She grinned, then turned to Travis. "And speaking of marriages, don't you have a tux fitting to see to?"

Color rose in the sheriff's cheeks. "I don't need you to keep track of my schedule, Addie," he said. "Right now I have a case to work on."

"You always have a case to work on," Adelaide said. "You only have one wedding." She whirled and stalked away.

Brodie settled back in his chair once more. "Do you have a tux fitting?" he asked.

"I canceled it."

"Unless you're going to get married in your uniform, are you sure that's a good idea?"

Travis scowled at Brodie. "They have my measurements. They don't need me." His phone rang and he answered it. "Hello?"

He listened for a moment, then said, "I've got Brodie in the office. I'm going to put you on speaker." He punched the keypad. "All right. Say that again."

"I've got what looks like another victim of the Ice Cold Killer," Deputy Dwight Prentice said. "Taped up, throat cut, left in her car near the top of Dixon Pass. Only, she's still alive. The ambulance is on its way."

Travis was already standing. "So are we," he said.

Chapter Four

The woman—a once-pretty brunette, her skin bleached of color and her hair matted with blood—stared up at them, glassy-eyed, her lips moving, but no sound coming out. "You're safe now," Brodie said, leaning over her. "We're going to take care of you." He stepped back as the EMTs moved in to transfer the woman to a waiting gurney.

"We've already called for a helicopter," the older of the two paramedics said. "I think this is more than the clinic in Eagle Mountain can handle. They've agreed to meet us at the ball fields, where it's open enough for them to land."

Brodie's gaze shifted to the woman again. She had closed her eyes and her breath came in ragged gasps. He wanted to grab her hand and encourage her to hang on, but he needed to move out of the way and let the paramedics do their job.

Travis, who had been talking to Dwight and highway patrolman Ryder Stewart, motioned for Brodie to join them. "Her name is Denise Switcher," Ryder said. "We found her driver's license in the purse on the passenger floorboard, and the registration on the car matches. Her address is in Fort Collins."

"Did she say anything about what happened?" Brodie asked.

"I don't think she can talk," Dwight said. "One of the EMTs said the vocal chords may be damaged."

Brodie winced. "How is it she's still alive?"

"I don't know," Travis said. "But I hope she stays that way." He nodded to Dwight. "You must have come along right after it happened. Did you see anything or anyone who might have been Alex?"

"No." Dwight hooked his thumbs over his utility belt and stared toward the EMTs bent over the woman. "A trucker who was pulled over taking off his tire chains flagged me down and said he spotted a car on the side of the road near the top of the pass. He didn't see anyone in it, but thought maybe I'd want to check." Dwight pulled a notebook from inside his leather coat. "Gary Ellicott. He was delivering groceries to Eagle Mountain and somehow missed that the road had been closed again. When he got to the barricades, he had to back down a ways before he could turn around. He thinks about fifteen minutes had passed between the time he spotted the car and when he talked to me."

"I don't think she was lying there very long," Brodie said. "A wound like that bleeds fast." If much more time had passed, she would have bled to death.

"The road closed seventy-five minutes ago," Ryder said. "There was a lot of traffic up here and it took maybe half an hour to clear out. If the killer was cutting her throat then, someone would have seen."

"So this most likely happened between thirty and forty-five minutes ago," Brodie said.

"But he would have had to have stopped the car before the road closed," Travis said. "The car is on the southbound side of the road, headed toward town. That seems to indicate she was arriving, not leaving."

"We'll need to find out if she was staying in town," Brodie said. "Maybe she has family in Eagle Mountain, was leaving and, like the truck driver, had to turn around because of the barricade."

"If this is Alex's work and not a copycat, that means he didn't leave town," Travis said.

The paramedics shut the door of the ambulance and hurried to the cab. Siren wailing, they pulled away, headed back toward town. "Let's take a look," Travis said, and led the way to the car, a gray Nissan sedan with Colorado plates. It was parked up against a six-foot berm of plowed snow, so close it was impossible to open the passenger side door. The snow around the vehicle had been churned by the footsteps of the paramedics and cops, to the point that no one shoe impression was discernable. "I took photographs of the scene before I approached," Dwight said. "But I can tell you there weren't any footprints. If I had to guess, I'd say the killer used a rake or shovel to literally cover his tracks."

Brodie continued to study the roadside. "I don't see any other tire impressions," he said.

"He could have parked on the pavement," Ryder said.

"Or he could have been on foot," Travis said.

"It's four miles from town up a half-dozen switchbacks," Ryder said. "That's a long way to walk. Someone would have noticed."

"Not if he stayed behind the snow." Travis kicked steps into the snowbank and scrambled to the top and looked down. "There's a kind of path stomped out over here."

Brodie climbed up beside him and stared down at the narrow trail. "It might be an animal trail."

"It might be. Or it could be how Alex made his way up to this point without being seen. Then he stepped out in the road and flagged down Denise and pretended to be a stranded motorist."

"How did he know the driver was a woman by herself?" Brodie asked.

"He could have studied approaching traffic with binoculars."

The two men descended once more to the others beside the car. "Why would any woman stop for him, knowing there's a killer on the loose?" Dwight asked.

"She was from Fort Collins," Travis said. "I don't know how much press these murders have been getting over there. It wouldn't be front-page news or the top story on a newscast."

"He's right," Brodie said. "I've seen a few articles in the Denver papers, but not much. It would be easy to miss."

"Alex is a good-looking young man," Travis said. "Clean-cut, well dressed. If he presented himself as a stranded motorist, stuck in the cold far from town, most people would be sympathetic."

"Maybe he dressed as a woman, the way Tim did when they were working together," Dwight said. "People would be even more likely to stop for a woman."

"Alex and Tim were both amateur actors, right?" Brodie asked, trying to recall information from the reports he had read.

"Yeah," Ryder said. "And we know that, at least a

few times, Tim dressed as a woman who was trying to escape an abusive boyfriend or husband. He flagged down another woman and asked for help, then Alex moved in to attack. One woman was able to escape and described the scenario for us."

Travis pulled on a pair of gloves, then opened the driver's-side door. He leaned in and came out with a woman's purse—black leather with a gold clasp. He pulled out the wallet and scanned the ID, then flipped through the credit cards until he came to a slim white card with an embossed photograph of a smiling brunette—Denise Switcher. "Looks like she worked at Colorado State University," he said.

The hair rose on the back of Brodie's neck. "Emily's school," he said. He didn't like another connection to Emily in this case.

"Alex's school." Travis slid the card back into the wallet. "I wonder if he chose her because he recognized her."

"That might have made her more likely to stop to help him out," Dwight said.

Travis returned the wallet to the purse and rifled through the rest of the contents. Expression grim, he pulled out a white business card, the words *ICE COLD* in black ink printed on one side.

The card taunted them—a reminder that, yes, they knew who attacked Denise Switcher, but they weren't any closer to catching him than they had ever been.

They were still silently contemplating the card when Travis's phone rang. He listened for a moment, then ended the call. "That was one of the paramedics," he said. "Denise Switcher coded before Flight for Life arrived. She's dead."

Brodie silently cursed the waste of a young woman's life, as well as their best chance to learn more about Alex's methods and motives. He turned to walk back toward the sheriff's department vehicle, but drew up short as a red Jeep skidded to a stop inches in front of him. The driver's door flew open and Emily stumbled out. "Is it true? Did the killer really get Denise?" she demanded, looking wildly around.

Brodie hurried to her. She wore only leggings and a thin sweater and tennis shoes, and was already shivering in the biting cold. He shrugged out of his jacket. "What are you doing here?" he asked.

She waved off his attempts to put his jacket around her. "You have to tell me. That ambulance I passed—was it Denise? Does that mean she's still alive?"

Travis joined them. "Emily, you shouldn't be here," he said.

"I was in the Cake Walk Café, waiting. Then Tammy Patterson came in and said she heard from a source at the sheriff's department that the Ice Cold Killer had attacked another woman. I had the most awful feeling it was Denise." She bit her bottom lip, her eyes fixed on Travis, her expression pleading.

He put a hand on her shoulder. "It was Denise Switcher," he said. "But how did you know?"

"Tammy said the woman was from Fort Collins. I was hoping that was just a coincidence, but…" She buried her face against Travis's shoulder.

"Emily?" Brodie approached, his voice gentle. "What was Denise doing in Eagle Mountain?"

She raised her head and wiped away tears. "I'm sorry. I thought I said. She was coming to see me."

BRODIE WORE WHAT Emily thought of as his cop face—grim determination and what felt like censure, as if he suspected her of withholding important information. She refused to give in to the temptation to cower against Travis, so she straightened and wiped the tears from her eyes.

Brodie, still scowling, thrust his jacket at her once more. "Put this on. You're freezing."

She would have liked nothing better than to refuse the offer, but the truth was, she was so cold she couldn't stop shaking. She'd been so upset she had left her own coat behind at the café. She mutely accepted his jacket and slipped into it, his warmth enveloping her, along with the scent of him, clean and masculine.

"Why was Denise coming to see you?" Travis asked.

"The lead on the research project I'm involved in had some files he wanted me to review," she said. "Denise volunteered to deliver them to me."

"She drove six hours to deliver files?" Brodie asked. "Why didn't they transmit them electronically? Or ask you to make the trip?"

"These are paper surveys students filled out," she said. "And the professor had already agreed I should stay here in Eagle Mountain until after the wedding." She hugged the coat more tightly around her. "Honestly, I don't think he would have bothered, except Denise wanted to come. She said it was a great excuse to get out of the office and spend at least one night in the mountains."

"The two of you were friends?" Travis asked.

She nodded, and bit the inside of her cheek to stave off the fresh wave of tears that threatened with that

one change of verb tense—*were*. "She's the adminis-
trative assistant in the economics department and she
and I really hit it off. I'd told her so much about Eagle
Mountain and the ranch that she was anxious to see
it." She swallowed hard. If Denise had stayed in Fort
Collins, she'd be alive now.

"When did you talk to her last?" Travis asked.

"She called me when she stopped for gas in Gun-
nison, and we agreed to meet at the Cake Walk for
lunch."

"What time was that?" Brodie asked.

"About ten thirty."

"Did Alex Woodruff know her?" Brodie asked.

Had Denise known her killer? Emily shuddered at
the thought, then forced herself to focus on the question. "Maybe," she said. "Students can register online
to participate in various research studies, but they can
also come into the office and fill out the paperwork
there. If Alex did that, he would have met Denise. And
a couple of times she's helped check people in for studies."

"So there's a good chance he did know her," Brodie said.

"Yes." She glanced toward the gray Nissan. "What
happened to her? I mean, I know she was killed, but
why up here?"

"It's possible Alex posed as a stranded motorist
in need of a ride," Travis said. "If your friend recognized him from school, do you think she would have
stopped?"

Emily nodded. "Yes. Denise was always pitching in
to help with fund-raisers or any extra work that needed

to be done. She would have stopped to help someone, especially someone she knew." Again, she struggled for composure. "I'm sure she has family in Denver. Someone will have to tell them."

"I'll take care of that," Travis said.

She wanted to hug her brother. He had had to break the awful news to too many parents and spouses and siblings since the killings had begun. "Why is Alex doing this?" she asked.

"We're hoping you can give us some insight into that," Brodie said. "You might talk to some of the professors who knew him. We could call them, but they might be more inclined to open up to you. You're one of them."

"What is that supposed to mean?" she asked.

"You're an academic," he said. "You speak their language. I'm just a dumb cop."

Under other circumstances, she might have laughed. Brodie was anything but dumb. But there was nothing funny about what had happened here today. "I'll see what I can find out," she said. "But I'm not promising I can help you."

"We'd appreciate it if you'd try." Travis patted her shoulder. "I'm sorry about your friend, but I think you'd better go home now. There's nothing you can do here."

She nodded, and slipped off the jacket and held it out to Brodie. "You keep it," he said. "I can get it tonight."

"Don't be silly," she said. "I'm getting back in my warm car, so I don't need it." And she didn't want to give him an excuse for looking her up again later.

He took the jacket, then turned toward her Jeep, frowning. "You drove up here by yourself?" he said.

"Yes."

"You shouldn't be out driving by yourself," he said. "Alex Woodruff targets women who are in their cars alone."

"I'm not going to stop if he tries to flag me down," she said. "I'm not stupid."

"He knows that," Brodie said. "He would use some subterfuge. He's done it before."

"Brodie's right," Travis said. "From now on, when you have to come to town, take someone else with you. And don't pull over for anyone—no matter what."

She stared at them, fear tightening her throat and making it hard to breathe. Of course she knew there was a killer preying on women. But it was hard to believe she was really in danger. That was probably what those other women had thought, too. She nodded. "All right," she said. "I won't go out alone, and I'll be careful."

Brodie followed her to the Jeep and waited while she climbed in. "I know you think Travis and I are overreacting," he said. "But until this man is caught, you're not going to be truly safe."

"I know." She didn't like knowing it, but there was no use denying facts. For whatever reason, Alex Woodruff was targeting women who were alone—women in her age group. "I do take this very seriously," she said. Having a brother who was sheriff and another brother who was a deputy didn't make her immune from the danger.

Chapter Five

Emily couldn't shake a sense of guilt over Denise's death. She could have refused her friend's offer to bring the student surveys to her. She could have at least warned Denise to be careful, and made sure she knew about the serial killer who had been targeting women in the area. But she couldn't change the past, and guilt wouldn't bring Denise back to her. All Emily could do was to try to help Travis and his officers find Alex and stop him before he killed again.

With this in mind, she called the professor who had taught several of the undergrad psychology courses she had taken at the university. "It's always wonderful to hear from a former student," Professor Brandt said, after Emily had introduced herself. "Even if you did forsake psychology for economics."

"I still have one foot in the psychology camp," she said. "And I use things you taught me almost every day."

Professor Brandt laughed. "You must want a big favor indeed if you're ladling out flattery like that," he said. "What can I do for you?"

"I'm calling about an undergrad, a psychology major who participated in some research I'm conducting," she said. "I need to get in touch with him, but I'm not having any luck. I'm wondering if you know how to reach him. His name is Alex Woodruff."

"Yes, I have had Alex in several classes," the professor said. "He was enrolled in my experimental psychology course this semester, but my understanding is that he never reported for classes."

"Do you know why?" she asked. "Has he been in touch with you?"

"No. There are always a number of students who drop out each semester for various reasons."

"Do you have any idea where he might be? Did he mention moving or anything like that?"

"No. But then, I doubt he would have confided in me. He wasn't the type to seek out faculty for conversation."

"What type was he?" Emily asked. "What were your impressions of him?"

"He was intelligent, good-looking. A bit arrogant. The type of student who doesn't have to work very hard or put forth much effort to get good grades. If I had to describe him in one word, I'd say he was superficial."

"Superficial?" she repeated. "What do you mean?"

"He was chameleonlike, adjusting himself to his circumstances. He could play the part of the studious scholar or the popular jock, but I always had the impression they were all just roles for him. Watching him was like watching an actor in a play. I never had a sense that he ever really revealed anything about himself."

"Yes, I saw that, too," Emily said, a chill shuddering up her spine. When she had met Alex, he had played the role of the eager research participant, an average student earning a little pocket change, no different from the majority of other students who filled out her questionnaires. But chances were his fantasies of murdering women had been well formed by then. The literature she had read about serial killers pointed to their compulsions building from a young age.

"I do remember one time the subject of future professions came up in class, and Alex said he wanted to go into law enforcement. He specifically mentioned becoming a profiler."

Another shudder went through her. "Did that strike you as odd?" she asked.

"Not really. Television has made the profession glamorous. I always point out to students that they'll need experience in some other branch of psychology before they can make the leap to criminal profiling."

"Did Alex have any particular friends at the university?" she asked. "A girlfriend?"

"I don't know," the professor said. "Why your interest in Alex? If you're unable to follow up with him, you can always discard his responses from your research."

"It seems odd to me that such a promising student would suddenly drop out of school," she said, grappling for some plausible explanation for her interest. "I know it's none of my business, but someone must know something. I guess I hate leaving a mystery unsolved."

"Now you've got me curious," he said. "I tell you what—I'll ask around a little and see what I can find out. Is this a good number for you?"

"Yes. I'm staying with my parents for my brother's wedding this weekend. I appreciate anything you can find out."

"I'll talk to you soon, then."

She ended the call and stared out the window at the snow-covered landscape. What role was Alex playing today? Was he safe and warm in the home of an unsuspecting friend, or hunkered down in a cave or a remote cabin, preparing to kill again? Why hadn't she—or the other people who knew him—seen in him the capacity to murder? Was it because he hid that side of himself so well—or because as humans they shied away from admitting the possibility that such evil lay in someone who was, after all, so very much like themselves?

BRODIE HAD NEVER thought of Emily as a serious person. He had a fixed image of her as young, fun and carefree. But maybe that was only because they had been like that when they had been a couple five years before. Time and the job had made him more somber, and he could see that in her also. He stood in the doorway of the sunroom that evening, studying her as she sat on a love seat across the room: legs curled under her, head bent over a thick textbook, dark hair in a knot on top of her head, brows drawn together in concentration. Travis's words to him earlier still stung—had she really been so hurt by their breakup? It had been what she wanted, wasn't it—to be rid of a man she couldn't see herself with permanently?

She looked up from the book and noticed him. "How long have you been standing there?" she asked.

"Not long." He moved into the room and held out the stack of file folders he had tucked under his arm. "I retrieved these from Denise Switcher's car. I think they're the files you said she was bringing to you." The box the files had been packed in had been spattered with blood, so he had removed them. No need to remind Emily of the violent way her friend had died.

She hesitated, then reached up to take the folders. "Thank you."

When he didn't leave, but stood in front of her, hands tucked in the pockets of his jeans, she motioned to the love seat across from her. "Do you want to sit down?"

He sat. "Are you okay?" he asked.

"Why wouldn't I be okay?" She pulled a pencil from the back of her head and her hair tumbled down around her shoulders. He'd always wondered how women did that—styled their hair with a pencil or a chopstick or whatever was handy.

"It's hard, losing a friend to murder," he said.

She nodded. "It's worse knowing someone you knew killed her." She shifted, planting her feet on the floor. "Did you have something to eat? I think Rainey kept back some dinner for you and Travis."

"I'll get it in a minute."

He let the silence stretch. It was a good technique for getting people to open up. He used it in interrogating suspects—though he wasn't interrogating Emily, and he didn't suspect her of anything more than being uncomfortable around him. He'd like to change that.

"I talked to one of Alex's professors," she said after a moment. She glanced at him through a veil of dark lashes—a look that might have been coy but wasn't. "I wasn't sure if I should let on that he's a murder suspect, so I pretended I was doing follow-up for the research he participated in for our department. I told the professor I hadn't been able to get hold of him—which isn't a lie. He confirmed that Alex didn't return to classes this semester."

"We already knew that. Did you find out anything else?"

"I'm getting to that."

"Sorry. Go on."

She sat up straighter, prepared to give a report. He

imagined her in the classroom, making a presentation. She was probably a good teacher—well-spoken and direct. Pleasant to listen to, which probably wasn't a requirement, but he was sure it helped. He liked listening to her, and he liked sitting across from her like this, breathing in the faint floral scent of her soap and enjoying the way the light of the lamp beside her illuminated her skin. "Alex is studying psychology," she said. "So I asked the professor what kind of person he thought Alex was. He said he was superficial."

Brodie considered the word. An unusual choice. "What do you think he meant?"

"He said Alex struck him as someone playing a part. He knew how to act like a serious student or a popular friend, but the professor always had the sense that beneath the surface, there wasn't much there. Or maybe, that there was something darker there that Alex didn't want to show to anyone else."

"Did you ask the professor if he thought Alex was a sociopath?"

"No. And I don't think he'd make that kind of diagnosis on the basis of their relationship. It wouldn't be professional."

"I'm no psychologist, but I'd say a man who kills eight women in cold blood doesn't have normal emotions or reactions."

"I wouldn't disagree." She met his gaze and he felt the zing of attraction. However else they had both changed in the past five years, they hadn't lost this sense of physical connection. He had always believed the physical side of a relationship was the most superficial, based on hormones and basic drives. With Emily, even this felt different.

"Did the professor say anything else?" he asked, determined to keep things loose and professional. He had meant what he said to Travis about coming here to do a job, not to resume a relationship with Emily. After all, she had made it clear when she had refused his proposal that she didn't see him as the kind of man she wanted to spend her life with.

"Only that Alex was very intelligent, made good grades when he applied himself and had expressed an interest in going into law enforcement work," she said. "Specifically, he mentioned he wanted to be a criminal profiler."

Another surprise. "That's interesting. And a little unnerving. I hate to think law enforcement would be attractive to someone like that."

"I don't know—if you wanted to commit crimes, doing it as a cop, where you would be privy to all the information about the investigation, would allow you to stay one step ahead of the people looking for you. You might even be able to guide them to look in the wrong direction."

"Now I'm a little unnerved that you've put so much thought into this." He tried for a teasing tone, letting her know he wasn't serious.

"You asked me to get inside Alex's head." She shifted position on the sofa. "Though I have to admit, it's not the most comfortable place to be."

"Do you have any ideas where he might be hiding out, or what his next move might be?" Brodie asked.

"I'm a researcher, not a clairvoyant," she said. "But I am working on it. The case feels really personal now, with Denise's death. I mean, I knew a lot of the women he's killed, but this hits a little close to home."

He nodded, but said nothing, debating whether he should mention his concerns about a connection to her.

She must have sensed his hesitation. She leaned toward him, her gaze searching. "What aren't you telling me?" she asked.

"I don't want to alarm you."

"I'm already alarmed."

He blew out a breath. Maybe if he shared his theories, she'd help blow them out of the water. "I'm wondering if you might be on Alex's radar as a possible target," he said. "If, in fact, you're what brought him to Eagle Mountain to begin with."

"Why would you think that?"

"Maybe he fixated on you."

"He's killed eight other women and hasn't even threatened me."

"Maybe he's biding his time, waiting for the right opportunity."

She didn't look frightened—only skeptical. "And the other women were what—practice?"

"The first one might have been. Then he discovered he liked killing. Or maybe he's done this before, someplace else."

"I'm sure Travis has already thought of that," she said. "I don't think he found any like crimes."

"You're right. And Alex is young. His first murder may very well have been Kelly Farrow."

"I think it's just a coincidence that he ended up here," she said. "He came here to ice climb with his friend, they got stranded by the snow and he killed Kelly—maybe he'd always had a sick fantasy about killing a woman and he thought doing so in this out-of-the-way place, with a small sheriff's department, would be easier."

Brodie nodded. "And once he started, he felt compelled to continue."

"From what I've read, that's how it works with many serial killers—they're fulfilling an elaborate, engrossing fantasy."

Brodie hoped she wasn't part of that fantasy, but decided not to share that with her. He didn't want to frighten her—only make her more aware of possible danger. "I told Travis I'd asked you to help with the case," he said.

"What did he say about that?"

"He reluctantly agreed to let you help, but I don't think he was too happy about getting his little sister involved." Or about any possible involvement between Brodie and Emily.

"He and Gage both tend to be overprotective. I've learned to humor them and do what I want, anyway."

"They have a right to be concerned. I hope you took what we said this afternoon—about not going anywhere alone—seriously."

"I did."

"It applies to all the women here at the ranch, and all the women you know."

"We do talk about this, you know? I don't know any woman who goes anywhere by herself without being alert to her surroundings."

"When you live in a peaceful place like Eagle Mountain, I can see how it would be easy to get complacent."

"But I don't live in Eagle Mountain," she said. "I live in Fort Collins. And I have two brothers who are

cops. I know more than I want to about how dangerous it can be out there."

"Point taken," he said. And maybe it was time to
shift the conversation to something more mundane and
less stressful. "How do you like living in the big city?
It's a lot different from life here on the ranch."

"I love it," she said. "I really enjoy my work, and I
like all the opportunities and conveniences of a bigger city."

Footsteps approached and they both turned toward
the door as Travis entered. He stopped short. "Brodie,
what are you doing here?"

"I dropped off the files from Denise Switcher's car,"
Brodie said. "The ones she was bringing to Emily."

"I could have brought them," Travis said. He was
studying Brodie as if he was a perp he suspected of
a crime.

"I'm sure Brodie didn't want to bother you with
such a little errand," Emily said. She turned to Brodie.
"Thanks again for bringing them to me."

"It's been a long day," Travis said. "I'm sure Brodie
wants to get to his cabin."

Brodie resisted the urge to needle Travis by pro-
testing that he wasn't tired in the least and had been
enjoying his visit with Emily. But the sheriff looked
in no mood for teasing. For whatever reason, Travis
still harbored hard feelings about Brodie and Emily's
breakup. At times, the sheriff seemed more upset with
Brodie than Emily did. Brodie stood. "Travis is right,"
he said. "And I've kept you long enough."

"I enjoyed your visit," Emily said. Brodie wondered
if she was saying so to goad her overprotective brother,
but she sounded as if she meant it.

"Yeah, we'll have to do it again sometime." He didn't miss the dark look Travis sent him, but sauntered past the sheriff, head up. Brodie hadn't come here intending to renew his relationship with Emily. But if that did end up happening, maybe it wouldn't be such a bad thing.

As long as the sheriff didn't decide to run him out of town first.

Chapter Six

Reviewing the student surveys would have to wait until after Wednesday's barbecue and bonfire, the latest in a series of events at the ranch that Emily was hosting in an attempt to entertain friends and family trapped in town by the weather. Wednesday morning found Emily in the kitchen with Bette and Rainey, reviewing the menu for the evening. "Good plain food to help warm folks up in the cold," Rainey declared after describing the chili she would make and the kabobs Bette would assemble. "The kind of food I've been making all my life."

The ranch cook was an angular woman in her late forties or early fifties, who had reigned over the Walker kitchen for the past decade. Though she shooed Emily and her friends out of the kitchen whenever they invaded that sacred territory, she had also been known to spoil the youngest Walker sibling with homemade cookies and grilled pimento cheese sandwiches at every opportunity. Rainey's son's recent incarceration had subdued the cook a little, but she had also confided to Emily's mother that she felt less stressed, since at least now she knew her son was somewhere safe, and not causing trouble for anyone else.

"Everything will be delicious," Emily said, and handed the menu back to Bette. "And I definitely want to keep this simple. This close to the wedding, I don't want to burden either one of you."

"She's got this, and the wedding, taken care of," Rainey said.

"Rainey has been a big help with the reception preparations," Bette said, quick to praise the woman who, on her initial arrival at the ranch, had been her biggest foe.

Emily's cell phone rang. She fished it from the back pocket of her jeans and her heart sped up when she saw Professor Brandt's number. "I have to take this," she said, and hurried from the room.

Alone in the sunroom, she answered the call. "Hello, Professor."

"Hello, Emily. I asked around about Alex Woodruff and I found out a few things, though I don't know if they'll help you much."

Emily grabbed a notebook and pen from the table and sat on the sofa. "I'm all ears."

"This is an odd situation," he said. "And I'll admit, I'm curious now, too. Alex doesn't have any close friends that I could find, though he spent more time with Tim Dawson than anyone else. Do you know him?"

"Yes."

"Oddly enough, Tim failed to return to school also," the professor said. "I wasn't able to learn anything about him. When I contacted his family, they didn't want to talk to me about him. His father hung up on me."

Maybe the Dawsons didn't want to reveal that their

son had been killed while committing a crime, or that he was a suspect in a series of murders. Emily was pretty sure Travis had talked to Tim's parents, but she had no idea what had come of that conversation. "What about Alex's family?" she asked.

"He's apparently estranged from them, though he has a trust fund that pays for his schooling and living expenses, and from what I gather, anything else he wants."

"Oh." That explained how he was able to spend a month in Eagle Mountain with no worries about money.

"I have a name for you, of a young woman he apparently dated for a while. Grace Anders. She's a student here. You understand I can't give you her contact information."

"I understand." If she couldn't figure out how to get hold of Grace on her own, Brodie or Travis could help her.

"When you return to school, you shouldn't have much trouble finding her here on campus, if you want to talk to her."

"Okay, thank you. Anything else?"

"No, that's all. But do me a favor and let me know what you find out. Like I said, I'm curious now."

"I'll do that." Though if things went well, Professor Brandt would be able to read about Alex and his arrest for murder in the Denver papers.

She hung up the phone and stared at the name she had written on her pad. Grace Anders. She could give the name to Travis and have him or Gage or one of his officers contact the young woman. They were trained to elicit information from witnesses. But would Grace really confide in them? Wouldn't she be more likely to open up to another woman at the university, someone close to her own age?

She picked up her phone again and punched in the number for the sheriff's department. Adelaide answered, all crisp professionalism. "The sheriff is out at the moment," she said, after Emily identified herself.

"It's really you I want to talk to," Emily said. "I'm doing a little job for Travis and I need help finding a phone number for a friend of Alex Woodruff. Grace Anders, in Fort Collins."

"Travis did mention something about you helping with the case," Adelaide said. "He wasn't too happy about the idea, if I recall."

"I'm staying safe, just making a few phone calls for him," she said. "Can you find Grace Anders's number for me?"

"Hold on a minute."

Emily doodled in her notebook while she waited for Adelaide. She was coloring in circles around the word *trust fund* when the older woman came back on the line and rattled off a phone number. "Thanks, Adelaide," Emily said, and hung up before the office manager could question her further.

Before she could lose courage, Emily dialed the number Adelaide had given her. On the third ring a young woman answered. "If you're trying to sell something, I'm not interested," she said.

"I'm not selling anything, I promise," Emily said. "I'm calling about Alex Woodruff."

The silence on the other end of the line was so complete, Emily feared Grace had hung up. "What about him?" she asked after a minute.

"My name is Emily Walker. I'm a grad student at the university. Is this Grace Anders?"

"Why are you calling me? What has Alex done?"

Emily thought it was interesting that Grace assumed Alex had done something. Something wrong? "I understand you dated him at one time."

"Not for months. I haven't had anything to do with him for months and I'd just as soon keep it that way."

No love lost in her tone, Emily decided. "I'm trying to help a friend who had a rather unpleasant encounter with Alex," she said. That wasn't a complete lie—Denise was her friend, and Alex had killed her. Emily was trying to help find him and see that he was punished for the crime.

"Sorry about your friend," Grace said. "Alex is a creep."

"But you went out with him."

"Because I didn't know he was a creep at first," Grace said. "He was good-looking and he could be charming. We had a good time, at first."

"But something happened to change that?" Emily prompted.

"What did he do to your friend? I mean, did he steal money from her or something?"

"Did he steal money from you?"

"No. He had plenty of money of his own. I just wondered."

"He didn't steal from my friend." How much should Emily say? She wanted Grace to feel comfortable confiding in her, but she couldn't say anything that might jeopardize Travis's case against Alex.

"Did he assault her?" Grace blurted. "I mean, rape her or something?"

"Or something."

Grace swore. "I knew it. I should have said something before, but what would I have said?"

"Did Alex rape you?" Emily asked, as gently as possible.

"No! Nothing like that. It was just… I got really bad vibes from him."

"What kind of vibes?" Emily asked. "I know that's a really personal question, but it could really help."

Grace sighed dramatically. "We had sex a couple of times and it was fine, and then he wanted to do things different." She paused, then continued, "It feels so icky even talking about it, but he wanted to choke me."

Emily gasped. "Choke you?"

"Yeah, you know that autoerotic thing some people do where they choke themselves while they're getting off. It's supposed to give you some super orgasm or something, but it's crazy. People have died like that."

"But he didn't want to choke himself—he wanted to choke you."

"You get how creepy that is, right? I told him no way. I was really freaked out."

"How did he react when you refused him?"

"He got all huffy. He really pressured me, and that made me freak out even more."

"Because you had a really bad vibe."

"Yeah. I guess. It just seemed to me that it wasn't the sex he was so into, but the choking. I was worried he might like it so much he wouldn't stop. Is that what happened to your friend?"

"Something like that. You've been really helpful. If the police were to contact you about this, would you be willing to talk to them?"

"I guess. I'm sorry about your friend."

"Do you know of any other women he dated?" she asked.

"No. Like I said, I've stayed as far away from him as I could. Somebody told me he didn't come back to school this semester. I was relieved to hear it."

"Did Alex ever threaten you?" Emily asked.

"No. I just never felt comfortable around him after the choking thing came up."

"You were smart to turn him down. You have good instincts."

"Maybe I've had too much practice dating creeps. I just want to meet a good guy, you know?"

They said goodbye and Emily reviewed the conversation, organizing her thoughts to present to Travis. Maybe Alex had merely been interested in experimenting sexually, but her instincts told her Grace had read him correctly—he wasn't so much interested in the sexual experience as he was in choking a woman and knowing what that felt like.

He hadn't choked his victims, but maybe he had ruled out that method after being turned down by Grace. Or maybe he had intended her to be his first victim. He could murder her, and if anyone found out, he could claim she had died accidentally while they were experimenting. He might even have been able to get away with it.

Maybe he *had* gotten away with it. Maybe somewhere in Denver was a young woman who had died at Alex's hands, though he hadn't yet been charged with the crime.

With trembling hands, Emily punched in Travis's

number. "Are you calling to tell me you've decided to cancel the bonfire tonight?" he asked.

"No! Why would I do that?"

"I told Lacy I thought you should. I'm concerned Alex will try to repeat his performance at the scavenger hunt."

"Alex is not invited to this party."

"That might not stop him."

"It's too late to cancel the bonfire," she said, trying to quell her annoyance and not succeeding. "All the invitations have already gone out, and the ranch hands have been accumulating a mountain of scrap wood and brush that needs to be burned. Not to mention Rainey and Bette have been cooking party food for days. I'm certainly not going to tell them their extra work will be wasted."

"Which is pretty much what Lacy said. But she agreed that I could station a deputy and one of the ranch hands at the gate to check the ID of every person who enters against your guest list. So I'll need a copy of the list, first chance you get."

"All right." Part of her thought this was overkill, but the rest of her was grateful for this extra measure of safety.

"If you didn't call about the party, why did you call?" Travis asked.

"I talked to a woman Alex used to date," she said. "She said they broke up when he tried to talk her into letting him strangle her while they had sex."

"That's interesting. Does she have any idea where he is right now?"

"No. She hasn't had anything to do with him for a couple of months. But do you think this is how he

started? What if some other woman agreed to his proposal and she died and everyone thought it was an accident, when really it was murder?"

"I haven't found anything like that in my research,
but I can add it to his file."

"You could call someone in Fort Collins and Denver and try to find out."

"I could. But that won't help us discover where Alex
is right now, and that's what I need to know if I'm going
to stop him."

"No one in Fort Collins knows where he is," she
said. "His professor told me he didn't have any friends
but Tim, and he's estranged from his parents. Oh, and
he has a big trust fund that pays for everything."

"Yes, we knew that."

"Then why did you even ask me to try to find out
about him?"

"You've learned useful information," Travis said. "I
don't want you to think I don't appreciate your help.
But we really need to focus on where Alex might be
hiding right now. Did he know anyone in Eagle Mountain before he arrived here? Does he have any relatives
who live here? Did he ever complete an outdoor survival course or express an interest in winter camping?"

If Travis wanted her to ask questions like that, why
hadn't he given her a list? "I don't think any of the people I talked to know those things," she said.

"Maybe no one does," Travis said. "But it's important to try everything we can think of. Is there anything else you need to tell me?"

"No."

"Then I have to go."

He ended the call and Emily frowned at her phone,

fighting frustration. She felt like she had learned something important about Alex, but Travis was right—it wasn't going to help them find him and stop him. The longer it took to locate him, the more time he had to attack and kill another woman.

She studied her notebook, hoping for inspiration that didn't come. "Emily?"

She turned toward the door, where Lacy stood. "The ranch hands brought up that load of hay bales you asked for," she said. "They want to know what to do with them."

"Sure thing." She jumped up, pushing aside thoughts of Alex for now. Time to distract everyone else—and herself—from the danger lurking just outside their doors.

FOR THE REST of the day, Emily focused on making sure the party was a success, and counted it a good sign that, though the highway was still closed due to multiple avalanches, no new snow had fallen in a couple of days, and clouds had receded to reveal a star-spangled night sky and an almost-full moon like a shining silver button overhead.

As an added bonus, though the wedding favors and guest book hadn't been delivered before the road closed again, Paige Riddell and her significant other, DEA agent Rob Allerton, had arrived and moved into the last empty guest cabin. Lacy was thrilled her friend had made it and had thanked Emily half a dozen times today for arranging the bonfire.

All the guests seemed happy to be here, gathering in a semicircle as Travis, Gage and Emily's father lit the bonfire, then cheering as it caught and blazed to life. Even before the blaze gave off much warmth, the sight of it made everyone more animated. The flames popped and crackled as they climbed the tower of old pallets, scrap wood and brush the ranch hands had spent days assembling; the sparks rose like glitter floating up into the black sky, the scent of wood smoke mingling with the aroma of barbecue and mulled cider.

From the fire, guests gravitated to a buffet set up under tents. Rainey and Bette had prepared big vats of chili, pans of corn bread and half a dozen different salads. They had also arranged skewers of kabobs and sausages guests could toast over the fire. Guests could opt for cookies for dessert, or create their own s'mores.

Seating was provided by hay bales draped in blankets and buffalo robes, shaped into surprisingly comfortable couches—some long enough for half a dozen people, others just the right size for cuddling for two. Two of the ranch hands played guitar and sang for the appreciative crowd. Alcoholic and nonalcoholic beverages added to the festivities.

"Travis tells me you're the genius behind all this." Brodie's voice, low and velvety, pulled Emily's attention from the music. She hoped the dim lighting hid the warm flush that seemed to engulf her body at his approach. He indicated the crowd around the bonfire. "It's a great party."

"Travis wanted to cancel the whole thing, but I had Lacy in my corner," she said.

"He doesn't look too upset right now." Brodie nodded toward the sheriff, who was slow dancing with Lacy on the edge of the firelight, her head on his shoulder, both dancers' eyes half-closed.

Emily couldn't help but smile at the lovebirds.

"They're so good together," she said. "It's great to see Travis so happy."

"Gage has found his match, too," Brodie said.

Emily shifted her attention from Travis to her other brother, who sat on a hay bale with his wife, Maya. The two were feeding each other toasted marshmallows and laughing, eyes shining as they gazed at one another. Emily sighed. "I never would have guessed my two brothers could be such romantics," she said.

"Are you kidding? When it comes to love, most men are completely at a woman's mercy. We may not always show our romantic side, but it's definitely there."

"I'm not talking about buying a woman flowers and delivering a convincing line to get her to go out with you—or to go to bed with you," Emily said.

"Neither am I. I think most people want to be in relationships, to love and be loved. Maybe one of the reasons a lot of men—and maybe women, too—have a hard time expressing that desire is that they know it's so important. They're really afraid of messing things up and getting it wrong."

Brodie was the last person in the world she had ever expected she'd have a philosophical conversation about love with. "Excuse me?" she asked. "Are you sure you're really Brodie Langtry? Mr. Heartbreaker?" He certainly hadn't hinted that he was so keen on that kind of deep relationship when the two of them had been together. And she still wasn't sure she believed he had never received the letter she had sent to him after their breakup. Pretending he'd never seen it made him look much better than if he had read the letter and decided to blow her off—which was what she had always believed.

"I grew up," he said, her own image shining back at her in the reflection of the firelight in his eyes. "We all do. Besides, I was never as shallow as you thought I was. When someone is important to me, I will do anything to protect them and support them."

Now he was getting really hard for her to believe. "Have you ever had a serious relationship with a woman in your life?" she asked.

"Once."

A sharp pain pinched her chest. Who was this woman who had captured his heart? And why did it hurt to hear about her? Emily wet her lips. "When was that?"

"A long time ago."

She thought she heard real regret in his voice, but why was she feeling sorry for him? "I don't believe you," she said. "You can have any woman you want. If you commit to one, you have to give up all the others, so why should you?"

"What about you?" he asked. "Are you serious about someone? Or have you ever been?"

He was the only man she'd made the mistake of falling for. "I'm getting my degree and focusing on my career. I don't have time for a relationship."

He moved closer, blocking the firelight, the sheepskin collar of his heavy leather coat brushing against the nylon of her down-filled parka. Layers of fabric separated them, yet she felt the contact, like current flowing through an electrical cord once it was plugged in. She couldn't make out his features in the darkness, but was sure he was watching her. "Now who's avoiding commitment?" he asked.

She told herself she should move away, but couldn't

make her feet obey the command. "I'm not avoiding anything," she said.

"Except me. You don't have to run from me, Emily. I would never hurt you."

Hurt wasn't always a matter of intent—maturity had taught her that, at least. This knowledge made it easier for her to forgive him, but she wasn't going to forget anytime soon how easily he had wounded her. She would have told anyone that she had gotten over him long ago, then he showed up here at the ranch and all the old feelings came surging back like the tide rushing in. No good would come of revisiting all that.

"I have to go check on the food," she said, finally forcing herself to take a step back, and then another.

He didn't come after her, just stood and watched her run away. Maybe he didn't pursue her because he didn't really want her, she told herself as she hurried toward the buffet table.

Or maybe he didn't chase her because he was so sure that if he bided his time, he could have her, anyway. That, on some level, she had never really stopped being his.

BRODIE LET EMILY walk away. Maybe what they both needed right now was space. He had never expected to be so drawn to her. He had thought he was over her years ago. He'd been angry and hurt when she turned down his marriage proposal, and had spent more than a few months nursing his hurt feelings and wounded pride.

And now that he was back in town, Emily's family acted as if he was the villain in the whole bad scene. Had Emily made up some story about him dumping her, instead of admitting that she'd turned him down? She didn't strike him as the type to lie about something like that, but as he had told her, they had both done a lot of growing up in the past five years.

He helped himself to a kabob from the buffet table and tried his hand grilling it over the fire. Gage, a skewered sausage in hand, joined him. Of the two brothers, Gage had been the friendliest since Brodie's return to Eagle Mountain. "How's it going?" Gage asked.

"Okay." Brodie glanced around to make sure no one could overhear. "I'm trying to figure out why your family is giving me the cold shoulder. I mean, they're all polite, but not exactly welcoming."

Gage slanted a look at him. "You dated Emily for a while, right?"

"Yes. Five years ago. And then we broke up. It happens. That doesn't make me the bad guy."

Gage rotated the sausage and moved it closer to the flames. "I was away at school when that all went down, so I don't know much about it," he said. "I do know when I asked about it when I came home for the holidays, everybody clammed up about it. I got the impression you dumped Emily and broke her heart. You were one of Travis's best friends, so I guess he saw it as some kind of betrayal."

"I asked your sister to marry me and she turned me down," Brodie said. "That's not exactly dumping her."

"Does Travis know that?"

"I'm sure he does. Emily didn't have any reason to lie about it."

Gage shook his head. "Then maybe you'd better ask Travis what's on his mind. You know him—he keeps his feelings to himself, most of the time."

"Maybe I will." But not tonight. Brodie looked across the fire to where Travis sat with Lacy in the golden glow of the fire, their heads together, whispering. The sheriff looked happier and more relaxed than he had since Brodie had arrived. Amazing what love could do for a person.

Someone shouting made him tense, and he turned to see Dwight helping Rob Allerton into the circle of firelight. Rob dropped onto a hay bale and pushed Dwight away, as Paige rushed to him. "What happened?" she asked, gingerly touching a darkening bruise on his forehead.

"I left my phone back in our cabin and decided to go get it so I could show someone some pictures I have on it," Rob said. "As I neared the ranch house, I noticed someone moving around by the cars. At first I thought it was someone leaving the party early, but as I drew nearer, the guy bolted and ran straight at me. He had a tire iron or a club or something like that in his hand." Rob touched the bruise and winced. "I guess I'm lucky he only struck me a glancing blow, but I fell, and by the time I got to my feet and went looking for him, he had vanished." He looked up and found Travis in the crowd gathered around him. "I think he did something to your sheriff's department SUV."

Brodie followed Travis, Gage and most of the rest of the guests over to the parking area in front of the house. Travis's SUV was parked in the shadows at the far end of a line of cars and trucks. The sheriff played the beam of a flashlight over the vehicle, coming to rest on the driver's-side door. Someone had spray-painted a message in foot-high, bright red letters: *ICE COLD*.

Chapter Seven

Emily dragged herself into the sheriff's department the next morning, the two cups of coffee she had forced down with breakfast having done little to put her in a better mood. She hadn't slept much after the party broke up last night—something she probably shared in common with everyone else in attendance at this meeting the sheriff had called. Most of the law enforcement personnel who gathered in the conference room had searched the ranch and surrounding area for Alex Woodruff late into the previous night. Once again, after leaving his blood-red taunt on Travis's SUV, he had disappeared into the darkness.

She took her place to Travis's left at the conference table, nodding in greeting at the others around the table and avoiding lingering too long when her gaze fell on Brodie. She had missed him at breakfast this morning. Her mother had mentioned that he'd left early with Travis. Though the two men hadn't been friendly since Brodie's arrival at the ranch, they did seem to work together well.

Her feelings for Brodie seemed to fluctuate between regret and relief. Regret that they couldn't pick up the easy exchange they had enjoyed Tuesday evening in the sunroom. Relief that she didn't have to revisit the tension between them beside the bonfire last night. Other people got through situations like this and were able to put the past behind them. She and Brodie would learn to do that, too.

Travis stood and everyone fell silent. "I think you all know my sister, Emily," he said. "She is acquainted with Alex Woodruff and is completing her master's degree in behavioral economics. I've asked her to sit in on some meetings, to help us try to get into Alex's mind in hopes of anticipating his next move."

"I pity you, being in that guy's mind," someone— she thought it might be Ryder Stewart—said from the other end of the table.

Travis ignored the comment and projected a map of Rayford County onto a wall screen. "As I believe all of you know, someone—we're operating on the assumption that it was Alex—vandalized my department SUV last night at my family's ranch during a party."

"How did he get by the security you had set up?" wildlife officer Nate Harris asked.

"He parked around a curve, out of sight of the guards," Travis said. "He approached the ranch house on foot, and circled around through the trees. We were able to trace his movements that far at first light."

"He must have run track." Rob Allerton had joined them this morning, the bruise on his forehead an angry purple, matching the half-moons under his eyes. "He raced out of there like a gazelle."

Travis projected a color photo of his SUV onto the wall screen. The large red letters stood out against the Rayford County Sheriff's logo. "He's always enjoyed taunting us. This seems to represent an acceleration of that."

"He knows we know who he is and he doesn't care," Ryder Stewart declared.

"He thinks he's better than all of us," Brodie said.

"We're looking for anywhere Alex might be hiding," Travis said. "We've ruled out the two sets of forest service summer cabins where we know he and Tim Dawson spent time before." He circled these sites in red on the image. "We know Alex and Tim used an unoccupied vacation home as a hideout previously, so we're working our way through unoccupied homes but we haven't hit anything there, either. We've also published Alex's picture in the paper, on posters around town and on all the social media outlets. We've alerted people to let us know if they spot him."

"If he's using someone's vacation home, the neighbors are bound to see him," Dwight said.

"Maybe he's using a disguise," Deputy Jamie Douglas said.

"Alex was in the drama club at the university," Emily said. "But I don't think he would hide in a place with a lot of people—not now when he knows you've identified him. He takes risks, but they're calculated risks." She had lain awake for a long time last night thinking about this, and searched for the right words to share her conclusions. "He knows you're looking for him, and he wants to be free to come and go as he pleases. That freedom is important to him—he has to be in charge, not allowing you to dictate his movements. Showing up at the ranch last night and vandalizing your vehicle is another way of asserting that freedom."

"He could have moved into an abandoned mine," Nate said from his seat beside Jamie. "There are plenty of those around."

Travis nodded. "We'll check those out."

"He could be in a cave," Dwight said.

"He could be," Travis said. "But remember—wherever he is has to be accessible by a road."

Emily leaned forward, trying to get a better look at the map. "What's that symbol on the map, near Dixon Pass?" she asked.

Travis studied the image, then rested the pointer on a stick figure facing downhill. "Do you mean this? I think it's the symbol for an old ski area."

"Dixon Downhill," Gage said. "I think it's been closed since the eighties. When they widened the highway in the nineties, they covered over the old access road into the place."

"I think part of the old ski lift is still there," Dwight said. "But I'm pretty sure they bulldozed all the buildings."

"Gage, you and Dwight check it out," Travis said. "See if there are any habitable buildings there where Alex might be holed up."

"I'd like to go with them," Brodie said.

"All right," Travis agreed. "Dwight, you and Nate can work on the mines." He gave out assignments to the others on the team.

"What would you like me to do?" Emily asked, as the others gathered up their paperwork and prepared to depart.

"You can go home and write up your thoughts on Alex," Travis said.

A report he would dutifully read, file away and consider his obligation to her met. Her brother might have agreed to let Brodie ask for her help, but that didn't mean he was going to let her get very involved. "I'd like to talk to Jamie," she said. "She spent time with Alex's partner, Tim, when the two kidnapped her and her sister."

"Her statement is in the file I gave you," Travis said.

"I want to talk to her," she said, with more force behind the words.

Travis gave her a hard look, but she looked him in the eye and didn't back down. "All right," he said. "Set it up with her."

"I'll see if she can meet me for lunch." She started to leave, but he stopped her.

"Emily?"

She turned toward him again. "Yes?"

"Alex Woodruff is very dangerous. Don't get any ideas about trying to get close to him on your own."

A shudder went through her. "Why would I want to get close to a man who's murdered eight women? Travis, do you really think I'm that stupid?"

"You're not stupid," he said. "But you tend to always think the best of people."

She wondered if he was talking about more than Alex now. Was he also warning her away from Brodie?

"I'll be careful," she said. "And I won't do anything foolish." Not when it came to either man.

To REACH WHAT was left of the Dixon Downhill ski area, Brodie and Gage had to park at the barricades closing off the highway, strap on snowshoes and walk up the snow-covered pavement to a break in a concrete berm on the side of the road, where an old emergency access road lay buried under snow. Reflectors on trees defined the route. The two men followed the reflectors to a bench that was the remains of the road that had once led to the resort.

The resort itself had been situated in a valley below the pass, with lift-accessed skiing on both sides. "You can still see the cuts for the old ski runs from here." Gage pointed out the wide path cut through stands of tall spruce and fir.

"Is that the lift line there?" Brodie indicated a cable running through the trees to their right. A couple of rusting metal chairs dangled crookedly from the braided line.

"I think so. There's the lift shack, at the top."

The small building that housed the engine that ran the old rope-tow lift really was a shack, cobbled together from rough lumber and tin, a rusting pipe jutting from the roof that was probably the engine exhaust. Brodie took out a pair of binoculars and glassed the area. From this angle, at least, it didn't look as if anyone had been down there in a long time.

"They used old car motors to power some of these things," Gage said. "I'd like to get a look at this one."

"Does the lift still run?" Brodie asked.

"I don't think so," Gage said. "Though if a mechanic messed with it, he might be able to get it going again. Those old motors weren't that sophisticated, and it's been out of the weather."

Gage led the way as they descended into the valley. With no traffic on the closed highway above, and thick snow muffling their steps, the only sounds were the occasional click of the ski poles they were using against a chunk of ice, and their labored breathing on the ascent.

Brodie tried not to think of the mountain of snow on either side of them. "Did you check with the avalanche center before we came down here?" he asked.

"No," Gage said. "We probably should have, but I was too eager to get down here and see what we could see." He stopped and glanced up toward the highway. "We'll be all right as long as he doesn't try to climb up and disturb the snowpack up there."

Brodie hoped Gage was right. After ten minutes of walking, they were forced to stop, the old road completely blocked by a snowslide, the wall of snow rising ten feet over their heads. "I think it's safe to say no one has been down here in a while," Gage said. "This didn't just happen." Dirt and debris dusted the top of the slide, and the ends of tree branches jutting out of the snow were dry and brown.

"At least now we know no one has been here," Gage said.

"Is this road the only way in?" Brodie asked.

"In summer, it might be possible to climb down the rock face from the highway," Gage said. "Though I wouldn't want to try it." He shook his head. "Even if Alex could get here, there's no place for him to stay. That lift shack isn't going to offer much shelter. At this elevation nighttime temperatures would be brutal. And the only way in and out is to go up this road—which is blocked—or scramble straight up."

"Wherever he is, it's somewhere he can go with ease," Brodie said. "This isn't it."

Gage clapped him on the back. "Come on. Let's go back."

The trip up was slower going, in deep snow up a steep grade. "We should have thought to bring a snowmobile," Gage said when they paused halfway up to rest.

Brodie took a bottle of water from his pack and drank deeply. "And then if Alex had been down there, he would have heard us coming miles away."

"He's not down there." Gage looked around at the world of white. "I wish I knew where he is."

Brodie started to replace the water bottle in his pack when a loud report made him freeze. "What was that?" he asked.

"It sounded like a gunshot." Gage put a hand on his weapon.

"Not close," Brodie said. "Maybe someone target shooting?"

"It sounded like it's up on the highway," Gage said. "Maybe a blowout on one of the road machines?"

"Let's get out of here," Brodie said. They started walking again, but had gone only a few steps when an ominous rumble sent his heart into his throat. He took off running, even as a wave of snow and debris flowed down the slope toward them.

Chapter Eight

Emily arranged to meet Deputy Jamie Douglas for lunch at a new taco place on the south end of town. The former gas station had half a dozen tables inside, and a busy drive-up window. Jamie, her dark hair in a neat twist at the nape of her neck, waved to Emily from one of the tables. "Thanks for agreeing to talk to me," Emily said, joining the deputy at the table.

"Sure. What can I do for you?"

"Let's order lunch and I'll fill you in."

They ordered at a window at the back of the room, then collected their food and returned to the table. "Travis asked me to put together a kind of profile of Alex Woodruff," Emily said when they were situated. "Not as an official profiler, but because I knew him slightly from the university and he hoped I'd have some insights. You probably spent more time with his partner, Tim, than anyone else, so I thought you might have some thoughts I could add to my assessment."

Jamie spooned salsa over her tacos. "I never even met Alex," she said.

"I know. But I think more information about Tim would help me clarify some things about their relationship."

"Sure. I'll try. What do you need to know?"

"I read your report, so I know the facts about what happened when Tim and Alex kidnapped you, but I'm more interested in other behavioral things."

"Like what?"

"When you came to, you and your sister were alone in the cabin with Tim?"

"Yes."

"And he told you he was waiting for Alex to return?"

"That's right. Well, he never named him, but we knew his partner was Alex."

"Did you get the impression that Alex was the leader—that Tim was looking to him to make the decisions?"

"Yes. Tim got a phone call from his partner—from Alex—who apparently told him he had to kill us by himself. Tim didn't like this, so then they agreed that Tim would bring us to wherever Alex was waiting, and they would kill us together."

"Do you think the idea of the killings started with Alex, or was it Tim's idea?"

"Definitely Alex. Tim said the first killing freaked him out, but then he started to like it. Or, at least, he liked getting away with the crimes."

"Alex must have recognized a similar personality to his own," Emily said.

Jamie nodded. "I guess it's like they say—birds of a feather flock together."

"My understanding is that Tim acted as the decoy, dressed as a woman, while Alex came up out of the woods and attacked women?" Emily asked.

"Yes. And Tammy Patterson's description of her ordeal confirms that." Tammy was a reporter for the *Eagle Mountain Examiner* who had managed to get away from Alex and Tim after they waylaid her one snowy afternoon.

"I don't think the two were equal partners," Emily said. "Alex was dominant. He's the man who chose the targets, and probably the one who did the actual killing. Tim was his helper. I wonder if Tim would have eventually killed on his own, without Alex around to goad him into doing it."

"I don't know," Jamie said. "But I believe Tim was prepared to kill me and Donna on his own. At least, that's what he told Alex."

"How is your sister doing after this ordeal?" Emily asked. Donna was a pleasant young woman with developmental disabilities who worked at Eagle Mountain Grocery.

"She's doing good." Jamie's smile at the mention of her sister was gentle. "She had some nightmares, but Nate has moved in with us and that's helped. She gets along really great with him, and she says having him in the house at night makes her feel safer." She blushed. "He makes me feel safer, too."

Emily hadn't missed that Jamie had been sitting next to Nate Harris at the meeting this morning. "It's great that the two of you got together," she said.

Jamie rotated the small diamond solitaire on the third finger of her left hand. "We're going to be married in the spring and Donna is almost more excited than I am."

"Congratulations." Emily couldn't quite hide her surprise. The last she had heard, Jamie and Nate had only recently started dating. "You obviously don't believe in long engagements."

"We were high school sweethearts, you know,"

Jamie said. "We broke up when he went away to college. I thought it was because he was eager to be free of me and date other people. He thought he was doing me a favor, not leaving me tied down to a man who wasn't around. Anyway, I guess we needed that time apart to really appreciate each other."

Emily nodded. So Jamie and Nate weren't strangers who just got together. They had dated and split up before—like her and Brodie. Except the situation with Brodie was entirely different. The circumstances of their split, and everything that had happened afterward, made things so much more awkward between them now.

Jamie's radio crackled with words that were, to Emily, unintelligible, but Jamie set down the glass of tea she had been sipping and jumped to her feet, her face pale. "I have to go," she said.

"What is it?" Emily asked, as the alarm from the fire station down the street filled the air. "What's happened?"

"An avalanche on Dixon Pass," Jamie said, already moving toward the door. "Gage and Brodie may be caught in it!"

As the wave of white moved down the hill toward him, Brodie tried to think what he was supposed to do. He had taken a backcountry rescue course once, and he struggled to recall what the instructor had said.

Then the avalanche of snow was on him, hitting him with the force of a truck, sending him sprawling, struggling for breath. Instinct took over and he began swimming in the snow, fighting to reach the surface before it hardened around him like concrete.

He fought hard for each stroke, his thoughts a jumble of images—of Gage's startled face just before the snow hit, of his mother the last time he had seen her and finally of Emily.

Emily, the hardness gone out of her eyes when she looked at him, head tilted to look up at him, lips slightly parted in a silent invitation for a kiss…

Then he popped to the surface of the snowslide, like a surfer thrust forward by the momentum of a wave, gasping in the achingly cold air. A tree branch glanced off his shoulder with a painful blow, then a rock bounced off his head, making him cry out.

Wrenching his head around, he saw that he was on the very edge of the slide, which had probably saved him. He struggled his way out of the snow's grip, like a man floundering out of quicksand. "Gage!" he screamed, then louder, "Gage!"

Relief surged through him as a faint cry greeted him. He fought his way toward it, clawing at the snow with numbed and aching hands, repeatedly calling, then waiting for the response to guide him in the right direction. "Gage! Gage!"

At last he located the source of the cries, and dug into the snow, first with his hands, then with a tree branch. He uncovered Gage's leg, the familiar khaki uniform twisted around his calf, then he dug his way up to Gage's head. When he had cleared away enough snow, he helped Gage sit up. They slumped together in the snow, gasping for air. A thin line of blood trickled from a cut on Gage's forehead, eventually clotting in the cold.

"We need to get out of here," Gage said after many minutes.

"We need help," Brodie countered, and shifted to

reach his cell phone. The signal wasn't good, but it might be enough. He dialed 911 and said the words most likely to rush help their way without long explanations. "Officer needs assistance, top of Dixon Pass."

The phone slipped from his numb grasp and he watched with an air of detachment as it skidded down the slope. Gage struggled to extract his own phone, then stared at the shattered screen. "They'll find us," he said, and lay back on the snow and closed his eyes.

Brodie wanted to join his friend in lying down for a nap. Fatigue dragged at him like a concrete blanket. He couldn't remember when he'd been so exhausted. But the danger of freezing out here in the snow was real. "Wake up, Gage," he said, trying to put some force behind the words. "You don't want to survive an avalanche only to die of hypothermia."

"There are worse ways to go," Gage said. But he sat up and looked up the slope, to the scarred area that showed the path of the avalanche.

"What do you think set it off?" Brodie asked.

"I don't know. Maybe that sound we heard earlier. That engine backfiring."

"Or the gunshot." The more Brodie thought about that report, the more it sounded to him like a gunshot.

"Somebody target shooting in the national forest?" Gage suggested. "Sound carries funny in the canyons."

"Maybe," Brodie said. "But what if someone set off the snowslide deliberately?"

"Why would they do that?"

"Because they didn't like us taking a look at the old ski resort?"

"I don't know who would object. And you saw yourself—no one has been down there in weeks. Since before that older snowslide."

"Can we find out when that snowslide happened?" Brodie asked.

"Probably," Gage said. "Maybe. I don't really know." He tilted his head. "Does that sound like a siren to you?"

It did, and half an hour later a search-and-rescue team had descended and was helping them back up the slope. The SAR director had wanted to strap Brodie and Gage into Stokes baskets and winch them up the slope, but the two victims had persuaded him they were capable of standing and walking out under their own power, with only a little help from the SAR volunteers.

An hour after that, Brodie was in his guest cabin on the Walker ranch, fortified with a sandwich and coffee, fresh from a hot shower and contemplating a nap.

A knock on the door interrupted those plans, however. He glanced through the peephole, then jerked open the door. "Emily, what are you doing here?" he asked.

She moved past him into the room, her face pale against her dark hair. "I wanted to make sure you were all right," she said.

"I'm fine." He rolled his shoulders, testing the statement. "A little bruised and tired, but okay."

She touched his arm, and the purpling bruise where he had collided with a tree branch or boulder in his frantic effort to escape the snowslide. That light, silken touch against his bare skin sent a current of heat through him.

He moved toward her, drawn by the scent of her mingling in the lingering steam from his shower. Her eyes widened, as if she was only just now seeing him—all of him, naked except for a pair of jeans, his skin still damp, droplets lingering in the hair on his chest.

She jerked her gaze back to his bruised arm. "You should put something on this," she said, her voice husky.

"Would you do it for me?"

"All right."

He retreated to the bathroom and fetched the ointment from his first-aid kit. Did he imagine her hand trembled when he handed it to her? Her touch was steady enough as she smoothed the ointment on, so careful and caring, and so incredibly sensuous, as if she was caressing not only his wound, but the invisible hurts inside of him.

She capped the tube of ointment and raised her eyes to meet his. Time stopped in that moment, and he had the sensation of being in a dream as he slid his arm around her waist and she leaned into him, reaching up to rest her fingers against the side of his neck, rising on her toes to press her lips to his.

He had a memory of kissing her when she had been a girl, but she kissed like a woman now, sure and wanting, telling him what she desired without the need for words. When she pressed her body to his, he pulled her more tightly against him, and when she parted her lips, he met the thrust of her tongue with his own. He willingly drowned in that kiss, losing himself until he had to break free, gasping, his heart pounding.

She opened her eyes and stared up at him with a dreamy, dazed expression. Then her vision cleared, eyes opening wider. She let out a gasp and pulled away.

"I can't do this," she said, and fled, out of his arms and out the door before he had time to react.

He wanted to go after her but didn't. He lay back on the bed and stared up at the ceiling, marveling at the twisted turn his life had taken, bringing him back here, to this woman, after so long.

And wondering where it all might lead.

Chapter Nine

Emily read through the first of the surveys her professor had sent for her to review—then read through it again, nothing having registered on the first pass. Her head was too full of Brodie—of the pressure of his lips on hers, the strength of his arms around her, the taste of his kisses. For all she had been enthralled by him five years ago, she had never felt such passion back then. The Brodie she had faced in his cabin yesterday had been more serious, with a depth she hadn't recognized before. He was stronger—and far more dangerous to her peace.

At this point in her life, she thought she could have handled a merely physical fling with a fun, hot guy. But she could never think of Brodie as merely a fling. And she didn't know if she would ever be able to completely trust him with her feelings. Even five years before, as crazy as she was about him, she had never been able to fully believe that his feelings for her were more than superficial. She was another conquest, another victim of his charm. He hadn't acted particularly torn up when she had turned down his marriage proposal, and he hadn't made any effort to persuade her to change her mind.

Even if he hadn't received the letter she had sent to
him later, if he had really loved her, wouldn't he have
kept in touch? He could have used his friendship with
Travis as an excuse to at least check on her. But he had
simply vanished from her life. That knowledge didn't
leave a good feeling behind, and it made getting involved with him again far too risky.

But she wasn't going to think about him now. She
had work to do. Determined to focus, she started reading through the survey once more. She had just finished her read-through and was starting to make notes
when her cell phone buzzed, startling her.

Half afraid it might be Brodie, she swiped open
the screen, then sagged with relief when she read her
brother's name. "Hi, Travis," she answered.

"There's someone here at the station I think you
should talk to," he said.

"Who is it?"

"Ruth Schultz. She says she knows you."

Emily searched her memory for the name, but came
up blank. "I don't think—"

"Hang on a minute… She says you knew her as
Ruth Parmenter."

"Ruthie!" Emily smiled. They had been classmates
in high school. "Why does she want to see me?"

"It has to do with the case. Could you come down
and talk to her?"

Puzzled, but intrigued, Emily glanced at the folder
full of surveys. Not exactly scintillating reading. And
not all that pressing, either, not with a murderer on
the loose. "Sure. Tell her I'll be there in half an hour."

Twenty-five minutes later, Adelaide looked up from
her desk when Emily entered the sheriff's department.

"Mrs. Schultz is in interview room one." Adelaide pointed down the hall. "She said she can stay until twelve thirty. That's when her youngest gets out of half-day kindergarten."

"All right." Emily headed past the desk, intending to stop by Travis's office first to ask what exactly she was supposed to be talking about with Ruthie, but before she could reach the sheriff's door, Brodie stepped out and intercepted her. "Travis had to leave, so he asked me to sit in with you and Mrs. Schultz," he said.

Running into him this way, when she hadn't had time to prepare, unsettled her. She took a deep, steadying breath, but that was a mistake, since all it did was fill her head with the masculine scent of him—leather and starch and the herbal soap that had surrounded them last night. She stared over his left shoulder and managed to keep her voice steady. "What is this all about?"

"She says her younger sister, Renee, is missing."

Emily had a vague memory of a girl who had been three years behind her in school—a pretty, sandy-haired flirt who had been popular with the older boys, and thus, unpopular with the older girls. "How long has she been missing?"

"Four days. At first Mrs. Schultz thought she had left town when the road opened and got caught when the road closed again. But she hasn't answered any calls or texts and that's not like her."

"Maybe her phone lost its charge or broke," Emily said. "Or maybe she's somewhere she doesn't want her sister to know about."

Brodie frowned. "Maybe. But Mrs. Schultz is worried because she said Renee knew Alex. She went out with him at least once."

Emily sucked in her breath. "That is a frightening thought. But why does she want to talk to me?"

"Because you knew Renee, and you know Alex. Travis explained you were helping us put together a profile of Alex and he thought the information she had might help. But most of all, I think she's looking for some reassurance from you that her sister is all right."

"I don't think I can give her that," Emily said.

"Probably not. But maybe telling her story to a friendly face—someone who isn't a cop—may help her."

"Then of course I'll talk to her."

Emily remembered Ruthie Parmenter as an elfin figure with a mop of curly brown hair and freckles, a star on the school track team, president of the debate club and senior class president. She had talked about going to college on the East Coast, then taking off for Europe with a camera, maybe becoming a war correspondent or a travel journalist or something equally exciting and adventurous.

The woman who looked up when Emily and Brodie entered the interview room was still lithe and freckle-faced, though her hair had been straightened and pulled back from her face by a silver clip. She wore a tailored blouse and jeans, and an anxious expression. "Emily, it's so good to see you," she said, standing and leaning over the table to give Emily a hug. "You still look just the same. I'd have recognized you anywhere."

Emily wasn't so sure she would have recognized Ruthie. Her former classmate looked older and more careworn, though maybe that was only from worrying about her sister. She indicated Brodie. "This is Agent Brodie Langtry, with the Colorado Bureau of Investigation."

"Yes, Brodie and I have met." The smile she gave him held an extra warmth, and Emily inwardly recoiled at a sudden pinch of jealousy. Seriously? Was she going to turn into that kind of cliché?

"Why don't we have a seat?" she said, pulling out a chair.

They sat, Brodie at the end of the table and the two women facing each other. "Brodie said you haven't been able to get in touch with your sister," Emily began.

"Yes. Not since Monday afternoon, when the road opened again for what was it—less than a day? I wasn't worried at first. I assumed she'd gone to Junction to shop and maybe take in a movie. But when I called the next day and she didn't answer, I was a little concerned. And when she didn't come to dinner last night, I knew something was wrong. It was my son's birthday—he just turned six. Renee would never have missed Ian's birthday."

"Was your sister dating anyone in particular?"

"No." She waved her hand, as if brushing aside the suggestion. "You know Renee—she always liked men, but she was never ready to settle down with anyone. She hasn't changed in that respect."

"But she had dated Alex Woodruff?" Emily asked.

"Yes." The faint lines on either side of her mouth deepened. "When I saw his picture in the paper and read that he was a person of interest in the Ice Cold Killer murders, my legs gave out and I had to sit down. And I knew I had to contact the sheriff. In case…" She paused and swallowed, then forced out the next words. "In case he's the reason Renee is missing."

Emily reached across and took Ruthie's hand and squeezed it. She could only imagine how worried Ruthie must be, but she wasn't going to offer hollow words of comfort. "When did Renee last go out with Alex?" she asked.

"I'm not positive, but I think they only had the one date. I think she would have told me if there was more than one—that was back on New Year's Eve. She went with him to the Elks' New Year's dance. My husband and I met them there."

"Was that their first date?" Emily asked.

"Yeah. She told me she met him at Mo's Pub a couple of nights before. He and a friend were there, playing pool, and she thought he was cute, so she asked him to the dance."

"She asked him?" Brodie asked. "He didn't approach her?"

"Not the way she told it." Ruthie shrugged. "That was Renee—she liked calling the shots in a relationship and wasn't afraid to make the first move."

"What did you think of him?" Emily asked.

Ruthie made a face. "I didn't like him. He struck me as too full of himself, and a phony. I told Renee that, too, and she said they had a lot of fun, but she didn't think she'd go out with him again—he wasn't her type. To tell you the truth, it surprised me she went out with him that one time. She generally likes older men who are a little rougher around the edges, you know? Outdoorsmen and daredevils. Alex was close to her age, and far too smooth."

"Did Renee mention anything that might have

happened later that night, maybe when Alex took her home—anything that seemed off or upsetting?" Emily asked.

"No. Nothing like that. She just said he wasn't her type. My husband didn't like Alex, either. In fact, he and I left the dance early. I was afraid if Bob had one too many drinks he might end up punching Alex. Alex kept popping off like he was an authority on everything and I could tell it was getting to Bob."

"You married Bob Schultz?" Emily asked, picturing the rancher's son who had never really been part of their group.

Ruthie smiled, her expression softening. "Yeah. I came home for Christmas after my first semester at Brown and he and I met up at a skating party my church had organized for the youth. We just really hit it off. I ended up transferring to Junction to finish my degree and we got married my sophomore year. We have two kids—Ian is six and Sophia is five."

"Wow," Emily said, trying—and failing—to hide her surprise.

Ruthie laughed. "I know! I was going to save the world and have all these adventures. But marriage and motherhood and running our ranch is adventure enough for me."

"You sound really happy."

"That's because I am." Her expression sobered once more. "Except, of course, I'm worried about Renee."

"Now that we know she's missing, we'll be looking for her," Brodie said. "You gave Travis a description of her vehicle, right?"

Ruthie nodded. "She drives a silver RAV4. Travis said he would put out a bulletin to let law enforcement all over the state know to be on the lookout for her. Maybe they will find her in Junction with some new guy she met." She smiled, but the expression didn't reach her eyes. "That would be just like Renee."

Brodie rose, and the women stood also. "Thank you for talking to me," Emily said.

Ruthie reached out and gripped Emily's wrist. "Be honest with me. Do you think this guy went after Renee?"

"I don't know," Emily said. "He hasn't had a previous relationship with any of the other women he's killed—at least not as far as we know. And all of them have been found very shortly after they were killed—within minutes, even." She gently extricated herself from Ruthie's grasp. "But people aren't always predictable. All I can tell you is that this doesn't follow his pattern so far."

Ruthie nodded. "I know you can't make any promises, but I'm holding out hope that it's just a sick coincidence that she knew this man." She shuddered. "I can't believe we spent a whole evening with him. I thought he was a bit of a jerk, but I never in a million years would have pegged him as a killer."

"If we could do that, we could prevent crimes before they happened," Brodie said. "But we can't."

They walked with Ruthie to the front door, where she offered Emily another hug. "We'll have to get together after this is all over," Ruthie said. "I'd like you to meet my family."

"I'd like that, too," Emily said.

Brodie waited until Ruthie was gone before he spoke. "What do you think?" he asked.

Emily worried her lower lip between her teeth.

"Alex went out with Michaela Underwood, too," she said. "So we know he has used asking women out as a way to get to them."

"But he killed Michaela on that first date. Renee Parmenter went out with him at least once and lived to tell the tale."

"That was about a week before he and Tim killed Kelly Farrow and Christy O'Brien," Emily said. "Maybe Alex was still working on his plan, or maybe killing women was still a fantasy for him then."

"She didn't tell her sister about anything unusual happening on the date, but that doesn't mean nothing did," Brodie said. "She might not have wanted to worry her sister."

"If Renee was wary of Alex, she probably wouldn't have gone out with him again," Emily said.

"So you don't think he used a second date as a way to get to her so he could kill her?" Brodie asked.

"I don't know," Emily said. "Maybe he charmed her. Or she was physically attracted to him in spite of her misgivings. Attraction can make people do things they know they shouldn't."

Her eyes met his, hoping he'd get the message that what had happened between them in his cabin yesterday was not going to be repeated. Brodie wasn't a bad person—far from it. But she didn't like the way he made her feel so out of control and not in charge of her decisions.

His gaze slid away from hers. "I hope Alex didn't murder Renee Parmenter. But I can't say I've got a good feeling about this."

"No, I don't, either," she admitted.

"Have you come up with any ideas about where he might be hiding—or what he intends to do next?"

"No, I haven't."

He clapped her on the back. "Then you'd better get to work. I still think you can give us something useful if you put your mind to it."

"Because of course you're always right."

"I've got good instincts. And so do you, if you'd pay attention to them."

He strode away, leaving her to wonder at his words—and at the look that accompanied them. She and Brodie seemed to specialize in nonverbal communication and mixed messages. It was probably time they cleared the air between them, but coming right out and saying what she felt wasn't something she had had much practice at. Like most people, she liked to protect her feelings. She had allowed herself to be vulnerable to a man exactly once, and the ending made her unwilling to do so again.

BRODIE HAD CLAIMED a desk in the corner of the sheriff's department conference room that had been turned into a situation room. The faces of the victims of the Ice Cold Killer surrounded him as he worked, and the scant evidence collected in the case crowded a row of folding tables against one wall. He hunched over his laptop, scanning databases, trying to trace Renee Parmenter's movements since her disappearance.

Travis had asked Ruth to run a notice in the paper, asking anyone who had any knowledge of Renee's whereabouts to contact the sheriff's department, but that wouldn't appear until tomorrow. As it was, Renee had been missing four days. Brodie feared they might already be too late.

The door to the room opened and Travis entered. He scanned the room, his gaze lingering a moment on the faces of the dead before he shifted his attention to Brodie. "Are you coming up with anything?"

Brodie pushed his chair back from the table that served as his desk. "The report from the CBI profiler came in a few minutes ago," he said.

"And?" Travis asked.

Brodie turned back to the computer, found the file and opened it. "I forwarded the whole thing to you, but the gist of it is, she thinks now that Alex is working alone, and he knows we know his identity, that's increasing the pressure on him. He's likely to kill more often and perhaps take more risks. He's trying to relieve the pressure and attempting to prove to us and to himself that we can't stop him."

"We have to find him in order to stop him," Travis said. "Does the profiler have any idea where he's likely to be hiding?"

"She doesn't mention that," Brodie said. "I'm still hoping Emily will come up with some ideas."

Travis shook his head. "I don't think my sister can help us with this one. We're going to have to keep looking and hope we catch a break."

"I've been working on trying to track Renee Parmenter," Brodie said. "It looks like she bought gas here in town, charging it to her credit card, the afternoon she disappeared. After that, there's nothing."

"Maybe she ran into Alex at the gas station, or he flagged down her car on the side of the road and she stopped because she recognized him," Travis said. "He asked her to give him a lift and he killed her."

"And then what?" Brodie asked. "Did he hide her car with the body? He's never done that before."

Travis rubbed his chin. "Hiding her doesn't fit with what we know about him, either," he said. "Alex wants us to know he's killed these women—that he got away with another murder. He wants to rub it in our faces that we aren't even slowing him down."

"He and Tim kidnapped Jamie and her sister and planned to kill them later," Brodie said. "Maybe that's a new MO for him."

"They kidnapped Jamie's sister in order to lure Jamie to them," Travis said. "Tim told her they wanted to kill a deputy as a way of getting to me. Fortunately, she was able to fight off Tim until we got to her."

"If Alex did kidnap Renee, he'd have to keep her somewhere," Brodie said. "We should consider that when we're focusing on places he might be hiding."

The phone on Brodie's desk beeped. He picked it up and Adelaide said, "Is the sheriff in there with you?"

"Yes."

"I've got a caller on the line who wants to talk to him. They were pretty insistent that I had to put them through to Travis. They won't give a name and I can't tell if it's a man or a woman."

"You record the incoming calls, right?" Brodie asked.

"Of course."

"Travis is right here." Brodie hit the button to put the call on speaker and handed the handset to Travis.

"Hello? This is Sheriff Walker."

After a second's pause, a wavery voice came on

the line. "I saw that girl you're looking for. She was hitchhiking on Dixon Pass. That's a dangerous thing to do, hitchhiking."

Travis's eyes met Brodie's. He could tell the sheriff was thinking the same thing he was—how did the caller know about Renee when the story hadn't even come out yet in the paper? "Who is calling?" Travis asked. "When did you see this hitchhiker?"

"Oh, it was a couple of days ago." The man... woman...sounded frail and uncertain. "I just wanted you to know."

"Could you describe her for me, please?" Travis asked. "And tell me exactly where you saw her."

But the call had already ended. Brodie took the handset and replaced it. "I'll contact the phone company and see if they can tell us anything about who made the call," he said.

Travis nodded. "I'd bet my next paycheck they don't find anything," he said. "I don't think that was a random Good Samaritan."

"Me, either," Brodie agreed. "Alex Woodruff is used to acting. It might not be too difficult for him to disguise his voice."

"Yes. Maybe he's annoyed that we haven't found Renee's body yet and decided to give us a hint."

"Or maybe he's set a trap."

"Come on," Travis said. "Let's go up to Dixon Pass and find out."

Chapter Ten

On the way up to the pass, Travis called Gage and let him know where they were headed and why. "I don't want the whole department up there in case this is a false alarm," Travis told his brother. "And I also don't put it past Alex to do something like this to draw us away from town. Just be alert if you don't hear from us in twenty minutes or so."

"Will do," Gage said. "But if that was Alex calling to give you a clue as to where to find Renee's body, it was a pretty vague one. Where are you going to look?"

"I have some ideas."

They parked Travis's sheriff's department SUV, which still bore faint traces of Alex's graffiti on the driver's side, at the barricades two-thirds of the way up the pass. They walked the rest of the way, past two dump trucks waiting to carry away loads of snow and an idling front-end loader. Travis stopped at the post that indicated the turnoff to the former ski area, most of the old road now buried under the avalanche that had almost killed Brodie and Gage. "The highway crews were able to clear this section of road pretty quickly," he said. "Apparently, most of the snow that came down was below this point."

"I still wonder what set off the slide," Brodie said. "Gage and I thought we heard a gunshot right before it came down."

"The road crew swears they had nothing to do with it," Travis said. "They were on a break when the avalanche happened. They don't remember seeing anyone around the road who wasn't supposed to be here, either."

Brodie continued to stare down at the river of snow. Sometimes things happened for no discernable reason, but the investigator in him didn't easily accept that.

"Gage said you didn't see anything suspicious down there before the slide," Travis said.

"No. It didn't look like anyone had been around for a while. I didn't see anywhere Alex might have been hiding—though we weren't able to get down there to take a closer look at the buildings. But if we couldn't get down there, neither could Alex, so I'd rule him out."

"Let's find someone to talk to about Renee Parmenter." They set out walking again. When they rounded the next curve, they could see a wall of blinding white, easily fifteen feet high, obliterating the roadway. A massive rotary snowblower was slowly chewing its way through the wall, sending a great plume of snow into the canyon below.

A man in a hard hat, blaze-orange vest over his parka, approached. "What can I do for you officers?" he asked.

"We're looking for a missing woman," Travis said.

The man scratched his head under the hard hat. "We haven't seen any women around here."

"What about cars?" Brodie asked. "Do you ever come across cars buried under these avalanches?"

"Sometimes. But we usually know they're there going in because someone reports it. If there was a driver or passenger in the vehicle, emergency services would have already worked to dig them out, and they usually flag the car for us so we can work around it. Hitting one could wreck a plow, but our guys watch out. There are all kinds of hazards that come down with the slides—rocks, trees. Once we found a dead elk."

"You might want to keep an eye out for a car up here," Travis said.

"What makes you think your missing woman is up here?" the man asked.

"We got a call," Travis said. "She's been missing since Monday—before the slide."

The man nodded. "Okay. We'll keep our eyes open."

He walked away and Travis and Brodie stood for a few minutes longer, watching the steady progress of the blower, until Brodie's ears rang with the sounds of the machinery. "Let's get out of here!" he shouted to be heard above the din. The noise, the endless snow and the eeriness of a highway with no traffic were beginning to get to him. Or maybe he was just twitchy after almost being buried alive in an avalanche.

Back in Travis's SUV, the sheriff didn't immediately start the vehicle. "If Alex killed Renee Parmenter, I have to believe he chose her because she knew him and was inclined to trust him," he said. "He took advantage of their previous relationship."

"Same with Denise Switcher," Brodie said. "She knew him from the university, so was more likely to stop when he flagged her down. He doesn't have Tim to help him lure and subdue his victims, so he's searching for easier prey—women who are more inclined to trust him."

Travis turned to Brodie. "Who else does he know who might trust him?" he asked. "Answer that question and we might be able to figure out who his next victim will be."

"We could start by interviewing single women in town, find out who else he—or Tim—might have dated in the weeks they've been here," Brodie said.

"Emily mentioned a woman he dated in Fort Collins," Travis said. "She dropped him because he wanted to strangle her while they were having sex."

Brodie scowled. "Maybe he planned to keep on choking her until she was dead." The more he learned about Alex, the greater his urgency to stop him.

"I'll ask to dig a little deeper. Maybe he had another girlfriend who came here for a visit and we haven't heard about her yet." He started the SUV and pulled out to turn around. But before he could make the turn, the man in the hard hat and orange vest ran toward them, waving his arms. Travis stopped and rolled down his window. "What is it?" he asked.

The man stopped beside the SUV, hands on his knees, panting. "We…found something," he gasped. "A car. And there's a woman inside."

"Poor Ruth." Emily's first thought on hearing of Renee Parmenter's death was of her sister. Yes, Renee had suffered at the hands of a murderer, but Ruth had to live with the knowledge that the person she loved had been taken so brutally. "I guess there's no doubt Renee was murdered?"

"No," Travis said. "She was killed just like the others."

"Alex even left his Ice Cold calling card," Brodie said. He and Travis flanked Emily on the living room sofa. A fire crackled in the woodstove across from them and a pile of wedding gifts that had been delivered when the road reopened waited on a table against the wall. Everything looked so ordinary and peaceful, which made the news of Renee's murder all the more disorienting.

"Have you told Ruth yet?" Emily asked.

"No," Travis said. "I was on my way there after I talked to you."

"I want to go with you," she said. "Maybe it will make it a little easier on her if she has a friend there."

"I was hoping you'd say that," Travis said. He stood. "Let's go see Ruth. If we wait too long, she might hear about this from someone else, and we don't want that."

By the time Ruth answered Travis's knock, Emily could see she had prepared herself for the worst. Her gaze slid past Emily and fixed on Travis. "Have you found her?" she asked, her voice tight, as if she had to force the words out.

"May we come in?" he asked.

She stepped back to let them pass. The house was an older one, with nineties-era blond wood and brass fixtures, the room cluttered with toys and shoes and a pile of laundry on one end of the sofa. A large window looked out onto pastures and hayfields, now covered with snow. "The kids are in school and my husband is out checking fences," Ruth said as she led the way to the sofa. She moved a child's book off the sofa and picked up a pillow from the floor, then sat, holding the pillow in her lap. "Tell me what you've found. It can't be anything worse than I've already imagined."

Travis removed his hat and sat across from Ruth while Emily settled in next to her. "We found your sister's body at the top of Dixon Pass, in her car," Travis said. "She was murdered—probably by Alex Woodruff."

Ruth made a short, sharp sound and covered her mouth with her hand. Emily took her other hand and squeezed it. Ruth held on tightly and uncovered her mouth. "When?" she asked.

"The car was buried by the avalanche that closed the road on Tuesday morning," Travis said. "She was killed before then."

Ruth closed her eyes, visibly pulling herself together. "Is there someone you'd like me to call?" Emily asked. "Your husband, or a friend?"

"Bob will be in soon." She opened her eyes, which shone with unshed tears. "If you know who did this, why don't you arrest him and stop him?" she asked.

"When we find Alex, we'll arrest him," Travis said. "Do you have any idea where he might be hiding? That night you and your husband met him, did he say anything at all that might give us a clue?"

She shook her head. "I'm sorry. We talked about school and the dance and the weather—just ordinary small talk among people who didn't know each other well."

"And you're sure Renee never mentioned seeing or talking to him after that night?" Travis asked.

"No. I really don't think she heard from him or saw him after that one date," Ruth said.

"You said you didn't like him," Travis said. "Maybe knowing that, she decided not to talk about him."

"Renee wasn't like that," Ruth said. "If she liked

someone and I didn't, she would have made a point of mentioning him, just to give me a hard time." She shook her head. "She was really definite about not wanting to see him again. If he had called and asked her out again, she would have been on the phone to me as soon as she hung up with him." Her breath caught, and she swallowed, then added, her voice fainter, "That's how we were. We talked about everything."

"I'm very sorry for your loss," Travis said. He stood, hat in hand. "Once the medical examiner has completed his autopsy, we'll release the body to the funeral home of your choice. Call my office if you have any questions."

Ruth stood and walked with them to the door. "Are you sure you don't want me to stay until your husband gets here?" Emily asked.

"I'll be okay." She took a shuddering breath. "I do better with this kind of stuff on my own—but thank you."

Emily squeezed her arm. "Call me if you need anything. Or if you just want to talk."

Ruth nodded, then looked at Travis again. "You'll find him and stop him, won't you?" she asked, the words more plea than query.

"Yes," he said.

He and Emily didn't say anything until they were almost back to the sheriff's department. "Denise was killed the same day," Emily said. "Right before the avalanche. And her car was found at the top of the pass."

"The first two murders—Kelly Farrow and Christy O'Brien—happened within hours of each other," Travis said.

"I think he gets a charge out of getting away with not one, but two killings," Emily said.

"The profiler from the Colorado Bureau of Investigation said he's feeling more pressure from us now that we know his identity," Travis said. "She believes he'll continue to kill, as a way to relieve the pressure."

Emily nodded. "Yes, that sounds right. And he wants to prove that he can still get away with the crimes—that you'll never catch him."

"He's by himself," Travis said. "Wherever he's hiding can't be that comfortable. We're doing everything we can to alert other people that he's dangerous, so he can't move safely around town, or rely on others for help. He's going to run out of victims he can fool also. We're going to run him to ground."

"I've been thinking," Emily said. "Maybe I can help you find him."

"Have you thought of someplace he might be hiding?"

"No. But he knows me. Maybe I could lure him out of hiding by agreeing to meet him."

"No." Travis didn't look at her, but the muscles along his jaw tightened.

"I'm serious," she said. Her brother wasn't the only stubborn member of this family. "I've lost too many friends to this man. I'll do whatever I can to stop him." Alex was a killer, but she knew him. Maybe she could get to him when no one else could.

Chapter Eleven

"Over my dead body."

So what if it was a cliché? Brodie thought, as soon as he had uttered those words. Travis's announcement that Emily wanted to try to lure Alex to her had prompted a visceral reaction that went beyond coherent speech. The thought of her anywhere near that monster made his blood freeze.

"I already told her the idea was out of the question," Travis said.

"It's a stupid idea." Brodie dropped into the chair across from Travis's desk at the sheriff's department, not sure if his legs were steady enough yet for him to remain standing. "What makes her think he'd come anywhere near her?"

"She fits the profile of the other women he's murdered," Travis said. "Alex knows her. And she's my sister. He's made it clear he enjoys getting back at me and my department—it's why he went after Jamie."

"How can you even look at this logically?" Brodie groused. "She's your sister."

"I made it clear it wasn't going to happen," he said.

"We don't even know where he is," Brodie said.

"What was she going to do—put an ad in the paper asking him to meet her? He'd see that as a trap right away."

"Maybe. Or maybe he'd be too tempted by the chance to get at her."

Brodie glared at the sheriff. "You've actually considered this, haven't you? You've run all the possibilities through your head."

Travis shifted in his chair. "It's not going to happen," he said again. "But if anyone is to blame for her coming up with the idea, it's you."

"Me?"

"You're the one who asked her to help with the case. You gave her the idea that she knows Alex better than anyone, and that her insight could help."

"Insight. Her thoughts. I never meant for her to put her life on the line—or anything close to it."

"I know. And I know she really wants to help. But this isn't the way to do it."

Brodie slid down farther in his chair. "I think this case is getting to us all."

Deputy Dwight Prentice stopped in the doorway to the office. "Abel Crutchfield just called in with a tip we ought to check out," he said.

"Who is Abel Crutchfield?" Brodie asked.

"He's a retired guy, spends a lot of time ice fishing in the area," Travis said. "He was the first one to report a blonde woman hanging around near where Michaela Underwood was murdered. That woman turned out to be Tim Dawson in disguise."

Brodie nodded and sat up straighter. "What's the tip?"

"He says he saw smoke coming from some caves over by Eagle Creek," Dwight said. "Like someone was camping up there. He figured we might want to check it out."

"Take Brodie over there with you and have a look," Travis said. "But call for backup if it looks like anyone is up there."

"Right." Brodie rose. "Much as I'd like to get hold of this guy, better not try to do it by ourselves."

"We should be able to get a good look from across the way," Dwight said. "Enough to see if it's worth going in. Maybe Abel just saw snow blowing off trees and mistook it for smoke."

The drive to Eagle Creek took twenty minutes, most of it on narrow, snow-packed forest service roads. "It doesn't look as if anyone lives out here," Brodie said, staring out at the landscape of snowy woodland.

"They don't," Dwight said. "This is all forest service land. A few snowmobilers or cross-country skiers use the road, and ice fishermen like Abel."

"Sounds like a good place for someone to hide out if he didn't want to be seen," Brodie said.

The caves themselves sat above the river in a limestone formation, centuries of dripping water having hollowed out the rock to form the openings. "Most of these caves are pretty shallow," Dwight said as he led the way through the snow along the riverbank. "There are only a couple that are deep enough to provide any real shelter."

"Deep enough to live in?" Brodie asked.

"Maybe. It wouldn't be very comfortable. You'd have to have a fire to keep from freezing to death, and there would be a lot of smoke and dampness. Not to mention bats, bugs and wild animals."

"It doesn't sound like Alex Woodruff's kind of

place," Brodie said. "He struck me as someone who likes his creature comforts."

"Yeah, but he's desperate now. He can't be as choosy."

They halted on a bench of land across the river from the largest opening. Dwight dug out a pair of binoculars and trained them on the cave. "The snow around the opening is churned up," he said. "Someone—or something—has been going in and out of there." He shifted the binoculars. "And there's a definite path leading up there."

Brodie sniffed the air. "I can smell smoke—like a campfire."

Dwight handed him the binoculars. "There's no smoke coming from there right now."

Brodie focused the glasses on the cave opening. It was impossible to see into the dark space, but there was definitely no movement at the entrance. He returned the binoculars to Dwight. "What do you think we should do now?"

"I'd like to get a little closer before we call in the cavalry," Dwight said. "We can approach from below and anyone inside wouldn't be able to see us until we were almost on him."

"Sounds good to me."

It took twenty minutes to retrace their steps along the river, negotiating over icy rock and snow-covered deadfall. They had to walk farther downstream to find a place to cross—a bridge of felled trees that required stepping carefully and balancing like a tightrope walker. But when they reached the other side, they found the worn path through the snow that they had glimpsed from the other side.

Weapons drawn, they moved cautiously up the path. The rushing water tumbling over rocks and downed trees drowned out all other sound. Dwight took the lead, while Brodie covered him, staying several yards behind. They reached a series of rock steps that led up to the cave and halted. "Let me go up first, while you stay down here," Dwight whispered. "I should be able to get right up on the entrance without being seen. You come up after me and we'll flank the entrance and demand whoever is in there to come out. If we don't get an answer, we'll shine a light in, maybe try to draw his fire."

Brodie agreed and Dwight started up, keeping close to the cliff side, placing each step carefully, the rush of the water below drowning out his approach. When he was safely up the steps and stationed on the left side of the cave entrance, he motioned for Brodie to follow.

Brodie moved up more quickly and took up a position on the opposite side of the cave entrance. "Is anyone in there?" Dwight called.

The words bounced off the canyon walls and echoed back at them, but no sound came from the cave.

"This is the Rayford County Sheriff's Department!" Dwight called. "You need to come out with your hands up!"

No answer or movement. Dwight unsnapped his flashlight from his utility belt and trained the powerful beam into the cave entrance. A rock fire ring sat about two feet inside, full of dark ash and a couple of pieces of charred wood. Brodie stooped, picked up a rock and tossed it inside the cave. It bounced off the stone floor and rolled toward the back, then all was silent again.

Dwight's eyes met Brodie's. He jerked his head toward the cave and indicated he was going in. Brodie nodded. Instincts could be wrong, but it didn't feel to him as if anyone was in there. Dwight swung the flashlight in ahead of him, then entered the cave, staying close to the wall. He had to duck to enter. Weapon ready, Brodie watched him disappear from sight.

"Come on in!" Dwight called a few seconds later. "There's no one in here."

Brodie unhooked his own flashlight and followed Dwight into the cave. He swept the light over the mostly empty space, coming to rest on a pile of garbage in the corner—tin cans, beer bottles and food wrappers. He moved closer to the fire. "Someone was here for a while," he said. "And not that long ago."

"The ashes in the firepit are still warm." Dwight crouched beside the rock ring and held his hand over the charred wood.

Brodie holstered his gun and played the flashlight over the scuffed dirt on the floor of the cave. The space was maybe ten feet deep and eight feet wide, tall enough to stand up in, but barely, with a ceiling of smoke-blackened rock and a dirt floor. It smelled of smoke, stale food and animal droppings. "Not exactly the Ritz," he said.

"No one would be camping here in the middle of winter unless he had to," Dwight said. "It has to be Alex."

Brodie trained his light on the garbage pile again. "He's buying food somewhere." He nudged a beer bottle with his toe. "Lots of craft beer, chips and canned pasta."

"That sounds like a college guy's diet," Dwight said. "If he's shopping, someone in Eagle Mountain must have seen him," Brodie said. "Why haven't they re-ported him to the sheriff's department?"

"He could be breaking into summer cabins," Dwight said. "Or shopping at the grocery store wearing a disguise."

"If he was here this morning, it doesn't look as if he intends to return," Brodie said. "There's no sleeping bag, no stash of food—not even any firewood."

"We'll watch the place for a couple of days, see if he comes back," Dwight said. "But I agree—it looks like he's cleared out. Maybe he saw Abel looking up this way and decided to leave."

"There's not much here, but we'd better look through it, see if we can find anything significant," Brodie said. He smoothed on a pair of gloves and began sifting through the garbage, while Dwight examined the firepit. He combed through half a dozen beer bottles, two empty ravioli cans, several candy bar wrappers and two chip bags, but found nothing that told them where Alex might be now. They took photographs and bagged everything as evidence. They might be able to get DNA off the beer bottles that would prove Alex was the person who had hidden in this cave, but Brodie didn't see how that would be useful in their case against him.

"I may have found something," Dwight said. He used a pen to lift something from the ashes and held it aloft. Brodie recognized the coiled binding of a pocket-size notebook. "The cover is gone, and the edge of the pages are charred, but most of it's intact," Dwight said. He spread the notebook on the ground and Brodie joined him in leaning over it. Dwight flipped through the pages, which appeared to contain everything from grocery lists—*chips, lunch meat, cookies, soda, razor*—to cryptic numbers and calculations. Most of the pages were blank.

"We'll have to go through this at the office and see if there's anything significant," Dwight said. He reached into his coat and pulled out a plastic evidence bag.

Brodie continued to flip through the pages. He found what looked like phone numbers, notes on what might have been climbing routes, then stopped on a page that was simply a column of letters—*KF, CO, FW, LG, AA, MU, TP, DD, JD, LW, RP, DS, EW.*

"What have you got there?" Dwight asked. "Are they some kind of abbreviations? For what?"

Brodie repeated the letters under his breath, then stopped in mid-syllable as the realization of what they represented hit him. "They're initials," he said. "Of all the women he's killed."

"Kelly Farrow, Christy O'Brien, Fiona Winslow, Lauren Grenado, Anita Allbritton, Michaela Underwood, Lynn Wallace, Renee Parmenter and Denise Switcher," Dwight said. "There's a line through *TP*— Tammy Patterson. She got away from him. Another line through *DD* and *JD*—Donna and Jamie Douglas. They escaped, too."

"They're in order of the attacks," Brodie said. "He must have killed Renee before Denise." He frowned at the last letters on the page. "Who is *EW*?"

"Is there a victim we haven't found yet?" Dwight asked. "Or someone he's gone after today?"

Brodie stood, his stomach heaving and a chill sweeping through him. "*EW* could be Emily Walker."

He clapped Dwight on the shoulder and shoved the notebook toward him. "Bag that and let's get out of here. We have to make sure Emily is all right."

Chapter Twelve

"I'm fine, and I think you're both overreacting." Emily had been up to her eyeballs in surveys to review when Brodie and Travis had burst in on her late Friday afternoon, demanding to know what she was doing and if she had talked to or seen Alex Woodruff. "Alex hasn't been anywhere near here, and as for what I'm doing, I'm working. And I don't need you interrupting."

"You could be in danger," Brodie said. "Promise me you won't go anywhere without me or Travis or Gage with you."

"What are you talking about?" She turned to Travis. "Why are you both here this time of day? What's happened?"

Travis pulled a plastic evidence envelope from his coat and held it out to her. "Brodie and Dwight found this in a cave over by Eagle Creek," he said. "We think it belongs to Alex."

She studied the half-charred notebook, and the list of letters inscribed on the page in front of her. "What does this have to do with me?"

"The letters on that page are the initials of the women Alex killed," he said. His face was pale and drawn, like a man in pain. "The crossed-out letters are the three women who got away."

She read through the list again and nodded. "All right. I can see that."

"The last letters are *EW,*" Brodie said. He put a hand on her shoulder. "Emily Walker."

This announcement elicited an astonished laugh from her. "*EW* could stand for anything," she said. "Ellen White. Elaine Wilson—there are a lot of women with those initials."

"What were those names again?" Brodie had pulled out a notebook and pen and was poised to write. "We'll need to check on those women, as well."

She shifted in her seat. "I don't actually know any women with those names," Emily said. "I was just giving you examples of women's names with those initials."

"We'll research tax rolls and any other records we can find for women with the initials *EW,*" Travis said. "But we wanted to be sure you're all right."

"I'm fine." Some of her annoyance receded, replaced by a cold undercurrent of fear. She thought Brodie and Travis were overreacting—but what if they weren't? "I'm smart enough to stay far away from Alex Woodruff," she said.

"Last I heard, you were volunteering to lure him to you," Brodie said.

"I did. But Travis persuaded me that was a bad idea." She shrugged. "It wouldn't work without the sheriff's department's cooperation. I mean, I'm not misguided enough to try to do something like that without a whole bunch of law enforcement watching my back."

Some of the tension went out of his shoulders. "I'm relieved you're all right," he said.

His real concern for her touched her, so that she had to look away. She focused on Travis. "I'm fine. It was sweet of you to worry, but don't."

"What are you doing the rest of the day?" Brodie asked.

She really wanted to tell him that was none of his business, but that would only lead to another argument. The man never took no for an answer. "Since the favors for the wedding didn't get here while the highway was open, a bunch of us are getting together with Lacy in a little while to make everything she needs. We're going to do crafts, drink wine, eat a lot of good things and stay right here on the ranch."

"Good." Travis tucked the evidence bag back into his pocket. "Don't say anything about this to anyone."

She shook her head. "Of course not."

"Come on, Brodie. Let's see about those other women."

They turned to leave, but she stopped them. "Did you say you found that in a cave?" she asked.

Travis nodded. "It looked like Alex had spent at least a couple of nights there, though he isn't there now. We've got a reserve deputy watching the place, in case he returns."

She wrinkled her nose. "That doesn't sound very comfortable—not like Alex."

"We agree," Brodie said. "It shows how desperate he's getting. The pressure on him is increasing."

"Then he's liable to become even more violent and unpredictable," she said.

"He's more likely to make mistakes," Travis said. "We're going to take advantage of that."

"Be careful," she said, but the two men were already turning away again.

She tried to put their visit, and the disturbing news about the list of initials, out of her mind and return her focus to the student surveys. But that proved impossible. She kept repeating the names of the murdered women, and picturing that *EW* at the bottom of the list. Surely that didn't stand for Emily Walker, but the idea that it *might* definitely shook her.

Travis and Brodie and Gage and her family and friends and everyone else she knew would protect her. They formed a living barricade between her body and anyone who might try to harm her. But could they really keep Alex away? He had proved so sly and elusive, slipping in and out of crime scenes unseen, leaving scarcely a trace of evidence. Every law enforcement officer in the county had been tracking him for weeks, yet they hadn't even touched him. Could he somehow get past all her defenses and take her down when she least expected it?

She shuddered and pushed the thought away. Alex wasn't a mythical boogeyman who could walk through walls. He was flesh and blood and as vulnerable as anyone. And she was safe. She was smart and wary and protected by all those who loved her.

She didn't believe Brodie loved her—not in the way she had once wanted him to. But she believed he would protect her. He might be glibly charming and socially superficial at times, but he took his duty as an officer of the law seriously. She tried to take comfort from that.

She was grateful when Lacy came to her and asked

for help setting up for their get-together with the other women in the wedding party. "This is so nice of everyone to help," Lacy said as she and Emily and Bette set out craft supplies and readied the refreshments.

"You deserve every bit of help we can give," Bette said, arranging paintbrushes at each place setting down the long dining room table, which had been spread with brown paper to protect its polished wood surface. "Besides, this is going to be fun."

At six o'clock, the other women began arriving: Lacy's mother and all the bridesmaids—Brenda Prentice, Gage's wife, Maya Renfro, and Paige Riddell— as well as wedding guests veterinarian Darcy Marsh, Deputy Jamie Douglas and her sister, Donna. Along with Emily, Travis's mom and Bette, they made a lively party. "We're going to be decorating fancy sugar cookies," Bette explained, passing a plate of cookies shaped liked butterflies and birds. "We're using colored frosting that's the consistency of paint. Use your paintbrushes to decorate the cookies however you wish. When the cookies are dry, we'll package them up with fancy wrappings."

"I'm not very artistic," Jamie said, looking doubtful. "What if my cookies turn out ugly?"

"Then we can eat them," Donna said, sending a ripple of laughter around the table.

"I don't know," Maya said. "That might be an incentive to mess up."

"They'll turn out great," Bette said. "And when we're done, we have more cookies and plenty of other yummy party food."

Emily dipped her paintbrush in a small pot of yellow icing and began to decorate a butterfly. Though she had never considered herself an artist, the results of her efforts pleased her. "Everyone is going to love these," she said.

"Probably more than the drink cozies and pens I ordered," Lacy said. She held up a purple humming-bird. "I kind of like the reminder of spring amid all this snow."

"The weather is breaking all kinds of records this year," Darcy said. "Ryder says no one he works with can remember the highway closing so often and for so long due to avalanches and the sheer volume of snow."

"The science classes have been measuring snow amounts and tracking the weather data," Maya, a high school teacher, said. "Word is forecasts look promis-ing for a shift in the weather to a drier pattern. That will give the snow time to settle and the highway de-partment to get the roads in good shape to stay open."

"That's good news." Emily turned to Lacy. "You shouldn't have any trouble getting away for your hon-eymoon."

"Travis has to catch the Ice Cold Killer first," Lacy said. "He'll never leave town with the case still open. I'll be lucky to drag him to the altar for a few hours."

"We're getting close," Jamie said. "Now that we have a good idea who the killer is, we have everyone in the county looking for him. Someone is going to see Alex and tip us off in time to arrest him."

"I just pray they find him before he kills someone else," Bette said. The others murmured agreement.

"Do any of you know a woman in town with the initials *EW*?" Emily asked. She had promised not to tell anyone about the notebook with Alex's supposed list—but that didn't mean she couldn't do a little digging of her own.

"You mean besides you?" Lacy asked. "Why?"

She shrugged. "No reason. Just wondering."

"That's not the kind of question a person asks for no reason," Brenda said. "What's going on? Does this have something to do with Alex?"

Emily grappled for some plausible story. "I, um, saw the initials in graffiti on the bathroom stall at Mo's Pub," she said. "I was just curious." She hoped the others didn't think the story was as lame as it sounded to her.

"There's Ellie Watkins," Maya said. "But she's only six—a classmate of my niece, Casey. So I don't think anyone would be writing about her on bathroom walls."

"Elaine Wulf is one of the museum volunteers," said Brenda, who managed the local history museum. "But she's at least eighty and I can't think she'd have been up to anything that would warrant writing about it on a bathroom wall."

The others laughed and Emily forced a weak smile. "It was probably only a tourist, then. Never mind."

"What did the message say?" Lacy asked. "It must have been pretty juicy if you're asking about it now."

"Oh, it was nothing." She held up her finished butterfly. "What do you think?"

They all complimented her and began showing off their own work, but Emily was aware of Lacy eyeing her closely.

When the women took a break to eat, Lacy pulled Emily aside. "What is going on?" she asked. "What was all that about a woman with the initials *EW*? And don't give me that lame story about graffiti in the restroom at Mo's Pub. There is no graffiti there. Mo wouldn't allow it."

Emily chewed her lip. "You have to promise not to let Travis know I told you this," she said.

"I can keep a secret—within reason."

"Dwight and Brodie checked out a cave where Alex might have been camping. They found a half-burned notebook in the fire ring. In it was a list of initials that matched the initials of all the women he's killed—or attempted to kill. The last set of initials on the list was *EW*."

Lacy's face paled. "Emily Walker—you!"

"It's not me!" Emily protested. "I mean, I'm not dead, and Alex hasn't tried to get to me, so it must be someone else. I was trying to figure out who it might be."

"I'm sure Travis is looking for her, too."

"Of course he is. I just thought with a room full of women here, someone might know a woman with those initials that Travis could check on—just to make sure she's all right."

Lacy rubbed her hands up and down her arms. "I hate to think the killer is out there stalking another woman."

"And I hate that I've upset you." Emily put her arm around her friend. "Come on. Let's go back to the others and do our best not to think about this anymore. Think about your wedding and how wonderful it's going to be when you and Travis are married."

For the rest of the evening, Emily did her best to put Alex out of her mind. She ate and drank, and listened as the married women in the group told stories of their own weddings—Travis's father had apparently been late to the altar because he got lost on the way to the church, and Lacy's father had proposed by hiding an engagement ring in a piece of cheesecake…and her mother had almost swallowed it.

After they ate, Bette led them in making wedding-themed wreaths to hang on all the outside doors of the ranch house, as well as the doors of the four guest cabins. They wrapped grapevine wreaths in white tulle and silver ribbon and added glittered snowflakes and feathers. The end result was surprisingly delicate and beautiful.

They wrapped the cookies and placed them in baskets, to be handed out at the wedding in two days. "They look like little works of art," Maya said.

"Definitely too pretty to eat," Brenda said.

"You have to eat them," Bette said. "They're delicious."

"They were!" Donna said. She, like everyone else, had eaten her share of "mistakes."

After everyone had left, Emily volunteered to help Bette hang the wreaths. "I'll get the cabins, if you'll do the doors in the house," she said, draping four of the wreaths over one arm.

The four guest cabins sat between the house and the barn, along a stone path through the snow. The porch lights of each cabin cast golden pools across the drifted snow, islands in the darkness that she headed for, the chill night air stinging her cheeks and turning her breath into frosty clouds around her head. Emily hung a wreath on each door, smiling at how festive each one looked. The last cabin in the row—the one farthest from the house—was where Brodie was staying. Emily approached it quietly, not anxious to disturb him. He'd been hovering over her even more than her brothers and all the attention made her uncomfortable. The sooner the case was solved and the wedding was over, the better for all of them. Brodie could go back to Denver, she'd return to Fort Collins and everyone could go about life as it had been before.

She hooked the wreath on the nail in the cabin's door and stepped back to make sure it wasn't crooked. Satisfied, she started to turn away, but the door opened and Brodie reached out and took hold of her arm. "Come inside," he said. "We need to talk."

She could have argued that she didn't want to talk to him, but arguing with Brodie never went well. He was too stubborn and determined to be right. If he had something he wanted to say to her, she might as well hear him out now. And then she'd make him listen to a few things she needed to say, too.

Once inside, he released his hold on her and she sat in the room's single chair, while he settled on the side of the bed. He didn't say anything right away, merely looked at her—or rather, looked through her, as if he was searching for some unspoken message in her face. "What did you want to talk about?" she asked, forcing herself to sit still and not fidget.

"Why did you turn down my proposal?" he asked.

She frowned. "Your proposal?"

"I asked you to marry me and you said no."

She couldn't have been more stunned if he had slapped her. "Brodie, that was five years ago."

"Yes, and it's been eating at me ever since. I figured it was past time we cleared the air between us."

Maybe he thought that was a good idea, but did she? Was she ready to share with Brodie all she'd been through—and maybe find out he'd known about her troubles all along? That he had received the letter she had sent to him, and chosen not to get involved? She pressed her lips together, searching for the right words. "I turned you down because I wasn't ready to get married yet—and neither were you."

"You said you loved me."

"I did! But marriage takes more than love. I was only nineteen—I had so many other things I needed to do first."

"What other things?"

Maybe he should have asked these questions five years ago, but he was asking them now, and maybe answering them would help her put herself back in that time and her mind-set then. "I was only a sophomore in college. I knew I needed to finish my education and get established in my career before I married."

"Why? Lots of people get married while they're still in school. I wouldn't have held you back."

"You would have, even if you didn't intend to." She shifted in her chair, trying to find the words to make him see. "You know my family places a lot of value on education and being successful in whatever you choose to do," she said.

"I think most families are like that," he said.

"Yes, but mine especially so. My mother has a PhD, did you know that? In entomology. And my father has built the Walking W into one of the largest and most successful ranches in the state. Travis is the youngest sheriff our county has ever had, and Gage is a decorated officer with a wall full of commendations."

"I wouldn't have held you back," he said again.

"You were established in a job that could require

you to move across the state at any time," she said. "In fact, you did move, right after we broke up."

"The department takes spouse's jobs into consideration," he said, for all the world as if he was making an argument all over again for her to marry him.

"You weren't ready to settle down," she said. "Not really."

"How do you know?" he asked.

She straightened. Why not come out and say what she had been thinking? "If you really loved me so much, you would have tried harder to persuade me to accept your proposal. Instead, after I said no, you simply walked away."

He stood and began to pace, his boot heels striking hard on the wood floor. "Did you really expect me to browbeat you into changing your decision—or worse, to beg?" He raked a hand through his hair and whirled to face her. "Did you ever think that I didn't walk away because I didn't love you, but because I respected you enough to know your own mind?"

His words—and the emotion behind them—hit her like a blow, knocking the breath from her. "I… I still don't think we were ready to marry," she managed to stammer. "So many other things could have happened to tear us apart."

"Like what?" His gaze burned into her, daring her to look away. "What would be so bad our love wouldn't have been enough to overcome it?"

She wet her lips and pushed on. "What if I'd gotten pregnant?"

"We'd have been careful, taken precautions."

"We didn't always do that before, did we?"

He stared at her, and she saw doubt crowd out defiance. He studied her, eyes full of questions. "Emily, is there something you're not telling me?" he asked, his voice so low she had to lean forward to catch all his words.

She was not going to cry. If she started, she might never stop. "I told you I wrote to you after you moved," she said, speaking slowly and carefully.

"And I told you, I never received your letter." He sank onto the edge of the bed once more, as if his legs would no longer support him. "Did you really think I would ignore you?"

"I didn't know. I didn't know what to think."

"What did the letter say?"

She sighed. Did this really matter now? It did to her—but would it to him? "After you left, I found out I was pregnant," she said.

"Emily." Just her name, said so softly, with such tenderness and sorrow the sound almost broke her. She blinked furiously, but couldn't hold back the tears. "My parents, of course, were very upset. Travis was furious. He's the one who insisted I contact you, though at first I refused."

"Why didn't you want me to know?" he asked. "I would have done the right thing. I already wanted to marry you."

"That's exactly why I didn't want you to know," she said. "I was going to have a baby, but I still didn't want to be married. And I didn't want you to marry me because you had to. It felt like I was trapping you into something I couldn't believe was right for either one of us."

He leaned forward and took her hand, his fingers warm and gentle as he wrapped them around her palm.

"What happened to the baby?" He swallowed. "To our baby?"

"I'm getting to that." She took a deep breath, steadying herself, but not pulling away from him. "My father finally persuaded me that you had a right to know you were going to be a father. So I tried to call and your number had changed. I wrote and the first letter came back, so Travis got your information from the CBI. The second letter didn't come back. I thought that meant you'd received it and decided to ignore it."

"I never would have ignored it." He moved from the bed to his knees in front of her. "I wouldn't ignore you."

"I was going to try to contact you again, but then…" She swallowed again. "Then I lost the baby."

He said nothing, only squeezed her hand and put his other hand on her knee.

She closed her eyes, the sadness and confusion and, yes, relief of those days rising up in her once more like water filling a well. "The doctor said it wasn't anything I'd done—that these things just happen sometimes. I was sad, but relieved, too. I went back to school and went on with my life. We…we never talked about what had happened again."

"Did Gage know this?" he asked, thinking of his conversation with Gage at the bonfire.

She shook her head. "No. He was away at school and then summer school. He knew that something had happened with us, but he never knew about the baby. Just my parents and Travis. I— It felt easier, the fewer people who knew."

"I would have wanted to know." He stroked her arm. "I would have wanted to be there for you."

She nodded, crying quietly now, more comforted by his sympathy than she could have imagined.

"No wonder Travis insists on keeping everything strictly business between us. He thinks I deserted you and our baby when you needed me most." He looked her in the eye, his gaze searching. "I wouldn't have done that, Emily. Never in a million years. I'm sick, hearing about this now."

She put her hand on his shoulder. "I believe that now," she said. Now that she had seen the real pain in his eyes. "I'm glad you know the truth. But we can't go back and change the past. Both of us are different people now."

"Different," he said. "Yet the same." His eyes locked to hers and she felt a surge of emotion, like a wave crashing over her. Brodie still attracted her as no other man ever had. But she was no longer the naive, trusting girl she had been five years ago. She didn't believe in fairy tales, or that either she or Brodie were perfect for each other.

But she did believe in perfect moments, and seizing them. She leaned toward him, and he welcomed her into his arms. She closed her eyes and pressed her lips to his, losing herself in sensation—the scent of him, herbal soap and warm male; the reassuring strength of him, holding her so securely; the taste of him, faintly salty, as she broke the kiss to trace her tongue along his throat.

"I don't want to let you go just yet," he said.

"I'm not going anywhere." She kissed him again, arching her body to his.

"Stay with me tonight," he murmured, his lips caressing her ear.

"Yes." She began to unbutton his shirt, kissing each inch of skin as it was exposed, peeling back the fabric to expose muscular shoulders and a perfectly sculpted chest. She pressed her lips over one taut nipple and he groaned, then dragged her away and began tugging at her clothes.

She laughed as he fumbled with her bra strap. "I never could get the hang of these things," he muttered as she pushed his hands away and removed the garment herself.

Together, they finished undressing and moved to the bed, where they lay facing each other, hands and eyes exploring. "You're even more beautiful than I remember," he said as he traced the curve of her hip.

"Mmm." She kissed her way along his shoulder, smiling to herself as she thought that he was exactly as she remembered him—strong and male and exciting. He slid his hands up her thighs, calluses dragging on her smooth skin. The heat of his fingers pressed into her soft flesh, and into the wetness between her legs.

He leaned into her, the hard ridge of his erection against her stomach making her gasp. He caught the sound in his mouth, his lips closing hungrily over hers, his fingers moving higher, parting her hot folds.

She squirmed and moaned, the sound muffled by the liquid heat of his tongue tangling with her own. He dipped his head to kiss her breasts—butterfly touches of his lips over and around the swelling flesh—then latched onto her sensitive, distended nipple, sucking hard, the pulling sensation reaching all the way to her groin, where she tightened around his plunging finger.

He slid his finger out of her and gripped her thighs, spreading her wide, cool air rushing across her hot, wet flesh, sending a fresh wave of arousal through her. "What do you want?" he whispered, his voice rough, as if he was fighting for control.

"I want you."

He leaned across her and jerked open the drawer of the bedside table. When he returned, he had a condom packet in his hand. He ripped it open with his teeth and smoothed on the sheath, then pushed her gently onto her back. "Are you ready?"

She nodded. More than ready.

He drove hard, but held her so gently, his fingers stroking, caressing, even as his hips pumped. The sensation of him filling her, stretching her, moving inside her, made her dizzy. "Don't stop," she gasped. "Please don't stop."

"I won't stop. I promise I won't stop." She slid her hands around to cup his bottom, marveling at the feel of his muscles contracting and relaxing with each powerful thrust.

He slipped his hand between them and began to fondle her, each deft move sending the tension within her coiling tighter. He kissed the soft flesh at the base of her throat. "I want to make it good for you," he murmured. "So good."

She sensed him holding back, waiting for her. When her climax overtook her, he swallowed her cries, then mingled them with his own as his release shuddered through them both.

"I'm glad you stopped fighting this," he said.

"I wasn't fighting," she said.

"You kept pushing me away."

Only because he had such power over her—power to make her forget herself. She didn't trust his motives—or her own.

Chapter Thirteen

Emily woke the next morning with the sun in her eyes and a smile on her face. Last night with Brodie had been better than her best fantasies—and better than she remembered from their younger alliance. There was something to be said for a little maturity when it came to sex.

She had remembered to text Lacy before she went to sleep last night, letting her know she was tucked in safely for the night, in case her friend worried. But she hadn't mentioned she was spending the night with Brodie. For now, she wanted to keep that information to herself. But she supposed she should get back to her own cabin soon, in case someone came looking for her.

She rolled over to face Brodie, who lay asleep on his back, dark stubble emphasizing the strong line of his jaw, his sensuous lips slightly parted. She was just about to lean over and give him a big kiss when pounding on the door shook the cabin. "Brodie, wake up!" a man shouted.

Brodie sat up, instantly alert. "Who is it?" he called.

"It's Travis," Emily whispered, even as her brother identified himself.

"Quick, go in the bathroom." Brodie urged her toward the one interior door in the cabin, then swung his feet to the floor and reached for the jeans he'd discarded last night.

Emily gathered the sheet around her and shuffled to the bathroom, only partially closing the door and positioning herself so that she could see out. Brodie opened the door and Travis—scarily pressed and polished as always—said, "They've found Lynn Wallace's car."

"Where?" Brodie held the door partially closed and stepped back. Emily realized he was attempting to kick the clothing she had left on the floor under the bed.

Travis frowned and tried to move into the cabin, but Brodie blocked the move. "Never mind. You can give me all the details on the way there. Just give me a minute to get dressed."

Brodie tried to shut the door, but Travis pushed past him. "What are you trying to hide?" he asked.

"Nothing, I—" Brodie protested, but Emily had heard enough. She moved out of the bathroom, still clutching the sheet around her.

"Brodie is trying to be a gentleman and hide me," she said. "But there's no need for that. We're all adults here."

Travis's face turned white, then red. "Emily, what do you think you're doing?" he finally snapped out.

As gracefully as she could, she bent and retrieved her clothes from the floor. "I'm going to get dressed so that I can come with you to look at Lynn's car."

"You are not coming with us," Travis said.

"I'm part of the investigative team," she said. "I want to see where the car was left and what kind of condition it's in. That may help me reach some more conclusions about Alex." Plus, she knew how annoyed

Travis would be at having her push her way in like this. Her brother was a good man, but he was far too up-tight, and she saw it as her duty to force him to loosen up a little.

"We don't need a civilian at a potential crime scene," Travis said.

"You can ride with me, but you have to stay in the vehicle until I clear you to get out," Brodie said.

Travis glared at him, no doubt perturbed at having Brodie overrule him. But Brodie didn't work for Travis, so Emily supposed he could make his own decisions.

"Okay." Clothes in hand, she turned back toward the bathroom.

"It is not okay," Travis said.

"Just give me a minute to get dressed," Brodie said. "I'm sure we can work this out."

Smiling to herself, Emily shut the bathroom door behind her. Later, she was sure she'd have to endure a lecture from her brother about how she was mak-ing a big mistake getting back together with Brodie. And maybe he was right. But at least this time she was going into the relationship with her eyes wide open. She would have a good time with Brodie now, and avoid thinking about forever.

TRAVIS INSISTED THE three of them travel together in his sheriff's department SUV. Brodie reluctantly agreed. He firmly believed in picking his battles, and argu-ing over how they were going to get to a crime scene wasn't on his list for today. Not with the promise of a bigger fight looming, judging by the icy stare Travis kept giving him. Fine. The two of them could clear the air later, preferably when Emily wasn't around.

As for the woman in question, Travis's little sister looked smug and satisfied, which should have felt more gratifying than it did. Brodie wasn't certain if she was so pleased with herself because of the fantastic sex they had enjoyed the night before—or because she'd managed to upset her usually unemotional brother.

Dwight met them at the barricade that blocked the still-closed road. He shifted the orange-and-white pylons to one side to allow Travis's vehicle to pass, then walked up to meet them after Travis had parked behind Dwight's cruiser.

Lynn Wallace's white Volvo sat crookedly across the northbound lane, both front doors open. "The crew working to clear the road found it like this when they reported for work this morning," Dwight said. "They left at about five o'clock yesterday, so someone drove it up here after that."

"Were the doors open like that, or did they open them?" Travis asked.

"They said they were open," Dwight said. "I think whoever dumped it here wanted to make sure it was noticed, and that people saw what was inside."

"What was inside?" Emily asked. She was pale and looked a little frightened, but stood her ground.

"Not another body, thank goodness," Dwight said. "Come take a look."

"Emily, you stay back here," Travis said.

"I won't compromise your crime scene," she said. "I know better than that." Not waiting for an answer, she started toward the car, so that Travis had to hurry to catch up with and pass her.

Brodie followed more slowly, so that by the time he arrived at the car, the others were gathered around, bent over and peering into the open doors. Emily took a step back and motioned for him to move in ahead of her.

The white upholstery of the Volvo, both front and back seats, had been slashed, long diagonal cuts leaving leather hanging in strips, stuffing pulled out and spilling onto the floor. Dull red liquid lay in pools on the seats and dripped onto the floor. "It's paint, not blood," Dwight said. "Regular latex. Most of it is still wet, probably from the cold. I took photos when I arrived, but the snow around the vehicle was pretty churned up. I think all the construction guys probably had a look."

The car's windshield had been smashed, the glass a spiderweb of cracks, green glass pebbles that had broken off from the cracks glittering on the dash.

Brodie rejoined Emily a short distance from the car. She stood with her arms folded across her stomach, staring at the pavement. "Are you okay?" he asked softly.

She nodded, but didn't speak until Travis joined them. "Alex is really angry," she said, looking at her brother. "Enraged. And he's coming apart."

"You think Alex did this?" Travis asked.

"Yes. I'm not an expert, but I think doing this, leaving the car up here like this, where it was sure to be found, he's sending you a message."

"What kind of message?" Brodie asked.

She glanced at him, then back at her brother. "The next woman he goes after, I think it's going to be more violent."

"And he's going to blame law enforcement for the violence," Brodie said. "We're making him do this because we won't leave him alone."

"Yes," Emily said. "I think you're right."

Travis looked back toward the Volvo, the silence stretching between them. Dwight shifted from one foot to the other. The rumble of the road machinery sounded very far away, muffled by distance and the walls of snow.

"Dwight, take Emily back to the ranch, please," Travis said. "Brodie and I will wait for the wrecker to tow the car to our garage for processing."

Emily stiffened, and Brodie expected her to argue with her brother, but she apparently saw the sense in not standing out here in the cold with nothing to do. She headed toward Dwight's cruiser, leaving the deputy to follow.

Brodie waited until Dwight had driven away and he and Travis were alone before he spoke. "If you have something to say to me, say it," he said.

Travis took a step toward Brodie, the brim of his hat shading his face, hiding his expression. Brodie braced himself for a dressing-down. Travis would tell him he had no business sleeping with Emily, that he was here to do a job and not to seduce his sister, that he had used their friendship to take advantage of Emily—nothing Brodie hadn't already told himself or heard before, five years ago, when he and Travis had also argued about Brodie's relationship with Emily. He would let Travis get out all his words and not try to defend himself. Once Travis had exhausted his anger, maybe they could have a civil discussion about Emily and Brodie's feelings for her.

But Travis didn't say anything. He reared back and belted Brodie in the chin, sending him staggering.

Brodie let out a yelp of surprise and managed to

stay upright. He rubbed his aching jaw and stared at the sheriff, who was flushed and breathing hard, hands at his sides, still balled into fists. "I reckon you think I deserve that," Brodie said.

"You don't think you do?"

"I had a long talk with your sister last night—before we went to bed together. She told me about the baby." He paused, gathering his emotions. The reality that Emily had been pregnant with his baby—that he could have been a father—was only just beginning to sink in. "I never knew, I swear. She said she wrote to me, but I never got the letter. If I had, you wouldn't have been able to keep me away from her."

Travis glared at him, wary.

"You know I asked her to marry me, right?" Brodie said.

Travis nodded.

"And she turned me down. I didn't dump her—she dumped me. But I would have come back to help her with the baby—in whatever way she wanted me to help."

He could tell the minute the fight went out of Travis. The sheriff's shoulders sagged and he bowed his head. "I'm sorry I let my temper get the best of me," he said.

Brodie rubbed his jaw again. "Maybe it was good for both of us." He offered his hand.

Travis stared at Brodie's hand. "Maybe it's none of my business, but what happens with you and Emily now?" he asked.

"I don't know. A lot of that is up to her. But it's not going to be a repeat of last time, I promise. Is that good enough for you?"

Travis grasped his hand, then pulled him close and

thumped him on the back. "You and Emily are adults, so what you do is your business," he said. He pulled away and his eyes met Brodie's—hard eyes full of meaning. "But if you hurt her again, I promise, I will hunt you down."

Brodie had no doubt of the truth behind those words. "You don't have to worry," he said. "Now come on. The killer is the only man you need to worry about hunting down right now."

"YOUR FIANCÉ ATE my prosciutto."

Saturday afternoon, Emily and Lacy looked up from the place cards they were hand-lettering for that night's wedding rehearsal dinner. The caterer, Bette, stood before them, hands on her hips and a stormy expression in her eyes. "How do you know Travis ate it?" Lacy asked.

"Because I caught him finishing off the last of it before he headed out the door this morning."

Lacy set aside the stack of place cards. "The poor man has been working so much, eating at odd hours. I hope you didn't fuss at him too much."

"I didn't. But I need that prosciutto for the dinner tonight."

"If you think the grocery in Eagle Mountain will have it, I can run and get it for you," Emily said. "I need to go to the office supply store, anyway."

"They don't have it," Bette said. "But Iris at the Cake Walk said she had some she would sell me. If you could fetch it for me, that would be a big help. I have too much to do to get ready for tonight to leave."

"Of course I'll get it." Emily looked at the place

cards spread out in front of her. "Lacy and I are almost finished here."

"Don't go to town by yourself," Lacy said. "Find one of the ranch hands to go with you."

"All right." Emily wanted to protest that she would be fine on her own, but the other women Alex had killed would have probably said the same thing. And the possibility that the *EW* on Alex's list might mean her made her even more cautious.

She and Lacy finished the place cards, each hand-lettered, with a tiny silk rose glued to the corner. "They turned out really nice," Emily said as she passed the last of the cards over to Lacy.

"They did." Lacy sighed. For a bride on the eve of her wedding day, she didn't look very happy.

"What's wrong?" Emily asked.

Lacy looked up, her eyes shiny with tears. "I'm being silly. I mean, women have died, and here I am, worrying about my wedding. It's ridiculous." She pressed her fingers to her eyes, blotting the tears.

"You're not being silly." Emily squeezed Lacy's hand. "The wedding is going to be beautiful. By tomorrow afternoon, you'll be married and it will be beautiful."

"I'm so worried something is going to happen to mess things up," she said. "Not just the wedding, but Travis—this killer hates him." She sniffed. "I know he has a dangerous job, and I told myself I could handle that, but when I think about something happening to him…" She pressed her lips together and looked away.

"Travis is smart and careful, and he loves you so much," Emily said. "Nothing is going to happen to him." She said a silent prayer that this would be true.

Lacy nodded and stood. "You're right. And my worrying won't accomplish anything." She gathered the place cards into a neat pile. "Thanks for your help with these. I think I'll go see if Bette needs me to do anything in the kitchen."

Emily wished she had had more to offer her friend than words. If only she could figure out where Alex was hiding. Finding and arresting him would allow Travis and Lacy to start their marriage off right, with a honeymoon away from all this stress and no lingering worries about local women dying.

She gathered her purse, slipped on her coat and went in search of someone to accompany her to town. She searched the barns and outbuildings, and stopped to check on Witchy, who was contentedly munching hay, her leg showing no signs of further inflammation. No one was at the bunkhouse or in the machine shed. Maybe the men had decided to make themselves scarce while the last frantic preparations for tomorrow's wedding were being completed.

On her way back from the barn she walked past the row of guest cabins. The door to Brodie's cabin opened and he stepped out onto the porch. Odd that he'd be here this time of day. "Brodie!" she called.

He turned to face her and she winced. The left side of his jaw was red and swollen. "What happened to you?" she asked, hurrying up the steps to him.

He gingerly touched his jaw. "I put ice on it, hoping to get the swelling down."

"What happened?" When she had left him and Travis on Dixon Pass, they had been waiting for the wrecker to arrive.

"It's no big deal." He took her arm and urged her

down the steps alongside him. "By tomorrow you won't even know it happened."

"You're not answering my question." She studied the injury more closely. She was no expert, but she was pretty sure someone had punched him. "Who hit you?"

"You don't want to know."

Had he tried to arrest someone and they fought back? No, he wouldn't bother hiding that information from her. In fact, she could think of only one person he might try to shield. "Did *Travis* punch you?" The last word came out as a squeak—she couldn't quite hold back her shock at the idea. Travis was so even-tempered. So aggravatingly calm almost all of the time.

But he definitely hadn't been pleased to find her and Brodie together this morning.

"It's no big deal," Brodie said again.

"Did you hit him back?" She clutched at his arm. "Lacy is going to be furious if you broke Travis's nose or something on the eve of the wedding."

"No, I didn't hit him back." He stopped walking and turned to face her. "I figured he needed the one punch to let off some of the pressure that's been building up with this case."

"Then he should go split wood or something—not punch you."

"Don't worry about it," he said. "We cleared the air, and everything is okay now."

"What did you tell him?"

He caressed her shoulders and spoke more softly. "I told him I never got your letter about the baby—that if I had, I never would have left you to deal with that alone. I still hate that you had to go through that by yourself."

The pain in his voice brought a lump to her throat.

She moved in closer and his arms went around her. They couldn't do anything to change the past, but at least now she knew he really hadn't deserted her when she needed him most. She wondered what would have happened if he had received her letter and come back to her. Would they have married, anyway? She knew she'd been right to turn down his proposal, but would knowing a child was on the way have changed her mind? She closed her eyes and pushed the thought away. The answer to that question didn't matter now.

Brodie patted her back. "What are you thinking?" he asked.

"Travis still shouldn't have hit you," she mumbled against his chest.

"It's okay," he said. "It was something we both needed, I think."

She raised her head to look at him. "Men are weird."

He laughed. "Now that that's settled, what are you up to?"

"I promised Bette I'd run to town and pick up some prosciutto for her. I was looking for someone to go with me. Want to volunteer?"

"Absolutely. What is Bette doing with prosciutto?"

"Something wonderful, I'm sure. It's for the rehearsal dinner tonight."

"I'd almost forgotten there's a wedding tomorrow."

"How could you forget? There's a big silver-and-white wreath on every door in the house—and the door of your cabin. Not to mention the wedding gifts in the hall and everyone running around like crazy people trying to get ready."

"I said almost. Besides, I've been focused on other things."

Right. Everything always came back to the killer.

Alex would probably be thrilled to know how much he was directing all their lives. She couldn't even go to the store by herself because of him. "Come on," she said. "Let's go. I have a million things to do before the dinner tonight."

On the way into town they didn't discuss Alex, or the wedding, or even the weather—all topics Emily felt had been exhausted in recent weeks. Instead, they talked about their lives on the other side of Colorado— she in Fort Collins and he in Denver. "In the spring there's a great farmers market every weekend," she told him. "I go sometimes just to hang out and people watch."

"Do you ever go hiking out around Horsetooth Falls?" he asked.

"It's been a while, but it's a great area."

"We should hike it together sometime," he said.

Her heart gave a funny little flutter. "Yeah. Yeah, we should."

He parked at the curb in front of the Cake Walk Café and followed Emily inside. The lunch crowd had dissipated, but people sat at a couple of tables, nursing cups of coffee or polishing off the last of a meal. The café's owner, Iris Desmet, waved from behind a counter at the back of the room. She disappeared into the kitchen and emerged a moment later with a paper-wrapped parcel. "I warned Bette that I've had this in my freezer for a while," she said as she punched keys on the cash register. "But she said she was desperate, so I told her she could have it for a discount."

"I'm sure it will be fine," Emily said. "Will we see you at the wedding tomorrow?"

"Of course. There's nothing like a wedding to cheer people up, and we could certainly use a little of that—

though I hear the road may open tomorrow, and the weather forecast doesn't show any more snow for a couple of weeks. Maybe the rest of the winter won't be as hard."

"I hope that's true." Emily handed over her credit card and waited while Iris swiped it, then she signed the receipt and tucked the package of prosciutto into her purse.

On the sidewalk, Dwight hailed them from across the street. "I thought you'd want to know what we found in the car once we started going through it," he said.

"Let me guess," Brodie said. "One of the Ice Cold calling cards."

Dwight nodded. "Better than that—we found some good prints in the paint. They match ones on file for Alex Woodruff."

"I don't think we had any doubt who was responsible, but it's nice to have more evidence," Brodie said.

"When you get a chance, we've got a couple of questions for the CBI profiler."

Emily put a hand on Brodie's back to get his attention. "You two talk shop. I'm going to the office supply store to pick up a few things."

Brodie frowned. "I'll only be a minute."

"And the store is only two doors down." She pointed to the building with the oversize gold paperclip over the door. "You can see it from here."

He nodded, then turned back to Dwight. Smiling to herself, she hurried toward the office supply. She couldn't say why she was so happy—there was still a killer on the loose, the highway leading out of town was still closed and everyone around her was keyed up over the wedding tomorrow. And it wasn't as if she and Brodie had resolved anything. She felt closer to him now, and they'd had a night of great sex. Maybe after this was all over, they'd get together again to hike or, who knows, maybe even go out on a real date. That was still no reason for the almost giddy lightness that made her want to skip down the sidewalk and had her fighting back a goofy smile.

The bells on the door of the Paperclip jangled as she entered. The owner, Eleanor Davis, who had taught Emily when she was in third grade, waved from in front of a display of earbuds and went back to assisting an older gentleman. Emily wandered down the aisles of office supplies, admiring a beautiful pen here or an attractive notebook there. She could have spent hours in here, running her hands over the displays and breathing in the scents of ink and paper, but settled for choosing a package of colorful note cards, a sturdy wire-bound journal and a purple gel ink pen. What could she say— some women experienced euphoria when buying new shoes, while office supplies did it for her.

Outside on the sidewalk, she almost collided with an elderly man. "So sorry, miss," he said, holding out his hands defensively. He stared out at her from behind thick glasses, his expression confused and his eyes bloodshot. His gray hair hung lank to his shoulders and a wisp of a gray beard stood out against sallow skin and sagging jowls. "Clumsy of me, I…" He looked around, blinking. "I think I need some help."

The poor dear looked really out of it. Emily glanced across the street, hoping to see Dwight and Brodie and wave them over, but they must have gone back into the café—probably to get out of the biting wind. She shifted her purchases to one hand. "What can I do to help you?" she asked.

"It's my car. There's something wrong with it."

"Let me call someone for you." She fumbled in her purse for her phone.

"No." He put out a hand to stop her. "Don't go to so much trouble. I know what's wrong. I just need to find the auto parts store."

"There's one out on the highway," she said. "Near the motel. But it's a little far to walk in this weather."

"You could give me a ride," he said. "I know it's a lot to ask, but it would help me so much."

She glanced toward the café again. "I'm with someone," she said. "But I'm sure he wouldn't mind giving you a ride—"

"No!" The man's hand clamped around her wrist—hard. Startled, she stared at him. The confused look had vanished from his eyes, and he no longer looked so old. Something sharp pricked her side—a knife. "Come with me now, and don't make a scene," he said.

Chapter Fourteen

Emily opened her mouth to scream, but no sound emerged. The old man put his arm around her, pulling her close. The odors of wood smoke and sweat stung her nose, and the knife dug into her side, so that it hurt to even breathe deeply. She dropped her purse, the contents spilling out onto the sidewalk, the package of ham coming to rest in a snowbank. "That's right, come along nice and easy," the man—she was sure it was Alex—crooned.

He still looked like an innocent old man, but nothing about him was harmless. He had a grip like iron—she imagined him breaking her wrist if she tried to jerk away. And then he would slash her open with the knife before she had time to run.

"Hey!" The shout boomed out, making her jump. Alex turned, dragging her around with him, and she stared as Brodie raced toward them. She had the sensation of being somewhere outside herself, watching a slow-motion movie—Alex opening his mouth to say something, Brodie reaching into his coat and pulling out a gun—the knife pressing harder against her side.

Then everything sped up. Someone screamed, Brodie shouted, then Alex shoved her away, so hard that she fell, slamming her knees into the concrete of the walkway. Brodie's boots thundered past her, then a woman knelt beside her, trying to help her to her feet.

But Emily didn't get up until Brodie returned. He bent over her, chest heaving, the gun out of sight now. For a long moment, neither of them said a thing, their eyes locked, his expression reflecting all the terror she felt. "Are you…all right?" he managed to gasp at last.

She nodded, though she still couldn't seem to speak. By now a crowd had gathered, everyone wanting to know what had happened, and if they could help. Brodie grasped Emily's hand and pulled her to her feet. She caught her breath at the sudden sharp pain in her side, and clamped her hand over the spot. "He had a knife," she said.

Brodie pushed her hand away, then yanked down the zipper of her coat and shoved it aside. She stared at the quarter-sized blossom of red against the white of her sweater. "We need to get you to the clinic," he said, then, without waiting for a reply, scooped her into his arms and started across the street.

"Brodie, put me down. Please!" She beat her fists against his chest, but his expression never changed. People called after them, a car braked to a halt as he stepped in front of it and horns honked, but Brodie appeared to hear none of it. He burst into the Eagle Mountain medical clinic and everyone in the small waiting room stared at them.

"She's hurt," he said. "She needs to see the doctor now."

She wanted to demand once more that he put her down, but doubted he would even hear her. When the door leading to the examination rooms opened, he carried her through it and into the closest empty room. A woman with a stethoscope followed them inside. "What is the meaning—"

But she got no further. Brodie took out his badge and shoved it at her, then pulled back Emily's coat to show the spot of blood. "She's been stabbed."

The woman's eyes widened, but she recovered quickly and took charge. She pushed Brodie out of the way, then eased the coat off Emily and pulled up the sweater.

In the end, Emily needed four stitches, a tetanus shot and some antibiotics to ward off infection. Brodie sat in a chair, scowling and silent, while the nurse practitioner on duty stitched up Emily. No one talked about what had happened, and Emily didn't know if she was relieved about that or not.

The nurse had just finished administering the tetanus vaccine when someone knocked on the door. "It's the sheriff," Travis said. "May I come in?"

"You might as well," the nurse practitioner said, and shifted so that Travis could squeeze in behind her.

"I'm fine," Emily said, sliding off the exam table, wincing a little at the pain in her side. "It was just a little cut."

Travis's answer was to pull her close and squeeze her so tight she couldn't breathe. Her brother wasn't much for words, but the concern in that hug made her tear up, and she had to force herself to smile and push him away. "I'm okay," she said. "Really."

Brodie stood and Travis turned to him. "I've got everyone available out looking for this guy, but I'm afraid he's done another disappearing act."

"Let's talk about this outside," Brodie said. He

picked up Emily's coat and helped her back into it. Then, one hand on her back, he followed her into the waiting room, where, once again, everyone stared at them.

"Someone brought these for you," the receptionist said, and handed over Emily's purse, the package of office supplies and the paper-wrapped parcel of prosciutto. Emily stared at the ham, teary again. It felt like hours since she had set out to run a simple errand for Bette, yet the prosciutto was still cold.

"Let's go to my office," Travis said, and escorted them out of the clinic. The three of them piled into his cruiser, Brodie in the back seat with her. She lay her head on his shoulder, closed her eyes and tried not to think about what had happened, although she knew she would have to give a statement to Travis. All she wanted was a few more minutes to pretend she hadn't just come within seconds of death.

At the station, Adelaide clucked over her and brought her a cup of tea. "Drink that," she ordered. "And don't let these two bully you into anything." She scowled at Brodie and Travis as if she blamed them for the attack, then left, closing the door to Travis's office behind her with a solid *Click!*

"I'm not going to bully you," Travis said. "But we need to know what happened. We got a description of the man who attacked you from a few people, but about all they said was that it was an old guy with a patchy beard, and none of them remembered seeing him before."

She took a long sip of the sweet, hot tea, then set the cup on the edge of the desk and took a deep breath. She could do this. She was alive and safe and what she had to say might help Travis and Brodie stop this man. "It was Alex," she said. "I didn't recognize him because he was wearing a disguise. A good one. But I'm sure it was him."

"Start with a description," Travis said. "We'll go from there."

She described the old man who had approached her—his glasses and long hair and saggy jowls. "He looked confused and harmless," she said. "Stooped over and a little shaky. I felt sorry for him. He wanted me to feel sorry for him, to not see him as a threat. I'm sure that's what he did with the other women, too."

"He didn't run like an old man," Brodie said. "He took off like a track star. He ducked down an alley and I lost him within seconds."

"He said he was having car trouble and asked me for a ride to the auto parts store," Emily said. "When I told him I was with someone, and started toward the café, he grabbed my wrist and stuck the knife in my side. His whole demeanor changed. That's when I knew it was Alex." She swallowed hard, remembered terror making her light-headed.

"I came out of the café with Dwight and saw Emily cozied up with this old guy," Brodie said. "Even though her back was to me, something about the situation didn't look right. When I called to them, the guy swung her around toward me. He looked angry—enraged—and I could see that Emily was terrified. I drew my weapon and ordered him to stop. At first I thought he would resist, or try to use Emily as a shield. Instead, he released her and took off running." He raked a hand through his hair. "I should have insisted you stay with me. And I never should have gone into the café with Dwight."

"I was in a public place with other people all around," Emily said. "What was Alex thinking?"

"He thinks he's invincible," Travis said. "That law enforcement is stupid and we'll never catch him. But we will."

A knock on the door interrupted them. "Come in," Travis called.

Dwight entered, a bundle of cloth in his hand. "We found these in the trash bins behind Mo's Pub," he said, and laid the bundle on the desk.

Emily stared at the drab shirt, thick glasses with scratched lenses, and thin gray beard and long hair. "That was his disguise," she said.

"I figure he ditched the clothes and either put on another disguise or walked away as himself," Dwight said.

"He's good at blending in," Emily said. "He can be noticed when he wants to be, but when he doesn't, he fades into the crowd."

"I interviewed some of his professors over the phone," Travis said. "Most of them didn't even remember him."

"He's decided to go after you now," Brodie said.

"But why? Because I knew him at school?"

"Maybe," Brodie said. "Or because you're Travis's sister. He wants to prove he's better than any cop."

She welcomed the anger that surged through her at the thought. It made her feel stronger. She stood. "I'm not going to sit quietly and play victim for his sick fantasies."

"No, you're not," Brodie agreed. "And he's not going

to get close enough to hurt you again." He stood also, and took her hand in his. "Because from now on, I'm not letting you out of my sight."

THAT EVENING, BRODIE sat in the Walkers' living room as Emily descended the stairs to the strains of Pachelbel's Canon. Something tugged hard at his chest as she paused at the bottom of the stairs and met his gaze, then she ducked her head and turned away to take her place in front of the fire, where the officiant, a plump woman with auburn hair, waited for the run-through of the wedding ceremony.

The other bridesmaids followed—Gage's wife, Maya, Paige Riddell and Brenda Prentice. The music switched to the traditional bridal entrance tune and Lacy, in a blue lace dress, carrying an imaginary bouquet, appeared at the top of the stairs. Even though this was only a rehearsal, Brodie and the other observers rose as Lacy descended the stairs.

Rather than watch the bride, Brodie kept his eyes on Travis, who stood with Gage, Ryder Stewart, Nate Harris and Cody Rankin in the archway between the living and dining room. The sheriff's stance was casual: hip cocked, face impassive. But as Lacy neared, Travis straightened, then reached out his hand to her. In that moment, Brodie was sure Travis wasn't thinking about a killer or the women who had died, or about anything but this woman and their future together.

Love had the power to do that—to push aside every worry and distraction, to focus attention on what mattered most, on life and hope, even in the midst of tragedy.

Brodie shifted his gaze to Emily. She was watching her brother and Lacy, eyes shiny with unshed tears, joy radiating from her smile. Brodie's heart hammered and he had trouble catching his breath, the knowledge of how much he loved her a sucker punch to the gut.

If only she would look at him, and let him see that she felt the same—that she loved him. But her eyes remained fixed on the bride and groom as the officiant explained what would happen next.

"You may practice kissing the bride if you like," the officiant said. Everyone laughed as Travis moved in to kiss Lacy and the spell was broken.

"Now that that's over, we can eat," Gage said, ignoring the scolding look from Maya.

Brodie stood and went to Emily. Though he was not a member of the wedding party, and had not even received an invitation to the wedding, Travis had embraced the idea of Brodie as Emily's bodyguard. He had also apparently persuaded his mother and father that Brodie was not the scoundrel they had assumed and now they, too, seemed happy to have him protecting their daughter.

As for Emily, he wasn't certain what she felt about him becoming, by default, her "plus-one" for the wedding. She smiled as he held her chair for her, next to his at the table, then quickly turned her attention to the other guests. Most of the wedding party was made up of other law enforcement officers and their spouses or significant others.

Travis and the bride-to-be sat side by side in the middle of the long table, Lacy smiling and beautiful, Travis stoic and tense, his smiles doled out sparingly for his beloved. He was putting on a good show, but Brodie knew his mind was back on Alex. Like Brodie, he was probably wondering if, while they ate and drank and toasted the happy couple, the Ice Cold Killer was claiming another victim.

The officiant, Reverend Winger, sat across the table. As Bette and the ranch cook, Rainey, set salads in front of the guests, she leaned across and asked, "Are you in law enforcement, too?"

"Yes, ma'am. I'm a detective with the Colorado Bureau of Investigation."

"This must be the safest place to be in the whole county right now," Reverend Winger said.

"Reverend Winger, I understand you vacationed in Italy last year." Lacy leaned across to address the pastor. "What was your favorite thing about that trip?"

As the reverend launched into a description of her visit to Tuscany, Brodie silently applauded Lacy. Before the rehearsal began, she had laid down the law—absolutely no discussion of the case tonight. *We're going to focus on the wedding and be happy*, she had insisted.

"The prosciutto doesn't look any worse for wear," Emily leaned over and whispered to Brodie as a plate of prosciutto-wrapped asparagus and petite sirloin steaks was set before each of them.

"No one will ever know," he said, and popped a bite of the asparagus into his mouth. No one would know what Emily had been through earlier that day, either. If he detected a little more tension around her eyes, that was only because he was so focused on her.

"You know, it's hard to eat when you're staring at me like that," she said.

"Sorry." He was tempted to say something about her being so beautiful he couldn't keep his eyes off her, but he was sure such a cheesy line would only make her groan. He focused on his own food. "This is delicious," he said. "Bette did a great job."

"She really did," Emily agreed. "Though in addition to the stress of my prosciutto problem, she had to deal with a no-show by the florist." She gestured toward the center of the table, where an arrangement of greens and pine cones, tied with silver ribbon, filled a silver vase. "This was a last-minute substitution."

"What did the florist have to say about the failed delivery?" he asked.

"By the time Bette had a chance to call, they were already closed. But she left a stern message—and she's going to double-check with them in the morning to make sure the wedding flowers get here in time."

"I'll be sure and tell her everything looks—and tastes—great."

"Speech! Speech!" Nate Harris, at one end of the table, tapped his spoon against his water glass.

Travis's father shoved back his chair and stood as the guests fell quiet. "Thank you, everyone, for coming here this evening," he said. "I especially want to thank Bette and Rainey for putting on such a lovely dinner."

Cries of "hear, hear" and light applause followed this remark.

Mr. Walker turned to Travis and Lacy. "Your mother and I have looked forward to tomorrow for a long time," he said. "We're so happy to welcome Lacy into the family and we wish you only the best." He raised his glass in a toast and everyone followed suit.

"Is this where everyone else in the wedding party feels compelled to also give a toast?" Emily whispered to Brodie. "If it is, I'm going to need more wine."

But instead of toasts, Bette arrived with dessert—a

baked Alaska that Brodie, at least, would have awarded first place in any bake-off.

Half an hour later, stuffed and happy, the guests who weren't staying on the ranch made their way to the door. Brodie stood with Emily, saying goodbye. When everyone was gone, Brodie led Emily aside, where they could talk without being overheard. "About the arrangements for tonight," he said. "I meant what I said before about not letting you out of my sight."

"So you're saying we have to sleep together?" He couldn't decide if the look in her eye was teasing or not.

"I'm saying I'm going to spend the night in the same room as you—sex is optional."

"Alex isn't going to come into this house and up to my bedroom," she said. "He wouldn't dare!"

"I wouldn't put anything past him at this point." After all, Alex had tried to crash the barbecue Wednesday night. Brodie took her arm and pulled her closer. "I'm not going to give him any opportunity to get to you again." The memory of her crumpled on the sidewalk, bleeding from Alex's knife, still made it hard to breathe.

"All right." Her smile made the tight band around his chest ease. "I was planning on sneaking out to your cabin later, anyway." She snuggled against him.

"Oh, you were?" He lowered his head to kiss her, but an uproar at the front door made them pull apart and turn toward the clamor. Lacy's parents, who had been among the first to leave, stood with Travis and Lacy— Mrs. Milligan in tears, her husband white-faced. "That poor woman," Mrs. Milligan moaned.

Brodie moved toward them, Emily close behind, as

Dwight shoved through the crowd. "The florist van is blocking the end of the driveway," he said. "The delivery driver is inside, dead."

Chapter Fifteen

Emily urged Brodie to go with Travis and the others to investigate the crime scene, but he insisted on staying by her side as she helped her mother and Lacy soothe the Milligans. She volunteered to let Lacy's parents stay in her room that evening. Her own parents didn't ask where she planned to spend the night, though she was aware of her mother watching her and Brodie more closely as the evening progressed.

Several hours passed before the other guests could leave. While they waited for the crime scene investigators and coroner to finish their work, for the ambulance to remove the body and for the wrecker to arrive to tow the van to the sheriff's garage, Emily poured coffee and served snacks that no one ate, and tried to make small talk about anything but the murders.

It was after midnight before she was able to retrieve her clothes and toiletries, along with a change of clothes for the next day, from her room and go with Brodie to his cabin. She should have been exhausted by the strain of the day, but instead felt hyperalert and on edge. Halfway down the path to the cabins, she put her arm out to stop Brodie. "Stop just a minute," she said. "This feels like the first time things have been quiet all day and I want to take it in."

She closed her eyes and breathed in deeply of the cold, clear air, then tilted her head back and stared up at the night sky, thousands of stars glittering against the velvet blackness.

"It's beautiful," Brodie said, standing behind her and wrapping his arms around her.

"It's surreal to think of violence in the midst of such peace," she said. "Especially while we were celebrating such a happy occasion."

He kissed the top of her head—such a sweet, gentle gesture. "Come on," he said. "You're shivering. It's warm in the cabin."

The cabin was warm and neat, the bed made and clutter put away. Was this because Brodie had been expecting her to stay with him tonight, or because he was a neat and organized guy? She suspected a little of both. "I want to change out of this dress and these heels," she said, staring down at her fashionable, but definitely chilly, attire.

"Go right ahead," Brodie said.

She retreated to the bathroom, where she changed into yoga pants and a T-shirt. She studied her reflection in the mirror over the sink, hesitating, then turned on the water and washed off her makeup, then brushed out her hair. It wasn't as if Brodie hadn't seen her like this before.

"How is your side doing?" he asked when she emerged from the bathroom. He had removed his shoes and untucked his shirt, and his gun lay on the table beside the bed.

She made a face. "It hurts some," she said. She had

been mostly successful at distracting herself from the pain. "It's more annoying than anything."

"Do you mind if I have a look?" he asked.

"All right."

He crossed the room to her and carefully lifted up the T. When she had changed for dinner earlier, she had removed the dressing, so that the stitches were exposed, the skin slightly puffy around the neat row of dark thread. Brodie studied the wound for a moment, then bent and gently kissed the skin above the stitches.

She threaded her fingers through his hair and held him to her for a moment, before dragging his face up to hers and kissing him. She molded her body to his, enjoying the feel of him so close, the anticipation of spending another night getting to know him even better like a pleasant hum through her.

"I don't want to hurt you," he murmured, his mouth against her hair.

"You won't." Not physically, at least. She wouldn't think about what might happen if he left her again.

They kissed again, heat building, and were moving toward the bed when someone knocked on the door. Brodie turned toward the sound. "It's Travis. Can I come in?"

Brodie opened the door and Travis entered. He looked cold and exhausted, Emily thought. He needed a hot drink and a good night's sleep, but she doubted he would get either. He glanced at Emily, then turned to Brodie. "I wanted to update you on what we found," he said.

"Emily will have to stay and hear." Brodie sat on the side of the bed and Emily settled next to him.

"All right." Travis took the chair and sat with his elbows on his knees, head down. "The woman is Sarah Geraldi, a part-time delivery person for the florist," he said. "She was killed like the others, hands and feet bound, the Ice Cold calling card tucked into her bra." He glanced at Emily again. "You were right. There was more violence this time. He cut her up pretty badly, and there was more blood."

"He would probably have blood on him," Brodie said. "He's not being as careful."

"He knows you know who he is," Emily said. "He's not trying to hide his identity anymore. In fact, I think he likes knowing you know that he's the one who's getting the better of you. At least, I think that's how he sees it."

Travis nodded. "The medical examiner thinks she was killed much earlier today, hidden in the van, then driven here a short time ago. The delivery van's engine was still warm."

"He killed her someplace else and brought her here to taunt you," Brodie said.

Travis nodded. "It looks that way."

"If Alex drove the van here with the body in it, how did he get away?" Brodie asked. "Has he recruited another accomplice? Stashed another vehicle somewhere? It's still seven miles to town."

"Maybe he didn't leave." Travis raised his head, his gaze steady, his expression grim. "Maybe he's still here, hiding somewhere."

TRAVIS'S ANNOUNCEMENT DID nothing to help Emily or Brodie sleep. They made love tenderly, but with an air of desperation, eager to suppress, at least for a little while, thoughts of the horror that might lurk outside the door. They both woke early and dressed without saying much, then made their way up the path to the house. Brodie walked with one arm around Emily, the other hand on his gun, constantly scanning around them for any sign of an intruder.

"I'm jumpy enough without you acting as if Alex is going to leap out of the bushes and grab me," she said. "You heard Travis—he had every extra man searching around here last night. Alex isn't here."

"I don't believe in taking chances when the stakes are so high," Brodie said.

The look he gave her had a lot of heat behind it, and she had to look away. She really needed to keep her emotions in check so that she could support Lacy today. She couldn't afford to let her confusing responses to Brodie reduce her to a sodden puddle of feelings.

The wedding was scheduled to take place at five o'clock. Before then, there was still a lot to do to prepare for the ceremony. Bette appeared in the doorway to the dining room as Emily and Brodie were finishing up breakfast. "I need you two to help with the decorations," she said.

"Sure." Emily handed her dirty dishes to Brodie, who had volunteered to carry them into the kitchen. "What can we do?"

"Give me those." Bette took the dishes, then dumped them in a bus tub on the end of the sideboard. "Needless to say, things are as chaotic at the florist's this morning as they are here, and we may not be getting all the flowers we ordered, so we're making some last-minute adjustments. Come with me."

She led them through the living room, where she had assembled a pile of evergreens, silver ribbon and a mass of white silk flowers. "I raided the attic and the rest of the house for every flower arrangement on the premises," Bette explained. "Now we're going to use them to transform this room into a woodland winter wonderland."

Under Bette's direction, Emily and Brodie began cutting and wiring the greenery to make garland. Bette came along behind them and attached ribbons and flowers. "I guess the florist was pretty upset when she got the news about her employee," Emily said as she snipped a section of pine branches.

"It's even worse than you think," Bette said. "The woman who was murdered was the shop owner's daughter."

"Oh, no!" Emily's chest tightened in sympathy for the poor woman.

"Believe me, I'd gladly throttle Alex Woodruff with my bare hands if I could find him." Bette yanked hard on the end of a silver bow. "Not only am I sick over all the women he's killed, but I hate that this has cast such a pall over the wedding. Lacy, of all people, deserves to be happy on this day."

"Of course she does," Emily murmured in sympathy. Travis deserved to be happy, too—and he wouldn't be until Alex was arrested and locked behind bars, where he couldn't hurt anyone else.

"Oh, Bette, it's going to look wonderful."

The three of them turned to see Lacy, dressed in black yoga pants and a too-large sweatshirt that had *Rayford County Sheriff's Dept.* emblazoned across the front, her hair rolled up in large foam rollers, her face pale from both lack of makeup and lack of sleep, and her eyes dull with a frazzled, distracted expression. She moved into the room and fingered a white silk rose, and a single tear rolled down her cheek.

"Oh, honey, it's going to be all right." Bette enfolded her friend in a hug.

Lacy gave in and sobbed on Bette's shoulder. "This is supposed to be the happiest day of my life," she said between tears. "And I'm so worried and scared and angry. What if something happens to Travis? What if someone else gets hurt? It's just so awful." And a fresh wave of weeping engulfed her.

Bette patted her back and looked over her shoulder at Emily and Brodie. "You two can finish up here, can't you?" she asked. "The garland is mostly done—you just need to add a few more bows and then put it around the archway." She indicated the arch between the living and dining room, where Lacy and Travis would stand to recite their vows.

"Of course we can," Emily said.

Bette nodded. "Come on, Lacy, let's go fix you a cup of tea and get something to take the puffiness out of your eyes," she said, leading the distraught bride away. "Everything is going to be fine."

Emily and Brodie finished the garland. Emily didn't think her bows looked as professional as Bette's, but she told herself everyone was going to be focused on the happy couple, and not the decorations. "You'll have to start attaching this over the archway," she said, handing Brodie a length of garland. "I'm not tall enough to do it without a ladder."

"What do I attach it with?" he asked.

She searched the table and spotted a staple gun. "Use this." She handed it to him. "If Mom complains later, I'll take the blame."

He positioned the garland, pressed the staple gun against it and...*click!* He frowned. "I think it's out of staples."

"I know where they are," she said, and raced to retrieve the box. Her mother kept all her household tools in an old pie safe at one end of the front porch. She hurried to the cabinet and found the box, half full of staples, and let out a sigh of relief. One less thing to worry about.

She was halfway back to the front door when a plaintive cry stopped her. She held her breath, listening, and it came again. "Tawny?" she called, and the cat answered, sounding even more distressed than before. She must have decided to have her kittens near the house, but where?

Emily moved to the end of the porch. "Tawny?"

The cry came again. Was the cat under one of the cars? Was she hurt? Heart hammering, Emily hurried toward the sounds of distress. "Tawny!" she called again, and bent to look underneath Brodie's SUV.

Strong arms grabbed her from behind, and a hand slapped over her mouth so that she couldn't cry out, and she couldn't move. She stared up into Alex's face. "Isn't this going to be a nice surprise for the sheriff on his wedding day?" he asked.

Chapter Sixteen

Brodie was about to go after Emily when Bette called to him from the other room. "Brodie, can you come in here a minute, please?"

He looked after Emily, who was closing the front door behind her.

"Lacy wants to speak to you," Bette said.

Telling himself Emily would be fine, he followed the sound of Bette's voice to the sunporch, where she and Lacy sat with teacups in hand. Lacy beckoned him. "I have a favor to ask," she said, and patted the love seat beside her.

"Of course." He perched on the edge of the seat, anxious to get this over with so he could check on Emily.

"Promise me you'll see that Travis gets to the altar for the wedding," she said. "There are plenty of other law enforcement officers here today who can handle things for a while. All I need are a couple of hours of Travis's undivided attention so that we can get married."

He nodded. "Of course." Though the sheriff was in charge of the case, there was no reason he couldn't take a break for a few hours.

"I'm going to find Gage and make him promise the same thing," Lacy said. "And any of the other officers who are here today." She set her teacup aside and stood. "And now I'd better get upstairs and take my bath. Paige is coming by soon to do my nails."

"I've got plenty to do, too," Bette said, standing also. "Brodie, did you and Emily finish the decorations?"

"Emily went to get more staples. I'll go find her." She had been gone much too long, he thought, quickening his pace through the house.

He grabbed his jacket from the hooks by the door and pulled it on as he stepped out onto the porch. The door to a cabinet at the end of the porch stood open. The cabinet contained a hammer and other small tools, paintbrushes, some flowerpots and other items that might be useful for minor repairs or outdoor decorating. Was this where Emily had retrieved the staples? But where was she?

A gray tabby cat came around the side of the house, heavily pregnant belly swaying from side to side. She jumped up onto the porch and rubbed herself against his legs. Brodie ignored her and stepped off the porch, studying the snow. Footprints overlaid each other in the snow on the edges of the shoveled path, but none stood out as particularly fresh, and he couldn't tell if any of them were Emily's.

A sheriff's department SUV pulled up in front of the house and Travis climbed out. "Are you hiding out here from the wedding chaos?" Travis asked.

Brodie opened his mouth to share his concern about Emily, then closed it again, remembering his promise to Lacy. Travis needed to focus on the wedding today. If Brodie needed help, there were plenty of other people around here who were qualified to give it. "What are you doing in uniform today?" he asked.

"I had to get a haircut and I stopped in the office to check on a few things," Travis said. "The wedding is hours away and there's not much for the groom to do but show up and say his lines when the time comes."

"I think Lacy is upstairs getting her nails done or something," Brodie said.

"That's okay. I really came by to take another look at the crime scene." Travis scanned the area around the house. "The searchers never found any sign of Alex last night, but I can't shake the feeling that he's hiding somewhere close by."

"We're all keeping an eye out for him," Brodie said.

Travis nodded. "I think I'll go in and check in with Lacy," he said. "She's a little stressed about all of this. I think she's worried I'm going to leave her at the altar or something."

"You wouldn't do that," Brodie said.

"Of course not." Travis moved past him. "Not permanently, anyway."

Brodie headed to his cabin, telling himself Emily might have gone there in search of something she had left behind the night before, maybe. But the place was empty, though the scent of her perfume lingered in the rumpled sheets on the bed, recalling their night together and how much she had come to mean to him.

He turned on his heel and headed to the barn. Maybe she had gone to check on her horse. But Witchy was contentedly munching hay in her stall. The mare swiveled her head to look at Brodie when he leaned over the stall door. She shook her head and whinnied, as if impatient that he was invading her home. "Next time,

I'll bring you a carrot," he said, and headed back to the house.

After checking that no one was lurking around to ask him what he was up to, he made his way up the stairs to Emily's bedroom. Five years ago, he had done much the same thing, sneaking past Emily's parents to rendezvous in her room, embracing the role of the dangerous bad boy up to no good with his best friend's sister.

He was cautious this time, not because he thought he had to hide what he was doing, but because he didn't want to upset and alarm the family if there was no need. He knocked softly on the door and relief surged through him as footsteps approached from the other side.

Mrs. Milligan blinked at him, her hair in curlers and some kind of greenish cream on her face. Brodie took a step back. "Have you, um, seen Emily?" he asked.

"No, I haven't."

"Thanks." He backed away, then turned and hurried down the stairs, heart pounding. Something had happened to Emily. She was gone. Now it was time to panic.

"Where are you taking me?"

Alex hadn't bothered to gag Emily, though he had bound her hands and feet with tape, holding her in an iron grip that had left bruises on her upper arms. He had dragged her through the woods to a dirty white van and belted her into the back seat, her head at an uncomfortable angle, every jolt of the vehicle on the uneven ground sending pain through her bound arms.

"You'll see." Alex, his head almost completely covered by a knit cap pulled low and a scarf wound over his mouth, nearly vibrated with suppressed elation. "The sheriff and his deputies were so sure they could stop me this time," he said. "They don't realize who they're dealing with. I'm an expert who's making them look like a bunch of amateurs."

"Why would you want to be an expert at murder?" Emily asked. "You're smart enough you could have excelled at almost anything." She figured it couldn't hurt to flatter him—and as long as they were talking, she could remain alive. Brodie would have missed her by now. He and the others would be looking for her. All she had to do was stay alive until they found her.

"Murder is the ultimate crime," Alex said. "The one that captures everyone's attention and focuses all the effort and money on the killer." He pounded the steering wheel with the heel of his hand. "Talk about a rush."

"Why come to Eagle Mountain?" Emily asked. "Couldn't you have gotten away with a lot more in Denver?"

Alex laughed—a maniacal chuckle that made the hair on the back of her neck stand on end. "You don't get it, do you?" he asked. "You're as clueless as the rest of them. Honestly, I expected better of you."

"Get what?"

"I came to this 'middle of nowhere' excuse for a town because of you!"

You came here to kill me. But she couldn't say the words.

"When we first met, I was intrigued," he said. "You were pretty and smart, and you had a certain *fragile* quality I appreciated. I thought about asking you out, but as I observed you, I noticed that you didn't appear to date anyone—male or female. If I asked you out, chances were you would turn me down. And sex wasn't what I was really after. No, I wanted a much deeper connection. Do you know what that is?"

"No." She had to force the single syllable out. Alex's words terrified her even more than his actions. He had seemed so normal on the outside, yet talking with him now, she understood clearly how unhinged he had become.

"Before I kill someone, I look into her eyes and she realizes her life—her very existence—is in my hands. It is the most profound connection I could ever have with another human being. The feeling I have at that moment, the power and, yes, the love, is incredible. I wanted to experience that with you."

She said nothing, no longer wanting to encourage him.

But he didn't need her encouragement. "I decided I needed to work my way up to you," he said. "I had to experiment and perfect my methods."

"What about Tim?" she asked, hoping to change the subject.

More stomach-turning laughter. "I asked him to come with me because I thought he could be my first victim. But he turned out to be useful."

"He helped you murder the first few women."

"He did. Turns out, he had a taste for killing and I was able to exploit that. Of course, he was nowhere near my level of genius. Which is why he was caught in the end." He giggled. That was the only way Emily could think to describe the sound he made, like a little child chuckling over a silly cartoon. "Things kept getting better and better for me after I came here. The local sheriff's department was as tiny as the town, and they had tiny brains, too. And then I found out your older brother was the sheriff. Such delicious synchronicity. As if this was all meant to be."

He had turned onto the highway up Dixon Pass. Emily craned her head to see out the window. "Is the pass open now?" she asked.

"It doesn't matter if it is," Alex said. "We're not going all the way to the top."

Emily strained forward, staring down the empty road. They passed a sign warning of the road closure, then the orange barricades loomed in sight. But before they reached the barricades, Alex jerked the steering wheel to the right and the van lurched to the side. Unable to brace herself with her bound hands and feet, she jerked painfully forward against the seat belt and her head bounced against the window. Tears stung her eyes from the pain.

The van jolted to a stop, the vehicle's nose buried in a snowbank. Alex shut off the engine, then came around and slid open the side door. He leaned in to unbuckle Emily and she wondered if she could find a way to fight him off. But then he was pulling her from the vehicle. He dumped her into the snow like an old suitcase and slammed the door shut behind her.

"Come on," he said, then grabbed her by the ankles and began dragging her through the snow.

She screamed, hoping to attract the attention of one of the highway workers who were clearing the pass. "Shut up," Alex said, no heat in the words. He climbed over a snowbank and came down in a narrow alley cut through the snow. The passage was just wide enough

for one person to walk. He strode down it, dragging
Emily by her heels after him. The packed snow scraped
her body and sent stabbing pains through her arms. The
cold bit into her until her teeth were chattering, and
tears streamed down her face from the pain as her head
repeatedly pounded against the ground. She wanted to
protest, to beg him to stop hurting her, but what difference would it make? He was going to kill her, unless Brodie and Travis and the others got here in time.

Then, as suddenly as he had started, Alex stopped.
Emily lay in the snow, staring up at the blue, blue sky,
wondering if this would be the last sight she would ever
see. Alex came and bent over her, the scarf no longer
hiding his face. "Wait for me at the bottom," he said,
then gave her a hard shove.

She flew down a steep slope, over the packed snow,
sliding on her back, and then she was falling, tumbling.
She pressed her arms tightly to her body and tried to
curl into a fetal position, sure she was going to break
something. Her body turned and bounced and slid some
more, until at last she came to rest in a drift of snow,
so cold she could no longer shake, numb with fear and
the certainty of impending death.

Then Alex was standing beside her. "Was that fun?"
he asked. "It looked like it might be." He hauled her upright and tossed her over his shoulder, as if she weighed
no more than a sack of flour. "One more trip and we'll
be home."

She heard the sound of a motor coming to life, and
the creak of turning gears. She craned her head to look
and saw an old ski lift with chairs wide enough for two
people. Alex shoved Emily into one of the chairs, then
sat beside her, and they started up at a rapid clip. She

thought of jumping from the lift, but the fall would probably hurt, and with her hands and feet still taped, she wouldn't be able to get away. "Is this where you've been living?" she asked.

"Pretty cool, huh?" he asked. "I got the old ski lift going, and I fixed up the lift shack at the top as a cozy little hideaway."

"Did you set off the avalanche the day Brodie and Gage came here?" she asked.

"They were stupid enough to come here when the avalanche danger was so high. I figure I did a public service, reminding them."

"Are you going to kill me up there?" Emily asked. Maybe it was a stupid question, but she wanted to know. If he answered yes, maybe she would risk jumping off the lift, and find a way to take him with her. With luck, he'd be the one to break a bone or hit his head when they landed.

"I'm going to kill you eventually," he said. "That's the point, isn't it? But not right away. First, we're going to wait."

"Wait for what?"

"For your brother and his men to come after you. I have a big surprise in store for them."

Chapter Seventeen

Brodie descended the stairs two at a time. He met Bette crossing the living room. "Have you seen Gage or Cody?" he asked.

"They and the other groomsmen went into town to pick up their tuxes. And I think they were all going to have lunch together. Why?"

He shook his head and went past her, back onto the porch. He could call Gage and break up the lunch—and probably end up disrupting the whole wedding. Or he could try to locate Emily and Alex on his own, and summon help then. He surveyed the empty porch again, then moved into the yard and parking area. He was staring at the ground, trying to find what might be Emily's footprints, when he spotted something he hadn't noticed before.

He picked up the box of staples, a cold piercing him that had nothing to do with the outside temperature. Something protruded from the corner of the box. He lifted the lid and shuddered as a small white card fluttered to the ground. He could read the words printed on it without bending over: *ICE COLD*.

Alex had Emily, and he wanted Brodie and the others to know he had her. Maybe he even wanted them to come after him.

Brodie picked up the card and tucked it back into the box of staples, then slipped them into his pocket. He surveyed the snow near where the card had fallen, the surface smooth and undisturbed. But a short distance away, he spotted an area of churned-up ice, with drag marks leading away from it.

He followed the marks for several hundred yards, to a wooded area on the edge of the Walker property. Someone had parked a vehicle here, the impressions from the tire tread making a distinctive pattern in the snow, dripping oil forming dark Rorschach blots between the treads. The tracks circled back to the road that led away from the ranch. When Brodie reached the road, he turned and jogged back toward the house to retrieve his truck. Travis's SUV was still parked in front of the house, but the sheriff must still be inside.

Good. Brodie would follow Alex, and once he found him, he'd call for help. And heaven help the man if he hurt one hair on Emily's head.

The oil drip made Alex's tracks relatively easy to follow. Brodie wondered once again if Alex had planned it that way. The man didn't seem to do anything by accident. Had he set up an ambush to take down any law enforcement who followed him? Did he really think he could defeat a whole phalanx of lawmen? Maybe he thought Emily would be enough of a shield to protect him.

The idea made Brodie's stomach churn, but he told himself if Alex intended to use Emily as a shield, he would keep her alive as long as she was useful to him.

And no matter what the murderer thought, he wasn't going to be able to outwit and outrun them much longer.

The oil drips turned onto the highway leading up to Dixon Pass. Brodie followed them, keeping his speed down, watching the roadsides for any sign of Alex or Emily, or anything that looked like a trap. Alex might be in disguise, or he might use other people to help him, as he had done before. But Brodie saw no other traffic or pedestrians as the road climbed toward the pass. He sped by the sign warning of the road closure, and was almost to the barricades when he spotted an old van, nose first in the snowbank that marked the site of the avalanche he and Gage had been caught in.

He pulled the truck in behind the van, blocking it, then sat for a long moment, staring at the empty vehicle, noting the puddle of oil beneath the rear axle and the opened passenger-side sliding door. The van had no license plate, and was scratched and battered, the bumper wired in place and a deep scratch running the length of the driver's side. Minutes passed, with no sign of life from the vehicle, and no sound but the ticking of the truck's cooling engine.

Weapon drawn, Brodie eased open the door and exited the truck, then approached the van. The vehicle was empty, the keys dangling in the ignition. A glance inside showed a roll of duct tape on the back floorboard, and a single long, dark hair caught in a tear in the upholstery on the back seat. Brodie stared at the hair, struggling to rein in his emotions. Emily had been in this van. So where was she now?

The deep snow made it easy to follow a set of footprints and drag marks from the van, up over a berm of snow to a perfectly carved channel, just wide enough for one man to pass through.

Brodie crept down this channel, the cold closing in around him, as if he were passing through a freezer. He kept his weapon drawn, alert for any activity over and above him. But the only sound was the heavy inhale and exhale of his own breath.

He emerged at the top of a rise and stared down at the old Dixon Downhill ski resort. As before, all was silent. A single chair dangled from the old lift and no life stirred below him.

Except... He sniffed the air. Yes, that was smoke, rising in a thin ribbon from a stovepipe on the other side of the canyon, where the old ski lift shack huddled at the top of the lift line. Brodie stared at the smoke, a vise clamped around his heart. Then he turned and walked back to his truck, where, fingers shaking so hard he could hardly make them work, he punched in Gage's number. After three rings, Gage answered. "What's up?" he asked, the sounds of laughter behind him.

"I've found Alex," Brodie said. "He's got Emily. We've got to stop him before it's too late."

ALEX FED MORE wood into the cast-iron stove that crouched at one end of the lift shack, until the flames leaped and popped, the heat almost overpowering, even though Emily was sprawled on the bench seat from an old pickup truck that had been placed in the opposite corner of the little wooden building. Alex—or someone else—had also brought in a rusting metal table, two wooden stools and a cot draped in blankets, presumably where Alex slept. "They should be able to see the smoke from the highway," he said, closing the door of the stove and standing. "I did everything I could to draw them here, but they're so dim, I need to practically lead them by the hand."

"There'll be more of them than there are you," she said. "You can't kill them all."

He turned to face her, firelight reflecting in his eyes, making him look as insane as he probably was. "But I can." He swept a hand toward the slope opposite them. "I've got explosives planted everywhere on that slope. I stole the dynamite and fuses from the highway crew. They use them to set off avalanches when the road is closed. There's enough gunpowder out there to take out half the mountain."

"If you do that, you'll be killed, too," she said.

"I'll be gone before it blows. Of course, you'll still be here." He tilted his head, studying her. "Do you think I should kill you before I go—or let you die with your brothers in the explosions?"

She closed her eyes, unwilling to look at his face any longer. The mania in his eyes frightened her. Had the insanity been there all along and she had simply failed to see it, believing he was just another undergrad, not someone she really noticed?

"They're here." She opened her eyes at his words, in time to see him pick up a rifle and carry it to the sliding window that filled half of one side of the shack. Originally, the window had allowed the lift operator a view of the lift line and the skiers unloading at the top of the lift. Now it gave Alex a view back toward the opposite slope, beyond which the van was parked. "They're really going to make this too easy for me," he said, sliding the window open a few inches.

She tried to rise up and look past him out the window, but the pain in her arms and legs made movement difficult. The best she could manage was a view of the sky and the back of his head.

Without warning, a blast echoed through the shack. Emily screamed. Alex steadied the rifle against his shoulder and fired again. The smell of gunpowder filled the air, and cold from the open window settled over her like an icy blanket. Alex straightened and laughed. "You should see them out there, running around like frightened rabbits," he said. "I can't believe they thought they were just going to walk up here and take me."

Emily closed her eyes again and said a silent prayer that no one had been hurt.

A melody full of Celtic pipes and drums filled the small shack. Alex whirled to face Emily once more. "What is that?"

"I... I think it's my phone." How was that even possible? She'd been carrying the phone in her back pocket when she stepped out onto the porch, but she would have thought it would have either fallen out or been damaged as she was dragged, and then pushed, down the snowy road.

The music continued to play. Still clutching the rifle, Alex stalked over, shoved Emily onto her side and extracted the phone from the back pocket of her jeans. He studied the screen, then swiped to answer. "Emily can't take your call," he said. "She's a bit tied up at the moment." He laughed, and her stomach churned.

Alex moved back to the window, his back to her. "Who do you think this is? This is the Ice Cold Killer. Who is this? Wait. I'm going to put you on speaker."

"What have you done to Emily?" Brodie's voice boomed over the phone. She choked back a sob, though whether of relief or panic, she couldn't say.

"I haven't done anything to her...yet." Alex held the phone out toward her. "Say hello to Agent Langtry," he said.

"Brodie, it's a trap," she said. "He's—" But before she could finish her warning, Alex hit her, hard, almost knocking her off the seat. She tasted blood from her split lip.

"Let her go now." Brodie's voice was louder, more urgent. "Release her and we can negotiate with you."

"You don't expect me to believe that, do you?" Alex said. "After all, you think I murdered ten women. Besides, I need her. The sheriff and his deputies won't dare hurt me if it means hurting his dear baby sister, too."

"Let her go and take me," Brodie said. "They won't hurt you with a fellow cop as a shield."

Emily held her breath, not sure she had heard correctly. Why would Brodie offer to take her place with a killer?

"Oh, you do tempt me," Alex said. "But I'm not interested in you. I came here originally to kill Emily and I believe in carrying through with my plans."

"What do you want from us?" Brodie asked.

"I want you to play a game with me. You won't win, but I'll try to make it challenging."

"What is the game?"

"Where is the sheriff?" Alex asked. "I want to talk to the sheriff."

"He isn't here."

"Why not? Does he think his wedding is more important than me? More important than his sister?"

"Tell me what you want," Brodie said.

"No. I'm done talking with you now. And I'm destroying this phone. Don't bother calling back." He hit the button to end the call, then jerked open the door to the stove and tossed the phone inside. The smell of burning plastic filled the air.

"Isn't that noble of him, wanting to take your place?" Alex said.

Emily didn't have words to explain how Brodie's offer made her feel. Was he only doing his job as an officer of the law, or did she really mean that much to him?

BRODIE, GAGE, DWIGHT, Jamie, Nate, Ryder and Marshal Cody Rankin gathered at the top of the rise looking down onto the ski lift, just out of range of Alex's rifle. Brodie punched Emily's number again and listened to it ring and ring. "He probably really did destroy the phone," Ryder, who was standing next to Brodie, said. "He doesn't strike me as one to bluff."

"Maybe we should get Travis out here to talk to him," Dwight said.

"Not yet," Gage said. "Rob is with him. His job is to keep him occupied and in the dark." DEA agent Rob Allerton was Paige Riddell's boyfriend and had the least involvement of any of them in this case.

"Alex might make a deal with Travis," Dwight said.

"He's more likely to kill him," Gage said. "I promised Lacy I'd do my best to see that she wasn't a widow before she was a wife."

"How are we going to get closer to him?" Nate asked.

"The snow down in the valley must be six feet deep," Jamie said. "You'd never get through there without a snow machine. Even if you could somehow manage on snowshoes, you'd have to climb down there first, and Alex would have plenty of time to see you and pick you off."

"How did he get up to the lift shack?" Brodie asked, studying the steep, rocky incline from the bottom of the lift to the top. "And how did he get Emily up there with him?"

"I think they rode the lift," Dwight said.

"The lift's broken," Gage said. "It hasn't worked in years."

"Maybe he figured out how to get it running," Brodie said. "Didn't you say it's powered by an old car motor?"

"That doesn't help us," Nate said. "If we try to start the lift, he'll just shoot us. He can let us get almost to him and pick us off."

"Maybe we could lure him out of the shack and pick him off with sniper fire," Ryder said.

"He'd never come out of that lift shack," Gage said. "Not without Emily as a shield. He's too smart for that."

"I still say we need to get Travis here to talk to him," Dwight said.

Brodie studied the scene below him while those around him debated the best approach. "What if instead of climbing up to him, we climb down?" he asked after a moment.

"Climb down from where?" Jamie asked.

"From above the lift shack." He indicated the cliff that rose behind the shack, part of a long ridge that formed the east side of the pass. "That may be how

Alex got down there in the first place. He's a rock climber, right?"

"How would you even get there?" Gage asked, squinting at the mountain that rose above the lift shack.

"There's an old mining road that runs along there, just above the ski area," Nate said. "See that narrow ledge." He pointed, and Brodie thought he could make out the relatively horizontal path along the cliff face. "Climbers use it in the summer. You can take a Jeep up there then, but you'd have to snowshoe in now."

"And if Alex did turn around and see someone up there, he could pick them off with that rifle." Gage shook his head. "It's too risky."

"He hasn't got a view of the slope behind him from the lift shack," Brodie said. "He'd have to step outside to see anyone up there, and we've already established he's unlikely to do that. The thing we need to do is keep him distracted."

"How?" Jamie asked.

"We could take turns approaching behind cover and taking potshots at him," Dwight said. "Or launch flares at him."

"Have to be careful with that," Nate said. "You don't want to set off another avalanche."

"Okay, so we could probably distract him," Dwight said. "But who are we going to get to make the climb? It looks pretty technical."

"I've done some climbing," Brodie said. All of it in a gym, but they didn't have to know that. He knew how to use the equipment, and he was desperate to get Emily out of there before she suffered even more than she already had.

"It's too risky." Gage shook his head.

"It's our best chance of getting to him," Brodie said. "He won't be expecting it because he sees himself as the expert and we're all the amateurs. He's probably made the climb, but he believes we'd never attempt it."

"He's right. You shouldn't attempt it," Dwight said.

"If it was Brenda trapped there, would you do it?" Brodie asked.

Dwight compressed his lips together. "I don't know," he said after a moment. "I'm just glad my wife isn't in there with him."

Emily wasn't Brodie's wife, but if things had worked out differently, she might have been. He wasn't going to let her die if he could do something—even a crazy, reckless stunt like rappelling down an icy cliff—to save her.

He turned to Gage. "Where can I get climbing gear?"

Nate clapped Brodie on the shoulder. "I've got a friend who can fix you up."

"Then let's go. We don't have any time to waste."

Chapter Eighteen

Alex paced back and forth across the floor of the lift shack, alternately cursing to himself and stopping to stare out the window. "Why aren't they doing anything?" he asked. "Nobody up there has moved for the past half an hour." He turned back to Emily. "Maybe they've decided to just let you die. What do you think about that?"

She swallowed and held her head up, though every movement sent pain shooting through her. Alex had let the fire go out and the cold made the pain worse. She couldn't stop shivering, but Alex, dressed in a fleece top and jeans, didn't seem to notice. "Maybe they went to get Travis," she said. "You burned my phone, so they don't have any way of letting you know."

"They better not be planning any tricks. They'll find out soon enough they can't trick me. Do you know why I chose this place for this standoff?" He put his face very close to hers, so that she could smell his stale body odor. It must have been a while since he had showered. How long had he been living up here in this primitive shack? "Do you know?" he demanded.

"No."

"It's because that road up there—" he gestured with

the rifle he still held "—that road is the only way in here." He laughed. "Unless they decided to try to land a helicopter down here. Not easy, and if they do, I'll just set off the explosives as soon as it touches down." He returned to watching out the window. "They can't get at me any other way."

"If they can't get in, how are you going to get out?" she asked.

He grinned, the expression in his eyes telling her he was long past any concrete grip on reality. "I'm going to climb out." He gestured behind them. "That cliff is a 5.9, maybe a 5.10 route. Expert only. But I've done it half a dozen times. I could do it with my eyes closed. By the time I make it to the top, they'll be trapped down here under tons of rock. I'll be far away from here, with a new identity, before anyone even starts to look for me."

"It sounds like you've thought of everything." She was back to flattery—anything to keep him talking and get on his good side.

"Of course I have. It's how I've been so successful so far. These country rubes aren't used to dealing with genius."

"You told them on the phone that you had a game for them to play," she said.

"For the sheriff. Of course, it's a game he can't win. I'm not stupid enough to design it any other way."

She wet her dry, cracking lips. "What is the game?"

"He has to guess the way I've planned for him to die."

"Why would he want to play a game like that?"

"If he guesses right, I'll slit your throat and you'll die quickly. If he guesses wrong…" He let the words trail away, leaving her to imagine the dozens of ways he might choose to make her suffer. She pushed the thoughts away. She wasn't dead yet. She wasn't going to give up hope. A person could live a long time on hope, or so she had read.

Hurry, she sent the thought to whatever rescuers might be mustering to help her. *Hurry, because I don't know how much longer I can hang on.*

"I'VE DONE THIS climb before, but not with the snow and ice." Nate's friend, a wiry thirtysomething who went by the single name Truman, handed Brodie a climbing helmet. "You're certifiable if you want to do it now."

"I don't have any choice." Brodie tugged the helmet on and fastened the chin strap, then reached for a pair of climbing gloves.

"We could try to bring in a helicopter," Nate said. "I bet he'd come outside when he heard that. We could probably get a good shot at him from inside the chopper."

"Or he could decide to kill Emily then and there." Brodie pulled a down jacket over his wool sweater. A Kevlar vest and thermal underwear added extra protection from the cold and gunfire, though he had doubts the vest would stop a bullet from a high-powered rifle—or prevent him from breaking every bone in his body if he fell from the cliff.

"The safety harness should protect you from a fall." Truman demonstrated hooking into the safety line. "It won't help if you bash into the rocks while you're swinging there, but if you lose contact with the cliff, we'll do our best to haul you up."

"I feel so much better now," Brodie said.

Truman made a face and ran through a checklist of the gear. None of the terms were new to Brodie, and he was beginning to feel more confident. "Come on," he said. "We need to get to the site where I'll start the downclimb." Every minute that passed was another minute that might cause Alex to lose patience and take his frustration out on Emily.

They drove as far as they could in Truman's Jeep, then strapped on snowshoes for the rest of the journey. They had to snowshoe almost two miles until they reached a point directly above the lift shack. Brodie peered down at the little tin-roofed building. "There's no smoke coming out of the stovepipe now," he said.

Nate was on the phone with Gage and relayed Brodie's observation. "Gage says Alex and Emily are still in there. He can see them through his binoculars."

"What are they doing?" Brodie asked.

"Just sitting there, he says. Waiting."

"Somebody's been climbing this route recently." Truman pulled back a tarp underneath a spindly fir to reveal a pair of snowshoes.

"Alex," Brodie said. "I figured he had to be getting to and from the shack this way, at least part of the time."

"Then you might be in luck," Truman said. "He may have set anchors in the rock that you can hook on to. Watch for areas cleared of snow—that might mark his hand-and footholds."

Brodie nodded and focused on checking and double-checking his safety harness.

"Why can't he just rappel down?" Nate asked. "It seems like that would be a lot faster."

"It would, if the cliff was straight down," Truman

said. "But it's not. There are a lot of rocks and trees and stuff that stick out. Try to rappel that and you'll just smash into stuff. No, our man is going to have to down-climb." He grinned at Brodie. "Sucks to be you, dude."

Brodie grunted and moved to the edge of the cliff. "You two just hang on if I slip."

Truman moved up beside him. "The route is hard to see from this angle," he said. "We're sort of jutting out over most of the area you'll be descending. But there's a ledge about fifteen feet down that will be a good place to stop and rest."

"If we can't see him, how are we going to know what to do to help him?" Nate asked.

"You can get a good idea of what's happening by the feel of the ropes." Truman clapped Brodie on the back. "Ready?"

Brodie nodded. His brain was telling him he was crazy to risk his life this way, but he was ignoring his brain. His heart was saying he didn't have a choice, and he was choosing to go with his heart. "Tell the others it's time to start whatever they've come up with to distract Alex."

"I've told them," Nate said. "Good luck."

The first step off the cliff, blindly groping for a foothold in the slick rock, was the worst. Relief surged through him as his foot found purchase and he was able to steady himself, but he couldn't stop to enjoy the sensation. He had to keep going. Glancing down, he could see the shallow rock ledge Truman had mentioned, and he focused on getting to it. One foot here, one hand there. Test the next foothold to see if it would support his weight. Reject another foothold as too weak or too slick. He wedged his foot into a niche in the rock. It felt secure, so he lowered himself down, searching for the next foothold.

Then the rock gave way. He flailed around, seeking purchase and finding none, swinging free against the rock face, like a pendulum in a crazy clock. Truman, very pale and very far away, looked over from the top. They had agreed that they couldn't shout to one another for fear of attracting Alex's attention. Nate also leaned out and gave him a thumbs-up. Truman pointed to the ledge and pantomimed lowering the rope. Brodie nodded. They were going to lower him to the ledge. Good idea.

Once safely on the ledge, he rested a moment, his body plastered to the rock, the cold seeping into him despite the layers of clothing. In contrast, the sun at his back burned. When he was breathing more or less regularly again, he tugged on the rope, a signal that he was ready to start down once more.

He fell three more times on the way down, each time the safety harness catching him, the rope stretching and bouncing him slightly. He learned to relax until the swaying slowed, then to find purchase in the rock once more. As Truman had guessed, Alex had hammered pitons into the rock face, allowing Brodie to clip into these as he moved down the cliff, untethering from Truman and Nate above.

About three-quarters of the way down he realized he was no longer afraid. He was actually doing this. The adrenaline rush was exhilarating, and if what awaited him at the end of the climb wasn't so important, he might have lingered to enjoy himself.

But he had no time to indulge himself. He moved

as quickly as possible. When he touched ground only a dozen feet behind the lift shack, his hand shook as he unhooked from the safety rope and climbed out of the harness. He took the time to roll up everything and stash it underneath a tree, not wanting to provide an escape route if Alex managed to make it out of the lift shack before Brodie got to him.

He straightened, drew his weapon and started toward the shack. His plan was to go in, surprise Alex and make an arrest with no one getting hurt. It was a good plan, but he had no idea if it would really work.

EMILY HAD FALLEN into a kind of stupor on the old car seat, while Alex slumped on a stool in front of the window, the rifle propped against the wall beside him. Earlier, she had spent some time groping around the seat, hoping to find a popped spring or a protruding bit of metal to cut the tape at her wrists or ankles, but no such luck. All she could do was wait and pray. She tried asking Alex questions about himself, but after a while he had stopped answering her.

Suddenly, he shoved back the stool and stood. "It's about time," he said.

Emily pushed herself up straighter. "What's happening?" she asked.

Alex gestured toward the window. "They've found a way to communicate."

By arching her back and craning her neck, Emily was able to make out someone holding what looked like a poster with writing on it. But it was too far away to read. "What does it say?" she asked.

Alex pulled out a pair of binoculars and studied the sign. "*THE SHERIFF IS READY TO TALK*."

"Travis is there?" Emily's heart pounded. Travis shouldn't be here! He should be with Lacy, getting married.

Alex scowled. "There's someone there in a sheriff's department uniform, with a big hat and a star on his chest, but I can't tell if it's your brother." He set down the binoculars and looked around the lift shack. "I need something to write on. I need to tell him to move in closer—and to take off the stupid hat."

"You should have thought of that before you burned up my phone." Emily braced herself for another blow, but Alex only scowled at her and began digging through the debris against the walls of the shack. Amazingly, he came up with a small whiteboard, roughly two-foot square. Emily recalled seeing similar boards at lift shacks at other resorts, used to convey messages such as "Mr. Reynolds, contact child care" or "New snow overnight 4 inches!"

In a drawer, Alex found a set of dry-erase markers. He scrawled his message, *COME CLOSER AND TAKE OFF THE HAT.*

"They're not going to be able to see that from in here," Emily said. "You'll have to go outside."

"And give them a clear shot at me?" Alex shook his head. "No, you'll go out." He pulled the knife from his belt and she shrank back in fear. But he bent and cut the tape from her ankles, then did the same for her wrists.

She cried out as she brought her hands in front of her again, the stabbing pain doubling her over. Alex chafed her ankles between his hands. "You'll be fine in a minute." He straightened and thrust the sign and the marker at her. "Go out there and hold this up. And don't try anything. If you run, I'll shoot you in the back." He held up the rifle.

She gripped the board with numb, aching fingers and he tucked the marker into the pocket of her jeans and hauled her to her feet. She could barely walk, much less run. Alex took her arm and dragged her toward the door of the lift shack. "Get out there!" he called, and thrust her out the door.

She landed sprawling in the snow, the sign facedown beside her. "Get up!" Alex shouted, and she looked back to see the rifle pointed at her.

Clenching her teeth, she shoved to her knees, then slowly stood, bringing the sign with her. Holding on to the lift shack for support, she made her way around to the side facing the road, moving through snow that came past her knees. Finally she stopped and held up the sign. Seconds later, an answer appeared: *YOU OKAY?* in letters large enough to be seen clearly even at that distance.

She nodded, hoping someone was watching through binoculars. Then she scrawled *YES* beneath Alex's message. A cold wind buffeted her, and she was shaking so badly she had trouble holding on to the sign. "Get back in here!" Alex shouted.

She wanted to ignore the command, to run as fast and as far as she could. But that wouldn't be very far. The snow here was several feet deep and she could scarcely move. She would be dead before she took more than a few steps.

"Get in!" Alex shouted again.

Instead, she moved up against the lift shack once more, the thick logs providing a barrier to the wind and, she hoped, bullets from the man inside. She sank into the snow and sat, arms wrapped around her knees. Alex couldn't see her from here, and he wouldn't be able to shoot her without coming outside—something he apparently was loath to do. She would sit here until her strength returned and some of the pain in her limbs subsided. By then, maybe someone below would have come up here to her, or found a way to get to her. Having her out of the way might even help them.

Alex was screaming now, a stream of profanities aimed at her. She closed her eyes and shut him out, focusing instead on the whistle of the wind around the corner of the lift shack, and the creak of the chair on the overhead cable.

And the sound of footsteps moving through the snow.

Her eyes snapped open, fear choking her. Alex's rage at her must have overcome his fear of leaving the shack. But instead of Alex, she was amazed to see Brodie standing at the corner of the shack, one finger to his lips. "How?" She had scarcely uttered the single syllable before he shook his head. He motioned for her to stay where she was, and indicated he intended to go inside the shack.

She shook her head. If Brodie went in there, Alex would kill him. He had the rifle, and a knife, and then there were the explosives everywhere on the mountain. How could she warn Brodie without Alex overhearing? She picked up the sign and rubbed out the message there with the sleeve of her sweater, then wrote, *HE HAS EXPLOSIVES ALL OVER THE MOUNTAIN. WILL DETONATE.*

Brodie read the message and nodded. Then his eyes met hers, and the determination and, yes, love in that single glance made her almost giddy. Then he was gone, around the back of the shack once more.

Emily shoved to her feet. She couldn't sit here, not knowing what was happening with Brodie and Alex. She followed Brodie around the back of the shack, floundering through the thick snow, which covered the sound of her approach. At the door of the shack he stopped, weapon raised, then burst inside.

She braced herself for the blast of gunfire or the sounds of a struggle, but only ringing silence followed. Cautiously, she moved forward, until she was just outside the open door. "What's happening?" she called.

"He isn't here," Brodie called. He stood over the table, examining the items scattered across it. "He must have slipped out while I was with you."

"A very good deduction," Alex said as he grabbed Emily from behind and put a knife to her throat.

This can't be happening, Emily thought, as Alex crushed her against him. The knife bit into her throat, but she scarcely felt it, as if her body was becoming immune to pain.

"Let her go," Brodie said, his gun leveled at Alex.

"Drop the gun or she dies now." Alex pulled her more tightly against him, so that she could hardly breathe, her body angled so that she was between his legs, one hand almost resting on his groin.

Brodie tossed the gun aside. It sank out of sight in the snow. "What now?" he asked.

"That's right," Alex said. "I'm calling the shots."

Emily gripped the dry-erase marker in her hand. As weapons went, it was pathetic. But it was all she had. Several years before, when she was an undergrad, she had attended a presentation on self-defense.

All she could remember was the instructor's advice to use whatever was at hand as a weapon. Most of the feeling had returned to her fingers. She made a fist around the marker, then drove it as hard as she could into Alex's groin.

The knife slid across her throat, but she was able to shove out of Alex's grasp as he doubled over. Brodie jumped on him and the two grappled in the snow. Emily knelt by the shack, watching in horror as blood stippled the pristine surface of the snow with red.

The two men rolled over and over in the snow, first Brodie on top, then Alex. With a cry of rage, Alex heaved Brodie off him and jumped to his feet. Then he was running, headed for the cliff. He began to climb, clambering up the steep slope without aid of harness or ropes or even gloves.

Brodie knelt beside Emily. "It's bleeding a lot, but I don't think the cuts are too deep," he said. He stripped out of his jacket, peeled off his sweater and wrapped it around her neck.

"There's a rifle in the shack," she said through chattering teeth. "You need to get it and go after him."

"It's okay," he said, one arm wrapped around her. "Nate and another man are waiting at the top of the cliff. He won't get away from them."

They stared as Alex scaled the cliff, swarming up the rock face. Emily gasped as he slipped, then regained his foothold. "He's going too fast," Brodie said. "He's being reckless."

He was almost to the top, where the rock jutted out and he had to pull himself over it. He had almost made it when something at the top caught his attention. "It's Nate," Brodie said. "He's got him covered."

A rope dropped over the edge of the cliff and dangled beside Alex. "Nate will pull him up and arrest him," Brodie said.

But Alex didn't take the rope. Instead, he looked back over his shoulder. He took one hand from the rock and balanced for a second, before releasing the other hand and falling backward.

Emily buried her face in Brodie's shoulder. Alex's cries echoed around them, then all fell silent. "Is he dead?" she asked.

"If he isn't, he's badly hurt." He stood. "Gage is sending a couple of snowmobiles down to get us. Let's go meet them."

"Can we sit here a little bit, until they get here?" she asked.

"Are you too weak to walk?" His voice rose in alarm. "Do you want me to carry you?"

"No, I don't want you to carry me." The idea made her want to laugh.

"What's so funny?"

"I'm wondering if there's a statute of limitations on proposals."

He hesitated, then said. "What do you mean?"

She pressed her palms to his chest, over his heart, and looked into his eyes. "I mean, I don't want you to carry me. But I might want you to marry me."

"Because I scaled a cliff and faced death to save you?"

"Because you did those things. And because I love you. More than I was willing to admit before."

"Why weren't you willing to admit it?"

"Are you always so full of questions?"

"I want to be sure you're not out of your mind from loss of blood."

"I turned down your proposal before because I was afraid of what I would have to give up if we married," she said. "Now I'm old enough to see that marriage isn't about giving things up—it's about gaining a partner who can help you get even more out of life."

He gently brushed her hair back from her face and looked into her eyes. "Emily Walker, will you marry me?" he asked.

Tears—of relief, and such joy she could hardly contain it—flooded her eyes and she pressed her lips to his.

The roar of an approaching snowmobile interrupted their kiss. Two more snowmobiles followed. They stopped nearby and Gage pulled off his helmet. "Are you okay?" he asked.

"Emily's wounded," Brodie said. "I'm fine." He looked toward the cliff. "Alex is either dead or wounded."

The man on the second snowmobile collected a medical kit from the back of the machine and started through the snow toward the cliff. The driver of the third snowmobile, a woman, approached Emily. "Let's take a look," she said, and began to unwind Brodie's sweater. She surveyed the wound. "It's mostly stopped bleeding. You might need a few stitches and you might be more comfortable wearing scarves for a while, but in a year or two I'll bet the scar hardly shows."

"I'll take a scar over the alternative," she said.

"I'll just get you cleaned up a bit," the woman said, and opened her medical kit.

The other paramedic returned, shaking his head. "That one doesn't need me anymore," he said.

Emily tried to feel some sympathy or sorrow for

the man Alex might have been—handsome, smart, with every advantage. But she felt only emptiness. She didn't have it in her to hate someone so twisted, but she could admit she was relieved he would never terrorize anyone else again.

The paramedic helped her to the snowmobile and assisted her in climbing on. Brodie rode behind Gage. They were at the top again before Emily remembered one of the most important questions of the day. She looked at Gage. "Where is Travis?"

Gage checked his watch. "I hope he's getting married about now."

"But you're the best man," she said. "And I'm one of the bridesmaids."

"I think they can finish the ceremony without us," Gage said.

"He's going to be furious when he finds out what happened," Emily said.

"He is. But he'll get over it."

"Get over what?"

They turned to see Travis, a leather duster pulled on over his tux, striding toward them. Lacy, a down parka over her wedding dress, and the rest of the wedding party trailed behind. "What are you doing here?" Gage demanded.

"I came to see this case to the finish." He turned to Emily. "Are you okay?"

She nodded. "I'll be fine." At least, she would be, given time to rest and heal.

Travis nodded and turned back to Gage. "Alex?"

"He's dead."

"He jumped off the cliff, rather than face arrest," Brodie said.

"It's over," Emily said, the impact just beginning to hit her. "It's really over."

"It is." Gage put one arm around his brother. "You can leave the mop-up to us. Now you can get on with the honeymoon."

"We have to get married first," Lacy said.

"You're not married yet?" Emily asked.

"We couldn't get married with most of the wedding party—and some of the guests—up here on the pass," she said.

"You all weren't coming to the wedding, so we decided to bring the wedding to you," Bette said. She indicated everyone around them. "We're all here, but it's a little chilly, so let's get going, why don't we?"

Emily put a hand to her throat. "But I'm not dressed for a wedding."

"No one is looking at you." Bette handed her a bouquet. "Now hold this, stand over there. Lacy, you stand here."

Bette arranged everyone, and within five minutes Emily was blinking back tears as her eldest brother and her dear friend promised to love, honor and cherish each other for the rest of their lives. The officiant pronounced them husband and wife and they kissed as a tinny rendition of the Wedding March—courtesy of someone's phone—serenaded them.

"Now everyone come back to the reception," Bette said. Gage started to object, but she held up a hand. "I know what you're going to say. You have a crime scene to process. I'll send refreshments back to you."

"If it's all right with you, I'll stay with Emily," Brodie said.

"You do that," Travis said. "I think I can trust you to take good care of her this time."

"This time, and for every time to come," he said.

The others piled into their vehicles and drove away, Travis and Lacy in a white pickup truck with tin cans tied to the back and *Just Married* scrawled across the back window. Then Brodie walked Emily to the ambulance and climbed in after her. "I don't think you ever gave me an answer to my proposal," he said, taking her hand.

"Yes," she said. "Yes, I'll marry you."

He held her gaze, steady and sure. "I never want to hold you back from your dreams," he said. "I only want to be part of them."

"You are." She kissed him, a sweet meeting of their lips full of promise and hope and all things she was determined to never give up again.

* * * * *

WEDDING AT CARDWELL RANCH

B.J. DANIELS

This is dedicated to my readers and my Facebook friends who shared their 'gaslighting' ideas and proved that they think as creepy me.

If you haven't already, come say hello on my author Facebook page at www.facebook.com/pages/BJ-Daniels/127936587217837

Chapter One

Allison Taylor brushed back a lock of her hair and willed herself not to scream.

"Is something wrong?" her brother-in-law asked from the kitchen doorway, startling her and making her jump.

She dropped the heavy covered pot she'd taken from the pantry a little too hard onto the counter. The lid shifted, but not enough that she could see inside.

"Didn't mean to scare you," Drew Taylor said with a laugh as he lounged against the kitchen door frame. "I was cravin' some of your famous chili, but I think maybe we should go out."

"I just need a minute. If you could see to Natalie…"

"She's still asleep. I just checked." Drew studied her for a long moment. Like his brother, he had russet-brown hair and dark brown eyes and classic good looks. His mother had assured both of her sons that they were wonderful. Fortunately Drew had taken it with a grain of salt—unlike his brother Nick.

"Are you okay, Allie? I've been so worried about you since Nick…"

"I'm fine." She didn't want to talk about her presumed-dead husband. She really just wanted her brother-in-law to go into the other room and leave her alone for a moment.

Drew had been a godsend. She didn't know what she would have done without him, she thought as she pulled a band from her jeans pocket and secured her long, blond hair in a single tail at the back of her head.

When she'd mentioned how nice his brother was to Nick shortly after they married, he'd scoffed.

"Just be glad he likes you. He's about the only one in my family," he had added with a laugh.

"Why don't you let me help you with that," Drew said now as he took a step toward her. He frowned as his gaze went to the pot and the pile of ingredients she'd already stacked up on the counter. The chili pot was the last thing she'd brought into the kitchen from the porch of the small cabin. "You kept the pot?"

So his mother had told him about the incident.

He must think I'm losing my mind just like his mother and sister do.

The worst part was she feared they were right.

Allie looked down at the heavy cast-iron pot with its equally heavy cast-iron lid. Her hand trembled as she reached for the handle. The memory of the last time she'd lifted that lid—and what she'd found inside—sent a shudder through her.

The covered cast-iron casserole pot, enameled white inside and the color of fresh blood on the outside, had been a wedding present from her in-laws.

"She does know how to cook, doesn't she?" her mother-in-law, Mildred, had asked all those years ago as if Allie hadn't been standing there. Mildred was a twig-thin woman who took pride in these things: her petite, slim, fifty-eight-year-old body, her sons and her standing in the community. Her daughter, Sarah, was just the opposite of her mother, overweight and dumpy by comparison. And Mildred was always making that comparison to anyone who would listen, including Sarah.

Mildred was on her fourth husband and lived in one of

the more modest mansions at Big Sky. Of her two sons, Nick had been the baby—and clearly her favorite.

Nick had laughed that day when his mother had asked if his new wife could cook. "She makes pretty good chili, I'll give her that," he told Mildred. "But that's not why I married her." He'd given Allie a side hug, grinning like a fool and making her blush to the roots of her hair.

Nick had liked to say he had the prettiest wife in town. "Just make sure you stay that way," he'd always add. "You start looking like my sister and you can pack your bags."

The red, cast-iron, covered pot she was now reaching for had become her chili pot.

"Allie, I thought you'd thrown that pot away!" Drew reached to stop her, knocking the lid off in the effort. It clattered to the counter.

Allie lunged back, her arm going up protectively to shield her face. But this time the pot was empty. No half-dead squirrel inside it.

"I'm throwing this pot in the trash," Drew announced. "If just the sight of it upsets you—"

"No, your mother will have a fit."

"Let her." He swept pot and lid off the counter and carried it out to the garbage can.

When he came back into the room, he looked at her and shook his head. "Allie, you've got to pull it together. Maybe you should go back to the doctor and see if there is something else he can give you. You're strung like a piano wire."

She shook her head. "I don't need a doctor." She just needed for whatever was happening to her to stop.

His gaze moved past her, his expression going from a concerned frown to a smile. "Hey, girl," he said as his five-year-old niece came into the kitchen. He stepped past Allie to swing Nat into his arms. "I came over to check on the two of you. Mama was going to cook us some dinner but I think we should go out to eat. What do you say?"

Allie started to argue that she couldn't let Drew do any more for them and she sure couldn't afford to go out to eat, but stopped as her daughter said, "Are you sick, Mama?" Her precious daughter looked to her with concern. Allie saw the worry in Nat's angelic face. She'd seen it too much lately. It was bad enough that Natalie had recently lost her father. Now more than ever she needed her mother to be sane.

"I'm fine, sweetie. It's too hot for chili, anyway. So let's go out, why not?" Allie said, relieved and thankful for Drew. Not just for coming by to check on them, but for throwing out the pot. She hadn't because her mother-in-law was upset enough and the Taylors were the only family she had, especially now.

"Just let me freshen up and change," she said as Drew took Nat to look for her shoes.

In the bathroom, Allie locked the door, turned on the shower and stripped off her clothes. She was still sweating from fear, her heart beating hard against her chest.

"You found a what in the chili pot?" her mother-in-law had asked in disbelief when Allie had called her—a huge mistake in retrospect. But at the time, she'd hoped her mother-in-law would understand why she couldn't keep the pot. Why she didn't want it in her house.

"I found a squirrel in that cast-iron pot you gave me. When I picked up the lid—"

"No way would a squirrel get into your cabin, let alone climb under a heavy lid like that. Why would it? You must have imagined it. Are you still on those drugs the doctor gave you after my Nicky died?"

Allie's husband had always been "my Nicky" to his mother while Mildred had insisted Allie call *her* "Mother Taylor."

"No, Mother Taylor, I told you." Allie's own mother had died when she was nineteen. Her father had moved, remarried and started a new family. They'd lost touch. "I quit taking the pills a long time ago."

"I think it's those pills," Mildred had said as if Allie hadn't spoken. "You said they had you seeing things that weren't there."

"The squirrel *was* there. I had to take it out back and—"

"If I were you, I'd talk to your doctor. Why do you need the pills, anyway? It isn't like you're still grieving over my Nicky. Charlotte Reynolds told me she saw you having lunch the other day, you and Natalie, and you were *laughing*."

Allie had closed her eyes, remembering the lunch in question. "I am trying to make things more normal for Nat."

"Well, it looks bad, you having a good time while your poor husband is barely cold in his grave."

She wanted to mention that Nick wasn't in his grave, but knew better than to bring that up. "It's been eight months."

"Like you have to tell me that!" Mildred sniffed and blew her nose. She'd cried constantly over the death of her favorite son and couldn't understand why Allie wasn't still doing the same.

"We all grieve in our own way and I have a young daughter to raise," Allie had said more times than she wanted to recall.

The phone call had ended with Mildred crying and talking about what a wonderful man her Nicky had been. A lie at best. He'd been a lousy husband and an even worse father, but now that he was dead, he would always be the wonderful man Mildred remembered.

After that, she'd learned her lesson. She kept the other crazy things that had been happening to herself. If Mildred knew, she would have her in a straitjacket. And little Nat...? She couldn't bear to think about Mildred having anything to do with raising her daughter.

"So," Drew said as she and Nat sat across from him in a

booth at a local café later that evening. "Did I hear you've gone back to work?"

It was impossible to keep anything a secret in this canyon, Allie thought. She had hoped to keep it from the Taylor family as long as possible.

"Dana Savage called me about doing a Western wedding up at her ranch for her cousin Tag and his soon-to-be wife, Lily." She didn't mention that she'd accepted the job several months ago. Or how badly she needed the money. With the investigation into Nick's presumed death still unresolved, the insurance company was holding off paying her. Not that it would last long if she didn't get back to work.

Her mother-in-law kept mentioning "that big insurance check my Nicky left you," but the insurance money would barely cover a couple years of Natalie's college, if that. And Allie hoped to invest it for that very use.

"I've been doing some work at Cardwell Ranch. Nice people to work for. But are you sure you're up to it?" Drew asked quietly, real concern in his tone. "Mother mentioned that she was worried about you. She said you were still taking the pills and they were making you see things?"

Of course Mildred told Drew and his sister, Sarah, everything. Allie tried not to show her irritation. She had no appetite, but she attempted to eat what she could. She didn't want Drew mentioning to his mother, even accidentally, that she wasn't eating much. Mildred would make it into her not taking care of herself.

"I'm fine. I'm *not* taking the pills. I told your mother—"

He held up his hand. "You don't have to tell me about my mother. She hears only what she wants to hear. I'm on your side. I think going back to work might be the best thing for you. So what do you plan to do with Natalie? I don't have to tell you what Mother is going to say."

"Nat's going with me," Allie said emphatically. "Dana

has children she can play with. As a matter of fact, Dana is going to teach Nat to ride a horse."

Natalie grinned and clapped her small hands excitedly. She was the spitting image of Allie at that age: straight, pale blond hair cut in a bob, green eyes with a pert little nose and deep dimples. Allie got the blond hair from her Scandinavian mother and the green eyes from her Irish father.

There was no sign of the Taylor family in her daughter, something that had caused a lot of speculation from not only Nick, but his mother.

Nat quickly told her uncle that it would be a very gentle horse and Dana's kids Hank and Mary were riding before they were even her age. "The twins are too young to ride yet," she announced.

"Dana wouldn't let Nat do it if she thought it wasn't all right," Allie added.

"I'm sure it will be fine," Drew said, but she could tell that he already knew what her mother-in-law was going to have to say about it. "Cardwell Ranch is where the wedding is going to be, I take it?"

"The wedding will be in a meadow on the ranch with the reception and a lot of other events in the large, old barn."

"You know that we've been invited," Drew said almost in warning.

The canyon was its own little community, with many of the older families—like Dana's—that dated back to the eighteen hundreds before there was even a paved road through it. Mildred Taylor must be delighted to be invited to a wedding of a family that was like old canyon royalty. Mother Taylor might resent the Cardwell clan, say things behind their back, but she would never outright defy them since everyone loved Dana Cardwell Savage and had held great respect for her mother, Mary Justice.

"How are things with you?" Allie asked.

"Everything's fine." He smiled but she'd seen the lines

around his eyes and had heard that his construction company was struggling without Nick.

He'd been so generous with her and Natalie that she feared he was giving away money he didn't have.

She was just thankful when the meal was over and Drew dropped her and Nat off at the small cabin in the Gallatin Canyon where she'd lived with Nick until his disappearance. *The canyon* as it was known, ran from the mouth just south of Gallatin Gateway almost to West Yellowstone, fifty miles of winding road that trailed the river in a deep cut through the mountains.

The drive along the Gallatin River was breathtaking, a winding strip of highway that followed the blue-ribbon trout stream up over the Continental Divide. In the summer as it was now, the Gallatin ran crystal clear over tinted green boulders. Pine trees grew dark and thick along its edge and against the steep mountains. Aspens, their leaves bright green, grew among the pines.

Sheer rock cliffs overlooked the highway and river, with small areas of open land. The canyon had been mostly cattle and dude ranches, a few summer cabins and homes—that was until Big Sky resort and the small town that followed developed at the foot of Lone Mountain.

Luxury houses had sprouted up all around the resort, with Mother Taylor's being one of them. Fortunately, some of the original cabins still remained and the majority of the canyon was National Forest so it would always remain undeveloped.

Allie's was one of the older cabins. Because it was small and not in great shape, Nick had gotten a good deal on it. Being in construction, he'd promised to enlarge it and fix all the things wrong with it. That hadn't happened.

After Drew left, Allie didn't hurry inside the cabin. It was a nice summer night, the stars overhead glittering brightly and a cool breeze coming up from the river.

She had begun to hate the cabin—and her fear of what might be waiting for her inside it. Nick had been such a force of nature to deal with that his presence seemed to have soaked into the walls. Sometimes she swore she could hear his voice. Often she found items of his clothing lying around the house as if he was still there—even though she'd boxed up his things and taken them to the local charity shop months ago.

Just the thought of what might be waiting for her inside the cabin this time made her shudder as she opened the door and stepped in, Nat at her side.

She hadn't heard Nick's voice since she'd quit taking the drugs. Until last night. When she'd come into the living room, half-asleep, she'd found his favorite shirt lying on the floor by the couch. She'd actually thought she smelled his aftershave even though she'd thrown the bottle away.

The cabin looked just as she'd left it. Letting out a sigh of relief, she put Nat to bed and tried to convince herself she hadn't heard Nick's voice last night. Even the shirt that she'd remembered picking up and thinking it felt warm and smelled of Nick before she'd dropped it over the back of the couch was gone this morning, proving the whole incident had been nothing but a bad dream.

"Good night, sweetheart," she said and kissed her daughter's forehead.

"Night," Nat said sleepily and closed her eyes.

Allie felt as if her heart was going to burst when she looked at her precious daughter. She couldn't let Mildred get her hands on Nat. But if the woman thought for a moment that Allie was incapable of raising her daughter...

She quickly turned out the light and tiptoed out of the room. For a moment, she stood in the small living area. Nick's shirt wasn't over the back of the couch so that was a relief.

So many times she had stood here and wished her life

could be different. Nick had been so sweet while they were dating. She'd really thought she'd met her Prince Charming—until after the wedding and she met the real Nick Taylor.

She sighed, remembering her decision soon after the wedding to leave him and have the marriage annulled, but then she'd realized she was pregnant. Had she really been so naive as to think a baby would change Nick into the man she'd thought she'd married?

Shaking her head now, she looked around the cabin, remembering all the ideas she had to fix the place up and make it a home. Nick had hated them all and they had ended up doing nothing to the cabin.

Well, she could do what she wanted now, couldn't she? But she knew, even if she had the money, she didn't have the heart for it. She would never be able to exorcize Nick's ghost from this house. What she really wanted was to sell the cabin and move. She promised herself she would—once everything with Nick's death was settled.

Stepping into her bedroom, she was startled to see a pile of her clothes on her bed. Had she taken them out of the closet earlier when she'd changed to go to dinner? Her heart began to pound. She'd been upset earlier but she wouldn't have just thrown her clothes on the bed like that.

Then how had they gotten there? She'd locked the cabin when she'd left.

Panicked, she raced through the house to see if anything was missing or if any of the doors or windows had been broken into. Everything was just as she'd left it—except for the clothes on her bed.

Reluctantly, she walked back into her bedroom half-afraid the clothes wouldn't still be on the bed. Another hallucination?

The clothes were there. Unfortunately, that didn't come as a complete relief. Tonight at dinner, she'd worn capris, a blouse and sandals since it was June in Montana. Why would she have pulled out what appeared to be almost everything she owned from the closet? No, she realized, not *everything*. These were only the clothes that Nick had bought her.

Tears blurred her eyes as she started to pick up one of the dresses. Like the others, she hated this dress because it reminded her of the times he'd made her wear it and how the night had ended. It was very low cut in the front. She'd felt cheap in it and told him so but he'd only laughed.

"When you've got it, flaunt it," he'd said. "That's what I say."

Why hadn't she gotten rid of these clothes? For the same reason she hadn't thrown out the chili pot after the squirrel incident. She hadn't wanted to upset her mother-in-law. Placating Mother Taylor had begun right after Allie had married her son. It was just so much easier than arguing with the woman.

"Nick said you don't like the dresses he buys you," Mildred had said disapprovingly one day when she'd stopped by the cabin and asked Allie why she wasn't wearing the new dress. "There is nothing wrong with looking nice for your husband."

"The dresses he buys me are just more revealing than I feel comfortable with."

Her mother-in-law had mugged a face. "You'd better loosen up and give my son what he wants or he'll find someone who will."

Now as she reached for the dress on the top of the pile, she told herself she would throw them out, Mother Taylor be damned.

But the moment she touched the dress, she let out a cry of surprise and panic. The fabric had jagged cuts down the front. She stared in horror as she saw other deep, angry-looking slices in the fabric. *Who had done this?*

Her heart in her throat, she picked up another of the dresses Nick had made her wear. Her sewing scissors clattered to the bedroom floor. She stared down at the scissors in horror, then at the pile of destroyed clothing. All of the dresses Nick had bought her had been ruined.

Allie shook her head as she dropped the dress in her hand and took a step back from the bed. Banging into the closed closet doors, she fought to breathe, her heart hammering in her chest. *Who did this?* Who *would* do this? She remembered her brother-in-law calling from out in the hall earlier, asking what was taking her so long before they'd gone to dinner. But that was because she'd taken a shower to get the smell of her own fear off her. It wasn't because she was in here cutting up the clothes her dead husband had made her wear.

Tears welled in her eyes, making the room blur. She shoved that bitter thought away and wiped at her tears. She wouldn't have done this. She *couldn't* have.

Suddenly, she turned and stared at the closed closet door with mounting fear. Slowly, she reached for the knob, her hand trembling. As the closet door came open, she froze. Her eyes widened in new alarm.

A half dozen new outfits hung in the otherwise nearly empty closet, the price tags still on them. As if sleepwalking, Allie reached for one of the tags and stared in shock at the price. Hurriedly, she checked the others. She couldn't afford any of them. So where had they come from?

Not only that, the clothes were what she would call "classic," the type of clothes she'd worn when she'd met Nick. The kind of clothes she'd pleaded with him to let her wear.

"I want other men to look at you and wish they were me," Nick had said, getting angry.

But when she and Nick went out and she wore the clothes and other men did look, Nick had blamed her.

"You must have given him the eye," Nick would say as

they argued on the way home. "Probably flipped your hair like an invitation. Who knows what you do while I'm at work all day."

"I take care of your daughter and your house."

Nick hadn't let her work after they'd gotten married, even though he knew how much she loved her wedding planning business. "Women who work get too uppity. They think they don't need a man. No wife of mine is going to work."

Allie had only the clothes he bought her. She'd purchased little since his death because the money had been so tight. Nick had wanted to know about every cent she'd spent, so she hadn't been able to save any money, either. Nick paid the bills and gave her a grocery allowance. He said he'd buy her whatever she needed.

Now she stared at the beautiful clothes hanging in her closet. Beautiful blouses and tops. Amazing skirts and pants and dresses. Clothes Nick would have taken out in the yard and burned. But Nick was gone.

Or was he? He still hadn't been declared legally dead. That thought scared her more than she wanted to admit. What if he suddenly turned up at her door one night?

Was that what was making her crazy? Maybe she *had* done this. She had yearned for clothing like this and hated the clothes Nick had bought her, so had she subconsciously...

Allie stumbled away from the closet, bumped into the corner of the bed and sat down hard on the floor next to it. Her hand shook as she covered her mouth to keep from screaming. Had she shoplifted these clothes? She couldn't have purchased them. Just as she couldn't have cut up the dresses and not remembered. There had to be another explanation. Someone was playing a horrible trick on her.

But even as she pondered it, more rational thoughts came on its heels. Did she really believe that someone had come into the cabin and done this? Who in their right mind would believe that?

Pushing herself up, she crawled over to where she'd dropped her purse as she tried to remember even the last time she'd written a check. Her checkbook wasn't in her purse. She frowned and realized she must have left it in the desk when she'd paid bills.

Getting up she walked on wobbly legs to the desk in the corner, opened the drawer and took out her checkbook. Her fingers shook with such a tremor that she could barely read what was written in it.

But there it was. A check for more than eight hundred dollars! The handwriting was scrawled, but she knew it had to be hers. She saw the date of the check. *Yesterday?*

She had dropped Nat off for a playdate and then gone into Bozeman… Could she account for the entire afternoon? Her heart pounded as she tried to remember everything she'd done and when she might have bought these clothes. She'd been wandering around in a daze since Nick's death. She couldn't account for every minute of yesterday, but what did that matter? The proof was staring her in the face.

Allie shoved the checkbook into the drawer and tried to pull herself together. She had to think about her daughter.

"You're fine," she whispered to herself. "Once you get back to work…" She couldn't have been more thankful that she had the Cardwell Ranch wedding. More than the money, she needed to do what she loved—planning weddings—and get her mind off everything else.

Once she was out of this house she'd shared with Nick… Yes, then she would be fine. She wouldn't be so…forgetful. What woman wouldn't feel she was losing her mind, considering what she'd been going through?

Chapter Two

"Who's that singing?" five-year-old Ford Cardwell asked as he and his father followed the sound.

Jackson Cardwell had parked the rental SUV down by his cousin Dana's ranch house when they'd arrived, but finding no one at home, they'd headed up the hill toward the barn and the van parked in front of it.

"I have no idea, son," Jackson said, but couldn't help smiling. The voice was young and sweet, the song beautiful. "It sounds like an angel."

"It *is* an angel," Ford cried and pointed past the barn to the corrals.

The girl was about his son's age, but while Ford had taken after the Cardwell side of the family with his dark hair and eyes, this child had pale blond hair and huge green eyes.

When she saw them, she smiled, exposing two deep dimples. Both children were adorable, but this little girl was hands down more angelic-looking and—Jackson would bet—*acting* than Ford.

She wore cowboy boots with a pale green-and-white-polka-dotted, one-piece, short jumpsuit that brought out the emerald-green of her eyes. Jackson saw that the girl was singing to several horses that had come up to the edge of the corral fence.

The girl finished the last of the lyrics before she seemed

to notice them and came running over. "If you're looking for my mother, she's in the barn working."

Next to him, Jackson saw that his son had apparently been struck dumb.

"I'm Nat," the girl announced. "My name is really Natalie, though." She shifted her gaze to the mute Ford. "Everyone calls me Nat, so you can if you want to."

"This is my son, Ford."

Nat eyed Ford for a moment before she stepped forward and took his hand. "Come on, Ford. You'll probably want to see the rest of the animals. There are chickens and rabbits and several mules along with all the horses. Don't worry," she added before Jackson could voice his concern. "We won't get too close. We'll just pet them through the corral fence and feed the horses apples. It's okay. Mrs. Savage showed me how."

"Don't go far," Jackson said as the precocious Nat led his son toward several low-slung buildings. The girl was busy talking as they left. Ford, as far as Jackson could tell, hadn't uttered a word yet.

As he turned back toward the barn, he saw the logo on the side of the van: Weddings by Allie Knight. The logo looked old as did the van.

The girl had said her mother was working in the barn. That must be where the wedding was going to be held. His brother Tag had mentioned something about his wedding to Lily McCabe being very *Western*.

"You mean like Texas meets Montana?" Jackson had joked.

"Something like that. Don't worry. You'll feel right at home."

His brother's wedding wasn't what had him worried. After talking to Tag for a few moments on the phone, he'd known his brother had fallen head over heels for Lily. He was happy for him.

No, what worried Jackson was nailing down the last of the plans before the wedding for the opening of a Texas Boys Barbecue joint in Big Sky, Montana. He had hoped that all of the brothers would be here by now. Laramie and Austin hadn't even flown up to see the space Tag had found, let alone signed off on the deal.

From the time the five brothers had opened their first restaurant in an old house in Houston, they'd sworn they would never venture outside of Texas with their barbecue. Even as their business had grown and they'd opened more restaurants and finally started their own franchise, they had stayed in the state where they'd been raised.

Jackson understood why Tag wanted to open one here. But he feared it had nothing to do with business and everything to do with love and not wanting to leave Montana, where they had all been born.

Before the wedding had seemed the perfect time for all of them to get together and finalize the deal. Hayes had come here last month to see if the restaurant was even feasible. Unfortunately, Hayes had gotten sidetracked, so now it was up to the rest of them to make sure Tag was doing the best thing for the business—and before the wedding, which was only four days away.

He hoped all his brothers arrived soon so they could get this over with. They led such busy lives in Texas that they hardly ever saw each other. Tag had said on the phone he was anxious to show him the building he'd found for the new restaurant. Tag and Hayes had already made arrangements to buy the building without the final okay from the other brothers, something else that made Jackson nervous.

Jackson didn't want this move to cause problems among the five of them. So his mind was miles away as he started to step into the dim darkness inside the barn.

The cool air inside was suddenly filled with a terrified scream. An instant later, a black cat streaked past him and out the barn door.

JACKSON RACED INTO the barn not sure what he was going to find. What he found was a blond-haired woman who shared a striking resemblance to the little girl who'd been singing outside by the corrals.

While Nat had been angelic, this woman was as beautiful as any he'd ever seen. Her long, straight, blond hair was the color of sunshine. It rippled down her slim back. Her eyes, a tantalizing emerald-green, were huge with fear in a face that could stop traffic.

She stood against the barn wall, a box of wedding decorations open at her feet. Her eyes widened in even more alarm when she saw him. She threw a hand over her mouth, cutting off the scream.

"Are you all right?" he asked. She didn't appear to be hurt, just scared. No, not scared, *terrified.* Had she seen a mouse? Or maybe something larger? In Texas it might have been an armadillo. He wasn't sure what kind of critters they had this far north, but something had definitely set her off.

"It was nothing," she said, removing her hand from her mouth. Some of the color slowly returned to her face but he could see that she was still trembling.

"It was *something,*" he assured her.

She shook her head and ventured a look at the large box of decorations at her feet. The lid had been thrown to the side, some of the decorations spilling onto the floor.

He laughed. "Let me guess. That black cat I just saw hightailing it out of here... I'm betting he came out of that box."

Her eyes widened further. *"You saw it?"*

"Raced right past me." He laughed. "You didn't think you imagined it, did you?"

"It happened so fast. I couldn't be sure."

"Must have given you quite a fright."

She let out a nervous laugh and tried to smile, exposing deep dimples. He understood now why his son had gone mute. He felt the same way looking at Natalie's mother. There was an innocence about her, a vulnerability that would make a man feel protective.

Just the thought made him balk. He'd fallen once and wasn't about to get lured into that trap again. Not that there was any chance of that happening. In a few days he would be on a plane back to Texas with his son.

"You know cats," he said, just being polite. "They'll climb into just about anything. They're attracted by pretty things." Just like some cowboys. Not him, though.

"Yes," she said, but didn't sound convinced as she stepped away from the box. She didn't look all that steady on her feet. He started to reach out to her, but stopped himself as she found her footing.

He couldn't help noticing that her eyes were a darker shade of green than her daughter's. "Just a cat. A black one at that," he said, wondering why he felt the need to fill the silence. "You aren't superstitious, are you?"

She shook her head and those emerald eyes brightened. That with the color returning to her cheeks made her even more striking.

This was how he'd fallen for Ford's mother—a pretty face and what had seemed like a sweet disposition in a woman who'd needed him—and look how that had turned out. No, it took more than a pretty face to turn his head after the beating he'd taken from the last one.

"You must be one of Tag's brothers," she said as she wiped her palms on her jeans before extending a hand. Along with jeans, she wore a checked navy shirt, the sleeves rolled up, and cowboy boots. "I'm Allie Taylor, the wedding planner."

Jackson quickly removed his hat, wondering where he'd

left his manners. His mother had raised him better than this. But even as he started to shake her hand, he felt himself hesitate as if he were afraid to touch her.

Ridiculous, he thought as he grasped her small, ice-cold hand in his larger, much warmer one. "Jackson Cardwell. I saw your van outside. But I thought the name on the side—"

"Taylor is my married name." When his gaze went to her empty ring finger, she quickly added, "I'm a widow." She pulled back her hand to rub the spot where her wedding band had resided not that long ago. There was a thin, white line indicating that she hadn't been widowed long. Or she hadn't taken the band off until recently.

"I believe I met your daughter as my son and I were coming in. Natalie?"

"Yes, my baby girl." Her dimpled smile told him everything he needed to know about her relationship with her daughter. He knew that smile and suspected he had one much like it when he talked about Ford.

He felt himself relax a little. There was nothing dangerous about this woman. She was a single parent, just like him. Only she'd lost her husband and he wished he could get rid of his ex indefinitely.

"Your daughter took my son to see the horses. I should probably check on him."

"Don't worry. Nat has a healthy respect for the horses and knows the rules. Also Warren Fitzpatrick, their hired man, is never far away. He's Dana's semi-retired ranch manager. She says he's a fixture around here and loves the kids. That seems to be his job now, to make sure the kids are safe. Not that there aren't others on the ranch watching out for them, as well. Sorry, I talk too much when I'm…nervous." She took a deep breath and let it out slowly. "I want this wedding to be perfect."

He could tell she was still shaken by the black cat episode. "My brother Tag mentioned that Dana and the kids had almost been killed by some crazy woman. It's good she has someone she trusts keeping an eye on the children, even with everyone else on the ranch watching out for them. Don't worry," he said, looking around the barn. "I'm sure the wedding will be perfect."

The barn was huge and yet this felt almost too intimate standing here talking to her. "I was just about to get Ford and go down to the house. Dana told me she was baking a huge batch of chocolate chip cookies and to help ourselves. I believe she said there would also be homemade lemonade when we got here."

Allie smiled and he realized she'd thought it was an invitation. "I really need to get these decorations—"

"Sorry. I'm keeping you from your work." He took a step back. "Those decorations aren't going to put themselves up."

She looked as if she wasn't so sure of that. The cat had definitely put a scare into her, he thought. She didn't seem sure of anything right now. Allie looked again at the box of decorations, no doubt imagining the cat flying out of it at her.

Glancing at her watch, she said, "Oh, I didn't realize it was so late. Nat and I are meeting a friend for lunch. We need to get going."

Jackson was suddenly aware that he'd been holding his hat since shaking Allie's hand. He quickly put it back on as they walked out of the barn door into the bright sunshine. "My son is quite taken with your daughter," he said, again feeling an unusual need to fill the silence.

"How old is he?"

"Ford's five."

"Same age as Nat."

As they emerged into the beautiful late-June day, Jackson saw the two children and waved. As they came running, Nat was chattering away and Ford was hanging on her every word.

"They do seem to have hit it off." Allie sounded surprised and pleased. "Nat's had a hard time lately. I'm glad to see her making a new friend."

Jackson could see that Allie Taylor had been having a hard time, as well. He realized she must have loved her husband very much. He knew he should say something, but for the life of him he couldn't think of what. He couldn't even imagine a happy marriage. As a vehicle came roaring up the road, they both turned, the moment lost.

"Hey, bro," Tanner "Tag" Cardwell called from the rolled down window of his pickup as he swung into the ranch yard. "I see you made it," he said, getting out to come over and shake his brother's hand before he pulled Jackson into a hug. Tag glanced over at Ford and Natalie and added with a laugh, "Like father like son. If there's a pretty female around, you two will find them."

Jackson shook his head. That had been true when he'd met Ford's mother. But since the divorce and the custody battle, he'd been too busy single-handedly raising his son to even think about women. That's why red flags had gone up when he'd met Allie. There was something about her that had pulled at him, something more than her obvious beauty.

"Dana's right behind me with the kids," Tag said. "Why don't I show you and Ford to your cabin, then you can meet everyone." He pointed up in the pines that covered the mountainside. "Let's grab your bags. It's just a short walk."

Jackson turned to say goodbye to Allie, but she and her daughter had already headed for the old van.

"COME ON, NAT, we're meeting Belinda for lunch," Allie said as the Cardwell men headed for the cabins on the mountain behind the barn. Working here had been a godsend. Nat was having a wonderful time. She loved Dana's children. Hank was a year older than Nat, with Mary being the same age. Dana's twin boys, Angus and Brick, were just over a year and her sister Stacy's daughter, Ella, was a year and a half. Dana had her hands full but Stacy helped out with the younger ones. All of them loved the animals, especially the horses.

True to her word, Dana had made sure Nat had begun her horseback riding lessons. Nat was a natural, Dana had said, and Allie could see it was true.

Their few days here so far had been perfect.

Until the cat, there hadn't been any other incidents.

Her friend Belinda Andrews was waiting for them at a little Mexican food place near Meadow Village at Big Sky. While other friends had gone by the wayside since she'd married Nick six years ago, Belinda hadn't let Nick run her off. Allie suspected that, like her, she didn't have a lot of friends and Nick, while he'd made it clear he didn't like Belinda, had grudgingly put up with her the times they'd crossed paths.

"I hope we didn't keep you waiting," Allie said as she and Nat met Belinda on the patio. "You didn't have any trouble getting off work for the wedding shoot?" Belinda worked for a local photographer, but freelanced weddings. It was how they'd met back when Allie had her own wedding planning business.

Belinda grinned. "All set for the Tag Cardwell and Lily McCabe wedding. I took Dana up on her offer. I'm moving into one of the guest cabins later today!"

Allie wasn't all that surprised. Dana had offered her a cabin, as well, while she was preparing everything for the wedding. But since she lived just down the highway a few miles, Allie thought it best to remain at home for Nat's sake. Her daughter had had enough changes in her life recently.

"You really are excited about this," Allie said, noticing how nice Belinda looked. Her friend was dressed in a crop top and cut-off jeans, her skin tanned. Her dark hair was piled haphazardly up on her head, silver dangly earrings tinkled from her earlobes and, while she looked makeup free, Allie could tell she wasn't.

Belinda looked enchanting, a trick Allie wished she could pull off, she thought. On the way here, she'd pulled her hair up in a ponytail and even though she'd showered this morning, she'd forgone makeup. Nick was always suspicious when she wore it when he wasn't around so she'd gotten out of the habit.

Inside the café, Nat asked if she could play in the nearby area for kids and Allie said she could as long as she didn't argue about coming back to eat when her meal came.

"You look…pale," Belinda said, studying her after they were seated outside on the patio under an umbrella so they could see Nat. "You haven't had anymore of those…incidents, have you?"

Allie almost laughed at that. "I just need to get more sun," she said and picked up her menu to hide behind.

"I know you too well," Belinda said, dragging down the menu so she could look into her eyes. "What's happened *now?*"

"A black cat jumped out of one of my decoration boxes and scared me just before I came over here. And guess what? Someone else saw it." *So there,* she wanted to say, *I don't need my head examined.*

Belinda nodded, studying her. "A *black* cat?"

"Yes, a *black* cat and I didn't imagine it. One of the Cardwell brothers saw it, as well." She couldn't even voice how much of a relief that had been.

"That's all that's happened?"

"That's it." She had to look down at the menu to pull off the lie and was just glad when Belinda didn't question her further. She hadn't told *anyone* about the shredded dresses from her closet or the new clothes she'd taken back. The sales associate hadn't remembered her, but said the afternoon when the clothing was purchased had been a busy one. None of the other sales associates remembered her, but agreed they'd been too busy to say for sure. She'd ended up keeping two of the outfits to wear while working the rehearsal dinner and the wedding.

"I already moved some of my things into the cabin," Belinda said.

Allie couldn't help being surprised. "Already? Why didn't you stop by the barn and say hello?" Allie had suggested Belinda as the wedding photographer and felt responsible and anxious since this was her first wedding in five years.

"You were busy," her friend said. "We can't keep each other from our jobs, right?"

"Right." She loved that Belinda understood that. In truth, Allie had been hesitant to suggest her friend. She didn't want to have to worry about Belinda, not with everything else that she had going on in her life right now. While her friend was a great photographer, sometimes she got sidetracked if a handsome man was around. But when she'd broached the subject with the bride-to-be, Lily had been delighted that it was one other thing she didn't have to worry about.

Dana had been kind enough to offer Belinda a cabin on the ranch for the five-day affair. "It will make it easier for you to get great shots if you're staying up here and experiencing all the wedding festivities," Dana had said. "And any friend of Allie's is a friend of ours."

She and Belinda had been friends since grade school. Lately they hadn't been as close, probably Allie's fault. Belinda was in between men right now, and much wilder, freer and more outspoken than Allie had ever been. But Belinda didn't have a five-year-old daughter, either.

"You have no idea what this means to me," Belinda said now. "I've been dying to photograph a Western wedding for my portfolio."

"Your portfolio?"

Belinda looked embarrassed as if she'd let the cat out of the bag, so to speak. "I'm thinking about opening my own studio."

"That's great." Allie was happy for her friend, although she'd wondered if Belinda had come into some money because it wouldn't be cheap and as far as she knew Belinda lived from paycheck to paycheck like everyone else she knew.

The waitress came and took their orders. A light breeze stirred the new leaves on the nearby trees. The smell of summer mixed with that of corn tortillas, the most wonderful smell of all, Allie thought. They sipped Mexican Cokes, munched on chips and salsa to the sound of Latin music playing in the background and Allie felt herself begin to relax.

"I wasn't going to bring this up," Belinda said, "but you know that psychic that I've seen off and on?"

Allie fought not to roll her eyes.

"I know you say you don't believe in this stuff, but she said something interesting when I mentioned you."

"You told her about *me?*" Allie hadn't meant for her voice to rise so high. Her daughter looked over. She smiled at Nat and quickly changed her tone. "I really don't want you talking to anyone about me, let alone a…" She tried to come up with a word other than *charlatan.*

Belinda leaned forward, unfazed. "She thinks what's happening to you is because of guilt. Simply put, you feel guilty and it is manifesting itself into these…*incidents.*"

Allie stared at her. Leave it to Belinda to get right to the heart of it.

Her friend lowered her voice as if afraid Nat might be listening. "It makes sense, if you think about it. Nick didn't know you were—" she glanced at Nat "—leaving him and going to file for custody of you-know-who, but *you* did know your plan. Then he goes and gets himself…" She grimaced in place of the word *killed*. "Something like that has to mess with your mind."

"Yes, losing your husband does mess with your mind no matter what kind of marriage you had." Fortunately, the waitress brought their food. Allie called Nat up to the table and, for a few moments, they ate in silence.

"The thing is…" Belinda said between bites.

"Can't we just enjoy our meal?" Allie pleaded.

Her friend waved that suggestion away, but didn't say more until they had finished and Nat had gone back to the play area.

"The psychic thinks there is more to it," Belinda said. "What if Nick *knew* about your…plan?"

"What are you saying?"

"Come on. You've been over Nick for a long time. His death wouldn't make you crazy—"

"I'm not crazy," she protested weakly.

"But what if he *did* know or at least suspected? Come on, Allie. We both know it was so not like Nick to go hunting up into the mountains alone, knowing that the grizzlies were eating everything they could get their paws on before hibernation." She didn't seem to notice Allie wince. "Didn't the ranger say Nick had food in his backpack?"

"He didn't take food to attract a bear, if that's what you're saying. He planned to stay a few days so of course he had food in his backpack."

"I'm not trying to upset you. But if he went up there to end it all, that was his choice. You can't go crazy because you feel guilty."

Her stomach turned at the thought of the backpack she'd been asked to identify. It had been shredded by the grizzly's claws. She'd been horrified to think of what the bear had done to Nick. She would never forget the officer who'd brought her the news.

"From what we've been able to assess at the scene, your husband was attacked by a grizzly and given the tracks and other signs—"

"Signs?"

"Blood, ma'am."

She'd had to sit down. "You're telling me he's...dead?"

"It certainly looks that way," the ranger said. Four days later, the search for Nick Taylor was called off because a winter storm had come in and it was believed that there was little chance he could have survived such an attack without immediate medical attention.

"Nick wouldn't," she managed to say now. In her heart of hearts, the man she knew so well, the man she'd been married to for more than six years, wouldn't purposely go into the woods with a plan to be killed by a grizzly.

But Nick had always been unpredictable. Moody and often depressed, too. The construction business hadn't been doing well even before Nick's death. What would he have done if he'd known she was leaving him and taking his daughter? Hadn't she been suspicious when Nick told her of his plan to go hunting alone? She'd actually thought he might be having an affair and wanted to spend a few days with his mistress. She'd actually hoped that was the case.

"You're going by yourself?" she'd asked. Nick couldn't even watch football by himself.

"I know things haven't been great with us lately," he'd said. That alone had surprised her. She really thought Nick hadn't noticed or cared. "I think a few days apart is just what we both need. I can tell you aren't happy. I promise you there will be changes when I get back and maybe I'll even come home with a nice buck." He'd cupped her face in his hands. "I don't think you know what you mean to me, but I promise to show you when I get back." He'd kissed her then, softly, sweetly, and for a moment, she'd wondered if Nick could change.

"You're wrong about Nick," she said now to Belinda. "If he was going to end it, he would have chosen the least painful way to do it. Not one—" she looked at Nat, who was swinging nearby, humming to herself and seemingly oblivious to their conversation "—that chose him. He had a gun with him he could have used."

"Maybe he didn't get the chance, but you're probably right," Belinda said and grabbed the check. "Let me get this. I didn't mean to upset you. It's just that you need to get a handle on whatever's been going on with you for you-know-who's sake." She cut her eyes to Nat, who headed toward them as they stood to leave.

"You're right about the guilt, though," Allie said, giving her friend that. She'd known as she'd watched Nick leave that day to go up into the mountains that nothing could change him enough to make her stay. She was going to ask him for a divorce when he came back.

Belinda changed the subject. "I saw your brother-in-law, Drew, earlier on the ranch."

Allie nodded. "He mentioned he was working up there. His construction company built the guest cabins."

"I'd forgotten that." Belinda frowned. "I was talking to Lily about photos at the rehearsal dinner. Did you know that Sarah is one of her bridesmaids?"

"My sister-in-law worked with Lily one season at her brother James's Canyon Bar." Allie had the impression that Lily didn't have a lot of female friends. Most of the math professors she knew were male, apparently. "I think James feels sorry for Sarah and you know Lily, she is so sweet."

"I have to hand it to Sarah, putting up with her mother day in and day out," Belinda said.

Allie didn't want to think about it. Along with fewer incidents the past few days, she'd also been blessed with no visits from her mother-in-law and Sarah.

"Sarah's a saint, especially—" Belinda lowered her voice

"—the way Mildred treats her. She is constantly bugging her about her weight and how she is never going to get a husband... It's awful."

Allie agreed.

"I don't understand why she doesn't leave."

"Where would she go and what would she do?" Allie said. "Sarah was in college when Mildred broke her leg. She quit to come home and take care of her mother. Mildred has milked it ever since. It used to annoy Nick, Sarah living in the guesthouse. He thought Sarah was taking advantage of his mother."

"Ha, it's the other way around. Sarah is on twenty-four-hour call. She told me that her mother got her out of bed at 2:00 a.m. one time to heat her some milk because she couldn't sleep. I would have put a pillow over the old nag's face."

Allie laughed and changed the subject. "You look especially nice today," she commented, realizing that her friend had seemed happier lately. It dawned on her why. "There's someone new in your life."

Belinda shrugged. She didn't like to talk about the men she dated because she thought it would jinx things for her. Not talking about them didn't seem to work, either, though. Belinda was so superstitious. Why else would she see a psychic to find out her future?

"This is going to be so much fun, the two of us working together again. Don't worry. I won't get in your way." Belinda took her hand. "I'm sorry I upset you. Sometimes I don't have the brains God gave a rock."

She didn't think that was the way the expression went, but said nothing. Belinda could be so...annoying and yet so sweet. Allie didn't know what she would have done without her the past few years. Belinda had been the only person she would talk freely to about Nick and the trouble between them.

"I'm just worried about you, honey," Belinda said, squeezing her hand. "I really think you should see some-one—"

"I don't need a shrink."

"Not a shrink. Someone more…spiritual who can help you make sense of the things that you say keep happening."

"Things *do* keep happening," she snapped. "I'm not mak-ing them up."

"So talk to this woman," Belinda said just as adamantly. She pressed a business card into Allie's hand.

She glanced at it and groaned. "Your psychic friend?"

"She might be the *only* person who can help you," Be-linda said cryptically. She gripped Allie's hand tighter. "She says she can get you in touch with Nick so you can get past this."

Allie stared at her for a moment before laughing out loud. "You have got to be kidding. What does she use? A Ouija board?"

"Don't laugh. This woman can tell you things that will make the hair on your head stand straight up."

That's all I need, she thought, reminded of Jackson Cardwell asking her if she was superstitious.

"Call her," Belinda said, closing Allie's fingers around the woman's business card. "You need closure, Allie. This woman can give it to you. She's expecting your call."

"I've been expecting your call, as well," said a sharp, older voice.

They both turned to see Mildred and her daughter. From the looks on their faces, they'd been standing there for some time.

Chapter Three

"Want to see the building for Montana's first Texas Boys Barbecue?" Tag asked after they'd dropped Jackson and Ford's luggage off at the small cabin on the side of the mountain and gone down to meet cousin Dana and her brood.

Dana Cardwell Savage was just as Tag had described her. Adorable and sweet and delighted that everyone was coming for the wedding.

"How is your cabin?" she asked after introducing him to her children with husband, Marshal Hud Savage. Hank was the spitting image of his father, Dana said, and six now. Mary was five and looked just like her mom. Then there were the twins, Angus and Brick, just a year and a half old with the same dark hair and eyes as all the Cardwells.

"The cabin is great," Jackson said as Ford instantly bonded with his second cousins. "Thank you so much for letting me stay there."

"Family is why we had them built," Dana said. "My Texas cousins will always have a place to stay when you visit. Or until you find a place to live in Montana when you realize you want to live up here," she added with a wink. "Isn't that right, Tag?"

"I would love to visit, but I'm never leaving Texas," Jackson said.

"Never say never," Tag commented under his breath.

"I was just about to take him down to see the restaurant location."

Ford took off with the other kids into a room full of toys and didn't even look back as his father left. Jackson almost felt as if he were losing his son to Montana and the Cardwell clan.

"Are you sure you don't want to wait until everyone gets here?" he asked as they left.

"Hayes and Laramie are flying in tomorrow. I was hoping you would pick them up at the airport. Austin is apparently on a case tying up some loose ends." He shrugged. Of the five of them, Austin was the loner. He was dedicated to his job and being tied up on a case was nothing new. "Anyway, it's your opinion I want. You're better at this than all three of them put together."

"So you haven't heard from Austin on the deal," Jackson guessed.

Tag shook his head. "You know how he is. He'll go along with whatever everyone else says. Come on," he said with a laugh when Jackson groaned. "I really do want your opinion."

"*Honest* opinion?" Jackson asked.

"Of course."

Jackson glanced around as they drove out of the ranch and down the highway to the turnoff to Big Sky. Being the youngest, he didn't remember anything about Montana. He'd been a baby when his mother had packed up her five sons and taken them to Texas.

Big Sky looked more like a wide spot in the road rather than a town. There were clusters of buildings broken only by sagebrush or golf greens.

"This is the lower Meadow Village," Tag told him. "There is also the Mountain Village higher up the mountain where the ski resort is. You really have to see this place in the winter. It's crazy busy around the holidays. There are a lot of second homes here so the residents fly in and spend a few weeks generally in the summer and the holidays. More and more people, though, are starting to live here year-round. There is opportunity here, Jackson."

Jackson wanted to tell his brother that he didn't need to sell him. He'd go along with whatever the others decided. In fact, he'd already spoken to Hayes about it. Once Hayes got on board, it was clear to Jackson that this was probably a done deal. The holdout, if there was one, would be Austin and only because he wouldn't be available to sign off on the deal. Even Laramie sounded as if he thought the restaurant was a good idea.

"Where does Harlan live?" Jackson asked as they drove past mansions, condos and some tiny old cabins that must have been there before anyone even dreamed of a Big Sky. He had only a vague recollection of his father from those few times Harlan had visited Texas when he was growing up.

"He lives in one of those cabins back there, the older ones. We can stop by his place if you like. More than likely he and Uncle Angus are down at the Corral Bar. It's their favorite watering hole. Maybe we could have a beer with them later."

"I'm sure I'll see him soon enough." Harlan was a stranger who hadn't even made Jackson's wedding, not that the marriage had lasted long, anyway. But he felt no tie to the man who'd fathered him and doubted he ever would. It was only when he thought about Ford that he had regrets. It would have been nice for Ford to have a grandfather. His ex-wife's family had no interest in Ford. So the only family his son had in Texas was Jackson's mother, Rosalee Cardwell and his brother Laramie. Tag had already moved to Montana and Hayes would be moving here soon.

"I'm getting to know Dad," Tag said. "He's pretty remarkable."

"Tell me about your wedding planner," Jackson said,

changing the subject then regretting the topic he'd picked when his brother grinned over at him. "I'm just curious about her." He hadn't told anyone about the cat or the terrified woman he'd found in the barn earlier. Her reaction seemed over the top given it had only been a cat. Though it *had* been a black one. Maybe she *was* superstitious.

"Allie's great. Dana suggested her. That's our Dana, always trying to help those in need. Allie lost her husband eight months ago. Terrible thing. He was hunting in the mountains and apparently killed by a grizzly bear."

"Apparently?"

"They never found his body. They think the bear dragged the body off somewhere. Won't be the first time remains have turned up years later in the mountains—if they turn up at all. They found his backpack and enough blood that he can be declared legally dead but I guess the insurance company has been dragging its feet."

Jackson thought of Allie and her little girl, Nat. "How horrible for them."

"Yeah, she's been having a hard time both emotionally and financially according to Dana, who suggested her for our wedding planner because of it. But Lily loves Allie and, of course, Natalie. That little girl is so darned bright."

"Yeah, Ford is definitely taken with her." But his thoughts were on Allie and her reaction to the cat flying out of that box of wedding decorations. It must have scared her half out of her wits in the emotional state she was in. "That was nice of Dana to hire her."

"Allie worked as a wedding planner before she married Nick Taylor. Dana offered Allie and Nat one of the new guest ranch cabins where we're staying. But I guess she thinks it would be better for Natalie to stay in their own home."

"Where do Allie and her daughter live now?"

"An old cabin down by the river. I'll show you on the

way back." Tag swung into a small complex and turned off the engine. "Welcome to the site of the next Texas Boys Barbecue joint."

"I THOUGHT YOU had a job," Mildred said to Allie over the sound of brass horns playing cantina music at the Mexican café.

"They allow lunch breaks," she said. "But I really need to get back." She excused herself to go to the ladies' room.

Mildred turned to Natalie, leaned down and pinched her cheek. "How is my sweetie today? Grandma misses you. When are you coming to my house?"

In the restroom, Allie splashed cold water on her face and tried to calm down. How much had they heard?

Enough that they had been looking at her strangely. Or was that all in her mind, as well? But if they heard Belinda trying to get her to see a psychic so she could reach Nick on the other side… Allie could well imagine what they would think.

She hurried, not wanting to leave Natalie with her grandmother for long. She hated it, but Mildred seemed to nag the child all the time about not spending enough time with her.

Leaving the restroom, she saw that Sarah and her mother hadn't taken a seat. Instead, they were standing at the takeout counter. There was no avoiding talking to them again.

"I couldn't help but overhear your…friend suggesting you see a…psychic?" Mother Taylor said, leaving no doubt that they had been listening. "Surely she meant a psychiatrist, which indicates that you are still having those hallucinations." She quirked an eyebrow, waiting for an answer.

"Belinda was only joking. I'm feeling much better, thank you."

Mildred's expression said she wasn't buying a minute of it. "Sarah, I left my sweater in the car."

"I'll get it, Mother." Sarah turned and headed for their vehicle parked out front.

"How is this…job of yours going?" Mildred asked. "I've never understood what wedding planners do."

Allie had actually told her once, listing about fifty things she did but Mildred clearly hadn't been listening.

"I'll have to tell you sometime," she said now. "But I need to get back to it. Come on, Natalie."

"You should let me have her for the rest of the day," Mildred said. "In fact, she can spend the night at my house."

"I'm sorry, but Natalie is getting horseback riding lessons this afternoon," Allie lied. "She's having a wonderful time with Dana's children."

"Well, she can still—"

"Not only that, I also prefer to have Nat with me right now. It's hard enough without Nick." Another lie followed by the biggest truth of all, "I need my daughter right now."

Mildred looked surprised. "That's the first time I've heard you mention my Nicky in months." She seemed about to cry. Sarah returned with her sweater, slipping it around her shoulders without even a thank-you from Mildred.

Nearby, Belinda was finishing up their bill.

"I really should get back to work." Allie tried to step past her mother-in-law, but the older woman grabbed her arm. "I worry that you are ill-equipped to take care of yourself, let alone a child. I need Natalie more than you do. I—"

Allie jerked her arm free. "Natalie would be heartbroken if she was late to her horseback riding lesson." She hurried to her daughter, picked up her purse off the table and, taking Nat's hand, left the restaurant, trying hard not to run.

She told herself to calm down. Any sign of her being upset and her in-laws would view it as her being unable to take care of Nat. But all she wanted was to get away and as quickly as possible.

But as she and Nat reached her van and she dug in her

purse for her keys, she realized they weren't there. Her heart began to pound. Since Nick's death, she was constantly losing her keys, her purse, her sunglasses…her mind.

"Forgetfulness is very common after a traumatic event," the doctor had told her when she'd gotten an appointment at her in-laws' insistence.

"It scares me. I try to remind myself where I put things so this doesn't happen, but when I go back to get whatever it was…I'm always so positive that's where I left it. Instead, I find it in some…strange place I could never imagine."

The doctor had chuckled and pulled out his prescription pad. "How are you sleeping?" He didn't even wait for her to answer. "I think once you start sleeping through the night, you're going to find that these instances of forgetfulness will go away."

The pills had only made it worse, though, she thought now as she frantically searched for her van keys. She could feel Nat watching her, looking worried. Sometimes it felt as if her five-year-old was taking care of her instead of the other way around.

"It's okay, sweetheart. Mama just misplaced her keys. I'm sure they're in here…."

"Looking for these?" The young waitress from the café came out the door, holding up her keys.

"Where did you find them?" Allie asked, thinking they must have fallen out of her purse at the table and ended up on the floor. That could happen to anyone.

"In the bathroom sink."

Allie stared at her.

"You must have dropped them while you were washing your hands," the young woman said with a shrug as she handed them over.

As if that was likely. She hadn't even taken her purse to

the restroom, had she? But she had it now and she couldn't remember. She'd been so upset to see Sarah and Mildred.

"Nat, what was Grandmother saying to you in the restaurant?"

"She wanted me to go to her house but I told her I couldn't. I'm going horseback riding when we get to the ranch," Nat announced. "Dana is taking me and the other kids." Her lower lip came out for a moment. "Grandma said she was really sad I wasn't going with her."

"Yes," Allie said as, with trembling fingers, she opened the van door. Tears stung her eyes. "But today is a happy day so *we* aren't going to be sad, right? There are lots of other days that you can spend with your grandmother." Nat brightened as she strapped her into her seat.

Just a few more minutes and she and Nat would be out of here. But as she started the van, she looked up to find Mother Taylor watching her from beside Sarah's pearl-white SUV. It was clear from her expression that she'd witnessed the lost-key episode.

From the front steps of the restaurant, Belinda waved then made the universal sign to telephone.

Allie knew Belinda didn't mean call her. Reaching in her pocket, she half expected the psychic's business card to be missing. But it was still there, she realized with sagging relief. As crazy as the idea of reaching Nick beyond the grave was, she'd do *anything* to make this stop.

WHEN ALLIE AND her daughter returned, Jackson was watching her from inside his cousin's two-story ranch house.

"She lost her husband some months back," Dana said, joining him at the window.

"I wasn't—"

"He went up into the mountains during hunting season," she continued, ignoring his attempt to deny he'd been wondering about Allie. "They found his backpack and his rifle and grizzly tracks."

"Tag mentioned it." Tag had pointed out Allie's small, old cabin by the river on their way back to the ranch. It looked as if it needed work. Hadn't Tag mentioned that her husband was in construction? "Tag said they never found her husband's body."

Dana shook her head. "But Nick's backpack was shredded and his rifle was half-buried in the dirt with grizzly tracks all around it. When he didn't show up after a few days and they had no luck finding him…"

"His remains will probably turn up someday," Hud said as he came in from the kitchen. Dana's husband, Hud, was the marshal in the canyon—just as his father had been before him. "About thirty years ago now, a hiker found a human skeleton of a man. He still hasn't been identified so who knows how long he'd been out there in the mountains."

"That must make it even harder for her," Jackson said.

"It was one reason I was so glad when she decided to take the job as wedding planner."

He watched Allie reappear to get a box out of the van. She seemed nervous, even upset. He wondered if something had happened at lunch. Now at least he understood why she had overreacted with the black cat.

Hud kissed his wife, saying he had to get back to work, leaving Dana and Jackson alone.

"Our fathers are setting up their equipment on the bandstand in the barn," Dana said. "Have you seen Harlan yet?"

"No," Jackson admitted. "Guess there is no time like the present, huh?"

Jackson hadn't seen his father in several years, and even then Harlan hadn't seemed to know how to act around him—or his other sons, for that matter. As they entered the barn, Tag joining them, he saw his father and uncle standing on the makeshift stage, guitars in their hands, and was surprised when he remembered a song his father had once sung to him.

He didn't know how old he'd been at the time, but he recalled Harlan coming into his bedroom one night in Texas and playing a song on his guitar for him. He remembered being touched by the music and his father's voice.

On stage, the two brothers began playing their guitars in earnest. His father began singing. It was the voice Jackson remembered and it was like being transported back to his childhood. It rattled him more than he wanted to admit. He'd thought he and his father had no connection. But just hearing Harlan sing made him realize that he'd been lying to himself about not only the lack of connection, but also his need for it.

Harlan suddenly broke off at the sight of his sons. He stared through the dim barn for a moment, then put down his guitar to bound off the stage and come toward Jackson. He seemed young and very handsome, belying his age, Jackson thought. A man in his prime.

"Jackson," he said, holding out his hand. His father's hand was large and strong, the skin dry, callused and warm. "Glad you made it. So where are the rest of your brothers?"

"They're supposed to fly in tomorrow. At least Laramie and Hayes are," Tag said. "Austin... Well, he said he would do his best to make it. He's tied up on a case, but I'm sure you know how that goes." At Christmas, Tag had found out what their father did besides drink beer and play guitar—and shared that amazing news with them. Both Harlan and his brother Angus had worked undercover as government agents and still might, even though they were reportedly retired.

"Duty calls sometimes," Harlan agreed. "I'm glad I'm retired."

"Until the next time someone gets into trouble and needs help," Tag said.

Harlan merely smiled in answer.

Jackson was glad to see that his brother and their father could joke. Tag, being the oldest, remembered the years living in Montana and their father more than his brothers.

"The old man isn't so bad," Tag had told them after his visit at Christmas. "He's starting to grow on me."

Jackson had laughed, but he'd been a little jealous. He would love for his son to have a grandfather. He couldn't imagine, though, how Harlan could be a part of his only grandson's life, even if he wanted to. Texas and Montana were just too far apart. And Harlan probably had no interest, anyway.

"Where's that bride-to-be?" Uncle Angus asked Tag as he hopped off the stage and came toward them.

"Last minute preparations for the wedding," Tag said. "You can't believe the lists she's made. It's the mathematician in her. She's so much more organized than I am. Which reminds me, Jackson and I have to drive down to Bozeman to pick up the rings."

"It took a wedding to get you Cardwell boys to Montana, I see." Uncle Angus threw an arm around Jackson. "So how are you liking it up here? I saw that boy of yours. Dana's got him riding horses already. You're going to have one devil of a time getting him to go back to Texas after this."

Didn't Jackson know it. He'd hardly seen his son all day. Even now Ford had been too busy to give Jackson more than a quick wave from the corral where he'd been with the kids and the hired man, Walker.

"Ford is going to sleep like a baby tonight after all this fresh air, sunshine and high altitude," Jackson said. "He's not the only one," he added with a laugh.

"It's good for him," Harlan said. "I was talking to him earlier. He's taken with that little girl."

"Like father like son," Tag said under his breath as Allie came in from the back of the barn.

Jackson saw her expression. "I think I'd better go check on my son," he said as he walked toward Allie. He didn't have time to think about what he was about to do. He moved to her, taking her arm and leading her back out of the barn. "What's wrong?"

For a moment she looked as if she were going to deny anything was. But then tears filled her eyes. He walked her around the far side of the barn. He could hear Dana out by the corral instructing the kids in horseback riding lessons. Inside the barn, his father and uncle struck up another tune.

"It's nothing, really," she said and brushed at her tears. "I've been so forgetful lately. I didn't remember that the band would be setting up this afternoon."

He saw that she held a date book in her trembling hand.

"It wasn't written down in your date book?"

She glanced at her book. "It was but for some reason I marked it out."

"No big deal, right?"

"It's just that I don't remember doing it."

He could see that she was still upset and wondered if there wasn't something more going on. He reminded himself that Allie had lost her husband only months ago. Who knew what kind of emotional roller coaster that had left her on.

"You need to cut yourself more slack," he said. "We all forget things."

She nodded, but he could see she was still worried. No, not worried, scared. He thought of the black cat and had a feeling it hadn't been her first scare like that.

"I feel like such a fool," she said.

Instinctively, he put his arm around her. "Give yourself time. It's going to be all right."

She looked so forlorn that taking her in his arms seemed not only the natural thing to do at that moment, but the only thing to do under the circumstances. At first she felt board-stiff in his arms, then after a moment she seemed to melt into him. She buried her face into his chest as if he were an anchor in a fierce storm.

Suddenly, she broke the embrace and stepped back. He followed her gaze to one of the cabins on the mountainside behind him and the man standing there.

"Who is that?" he asked, instantly put off by the scowling man.

"My brother-in-law, Drew. He's doing some repairs on the ranch. He and Nick owned a construction company together. They built the guest cabins."

The man's scowl had turned into a cold stare. Jackson saw Allie's reaction. "We weren't doing anything wrong."

She shook her head as the man headed down the mountainside to his pickup parked in the pines. "He's just very protective." Allie looked as if she had the weight of the world on her shoulders again.

Jackson watched her brother-in-law slowly drive out of the ranch. Allie wasn't the only one the man was glaring at.

"I need to get back inside," she said and turned away.

He wanted to go after her. He also wanted to put his fist into her brother-in-law's face. Protective my butt, he thought. He wanted to tell Allie to ignore all of it. Wanted... Hell, that was just it. He didn't know what he wanted at the moment. Even if he did, he couldn't have it. He warned himself to stay away from Allie Taylor. Far away. He was only here for the wedding. While he felt for the woman, he couldn't help her.

"There you are," Tag said as he came up behind them. "Ready to go with me to Bozeman to get the rings?"

Jackson glanced toward the barn door Allie was stepping through. "Ready."

Chapter Four

As Jackson started to leave with his brother, he turned to look back at the barn. Just inside the door he saw Allie. All his survival instincts told him to keep going, but his mother had raised a Texas cowboy with a code of honor. Or at least she'd tried. Something was wrong and he couldn't walk away.

"Give me just a minute," he said and ran back. As he entered the barn, he saw Allie frantically searching for something in the corner of the barn. His father and brother were still playing at the far end, completely unaware of them.

"What are you looking for?"

She seemed embarrassed that he'd caught her. He noticed that she'd gone pale and looked upset. "I know I put my purse right there with my keys in it."

He glanced at the empty table. "Maybe it fell under it." He bent down to look under the red-and-white-checked tablecloth. "The barn is looking great, by the way. You've done a beautiful job."

She didn't seem to hear him. She was moving from table to table, searching for her purse. He could see that she was getting more anxious by the moment. "I know I put it right there so I wouldn't forget it when I left."

"Here it is," Jackson said as he spied what he assumed had to be her purse not on a table, but in one of the empty boxes that had held the decorations.

She rushed to him and took the purse and hurriedly looked inside, pulling out her keys with obvious relief.

"You would have found it the moment you started loading the boxes into your van," he said, seeing that she was still shaken.

She nodded. "Thank you. I'm not usually like this."

"No need to apologize. I hate losing things. It drives me crazy."

She let out a humorless laugh. "Crazy, yes." She took a deep breath and let it out slowly. Tears welled in her eyes.

"Hey, it's okay."

He wanted to comfort her, but kept his distance after what had happened earlier. "It really is okay."

She shook her head as the music stopped and quickly wiped her eyes, apologizing again. She looked embarrassed and he wished there was something he could say to put her at ease.

"Earlier, I was just trying to comfort you. It was just a hug," he said.

She met his gaze. "One I definitely needed. You have been so kind…."

"I'm not kind."

She laughed and shook her head. "Are you always so self-deprecating?"

"No, just truthful."

"Well, thank you." She clutched the keys in her hand as if afraid she would lose them if she let them out of her sight.

At the sound of people approaching, she stepped away from him.

"Let me load those boxes in your van. I insist," he said before she could protest.

As Dana, Lily and the kids came through the barn door they stopped to admire what Allie had accomplished. There were lots of oohs and ahhs. But it was Lily whose face lit up as she took in the way the barn was being transformed.

Jackson shifted his gaze to Allie's face as she humbly accepted their praise. Dana introduced Jackson to Lily. He could see right away why his brother had fallen for the woman.

"Please come stay at one of the guest cabins for the rest of the wedding festivities," Dana was saying to Allie.

"It is so generous of you to offer the cabin," Allie said, looking shocked at the offer.

"Not at all. It will make it easier for you so you don't have to drive back and forth. Also I'm being selfish. The kids adore Natalie. It will make the wedding a lot more fun for them."

Allie, clearly fighting tears of gratitude, said she would think about it. Jackson felt his heartstrings pulled just watching. "I'll work hard to make this wedding as perfect as it can be. I won't let you down."

Lily gave her a hug. "Allie, it's already perfect!"

Jackson was surprised that Lily McCabe had agreed to a Western wedding. According to the lowdown he'd heard, Lily taught mathematics at Montana State University. She'd spent her younger years at expensive boarding schools after having been born into money.

Jackson wondered if the woman had ever even been on a horse—before she met the Cardwells. Apparently, Allie was worried that a Western wedding was the last thing a woman like Lily McCabe would want.

"Are you sure this is what *you* want?" Allie asked Lily. "After all, it is *your* wedding."

Lily laughed. "Just to see the look on my parents' faces will make it all worthwhile." At Allie's horrified look, she quickly added, "I'm kidding. Though that is part of it. But when you marry into the Cardwell family, you marry into ranching and all that it comes with. I want this wedding to be a celebration of that.

"This is going to be the best wedding ever," Lily said as

she looked around the barn. "Look at me," she said, holding out her hands. "I'm actually shaking I'm so excited." She stepped to Allie and gave her another hug. "Thank you so much."

Allie appeared taken aback for a moment by Lily's sudden show of affection. The woman really was becoming more like the Cardwells every day. Or at least Dana Cardwell. That wasn't a bad thing, he thought.

"We should probably talk about the other arrangements. When is your final dress fitting?"

"Tomorrow. The dress is absolutely perfect, and the boots!" Lily laughed. "I'm so glad Dana suggested red boots. I love them!"

This was going to be like no wedding Allie had ever planned, Jackson thought. The Cardwells went all out, that was for sure.

He looked around the barn, seeing through the eyes of the guests who would be arriving for the wedding. Allie had found a wonderful wedding cake topper of a cowboy and his bride dancing that was engraved with the words: *For the rest of my life.* Tag had said that Lily had cried when she'd seen it.

The cake was a little harder to nail, according to Tag. Jackson mentally shook his head at even the memory of his brother discussing wedding cakes with him. Apparently, there were cake designs resembling hats and boots, covered wagons and cowhide, lassoes and lariats, spurs and belt buckles and horses and saddles. Some cakes had a version of all of them, which he could just imagine would have thrown his brother for a loop, he thought now, grinning to himself.

"I like simple better," Lily had said when faced with all the options. "It's the mathematician in me."

Allie had apparently kept looking until she found what she thought might be the perfect one. It was an elegant white, frosted, tiered cake with white roses and ribbons in a similar design as Lily's Western wedding dress.

"I love it," Lily had gushed. "It's perfect."

They decided on white roses and daisies for her bouquet. Bouquets of daisies would be on each of the tables, the vases old boots, with the tables covered with red-checked cloths and matching napkins.

Jackson's gaze returned to Allie. She seemed to glow under the compliments, giving him a glimpse of the self-assured woman he suspected she'd been before the tragedy.

"Jackson?"

He turned to find Tag standing next to him, grinning.

"I guess you didn't hear me. Must have had your mind somewhere else." Tag glanced in Allie's direction and then wisely jumped back as Jackson took a playful swing at him as they left the barn.

"You sure waited until the last minute," Jackson said to his brother as they headed for Tag's vehicle. "Putting off the rings…" He shook his head. "You sure you want to go through with this?"

His brother laughed. "More sure than I have been about anything in my life. Come on, let's go."

"I'll see if Ford wants to come along," Jackson said. "I think that's enough cowboying for one day."

But when he reached the corral, he found his son wearing a straw Western hat and atop a huge horse. Jackson felt his pulse jump at the sight and his first instinct was to insist Ford get down from there right away.

But when he got a good look at his son's face, his words died on a breath. He'd never seen Ford this happy. His cheeks were flushed, his eyes bright. He looked…proud.

"Look at me," he called to his father.

All Jackson could do was nod as his son rode past him. He was incapable of words at that moment.

"Don't worry about your son," his father said as he joined him at the corral fence. "I'll look after him until you get back."

ALLIE LISTENED TO Jackson and Tag joking with each other as they left the barn. Jackson Cardwell must think her the most foolish woman ever, screaming over nothing more than a cat, messing up her date book and panicking because she'd misplaced her purse.

But what had her still upset was the hug. It had felt so good to be in Jackson's arms. It had been so long since anyone had held her like that. She'd felt such an overwhelming need...

And then Drew had seen them. She'd been surprised by the look on his face. He'd seemed...angry and upset as if she was cheating on Nick. Once this investigation was over, maybe they could all put Nick to rest. In the meantime, she just hoped Drew didn't go to his mother with this.

Instinctively, she knew that Jackson wouldn't say anything. Not about her incidents or about the hug.

Dana announced she was taking the kids down to the house for naptime. Allie could tell that Nat had wanted to go down to the house—but for lemonade and cookies. Nat probably needed a nap, as well, but Allie couldn't take her up to the cabin right now. She had work to do if she hoped to have the barn ready for the rehearsal dinner tomorrow night.

"I really need your help," she told her daughter. Nat was always ready to give a helping hand. Well, she was before the Cardwell Ranch and all the animals, not to mention other kids to play with.

"Okay, Mama." She glanced back at the barn door wistfully, though. Nat had always wanted brothers and sisters, but they hadn't been in Allie's plans. She knew she could take care of one child without any help from Nick. He'd wanted a boy and insisted they try for another child soon after Nat was born.

Allie almost laughed. Guilt? She had so much of it where Nick and his family were concerned. She had wanted to enjoy her baby girl so she'd gone on the pill behind Nick's back. It had been more than dishonest. He would have killed her if he had found out. The more time that went by, the less she wanted another child with her husband so she'd stayed on the pill. Even Nick's tantrums about her not getting pregnant were easier to take than having another child with him.

She hadn't even told Belinda, which was good since her friend was shocked when she told her she was leaving Nick and moving far away.

"Divorcing him is one thing," Belinda had said. "But I don't see how you can keep his kid from him or keep Nat from his family."

"Nick wanted a son. He barely takes notice of Nat. The only time he notices her is when other people are around and then he plays too rough with her. When she cries, he tells her to toughen up."

"So you're going to ask for sole custody? Isn't Nick going to fight you?"

Allie knew it would be just like Nick to fight for Nat out of meanness and his family would back him up. "I'm going to move to Florida. I've already lined up a couple of jobs down there. They pay a lot more than here. I really doubt Nick will bother flying that far to see Nat—at least more than a few times."

"You really are going to leave him," Belinda had said. "When?"

"Soon." That had been late summer. She'd desperately wanted a new start. Nick would be occupied with hunting season in the fall so maybe he wouldn't put up much of a fight.

Had Belinda said something to Nick? Or had he just seen something in Allie that told him he had lost her?

"How can I help you, Mama?" Nat asked, dragging her from her thoughts.

Allie handed her daughter one end of a rope garland adorned with tiny lights in the shape of boots. "Let's string this up," she suggested. "And see how pretty it looks along the wall."

Nat's eyes lit up. "It's going to be beautiful," she said. *Beautiful* was her latest favorite word. To her, most everything was beautiful.

Allie yearned for that kind of innocence again—if she'd ever had it. But maybe she could find it for her daughter. She had options. She could find work anywhere as a wedding planner, but did she want to uproot her daughter from what little family she had? Nat loved her Uncle Drew and Sarah could be very sweet. Mildred, even as ungrandmotherly as she was, was Nat's only grandmother.

Allie tried to concentrate on her work. The barn was taking shape. She'd found tiny cowboy boot lights to put over the bar area. Saddles on milk cans had been pulled up to the bar for extra seating.

Beverages would be chilling in a metal trough filled with ice. Drinks would be served in Mason jars and lanterns would hang from the rafters for light. A few bales of hay would be brought in around the bandstand.

When they'd finished, Allie plugged in the last of the lights and Nat squealed with delight.

She checked her watch. "Come on," she told her daughter. "We've done enough today. We need to go into town for a few things. Tomorrow your aunt Megan will be coming to help." Nat clapped in response. She loved her auntie Megan, Allie's half sister.

After Allie's mother died, her father had moved away, remarried and had other children. Allie had lost touch with her father, as well as his new family. But about a year ago, her stepsister Megan had found her. Ten years younger, Megan was now twenty-three and a recent graduate in design. When she'd shown an interest in working on the Cardwell Ranch wedding, Allie had jumped at it.

"I really could use the help, but when can you come down?" Megan lived in Missoula and had just given her two weeks' notice at her job.

"Go ahead and start without me. I'll be there within a few days of the wedding. That should be enough time, shouldn't it?"

"Perfect," Allie had told her. "Natalie and I will start. I'll save the fun stuff for you." Natalie loved Megan, who was cute and young and always up for doing something fun with her niece.

The thought of Megan's arrival tomorrow had brightened Natalie for a moment, but Allie now saw her looking longingly at the Savage house.

"How about we have something to eat while we're in Bozeman?" Allie suggested.

Nat's eyes widened with new interest as she asked if they could go to her favorite fast-food burger place. The Taylors had introduced her daughter to fast food, something Allie had tried to keep at a minimum.

But this evening, she decided to make an exception. She loved seeing how happy her daughter was. Nat's cheeks were pink from the fresh air and sunshine.

All the way into town, she talked excitedly about the horses and the other kids. This wedding planner job at Cardwell Ranch was turning out to be a good thing for both of them, Allie thought as they drove home.

By the time they reached the cabin Nat had fallen asleep in her car seat and didn't even wake up when Allie parked out front. Deciding to take in the items she'd purchased first, then bring in her daughter, Allie stepped into the cabin and stopped dead.

At the end of the hall, light flickered. A candle. She hadn't lit a candle. Not since Nick. He liked her in candlelight. The smell of the candle and the light reminded her of the last time they'd had sex. Not made love. They hadn't made love since before Natalie was born.

As she started down the hallway, she told herself that she'd thrown all the candles away. Even if she'd missed one, she wouldn't have left a candle burning.

She stopped in the bedroom doorway. Nick's shirt was back, spread on the bed as if he were in it, lying there waiting for her. The smell of the sweet-scented candle made her nauseous. She fought the panicked need to run.

"Mama?" Nat's sleepy voice wavered with concern. "Did Daddy come back?" Not just concern. Anxiety. Nick scared her with his moodiness and surly behavior. Nat was smart. She had picked up on the tension between her parents.

Allie turned to wrap her arms around her daughter. The warmth of her five-year-old, Nat's breath on her neck, the solid feel of the ground under her feet, those were the things she concentrated on as she carried Natalie down the hallway to her room.

Her daughter's room had always been her haven. It was the only room in the house that Nick hadn't cared what she did with. So she'd painted it sky-blue, adding white floating clouds, then trees and finally a river as green and sunlit as the one out Nat's window.

Nick had stuck his head in the door while she was painting it. She'd seen his expression. He'd been impressed—and he hadn't wanted to be—before he snapped, "You going to cook dinner or what?" He seemed to avoid the room after that, which was fine with her.

Now, she lay down on the bed with Nat. It had been her

daughter's idea to put stars on the ceiling, the kind that shone only at night with the lights out.

"I like horses," Nat said with a sigh. "Ms. Savage says a horse can tell your mood and that if you aren't in a good one, you'll get bucked off." She looked at her mother. "Do you think that's true?"

"I think if Ms. Savage says it is, then it is."

Nat smiled as if she liked the answer.

Allie could tell she was dog-tired, but fighting sleep.

"I'm going to ride Rocket tomorrow," Natalie said.

"Rocket? That sounds like an awfully fast horse." She saw that Nat's eyelids had closed. She watched her daughter sleep for a few moments, then eased out of bed.

After covering her, she opened the window a few inches to let the cool summer night air into the stuffy room. Spending time with her daughter made her feel better, but also reminded her how important it was that she not let anyone know about the things that had been happening to her.

She thought of Jackson Cardwell and the black cat that had somehow gotten into her box of decorations. She hadn't imagined that. She smiled to herself. Such a small thing and yet…

This time, she went straight to her bedroom, snuffed out the candle and opened the window, thankful for the breeze that quickly replaced the sweet, cloying scent with the fresh night air.

On the way out of the room, she grabbed Nick's shirt and took both the shirt and the candle to the trash, but changed her mind. Dropping only the candle in the trash, she took the shirt over to the fireplace. Would burning Nick's favorite shirt mean she was crazy?

Too bad, she thought as she dropped the shirt on the grate and added several pieces of kindling and some newspaper. Allie hesitated for only a moment before lighting the paper with a match. It caught fire, crackling to life and forcing her to step back. She watched the blaze destroy the shirt and reached for the poker, determined that not a scrap of it would be left.

She had to get control of her life. She thought of Jackson Cardwell and his kindness. He had no idea how much it meant to her.

As she watched the flames take the last of Nick's shirt, she told herself at least this would be the last she'd see of that blamed shirt.

Chapter Five

Jackson met Hayes and Laramie at the airport, but while it was good to see them, he was distracted.

They talked about the barbecue restaurant and Harlan and the wedding before McKenzie showed up while they were waiting for their luggage to pick up Hayes. Hayes had been in Texas tying up things with the sale of his business.

Jackson had heard their relationship was serious, but seeing McKenzie and Hayes together, he saw just how serious. Another brother falling in love in Montana, he thought with a shake of his head. Hayes and McKenzie would be joining them later tonight at the ranch for dinner.

He and Laramie ended up making the drive to Cardwell Ranch alone. Laramie talked about the financial benefits of the new barbecue restaurant and Jackson tuned him out. He couldn't get his mind off Allie Taylor.

Maybe it was because he'd been through so much with his ex, but he felt like a kindred spirit. The woman was going through her own private hell. He wished there was something he could do.

"Are you listening?" Laramie asked.

"Sure."

"I forget how little interest my brothers have in the actual running of this corporation."

"Don't let it hurt your feelings. I just have something else on my mind."

"A woman."

"Why would you say that, knowing me?"

Laramie looked over at him. "I was joking. You swore off women after Juliet, right? At least that's what you... Wait a minute, has something changed?"

"Nothing." He said it too sharply, making his brother's eyebrow shoot up.

Laramie fell silent for a moment, but Jackson could feel him watching him out of the corner of his eye.

"Is this your first wedding since...you and Juliet split?" Laramie asked carefully.

Jackson shook his head at his brother's attempt at diplomacy. "It's not the wedding. There's this...person I met who I'm worried about."

"Ah. Is this person—"

"It's a woman, all right? But it isn't like that."

"Hey," Laramie said, holding up his hands. "I just walked in. If you don't want to tell me—"

"She lost her husband some months ago and she has a little girl the same age as Ford and she's struggling."

Laramie nodded. "Okay."

"She's the wedding planner."

His brother's eyebrow shot up again.

"I'll just be glad when this wedding is over," Jackson said and thought he meant it. "By the way, when is Mom flying in?" At his brother's hesitation, he demanded, "What's going on with Mom?"

ALLIE HAD UNPACKED more boxes of decorations by the time she heard a vehicle pull up the next morning. Natalie, who had been coloring quietly while her mother worked, went running when she spotted her aunt Megan. Allie smiled as Megan picked Nat up and swung her around, both of them laughing. It was a wonderful sound. Megan had a way with Natalie. Clearly, she loved kids.

"Sorry I'm so late, but I'm here and ready to go to work." Megan was dressed in a T-shirt, jeans and athletic shoes. She had taken after their father and had the Irish green eyes with the dark hair and complexion. She was nothing short of adorable, sweet and cute. "Wow, the barn is already looking great," she exclaimed as she walked around, Natalie holding her hand and beaming up at her.

"I helped Mama with the lights," Nat said.

"I knew it," Megan said. "I can see your handiwork." She grinned down at her niece. "Did I hear you can now ride a horse?"

Natalie quickly told her all about the horses, naming each as she explained how to ride a horse. "You have to hang on to the reins."

"I would imagine you do," Megan agreed.

"Maybe you can ride with us," Nat suggested.

"Maybe I can. But right now I need to help your mom."

Just then Dana stuck her head in the barn doorway and called to Natalie. Allie introduced Dana to her stepsister, then watched as her daughter scurried off for an afternoon ride with her friends. She gave a thankful smile to Dana as they left.

"Just tell me what to do," Megan said and Allie did, even more thankful for the help. They went to work on the small details Allie knew Megan would enjoy.

Belinda stopped by to say hello to Megan and give Allie an update on the photos. She'd met with Lily that morning, had made out a list of photo ideas and sounded excited.

Allie was surprised when she overheard Belinda and Megan discussing a recent lunch. While the three of them had spent some time together since Megan had come back into Allie's life, she hadn't known that Belinda and Megan had become friends.

She felt jealous. She knew it was silly. They were both

single and probably had more in common than with Allie, who felt as if she'd been married forever.

"How are you doing?" Megan asked after Belinda left.

"Fine."

"No, really."

Allie studied her stepsister for a moment. They'd become close, but she hadn't wanted to share what was going on. It was embarrassing and the fewer people who knew she was losing her mind the better, right?

"It's been rough." Megan didn't know that she had been planning to leave Nick. As far as her sister had known, Allie had been happily married. Now Allie regretted that she hadn't been more honest with Megan.

"But I'm doing okay now," she said as she handed Megan another gift bag to fill. "It's good to be working again. I love doing this." She glanced around the barn feeling a sense of satisfaction.

"Well, I'm glad I'm here now," Megan said. "This is good for Natalie, too."

Good for all of us, Allie thought.

JACKSON LOOKED AT his brother aghast. "Mom's dating?" He should have known that if their mom confided in anyone it would be Laramie. The sensible one, was what she called him, and swore that out of all her sons, Laramie was the only one who she could depend on to be honest with her.

Laramie cleared his throat. "It's a little more than dating. She's on her honeymoon."

"Her *what?*"

"She wanted it to be a surprise."

"Well, it sure as hell is that. Who did she marry?"

"His name is Franklin Wellington the Fourth. He's wealthy, handsome, very nice guy, actually."

"*You've* met him?"

"He and Mom are flying in just before the wedding on his private jet. It's bigger than ours."

"Laramie, I can't believe you would keep this from the rest of us, let alone that Mom would."

"She didn't want to take away from Tag's wedding but they had already scheduled theirs before Tag announced his." Laramie shrugged. "Hey, she's deliriously happy and hoping we will all be happy for her."

Jackson couldn't believe this. Rosalee Cardwell hadn't just started dating after all these years, she'd gotten married?

"I wonder how Dad will take it?" Laramie said. "We all thought Mom had been pining away for him all these years...."

"Maybe she was."

"Well, not anymore."

"BUT YOU *HAVE* to go on the horseback ride," Natalie cried.

As he stepped into the cool shade, Jackson saw Allie look around the barn for help, finding none. Hayes was off somewhere with his girlfriend, McKenzie, Tag was down by the river writing his vows, Lily was picking her parents up at the airport, Laramie had restaurant business and Hud was at the marshal's office, working. There had still been no word from Austin. Or their mother.

Wanting to spend some time with his son, Jackson had agreed to go on the short horseback ride with Dana and the kids that would include lunch on the mountain.

"Dana promised she would find you a very gentle horse, in other words, a really *old* one," Megan joked.

Natalie was doing her "please-Mama-please" face.

"Even my dad is going to ride," Ford said, making everyone laugh.

Allie looked at the boy. "Your dad is a cowboy."

Ford shook his head. "He can't even rope a cow. He tried

once at our neighbor's place and he was really bad at it. So it's okay if you're really bad at riding a horse."

Jackson smiled and ruffled his son's hair. "You really should come along, Allie."

"I have too much work to—"

"I will stay here and get things organized for tomorrow," Megan said. "No more arguments. Go on the ride with your daughter. Go." She shooed her toward the barn door.

"I guess I'm going on the horseback ride," Allie said. The kids cheered. She met Jackson's gaze as they walked toward the corral where Dana and her ranch hand, Walker, were saddling horses. "I've never been on a horse," she whispered confidentially to Jackson.

"Neither had your daughter and look at her now," he said as he watched Ford and Natalie saddle up. They both had to climb up the fence to get on their horses, but they now sat eagerly waiting in their saddles.

"I'll help you," Jackson said as he took Allie's horse's reins from Dana. He demonstrated how to get into the saddle then gave her a boost.

"It's so high up here," she said as she put her boot toes into the stirrups.

"Enjoy the view," Jackson said and swung up onto his horse.

They rode up the mountain, the kids chattering away, Dana giving instructions to them as they went.

After a short while, Jackson noticed that Allie seemed to have relaxed a little. She was looking around as if enjoying the ride and when they stopped in a wide meadow, he saw her patting her horse's neck and talking softly to it.

"I'm afraid to ask what you just said to your horse," he joked as he moved closer. Her horse had wandered over to some tall grass away from the others.

"Just thanking him for not bucking me off," she admitted shyly.

"Probably a good idea, but your horse is a she. A mare."

"Oh, hopefully, she wasn't insulted." Allie actually smiled. The afternoon sun lit her face along with the smile.

He felt his heart do a loop-de-loop. He tried to rein it back in as he looked into her eyes. That tantalizing green was deep and dark, inviting, and yet he knew a man could drown in those eyes.

Suddenly, Allie's horse shied. In the next second it took off as if it had been shot from a cannon. To her credit, she hadn't let go of her reins, but she grabbed the saddlehorn and let out a cry as the mare raced out of the meadow headed for the road.

Jackson spurred his horse and raced after her. He could hear the startled cries of the others behind him. He'd been riding since he was a boy, so he knew how to handle his horse. But Allie, he could see, was having trouble staying in the saddle with her horse at a full gallop.

He pushed his harder and managed to catch her, riding alongside until he could reach over and grab her reins. The horses lunged along for a moment. Next to him Allie started to fall. He grabbed for her, pulling her from her saddle and into his arms as he released her reins and brought his own horse up short.

Allie slid down his horse to the ground. He dismounted and dropped beside her. "Are you all right?"

"I think so. What happened?"

He didn't know. One minute her horse was munching on grass, the next it had taken off like a shot.

Jackson could see that she was shaken. She sat down on the ground as if her legs would no longer hold her. He could hear the others riding toward them. When Allie heard her daughter calling to her, she hurriedly got to her feet, clearly wanting to reassure Natalie.

"Wow, that was some ride," Allie said as her daughter came up.

"Are you all right?" Dana asked, dismounting and joining her.

"I'm fine, really," she assured her and moved to her daughter, still in the saddle, to smile up at her.

"What happened?" Dana asked Jackson.

"I don't know."

"This is a good spot to have lunch," Dana announced more cheerfully than Jackson knew she felt.

"I'll go catch the horse." He swung back up into the saddle and took off after the mare. "I'll be right back for lunch. Don't let Ford eat all the sandwiches."

ALLIE HAD NO idea why the horse had reacted like that. She hated that she was the one who'd upset everyone.

"Are you sure you didn't spur your horse?" Natalie asked, still upset.

"She isn't wearing spurs," Ford pointed out.

"Maybe a bee stung your horse," Natalie suggested.

Dana felt bad. "I wanted your first horseback riding experience to be a pleasant one," she lamented.

"It was. It is," Allie reassured her although in truth, she wasn't looking forward to getting back on the horse. But she knew she had to for Natalie's sake. The kids had been scared enough as it was.

Dana had spread out the lunch on a large blanket with the kids all helping when Jackson rode up, trailing her horse. The mare looked calm now, but Allie wasn't sure she would ever trust it again.

Jackson met her gaze as he dismounted. Dana was already on her feet, heading for him. Allie left the kids to join them.

"What is it?" Dana asked, keeping her voice down.

Jackson looked to Allie as if he didn't want to say in front of her.

"Did I do something to the horse to make her do that?" she asked, fearing that she had.

His expression softened as he shook his head. "You didn't do *anything*." He looked at Dana. "Someone shot the mare." He moved so Dana could see the bloody spot on the horse. "Looks like a small caliber. Probably a .22. Fortunately, the shooter must have been some distance away or it could have been worse. The bullet barely broke the horse's hide. Just enough to spook the mare."

"We've had teenagers on four-wheelers using the old logging roads on the ranch," Dana said. "I heard shots a few days ago." Suddenly, all the color drained from Dana's face. "Allie could have been killed," she whispered. "Or one of the kids. When we get back, I'll call Hud."

JACKSON INSISTED ON riding right beside Allie on the way back down the mountain. He could tell that Allie had been happy to get off the horse once they reached the corral.

"Thank you for saving me," she said. "It seems like you keep doing that, doesn't it?" He must have looked panicked by the thought because she quickly added, "I'm fine now. I will try not to need saving again." She flashed him a smile and disappeared into the barn.

"Ready?" Tag said soon after Jackson had finished helping unsaddle the horses and put the tack away.

Dana had taken the kids down to the house to play, saying they all needed some downtime. He could tell that she was still upset and anxious to call Hud. "Don't forget the barbecue and dance tonight," she reminded him. "Then tomorrow is the bachelor party, right?"

Jackson groaned. He'd forgotten that Tag had been waiting for them all to arrive so they could have the party. The last thing he needed was a party. Allie's horse taking off like that... It had left him shaken, as well. Dana was convinced it had been teenagers who'd shot the horse. He hoped that was all it had been.

"Glad you're back," Tag said. "We're all going down to the Corral for a beer. Come on. At least four of us are here. We'll be back in time for dinner."

Ford was busy with the kids and Dana. "Are you sure he isn't too much?" Jackson asked his cousin. "I feel like I've been dumping him on you since we got here."

She laughed. "Are you kidding? My children adore having their cousin around. They've actually all been getting along better than usual. Go have a drink with your brothers. Enjoy yourself, Jackson. I suspect you get little time without Ford."

It was true. And yet he missed his son. He told himself again that he would be glad when they got back to Texas. But seeing how much fun Ford was having on the ranch, he doubted his son would feel the same.

ALLIE STARED AT her date book, heart racing. She'd been feeling off balance since her near-death experience on the horse. When she'd told Megan and Belinda about it on her return to the barn, they'd been aghast.

She'd recounted her tale right up to where Jackson had returned with the mare and the news that it had been shot.

"That's horrible," Megan said. "I'm so glad you didn't get bucked off. Was the mare all right?"

Belinda's response was, "So Jackson saved you? Wow, how romantic is that?"

Needing to work, Allie had shooed Belinda out of the barn and she and Megan had worked quietly for several hours before she'd glanced at her watch and realized something was wrong.

"The caterer," Allie said. "Did she happen to call?"

Megan shook her head. "No, why?"

"Her crew should have been here by now. I had no idea

it was so late." Allie could feel the panic growing. "And when I checked my date book…"

"What?" Megan asked.

"I wouldn't have canceled." But even as she was saying it, she was dialing the caterer's number.

A woman answered and Allie quickly asked about the dinner that was to be served at Cardwell Ranch tonight.

"We have you down for the reception in a few days, but… Wait a minute. It looks as if you did book it."

Allie felt relief wash through her, though it did nothing to relieve the panic. She had a ranch full of people to be fed and no caterer for the barbecue.

"I'm sorry. It says here that you called to cancel it yesterday."

"That's not possible. It couldn't have been me."

"Is your name Allie Taylor?"

She felt her heart drop. "Yes."

"It says here that you personally called."

Allie dropped into one of the chairs. She wanted to argue with the woman, but what good would it do? The damage was done. And anyway, she couldn't be sure she hadn't called. She couldn't be sure of anything.

"Just make sure that the caterers will be here on the Fourth of July for the wedding reception and that no one, and I mean not even me, can cancel it. Can you do that for me?" Her voice broke and she saw Megan looking at her with concern.

As she disconnected, she fought tears. "What am I going to do?"

"What's wrong?"

Her head snapped up at the sound of Jackson's voice. "I thought you were having beers with your brothers?"

"A couple beers is all I can handle. So come on, what's going on?"

She wiped at her eyes, standing to turn her back to him until she could gain control. What the man must think of her.

"The caterer accidentally got canceled. Looks like we might have to try to find a restaurant tonight," Megan said, reaching for her phone.

"Don't be ridiculous," Jackson said, turning Allie to look at him. "You have some of the best barbecue experts in the country right here on the ranch. I'll run down to the market and get some ribs while my brothers get the fire going. It's going to be fine."

This last statement Allie could tell was directed at her. She met his gaze, all her gratitude in that one look.

Jackson tipped his hat and gave her a smile. "It's going to be better than fine. You'll see."

"I HOPE YOU don't mind," Allie heard Jackson tell Dana and Lily. "I changed Allie's plans. I thought it would be fun if the Cardwell boys barbecued."

Dana was delighted and so was Lily. They insisted she, Natalie, Megan and Belinda stay and Allie soon found herself getting caught up in the revelry.

The Texas Boys Barbecue brothers went to work making dinner. Allie felt awful that they had to cook, but soon saw how much fun they were having.

They joked and played around while their father and Dana's provided the music. All the ranch hands and neighbors ended up being invited and pretty soon it had turned into a party. She noticed that even Drew, who'd been working at one of the cabins, had been invited to join them.

The barbecue was amazing and a lot more fun than the one Allie had originally planned. Everyone complimented the food and the new restaurant was toasted as a welcome addition to Big Sky.

Allie did her best to stay in the background. The day had left her feeling beaten up from her wild horseback ride to the foul-up with the caterer, along with her other misadventures. She was just happy to sit on the sidelines. Megan and Belinda were having a ball dancing with some of the ranch hands. All the kids were dancing, as well. At one point, she saw Jackson showing Ford how to do the swing with Natalie.

Someone stepped in front of her, blocking her view of the dance floor. She looked up to see Drew.

"I don't believe you've danced all night," he said.

"I'm really not—"

"What? You won't dance with your own brother-in-law? I guess you don't need me anymore now that you have the Cardwells. Or is it just one Cardwell?"

She realized he'd had too much to drink. "Drew, that isn't—"

"Excuse me," Jackson said, suddenly appearing beside her. "I believe this dance is mine." He reached for Allie's hand.

Drew started to argue, but Jackson didn't give him a chance before he pulled Allie out onto the dance floor. The song was a slow one. He took her in his arms and pulled her close.

"You really have to quit saving me," she said only half joking.

"Sorry, but I could see you needed help," Jackson said. "Your brother-in-law is more than a little protective, Allie."

She didn't want to talk about Drew. She closed her eyes for a moment. It felt good in the cowboy's arms. She couldn't remember the last time she'd danced, but that felt good, too, moving to the slow country song. "You saved my life earlier and then saved my bacon tonight. Natalie thinks you're a cowboy superhero. I'm beginning to wonder myself."

He gave her a grin and a shrug. "It weren't nothin', ma'am," he said, heavy on the Texas drawl. "Actually, I don't know why my brothers and I hadn't thought of it before. You did me a favor. I'd missed cooking with them. It was fun."

"Did I hear there is a bachelor party tomorrow night?"

Jackson groaned. "Hayes is in charge. I hate to think." He laughed softly. "Then the rehearsal and dinner the next night and finally the wedding." He shook his head as if he couldn't wait for it to be over.

Allie had felt the same way—before she'd met Jackson Cardwell.

Drew appeared just then. "Cuttin' in," he said, slurring his words as he pried himself between the two of them.

Jackson seemed to hesitate, but Allie didn't want trouble. She stepped into Drew's arms and let him dance her away from the Texas cowboy.

"What the hell do you think you're doing?" Drew demanded as he pulled her closer. "My brother is barely cold in his grave and here you are actin' like—"

"The wedding planner?" She broke away from him as the song ended. "Sorry, but I'm calling it a night. I have a lot of work to do tomorrow." With that she went to get Natalie. It was time to go home.

Chapter Six

Allie was getting ready to go to the ranch the next morning when she heard a vehicle pull up. She glanced out groaning when she saw it was Drew. Even more disturbing, he had his mother with him. As she watched them climb out, she braced herself for the worst. Drew had been acting strangely since he'd seen her with Jackson that first time.

"Hi," she said opening the door before either of them could knock. "You just caught me heading out."

"We *hoped* to catch you," Mildred said. "We're taking Natalie for the day so you can get some work done."

Not may we, but *we're taking*. "I'm sorry but Natalie already has plans."

Mildred's eyebrow shot up. "Natalie is five. Her plans can change."

"Natalie is going with the Cardwells—"

"The Cardwells aren't family," Mildred spat.

No, Allie thought, *but I wish they were.* "If you had just called—"

"I'm sure Nat would rather spend the day with her grandmother than whatever you have planned for—" Mildred broke off at the sound of a vehicle coming up the road toward them.

Who now? Allie wondered, fearing she was about to lose this battle with her in-laws—and break her daughter's heart. Her pulse did a little leap as she recognized the SUV as the one Jackson Cardwell had been driving yesterday. But what was he doing here? Allie had said she would bring Nat to the ranch.

Jackson parked and got out, Ford right behind him. He seemed to take in the scene before he asked, "Is there a problem?"

"Nothing to do with you," Drew said.

"Jackson Cardwell," he said and held out his hand. "I don't believe we've been formally introduced."

Drew was slow to take it. "Drew Taylor." Allie could see her brother-in-law sizing up Jackson. While they were both a few inches over six feet and both strong-looking, Jackson had the broader shoulders and looked as if he could take Drew in a fair fight.

Mildred crossed her arms over her chest and said, "We're here to pick up my granddaughter."

"That's why *I'm* here," Jackson said. Just then Natalie came to the door. She was dressed for the rodeo in her Western shirt, jeans and new red cowboy boots. Allie had braided her hair into two plaits that trailed down her back. A straw cowboy hat was perched on her head, her smile huge.

"I'm going to the rodeo with Ford and Hank and Mary," Nat announced excitedly. Oblivious to what was going on, she added, "I've never been to a rodeo before."

"Hop into the rig with Ford. I borrowed a carseat from Dana," Jackson said before either Drew or Mildred could argue otherwise.

With a wave, Nat hurried past her grandmother and uncle and taking Ford's hand, the two ran toward the SUV.

Allie held her breath as she saw Drew ball his hands into fists. She'd never seen him like this and realized Jackson was right. This was more than him being protective.

Jackson looked as if he expected Drew to take a swing— and was almost daring him to. The tension between the two men was thick as fresh-churned butter. Surely it wouldn't come to blows.

"Are you ready?" Jackson said to her, making her blink in surprise. "Dana gave me your ticket for the rodeo."

He *knew* she wasn't planning to go. This wedding had to be perfect and let's face it, she hadn't been herself for some time now.

"Going to a rodeo is part of this so-called wedding planning?" Mildred demanded. She lifted a brow. "I heard it also entails dancing with the guests."

"All in a day's work," Jackson said and met Allie's gaze. "We should get going. Don't want to be late." He looked to Drew. "Nice to meet you." Then turned to Mildred. "You must be Allie's mother-in-law."

"Mildred." Her lips were pursed so tightly that the word barely came out.

"I just need to grab my purse," Allie said, taking advantage of Jackson's rescue, even though she knew it would cost her.

When she came back out, Jackson was waiting for her. He tipped his hat to Drew and Mildred as Allie locked the cabin door behind her. She noticed that Mother Taylor and Drew were still standing where she'd left them, both looking infuriated.

She hated antagonizing them for fear what could happen if they ever decided to try to take Natalive from her. If they knew about just a few of the so-called incidents...

Like Nat, Allie slipped past them out to the SUV and didn't let out the breath she'd been holding until she was seated in the passenger seat.

"That looked like an ambush back there," Jackson said as they drove away.

She glanced back knowing she might have escaped this time, but there would be retribution. "They mean well."

JACKSON GLANCED OVER at her. "Do they?"

She looked away. "With Nick gone… Well, we're all adjusting to it. I'm sure they feel all they have left of him is Nat. They just want to see more of her."

He could see that she felt guilty. His ex and her family had used guilt on him like a club. He remembered that beat-up, rotten feeling and hated to see her going through it.

In the backseat, Natalie was telling Ford about something her horse had done yesterday during her ride. They both started laughing the way only kids can do. He loved the sound.

"Thank you for the rescue, but I really can't go to the rodeo. You can drop me at the ranch," Allie said, clearly nervous. "I need to check on things."

"You've done a great job. A few hours away at the rodeo is your reward. Dana's orders. She's the one who sent me to get you, knowing you wouldn't come unless I did."

"I really should be working."

"When was the last time you were at a rodeo?" he asked.

She chewed at her lower lip for a moment. "I think I went with some friends when I was in the fifth grade."

He smiled over at her. "Well, then it is high time you went again."

"I want an elephant ear!" Ford cried from the backseat.

"An elephant ear?" Nat repeated and began to giggle.

"So Nat's never been to a rodeo, either?" Jackson asked.

"No, I guess she hasn't."

"Well, she is going today and she and her mother are going to have elephant ears!" he announced. The kids laughed happily. He was glad to hear Ford explaining that an elephant ear really was just fried bread with sugar and cinnamon on it, but that it was really good.

Allie seemed to relax, but he saw her checking her side mirror. Did she think her in-laws would chase her down? He wouldn't have been surprised. They'd been more than overbearing. He had seen how they dominated Allie. It made him wonder what her husband had been like.

When they reached the rodeo grounds, Dana and Hud were waiting along with the kids and Tag and Lily and Hayes and McKenzie and Laramie.

"Oh, I'm so glad you decided to come along," Dana said when she saw Allie. "Jackson said he wasn't sure he could convince you, but he was darned sure going to try." She glanced at her cousin. "He must be pretty persuasive."

"Yes, he is," Allie said and smiled.

Jackson felt a little piece of his heart float up at that smile.

Easy, Texas cowboy, he warned himself.

But even as he thought it, he had to admit that he was getting into the habit of rescuing this woman—and enjoying it. Allie needed protecting. How badly she needed it, he didn't yet know.

It was the least he could do—until the wedding. And then he and Ford were headed back to Texas. Allie Taylor would be on her own.

Just the thought made him scared for her.

ALLIE COULDN'T REMEMBER the last time she'd had so much fun. The rodeo was thrilling, the elephant ear delicious and the Cardwells a very fun family. She'd ended up sitting next to Jackson, their children in front of them.

"I want to be a barrel racer," Natalie announced.

"We'll have to set up some barrels at the ranch," Dana said. "Natalie's a natural in the saddle. She'd make a great barrel racer."

"Well, I'm not riding the bulls," Ford said and everyone laughed.

"Glad you came along?" Jackson asked Allie as he offered some of his popcorn.

She'd already eaten a huge elephant ear and loved every

bite, but she still took a handful of popcorn and smiled. "I am. This is fun."

"You deserve some fun."

Allie wasn't so sure about that. She wasn't sure what she deserved, wasn't that the problem? She leaned back against the bleachers, breathing in the summer day and wishing this would never end.

But it did end and the crowd began to make their way to the parking lot in a swell of people. That's when she saw him.

Nick. He was moving through the crowd. She'd seen him because he was going in the wrong direction—in their direction. He wore a dark-colored baseball cap, his features lost in the shadow of the cap's bill. She got only a glimpse— Suddenly, he turned as if headed for the parking lot, as well. She sat up, telling herself her eyes were deceiving her. Nick was dead and yet—

"Allie, what it is?" Jackson asked.

In the past when she'd caught glimpses of him, she'd frozen, too shocked to move. She sprang to her feet and pushed her way down the grandstand steps until she reached the ground. Forcing her way through the crowd, she kept Nick in sight ahead of her. He was moving fast as if he wanted to get away.

Not this time, she thought, as she felt herself gaining on him. She could see the back of his head. He was wearing his MSU Bobcat navy ball cap, just like the one he'd been wearing the day he left to go up into the mountains—and his favorite shirt, the one she'd burned.

Her heart pounded harder against her ribs. She told herself she wasn't losing her mind. She couldn't explain any of this, but she knew what she was seeing. Nick. She was within yards of him, only a few people between them. She could almost reach out and grab his sleeve—

Suddenly, someone grabbed her arm, spinning her

around. She stumbled over backward, falling against the person in front of her, tripping on her own feet before hitting the ground. The fall knocked the air from her lungs and skinned her elbow, worse, her pride. The crowd opened a little around her as several people stopped to see if she was all right.

But it was Jackson who rushed to help her up. "Allie, are you all right?"

All she could do was shake her head as the man she thought was Nick disappeared into the crowd.

"WHAT'S GOING ON?" Jackson asked, seeing how upset she was. Had he said or done something that would make her take off like that?

She shook her head again as if unable to speak. He could tell *something* had happened. Drawing her aside, he asked her again. The kids had gone on ahead with Dana and her children.

"Allie, talk to me."

She looked up at him, those green eyes filling with tears. "I saw my husband, Nick. At least I think I saw him." She looked shocked as she darted a glance at the crowd, clearly expecting to see her dead husband again.

"You must think I'm crazy. *I* think I'm crazy. But I saw Nick. I know it couldn't be him, but it looked so much like him...." She shivered, even though the July day was hot. "He was wearing his new ball cap and his favorite shirt, the one I burned..." She began to cry.

"Hey," he said, taking her shoulders in his hands to turn her toward him. "I don't think you're crazy. I think you've had a horrible loss that—"

"I didn't *love* him. I was *leaving* him." The words tumbled out in a rush. "I...I...*hated* him. I *wanted* him gone, not dead!"

Jackson started to pull her into his arms, but she bolted

and was quickly swept up in the exiting crowd. He stood for
a moment, letting her words sink in. Now, more than ever,
he thought he understood why she was letting little things
upset her. Guilt was a powerful thing. It explained a lot,
especially with her relationship with her in-laws that he'd
glimpsed that morning. How long had they been browbeat-
ing her? he wondered. Maybe her whole marriage.

He found himself more curious about her husband, Nick
Taylor. And even more about Allie. Common sense told him
to keep his distance. The wedding was only days away, then
he and Ford would be flying back to Houston.

Maybe it was because he'd gone through a bad marriage,
but he felt for her even more now. Like her, he was raising his
child alone. Like her, he was disillusioned and he'd certainly
gone through a time with his ex when he thought he was losing his mind. He'd also wished his ex dead more than once.

ALLIE CAUGHT UP to Dana as she was loading all the kids
into her Suburban. Hud had brought his own rig since he
had to stop by the marshal's office.

"Mind if I catch a ride with you?" Allie asked. "Jackson
had some errands to run in town." The truth was that after
her outburst, she was embarrassed and knew Dana had room
for her and Nat in the Suburban.

"Of course not."

Allie had stopped long enough to go into the ladies' room
and wash her face and calm down. She knew everyone had
seen her take off like a crazy woman. She felt embarrassed
and sick at heart, but mostly she was bone-deep scared.

When she'd seen Jackson heading for the parking lot,
she'd motioned that she and Nat were going with Dana.
He'd merely nodded, probably glad.

Dana didn't comment on Allie's red eyes or her im-
promptu exit earlier, though as she joined them at the
Suburban. Instead, Dana made small talk about the rodeo,
the weather, the upcoming wedding.

They were almost back to the ranch before Dana asked, "How are things going?" over the chatter of the kids in the back of the SUV.

Allie could tell that she wasn't just making conversation anymore. She really wanted to know. "It's been hard. I guess it's no secret that I've been struggling."

Dana reached over and squeezed her hand. "I know. I feel so bad about yesterday. I'm just so glad you weren't hurt." She smiled. "You did a great job of staying on that horse, though. I told Natalie how proud I was of you."

Allie thought of Jackson. He'd saved her life yesterday. She remembered the feel of his arms as he'd pulled her from the horse—and again on the dance floor last night. Shoving away the memory, she reminded herself that once the wedding was over, he and Ford would be leaving. She was going to have to start saving herself.

"Did Hud find out anything about who might have shot the horse?" she asked, remembering Hud talking to the vet when he'd stopped by to make sure the mare was all right.

"Nothing yet, but he is going to start gating the roads on the ranch. We can't keep people from the forest service property that borders the ranch, but we can keep them at a distance by closing off the ranch property. In the meantime, if there is anything I can do to help you…"

"Dana, you've already done so much. Letting Natalie come to the ranch and teaching her to ride…" Allie felt overwhelmed at Dana's generosity.

"Let's see if you thank me when she's constantly bugging you about buying her a horse," Dana joked. "Seriously, she can always come up to the ranch and ride. And if someday you do want a horse for her…"

"Thank you. For everything."

"I love what you've done to the barn," Dana said, changing the subject. "It is beyond my expectations and Lily can't say enough about it. I'm getting so excited, but then I'm a sucker for weddings."

"Me, too," Allie admitted. "They are so beautiful. There is so much hope and love in the air. It's all like a wonderful dream."

"Or fantasy," Dana joked. "Nothing about the wedding day is like marriage, especially four children later."

No, Allie thought, but then she'd had a small wedding in Mother Taylor's backyard. She should have known then how the marriage was going to go.

"Have you given any more thought to moving up to a guest cabin?" Dana asked.

"I have. Like I said, I'm touched by the offer. But Natalie has been through so many changes with Nick's death, I think staying at the cabin in her own bed might be best. We'll see, though. She is having such a great time at the ranch and as the wedding gets closer…"

"Just know that I saved a cabin for you and Natalie," Dana said. "And don't worry about your daughter. We have already adopted her into the family. The kids love her and Ford…." She laughed and lowered her voice, even though the kids weren't paying any attention behind them. "Have you noticed how tongue-tied he gets around her?"

They both laughed, Allie feeling blessed because she felt as if she, too, had been adopted into the family. The Cardwells were so different from the Taylors. She pushed that thought away. Just as she did the memory of that instant when she would have sworn she saw Nick at the rodeo.

Every time she thought she was getting better, stronger, something would happen to make her afraid she really was losing her mind.

"HEY," BELINDA SAID, seeming surprised when Allie and Nat walked into the barn that afternoon. "Where have you been? I thought you'd be here working."

"We went to the rodeo!" Natalie said. "And now I'm

going to go ride a horse!" With that she ran out of the barn to join the other kids and Dana.

"You went to the rodeo?"

"You sound like my in-laws," Allie said. "Yes, I was invited, I went and now I will do the last-minute arrangements for the rehearsal dinner tomorrow and it will all be fine."

Belinda lifted a brow. "Wow, what a change from the woman who was panicking because she couldn't find her keys the other day. Have you been drinking?"

"I'm taking my life back." She told her friend about the candle, Nick's shirt and what she did with it. Also about chasing the man she thought was Nick at the rodeo. "I almost caught him. If someone hadn't grabbed my arm…"

Belinda's eyes widened in alarm. "Sorry, but doesn't that sound a little…"

"Crazy? Believe me, I know. But I was sick of just taking it and doing nothing."

"I can see you thinking you saw someone who looked like Nick at the rodeo…."

"He was wearing his favorite shirt and his new ball cap."

Belinda stared at her. "The shirt you'd burned a few nights ago, right?"

Allie regretted telling her friend. "I know it doesn't make any sense. But all these things that have been happening? I'm not imagining them." From her friend's expression, she was glad she hadn't told her about the dresses or the new clothes she'd found in her closet.

"Sweetie," Belinda asked tentatively. "Did you give any more thought to making that call I suggested?"

"No and right now I have work to do."

"Don't we all. Some of us didn't spend the day at the rodeo."

Her friend actually sounded jealous. Allie put it out of her mind. She had to concentrate on the wedding. The barn looked beautiful. After the rehearsal dinner tomorrow night, she would get ready for the wedding. All she had to do was hold it together until then.

Megan came in with her list of last-minute things that needed to be tended to before the wedding rehearsal.

"I'll meet you down in the meadow in a few minutes." Left alone, Allie looked around the barn. She was a little sad it would be over. Jackson and Ford would be returning to Texas. Nat was really going to miss them.

And so are you.

ALLIE WASN'T SURE what awakened her. Dana had insisted she take the rest of the day off and spend it with Natalie.

"You have accomplished so much," Dana had argued. "Tomorrow is another day. The men are all going with Tag for his bachelor party tonight. I plan to turn in early with the kids. Trust me. We all need some downtime before the wedding."

Emotionally exhausted, Allie had agreed. She and Nat had come back to the cabin and gone down to the river until dinner. Nat loved building rock dams and playing in the water.

After dinner even Natalie was exhausted from the full day. After Allie had put her down to sleep, she'd turned in herself with a book. But only a few pages in, she had turned out the light and gone to sleep.

Now, startled awake, she lay listening to the wind that had come up during the night. It was groaning in the boughs of the pine trees next to the cabin. Through the window, she could see the pines swaying and smell the nearby river. She caught only glimpses of the moon in a sky filled with stars as she lay listening.

Since Nick's death she didn't sleep well. The cabin often woke her with its creaks and groans. Sometimes she would hear a thump as if something had fallen and yet when she'd gone to investigate, she would find nothing.

One time, she'd found the front door standing open. She had stared at it in shock, chilled by the cold air rushing in—and the knowledge that she distinctly remembered locking it before going to bed. Only a crazy woman would leave the front door wide open.

Now, though, all she heard was the wind in the pines, a pleasant sound, a safe sound. She tried to reassure herself that everything was fine. She thought of her day with the Cardwell family and remembered how Jackson had saved her by having the Cardwell brothers make their famous Texas barbecue for supper. She smiled at the memory of the brothers in their Texas Boys Barbecue aprons joking around as they cooked.

She'd overheard one of the brothers say he was glad to see Jackson loosening up a little. Allie found herself watching him earlier at the rodeo, wondering how he was doing as a single father. She didn't feel as if she'd done very well so far as a single mother.

Ford was having a sleepover at the main house at the ranch again tonight. Allie knew if Nat had known about it, she would have wanted to stay, as well. But she suspected that Dana had realized that she needed her daughter with her tonight. What a day! First a run-in earlier with Mildred and Drew... Allie felt a chill at the memory. They had both been so furious and no doubt hurt, as well. Then thinking she saw Nick. She shook her head and, closing her eyes, tried to will herself to go back to sleep. If she got to thinking about any of that—

A small thump made her freeze. She heard it again and quickly swung her legs over the side of the bed. The sound had come from down the hall toward the bedroom where Natalie was sleeping.

Allie didn't bother with her slippers or her robe; she was too anxious as she heard another thump. She snapped on the hall light as she rushed down the short, narrow hallway to her daughter's room. The door she'd left open was now closed. She stopped in front of it, her heart pounding. The wind. It must have blown it shut. But surely she hadn't left Nat's window open that much.

She grabbed the knob and turned, shoving the door open with a force that sent her stumbling into the small room. The moon and starlight poured in through the gaping open window to paint the bedroom in silver as the wind slammed a loose shutter against the side of the cabin with a thump.

Allie felt her eyes widen as a scream climbed her throat. Nat's bed was empty.

Chapter Seven

Jackson felt at loose ends after the bachelor party. Part of the reason, he told himself, was because he'd spent so little time with his son. Back in Texas on their small ranch, he and Ford were inseparable. It was good to see his son having so much fun with other children, but he missed him.

Tonight Ford was having a sleepover at the main house with Dana's brood. He'd wanted to say no when Dana had asked, but he had seen that Ford had his heart set and Jackson had no choice but to attend Tag's bachelor party.

Fortunately, it had been a mild one, bar-hopping from the Corral to Lily's brother's bar at Big Sky, The Canyon Bar. They'd laughed and joked about their childhoods growing up in Texas and talked about Tag's upcoming wedding and bugged Hayes about his plans with McKenzie. Hayes only grinned in answer.

Hud, as designated driver, got them all home just after midnight, where they parted company and headed to their respective cabins. That was hours ago. Jackson had slept for a while before the wind had awakened him.

Now, alone with only his thoughts, he kept circling back to Allie. She'd had fun at the rodeo—until she'd thought she'd seen her dead husband. He blamed her in-laws. He figured they'd been laying a guilt trip on her ever since Nick Taylor had been presumed dead. Her run-in with them that morning must have made her think she saw Nick. He wanted to throttle them for the way they treated Allie and shuddered at the thought of them having anything to do with raising Natalie.

Allie was too nice. Did she really believe they meant well? Like hell, he thought now. They'd been in the wrong and yet they'd made her feel badly. It reminded him too much of the way his ex had done him.

It had been fun cooking with his brothers again—just as they had when they'd started their first barbecue restaurant. Allie'd had fun at the barbecue, too. He'd seen her laughing and smiling with the family. He'd enjoyed himself, as well. Of course Austin still hadn't arrived. But it was nice being with the others.

As much as he'd enjoyed the day, he felt too antsy to sleep and admitted it wasn't just Ford who was the problem. He tried to go back to sleep, but knew it was impossible. He had too much on his mind. Except for the wind in the pines, the ranch was quiet as he decided to go for a walk.

Overhead the Montana sky was a dazzling glitter of starlight with the moon peeking in and out of the clouds. The mountains rose on each side of the canyon, blacker than midnight. A breeze stirred the dark pines, sending a whisper through the night.

As he neared his rental SUV, he decided to go for a ride. He hadn't had that much to drink earlier and, after sleeping for a few hours, felt fine to drive.

But not far down the road, he found himself slowing as he neared Allie's cabin. The cabin was small and sat back from the highway on the river.

He would have driven on past, if a light hadn't come on inside the cabin.

Something about that light coming on in the wee hours of the morning sent a shiver through him. He would have said he had a premonition, if he believed in them. Instead, he didn't question what made him turn down her road.

Just as he pulled up to the cabin, Allie came running out.

At first he thought she'd seen him turn into her yard and that was why she'd come running out with a flashlight. But one look at her wild expression, her bare feet and her clothed in nothing but her nightgown, and he knew why he'd turned into her cabin.

"Allie?" he called to her as he jumped out. "Allie, what's wrong?"

She didn't seem to hear him. She ran toward the side of the cabin as if searching furiously as her flashlight beam darted into the darkness. He had to run after her as she headed around the back of the cabin. He grabbed her arm, thinking she might be having a nightmare and was walking in her sleep.

"Allie, what's wrong?"

"Nat! She's gone!"

He instantly thought of the fast-moving river not many yards out the back door. His gaze went to Allie's feet. "Get some shoes on. I'll check behind the house."

Taking her flashlight, he pushed her toward the front door before running around to the back of the cabin. He could hear and smell the river on the other side of a stand of pines. The July night was cool, almost cold this close to the river. Through the dark boughs, he caught glimpses of the Gallatin River. It shone in the moon and starlight, a ribbon of silver that had spent eons carving its way through the granite canyon walls.

As he reached the dense pines, his mind was racing. Had Natalie gotten up in the night and come outside? Maybe half-asleep, would she head for the river?

"Natalie!" he called. The only answer was the rush of the river and moan of the wind in the pine boughs overhead.

At the edge of the river, he shone the flashlight beam along the edge of the bank. No tracks in the soft earth. He flicked the light up and down the area between the pines, then out over the water. Exposed boulders shone in the light as the fast water rushed over and around them.

If Natalie had come down here and gone into the swift current…

At the sound of a vehicle engine starting up, he swung his flashlight beam in time to see a dark-colored pickup take off out of the pines. Had someone kidnapped Natalie? His first thought was the Taylors.

As he ran back toward the cabin, he tried to tell himself it had probably been teenagers parked down by the river making out. Once inside, he found Allie. She'd pulled on sandals and a robe and had just been heading out again. She looked panicked, her cheeks wet with tears.

"You're sure she isn't somewhere in the house," he said, thinking about a time that he'd fallen asleep under his bed while his mother had turned the house upside down looking for him.

The cabin was small. It took only a moment to search everywhere except Nat's room. As he neared the door to the child's bedroom, he felt the cool air and knew before he pushed open the door that her window was wide open, the wind billowing the curtains.

He could see the river and pines through the open window next to the bed. No screen. What looked like fresh soil and several dried pine needles were on the floor next to the bed. As he started to step into the room, a sound came from under the covers on the bed.

Jackson was at the bed in two long strides, pulling back the covers to find a sleeping Natalie Taylor curled there.

Had she been there the whole time and Allie had somehow missed her?

Allie stumbled into the room and fell to her knees next to her daughter's bed. She pulled Nat to her, snuggling her face into the sleeping child.

Jackson stepped out of the room to leave them alone for

a moment. His heart was still racing, his fear now for Allie rather than Nat.

A few minutes later, Allie came out of her daughter's room. He could see that she'd been crying again.

"She's such a sound sleeper. I called for her. I swear she wasn't in her bed."

"I believe you."

"I checked her room. I looked under her bed...." The tears began to fall again. "I looked in her closet. I called her name. *She wasn't there.* She wasn't anywhere in the cabin."

"It's all right," Jackson said as he stepped to her and put his arms around her.

Her voice broke as she tried to speak again. "What if she was there the whole time?" she whispered against his chest. He could feel her trembling and crying with both relief and this new fear. "She can sleep through anything. Maybe—"

"Did you leave the window open?"

"I cracked it just a little so she could get fresh air...."

"Natalie isn't strong enough to open that old window all the way like that."

Allie pulled back to look up at him, tears welling in her green eyes. "I *must* have opened it. I *must* have—"

He thought of the pickup he'd seen leaving. "There's something I need to check," he said, picking up the flashlight from where he'd laid it down just moments before. "Stay here with Natalie."

Outside he moved along the side of the house to the back, shining the flashlight ahead of him. He suspected what he would find so he wasn't all that surprised to discover the boot prints in the soft dirt outside Nat's window.

Jackson knelt down next to the prints. A man-size boot. He shone the light a few feet away. The tracks had come up to the window, the print a partial as if the man had sneaked up on the toes of his boots. But when the prints retreated from the child's window, the prints were full boot tracks, deep in the dirt as if he'd been carrying something. The tracks disappeared into the dried needles of the pines, then reappeared, this time headed back to the house. When the man had returned Natalie to her bed—and left dried pine needles and dirt on the bedroom floor.

ALLIE SAT ON the edge of her daughter's bed. She'd always loved watching Natalie sleep. There was something so incredibly sweet about her that was heightened when she slept. The sleep of angels, she thought as she watched the rise and fall of her daughter's chest.

Outside the now closed window, Jackson's shadow appeared and disappeared. A few minutes later, she heard him come back into the cabin. He came directly down the hall, stopping in Nat's bedroom doorway as if he knew she would be sitting on the side of the bed, watching her daughter sleep. That was where he would have been if it had been his son who'd gone missing, he thought.

She was still so shaken and scared. Not for Natalie, who was safe in her bed, but for herself. How could she have thought her daughter was missing? She really was losing her mind. Tucking Nat in, she checked to make sure the window was locked and left the room, propping the door open.

Jackson followed her into the small living room. She held her breath as she met his gaze. He was the one person who had made her feel as if she was going to be all right. He'd seen the black cat. He'd sympathized with her when she'd told him about misplacing her car keys and messing up her date book.

But earlier he'd looked at her as if she were a hysterical woman half out of her mind. She *had* been. Maybe she *was* unstable. When she'd found Nat's bed empty— Just the thought made her blood run cold again.

"I swear to you she wasn't in her bed." She could hear how close she was to breaking down again.

He must have, too, because he reached over and gripped her arm. "You didn't imagine it any more than you did the black cat."

She stared at him. "How can you say that?"

"Someone was outside Natalie's window tonight. There were fresh tracks where he'd stood. He took Natalie."

Her heart began to thunder in her ears. "Someone tried to…" She couldn't bring herself to say the words as she imagined a shadowed man taking her baby girl out through the window. "But why…?"

"He must have heard me coming and changed his mind," Jackson said.

"Changed his mind?" This all felt too surreal. First Nick's death then all the insane incidents, now someone had tried to take her child?

"Why don't you sit down," Jackson suggested.

She nodded and sank into the closest chair. He took one and pulled it next to hers.

"Is there someone who would want to take your daughter?" he asked.

Again she stared at him, unable to speak for a moment. "Why would anyone want to kidnap Natalie? I don't have any money."

He seemed to hesitate. "What about your husband's family?"

JACKSON SAW THAT he'd voiced her fear. He'd seen the way her in-laws had been just that morning. It wasn't much of a stretch that they would try to take Natalie. But through an open window in the middle of the night?

"They've made no secret that they want to see her more, but to steal her from her bed and scare me like this?"

Scare her. He saw her eyes widen in alarm and he took a guess. "There have been other instances when something happened that scared you?"

Her wide, green eyes filled with tears. "It was nothing. Probably just my imagination. I haven't been myself since…"

"Tell me about the incidents."

She swallowed and seemed to brace herself. "I found a squirrel in my cast-iron pot that has a lid."

"A live squirrel?"

"Half dead. I know it sounds crazy. How could a squirrel get under a heavy lid like that?"

"It couldn't. What else?"

She blinked as if stunned that he believed her, but it seemed to free her voice. "My husband used to buy me clothes I didn't like. I found them all cut up but I don't remember doing it. My brother-in-law took Nat and me out for dinner and when I got back they were lying on the bed and there were new clothes in the closet, eight hundred dollars' worth, like I would have bought if…"

"If you had bought them. Did you?"

She hesitated. "I don't think so but there was a check missing from my checkbook and when I took them back to the store, the clerks didn't remember who'd purchased them."

"No one was ever around when any of these things happened?"

She shook her head. "When I told my mother-in-law about the squirrel in the pot…she thought I was still taking the drugs the doctor gave me right after Nick's death. The drugs did make me see things that weren't there.…" Her words fell away as if she'd just then realized something. "Unless the things *had* been there."

Allie looked up at him, tears shimmering in her eyes. "Like the black cat.… I wasn't sure I'd even seen it until you…"

It broke his heart. For months after her husband's death, she'd been going through this with no one who believed her.

"I don't think you imagined any of these things that have been happening to you," he said, reaching for her hand. "I think someone wants you to *believe* you are losing your mind. What would happen if you were?"

She didn't hesitate an instant. "I would lose Natalie."

As RELIEVED AS she was, Allie had trouble believing what he was saying. She got up and started to make a fire.

"Let me do that," Jackson said, taking a handful of kindling from her.

Allie moved restlessly around the room as he got the blaze going. "You think it's someone in Nick's family?"

"That would be my guess. It's clear they want Natalie, especially your mother-in-law. Would her son, Drew, help her?"

She shook her head. "Nick would do whatever his mother wanted. But Drew…" She didn't want to believe it, but he seemed to have turned against her lately. She felt sick at the thought that she might have been wrong about him all this time.

"You must think I'm such a fool."

"My mother said be careful what family you're marrying into. I didn't listen. I didn't even *know* the woman I was really marrying. But then she hid it well—until we were married."

"I know exactly what you're saying."

His chuckle held no humor. "I learned the hard way."

"So did I. I would have left Nick, if he hadn't disappeared…. I suppose you heard that he went hiking up in the mountains late last fall and was believed killed by a grizzly."

He nodded. "I'm sorry. You must have all kinds of conflicting emotions under the circumstances."

Allie let out a sigh. "You have no idea. Or maybe you do. My friend Belinda says my so-called incidents are brought on by my guilt. She's even suggested that I see a psychic to try to contact Nick on the other side to make the guilt go away."

He shook his head. "I think there is a very sane explanation that has nothing to do with guilt, and the last thing you need is some charlatan who'll only take your money."

She laughed. "That was exactly what I thought." She couldn't believe how much better she felt. She hadn't felt strong for so long. Fear had weakened her, but Jackson's words brought out some of the old Allie, that strong young woman who'd foolishly married Nick Taylor.

He hadn't broken her at first. It had taken a few years before she'd realized what he'd done to her. She no longer had her own ideas—if they didn't agree with his. He dressed her, told her what friends he liked and which ones he didn't.

He'd basically taken over her life, but always making it seem as if he were doing her a favor since he knew best. And she had loved him. At least at first so she'd gone along because she hadn't wanted to upset him. Nick could be scary when he was mad. She'd learned not to set him off.

When Nick had been nice, he'd been so sweet that she had been lulled into thinking that if she was just a little more accommodating he would be sweet all the time.

"Belinda thinks Nick knew that I was leaving him and went up in the mountains to…"

"Kill himself? What do you think?" Jackson asked.

"Nick did say he wanted to change and that he was sorry about the way he'd acted, but…"

"You didn't believe it?"

She shook her head. "The Nick I knew couldn't change even if he'd wanted to."

So why had Nick Taylor gone up into the mountains last fall and never come back? Jackson wondered.

The fact that his body hadn't been found made Jackson more than a little suspicious. If the man had purposely

gone to the mountains intending to die and leave his wife
and child alone, then he was a coward. If he set the whole
thing up and was now trying to have his wife committed...

The timing bothered him. His stomach roiled with anger
at the thought. "Is there any chance he knew of your plans?"

"I didn't think so. For months I'd been picking up any
change he left lying around. I also had been skimping on
groceries so I could save a little. He might have noticed."
She looked away guiltily. "I also took money out of his wallet if he'd been drinking. I figured he wouldn't know how
much he spent. He never said anything."

Jackson hoped this bastard was alive because he planned
to punch him before the man went to prison for what he was
doing to this woman. Not letting her have her own money
was a sin in any marriage, no matter what some head-of-
the household types said.

"I hate to even ask this, but is there any chance—"

"Nick is still alive?" She stood and paced around the
room. "That would explain it, wouldn't it? Why I think I
see him or why I smell his aftershave in the house, even
though I threw out the bottle months ago. Why when I start
feeling better, he shows up."

"Like at the rodeo?" Jackson asked, feeling his skin crawl
at the thought of the bastard. "This only happens when there
is no one else around who sees him, right?"

She nodded. "It all happens in a split second so I can't be
sure. At the rodeo, though, I almost caught him. Just a few
more yards..." Allie's eyes suddenly widened. "I remember now. Someone grabbed my arm and spun me around.
That's why I fell."

"You think it was someone who didn't want you to catch
him."

"Did you see anyone you recognized in the crowd before
you found me?"

He thought for a moment. "I wasn't looking for anyone

but you, I'm sorry. Allie, all of this is classic gaslighting. Someone wants to unnerve you, to make you think you're imagining things, to make you doubt your own reality and ultimately make you doubt your own sanity."

She met his gaze. Her eyes filled with tears. "You think it's Nick?"

"I think it's a possibility. If he suspected you were going to leave him and take Natalie…he might have staged his death. He had the most to lose if you left him and with his body never being found…"

NICK ALIVE? ALLIE felt a chill move through her. Her husband had been a ghost, haunting her from his mountain grave for months. Now he had taken on an even more malevolent spirit.

She got up and threw another log on the fire. But not even the hot flames could chase away the icy cold that had filled her at the thought of Nick still alive. Not just alive but stalking her, trying to make her think she was crazy. Still, why—

"You think he's after Natalie," she said and frowned. "He's never cared that much about her. He wanted a son and when he didn't get one…"

"Believe me. I know what it's like to have a vindictive spouse who would do anything to hurt me—including taking a child she didn't really want."

"Oh, Jackson, I'm so sorry."

"If your husband is alive, you can bet he is behind all of this."

If Nick really was alive, then Drew would know. It would also explain why Drew was being so protective and acting jealous over Jackson.

Jackson stepped to her. "There is one thing you can count on. It's going to get worse. Nick will have to escalate his plan. He probably has a story already planned for when he comes stumbling out of the mountains after being attacked and having no memory for months. But that story won't hold up if it goes on much longer. I don't want to scare you, but if whoever is behind this can't drive you crazy, they might get desperate and decide the best way to get Natalie is to get rid of her mother for good."

She shuddered.

"Sorry," he said. "I know it seems like a leap…"

Jackson looked to the dark window before returning his gaze to her. "But if your husband is alive, then you have to assume he is watching your every move."

If Nick wasn't, then Drew was doing it for him, she realized. "You really think it's possible?" she asked in a whisper as if not only was he watching but he was listening, as well.

"Given what has been happening to you and the fact that his body was never found?" Jackson nodded. "But if he is alive, we can't let him know that we're on to him."

We. That had such a wonderful sound. She had felt so alone in all this. Suddenly, she wasn't. Jackson believed her. He didn't think she was crazy. Far from it. He thought all of this was happening because someone wanted her to *believe* she was crazy. Maybe not just *someone,* but the man she'd married.

She swallowed back the bile that rose in her throat at the thought of how far her husband had gone and to what end? "He must have known I was leaving him and taking Natalie."

"That would be my guess. With you in the nuthouse, he could reappear and take your daughter."

The thought of Natalie with a man who would do something like that turned her blood to ice.

"But if he is alive, then—" Jackson seemed to hesitate "—then I really can't see how he could have pulled this off without help."

Allie knew what he was saying. Not just Drew but Mildred and Sarah might be in on this. "His brother, Drew, has been around a lot since Nick…disappeared and has helped out financially until the investigation is over. His mother's never liked me and didn't believe me when I've told her about only some of the things that have been happening. Or at least she pretended not to."

Jackson nodded. "What about Drew's sister, Sarah?"

"She's afraid of Mother Taylor, not that I can blame her."

He looked away for a moment. "What about the two women working with you on the wedding?"

"*Belinda and Megan?* Belinda's the only friend who stuck with me after I married Nick. He tried to run her off but she wasn't having any of it." Allie didn't want to believe it. Refused to. She shook her head. "She's been on my side against them. And Megan? She's my *stepsister* I never knew until…"

"Until?" he prompted.

"I guess it was right before Nick died. Megan contacted me. She was just finishing up her college degree at the University of Montana in Missoula. After my mother died, my father remarried several times and had more children. He moved away and I lost track of him and my step-siblings. Megan was like a gift coming into our lives when she did. Nat adores her. I adore her. You can't think she is somehow involved in any of this."

Jackson didn't say anything. He didn't have to. His skepticism was written all over his face. "It's the timing that bothers me."

She nodded. He thought she was naive. She'd always been too trusting. Isn't that what Nick had told her time and time again?

Allie quickly turned away as she felt hot tears scald her eyes. All of this was just too much. She thought of her daughter and hurriedly wiped at her tears. Straightening her back, she felt a surge of anger and turned back to face Jackson.

"Whoever is doing this, they aren't going to win. What do we do?" she asked.

"We catch them. Do you have a photograph of Nick?"

As she left the room, she noticed that the sun had come up. She came back with a snapshot. "This is the only one I could find. It's one of Nick and his brother, Drew. Nick is the one on the right."

Jackson looked down at the photo. "They look alike."

"Do they?" she said, looking at the snapshot he was holding. "I guess they do a little," she said, surprised that she hadn't noticed it because their personalities were so different. "Drew was always the quiet one. Nick was his mother's favorite. I'm sure that had something to do with why he was so cocky and smart-mouthed. Drew was the one always standing back watching."

"Did Drew resent that?" Jackson asked.

Allie frowned. "I don't know. He didn't seem to. Just the other day he was telling me how hard it was to keep the business going without Nick."

Jackson turned thoughtful for a moment. "You mentioned something about Belinda wanting you to see some psychic so you could reach Nick on the other side? I think you should do it."

Allie blinked in surprise. "Seriously? You don't think I'm messed up enough?"

"It's Belinda's idea, right? If she is involved, then this séance with the psychic is a trap. But since we are on to them now, it would help to know what they have planned for you. I suspect it won't be pleasant, though. I'm sure it is supposed to push you over the edge, if you aren't already dangling there. Do you think you can handle it?"

She raised her chin, her eyes dry, resolve burning in her like a blazing fire. She thought of the people who had been tricking her for months. Anger boiled up inside her along with a steely determination. She hadn't felt this strong in years. "I can handle it."

Jackson smiled at her. "Good." He checked his watch. "Give the psychic a call. Calling this early she will think you are desperate to see her, exactly what we want her to think."

Allie dug the card out, glad now that she'd saved it. She took a breath, let it out and dialed the number. Jackson stepped closer so he could hear.

She was surprised when a young-sounding woman answered after three rings.

"I'm sorry to call so early but I need your help. My friend Belinda suggested I call you." Jackson gave her a thumbs-up.

"You must be Allie. I was hoping you'd call. You're in danger—and so is your daughter. I need to see you as soon as possible."

"Is today too soon, then?" Allie asked.

"Why don't you come this evening, say about eight? Will that work for you?"

Allie met Jackson's gaze. He nodded. "That would be fine. I hope you can help me."

"I will do my best but ultimately it will be up to the spirits."

Jackson swore softly as Allie disconnected. "Spirits my ass. Between now and then, I will try to find out everything I can about the people with access to you." He reached over and took her hand. "Don't worry. We're going to catch these bastards."

Chapter Eight

When Jackson returned to the ranch, he found his brothers, told them what he thought was going on and asked for their help. He no longer kidded himself that he wasn't involved.

"I can talk to the cops about what they found in the mountains," Hayes said. "You say Nick Taylor's body still hasn't been found? Isn't that odd? He died late last fall and even with hikers in the area, no remains have turned up?"

"No, that's what makes me suspicious," Jackson said. "His claw-shredded backpack and rifle were discovered at the scene with grizzly prints in the dirt and enough blood to make them believe he was killed there. But still no remains of any kind."

Hayes nodded. "I'll get right on it."

"What can I do?" Laramie asked.

"Financials on everyone involved including Allie's friend Belinda Andrews and her stepsister, Megan Knight, as well as all of the Taylor family. Nick and his brother, Drew, were partners in a construction company called Gallatin Canyon Specialty Construction."

"You got it," Laramie said. "What about Allie herself?"

"Sure, and Nick, just in case he had something going on that she didn't know about," Jackson said.

"Wait a minute," Tag said. "What about me?"

"You, brother dear, are getting married. You just concentrate on your lovely bride-to-be," Jackson told him. Tag started to object. "If you're going to be hanging around the ranch here, then do me a favor. Keep an eye on Drew Taylor. He's apparently doing some repairs here."

Jackson stopped by the barn to find Allie and Megan hard at work putting together centerpieces for the tables. Allie pretended she needed something from her van and got up to go outside with him.

"No more trouble last night?" he asked, seeing worry in her gaze.

"None. I'm just having a hard time believing any of that happened last night." She glanced around as if she expected Nick to materialize before her gaze came back to him. Or maybe she was worried about her brother-in-law, Drew, seeing them together again. "I can't believe Belinda or Megan—"

"Have you seen Belinda?"

"She had to go into Bozeman. She left about twenty minutes ago, why?"

He shook his head. "You better get back inside. Try not to let on that you're suspicious."

She sighed. "You don't know how hard that is."

"I can imagine." He gave her an encouraging smile. "Just be your usual sweet self." He loved it when she returned his smile and those gorgeous dimples of hers showed.

As she went back into the barn and rejoined Megan, he headed up the hillside. Belinda was staying in the last guesthouse to the east. Each cabin was set away from the others in the dense pines for the most privacy.

A cool pine-scented breeze restlessly moved the boughs over his head as he walked on the bed of dried needles toward Belinda's cabin. He could hear the roar of the river and occasionally the sound of a semi shifting down on the highway far below. A squirrel chattered at him as he passed, breaking the tranquility.

He was almost to her cabin when he heard the crack of a twig behind him and spun around in surprise.

His brother Hayes grinned. "I would imagine the cabin will be locked," he said as he stepped on past to climb the steps to the small porch and try the door. "Yep, I know your lock-picking skills are rusty at best." He pulled out his tool set.

Jackson climbed the steps and elbowed his brother out of the way. "I told Dana I was locked out. She gave me the master key." He laughed and opened the door.

"You know I do this for a living, right?" his brother asked.

"I'd heard that. But are you any good?"

Hayes shot him a grin and headed for the log dresser in the room with the unmade bed.

Jackson glanced around the main room of the cabin and spotted Belinda's camera bag. He could hear his brother searching the bedroom as he carefully unzipped the bag. There were the usual items found in a professional photographer's large bag. He carefully took out the camera, lens and plastic filter containers and was about to put everything back, thinking there was nothing to find when he saw the corner of a photo protruding from one of the lower pockets.

"What did you find?" Hayes asked as he returned after searching both bedrooms.

Jackson drew out the photos and thumbed through them. They were shots taken with apparent friends. Each photo had Belinda smiling at the camera with her arm around different friends, all women. He was thinking how there wasn't one of her and Allie, when he came to the last photo and caught his breath.

"Who is that?" Hayes asked.

"Allie's husband, Nick, and her best friend Belinda Andrews. Allie said that Nick never liked Belinda." The snapshot had been taken in the woods along a trail. There was a sign in the distance that said Grouse Creek Trail. Nick had his arm possessively around Belinda. Both were smiling at each other rather than the camera the way lovers do.

"Apparently, they liked each other a lot more than Allie knew," Hayes said. "But you know what is really interesting about that photo? That trailhead sign behind them."

"Let me guess. Up that trail is where Nick Taylor was believed to have been killed."

WHEN THEY'D FINISHED the centerpieces, Allie sent Megan into Bozeman for an order of wedding items that had been delayed. It had been difficult working with her and suspecting her of horrible things. Allie was relieved when she was finally alone in the barn.

Everything was coming along on schedule. It had been Dana's idea to start days early. "I don't want you to feel any pressure and if you need extra help, you just let me know," Dana had said.

"No, I'm sure that will be fine."

"I want you to have some free time to go for a horseback ride or just spend it on the ranch with your daughter."

"You are so thoughtful," Allie had said.

"Not at all. I just know what it's like with a little one, even though Natalie isn't so little anymore," she said with a laugh. "I promise I will keep your daughter busy so you can work and not have to worry about her having a good time."

Dana had been good to her word. Allie stepped outside the barn now to check on Natalie only to find her on the back of a horse about to take a short ride up the road for another picnic with Dana and the other children.

"Come along," Dana encouraged. "Warren would be happy to saddle you a horse. You know what they say about almost falling off a horse, don't you?" she asked with a smile. "You have to get back on."

Allie laughed, thinking that was exactly what she was

doing with her life, thanks to Jackson. She was tempted to go on the ride until she saw him headed her way. "Next time."

"We're going to hold you to it," Dana said. "In fact, we're all going on a ride tomorrow before the rehearsal dinner. Plan on coming along." With that they rode off, the kids waving and cheering as they disappeared into the pines.

Jackson waved to his son, making the same promise before he continued on down the mountainside toward her.

When she saw his expression, her heart fell. He'd discovered something and whatever it was, it wasn't good.

"Let's go up to my cabin," Jackson said as he glanced around. "We can talk there."

They made the short hike up the mountainside. His cabin faced the river, sheltered in the pines and was several dozen yards from the closest cabin where his brothers were staying together.

"What is it?" Allie asked the moment they were inside.

Jackson handed her a snapshot in answer.

She looked down at her smiling husband and her best friend. There was no doubt what she was looking at but still she was shocked and found it hard to believe. For more than six years Belinda and Nick had acted as if they couldn't stand each other. Had it been a lie the entire time?

"When was this taken?" she asked.

Jackson shook his head. "There isn't a date. I found it in her camera bag with a lot of other photos of her with friends."

Allie raised an eyebrow. "You aren't going to try to convince me that they are just friends."

He shook his head. "You weren't at all suspicious?"

She laughed as she made her way to the couch and sat down. The ground under her feet no longer felt stable. "Nick always said I was too trusting. Belinda was the only friend who could put up with Nick. So I guess a part of me suspected that Nick liked her more than he let on."

"I'm sorry."

"Don't be. I stopped loving Nick Taylor the year we got married. If I hadn't gotten pregnant with Nat…" She tossed the photo on the coffee table in front of her.

"She was the only one you told about your plans to leave Nick?" he asked as he took a seat across from her.

Allie let out a laugh. "So of course she told him."

"More than likely," he agreed. "There's more." He took a breath and let it out as he studied her. "You sure you want to hear all of this?"

She sat up straighter. "Let me have it."

"I got my brothers to help me. They have the expertise in their chosen fields that we needed. Hayes talked to the cops who had a copy of Nick's file with reports from the hiker who found the backpack and rifle to the warden who investigated the initial scene. He reported that there was sufficient evidence to assume that Nick was dead based on the shredded backpack and the amount of blood soaked into the pine needles."

"So…he's dead?"

"Or he made it look that way," Jackson said. "No DNA was tested at the scene because there didn't appear to be a need to do so. But there are still a lot of questions. No shots were fired from the rifle, leading the investigators to believe he didn't have time to get off a shot before he was attacked by the bear. Or he could have staged the whole thing. But the incidents you've been having with things disappearing and reappearing, those can't be Nick. If he's alive, he has to keep his head down."

"So we're back to my in-laws and Belinda and Megan."

"I'm afraid so. Belinda, if involved with Nick, would be the obvious one. Was she around before any of the incidents happened?"

Allie thought back to when her keys had ended up in the bathroom sink at the Mexican restaurant. She'd left her purse at the table, but then Sarah and her mother had been there, too. She sighed, still refusing to believe it, even after seeing the photo. "Yes, but Belinda wouldn't—"

"Wouldn't have an affair with your husband behind your back?"

"She's been so *worried* about me."

Jackson raised a brow.

Allie hugged herself against the thought of what he was saying. Belinda *had* apparently betrayed her with Nick. Maybe Jackson was right. Then she remembered something. "Belinda has a new man in her life. I know the signs. She starts dressing up and, I don't know, acting different. The man can't be Nick. That photo doesn't look recent of her and Nick. Why would she be acting as if there was someone new if it was Nick all these months?"

"Maybe he's been hiding out and has only now returned to the canyon."

That thought turned her stomach. "If he's come back…"

"Then whoever has been gaslighting you must be planning on stepping up their plan," Jackson said.

She turned to look at him as a shiver raced through her. "The psychic. Maybe this is their grand finale, so to speak, and they have something big planned tonight to finally send me to the loony bin."

"Maybe you shouldn't go—"

"No. Whatever they have planned, it won't work. They've done their best to drive me crazy. I know now what they're up to. I'll be fine."

"I sure hope so," Jackson said.

"WHAT IS THE lowdown on the Taylor family?" Jackson asked Hud after dinner that evening at the ranch. They'd had beef steaks cooked on a pitchfork in the fire and eaten on the wide porch at the front of the house. The night had been beautiful, but Jackson was too antsy to appreciate it. He was worried about Allie.

She'd dropped Natalie by before she and Belinda had left. He hadn't had a chance to speak with her without raising suspicion. All he could do was try his best to find out who was behind the things that had been happening to her.

"Old canyon family," Hud said. "Questionable how they made their money. It was rumored that the patriarch killed someone and stole his gold." Hud shrugged. "Mildred? She married into it just months before Bud Taylor died in a car accident. She's kept the name even though she's been through several more husbands. I believe she is on number four now. Didn't take his name, though. He's fifteen, twenty years older and spends most of his time with his grown children back in Chicago."

"And the daughter?"

"Sarah?" Hud frowned. "Never been married that I know of. Lives in the guesthouse behind her mother's. No visible means of support."

"The brothers had a construction company together?"

"They did. Nick was the driving force. With him gone, I don't think Drew is working all that much."

"Just between you and me, Allie was planning to leave Nick Taylor before he went up in the mountain and disappeared," Jackson said, taking the marshal into his confidence.

Hud looked over at him. "What are you getting at?"

"Is there any chance Nick Taylor is alive?"

Hud frowned. "You must have some reason to believe he is."

"Someone has been gaslighting Allie."

"For what purpose?"

"I think someone, probably in the Taylor family, wants to take Natalie away from her."

"YOU SEEM BETTER," Belinda noted on the drive out of the canyon. She'd insisted on driving Allie to the psychic's house, saying she didn't trust Allie to drive herself if the psychic said anything that upset her.

Allie had been quiet most of the drive. "*Do* I seem better?" Did her friend seem disappointed in that?

"Maybe this isn't necessary."

That surprised her. "I thought you were the one who said I had to talk to this psychic?"

"I thought it would help."

"And now?" Allie asked.

"I don't want her to upset you when you seem to be doing so well."

"That's sweet, but I'm committed…so to speak."

Belinda nodded and kept driving. "Seriously, you seem so different and the only thing that has changed that I can tell is Jackson Cardwell showing up."

Allie laughed. "Just like you to think it has to be a man. Maybe I'm just getting control of my life."

Her friend looked skeptical. "Only a few days ago you were burning Nick's favorite shirt so it didn't turn up again."

"Didn't I tell you? The shirt *did* turn up again. I found it hanging in the shower this morning. Now I ask you, how is that possible?"

"You're sure you burned it? Maybe you just—"

"Dreamed it?" Allie smiled. That was what they wanted her to think. She looked over at Belinda, worried her old friend was up to her neck in this, whatever it was.

Allie fought the urge to confront her and demand to know who else was behind it. But Belinda turned down a narrow road, slowing to a stop in front of a small house with a faint porch light on.

Showtime, Allie thought as she tried to swallow the lump in her throat.

Chapter Nine

Belinda's apartment house was an old, five-story brick one a few blocks off Main Street in Bozeman.

Laramie waited in the car as lookout while Jackson and Hayes went inside. There was no password entry required. They simply walked in through the front door and took the elevator up to the third floor to room 3B. It was just as Allie had described it, an apartment at the back, the door recessed so even if someone had been home on the floor of four apartments, they wouldn't have seen Hayes pick the lock.

"You're fast," Jackson said, impressed.

Hayes merely smiled and handed him a pair of latex gloves. "I'm also smart. If you're right and Nick Taylor is alive and this becomes a criminal case... You get the idea. It was different up on the ranch. This, my brother, is breaking and entering."

Jackson pulled on the gloves and opened the door. As he started to draw his flashlight out of his pocket, Hayes snapped on an overhead light.

"What the—"

"Jackson," his brother said and motioned toward the window. The curtains were open, the apartment looking out onto another apartment building. While most of the curtains were drawn in those facing this way, several were open.

Hayes stepped to the window and closed the curtains.

"Nothing more suspicious than two dudes sneaking around in a woman's apartment with flashlights."

He had a point. "Let's make this quick."

"I'm with you," Hayes said and suggested the best place to start.

"If I didn't know better, I'd think you'd done this before," Jackson joked.

Hayes didn't answer.

In the bedroom in the bottom drawer of the bureau under a bunch of sweaters, Jackson found more photos of Belinda and Nick, but left them where he'd found them.

"So you think I'm right and Nick is alive," Jackson said.

Hayes shrugged.

Jackson finished the search of the bedroom, following his brother's instructions to try to leave everything as he had found it.

"Find anything?" he asked Hayes when he'd finished.

"She recently came into thirty-eight thousand dollars," Hayes said, thumbing through a stack of bank statements he'd taken from a drawer.

"Maybe it's a trust fund or an inheritance."

"Maybe. Or blackmail money or money Nick had hidden from Allie," Hayes said as he put everything back. "Laramie would probably be able to find out what it was if we had more time. Did you put the photos back?"

"All except one. I want to show it to Allie. It looks more recent to me."

Hayes looked as if he thought that was a bad idea. "You're messing with evidence," he reminded him.

"I'll take that chance," Jackson said.

His brother shook his head as he turned out the light and moved to the window to open the curtains like he'd found them.

"Does anyone else know how involved you are with the wedding planner?" Silence. "I didn't think so. Better not let cousin Dana find out or there will be hell to pay. She is very protective of people she cares about. She cares about that woman and her child. If you—"

"I'm not going to hurt her." He couldn't see his brother's expression in the dark. He didn't have to.

ALLIE BRACED HERSELF. She hadn't shared her fears about the visit with the psychic with Jackson before she'd left. She hadn't had to. She'd seen the expression on his face as he watched her leave. He was terrified for her.

For months someone had been trying to push her over the edge of sanity. She had a bad feeling that the psychic was part of the master plan, a shocker that was aimed at driving her insane. By now, they probably thought she was hanging on by a thread. While she was stronger, thanks to Jackson and his determination that she was perfectly sane and those around her were the problem, there was a part of her that wasn't so sure about that.

Just this morning, she'd stepped into the bathroom, opened the shower curtain and let out a cry of shock and disbelief. Nick's favorite shirt was hanging there, the same shirt she'd burned in the fireplace a few nights ago. Or at least one exactly like it. Worse, she smelled his aftershave and when she opened the medicine cabinet, there it was in the spot where he always kept it—right next to his razor, both of which she had thrown out months ago.

Had he hoped she would cut her wrists? Because it had crossed her mind. If it hadn't been for Natalie…and now Jackson…

"Remember, you're that strong woman you were before you met Nick Taylor," Jackson had said earlier.

She'd smiled because she could only vaguely remember that woman. But she wanted desperately to reacquaint herself with her. Now all she could do was be strong for her daughter. She couldn't let these people get their hands on Natalie.

Belinda parked in front of a small house and looked over at her. "Ready?"

Allie could hear reluctance in her friend's voice. If Jackson was right and Nick was behind this, then Allie suspected he was forcing Belinda to go through with the plan no matter what.

But that's what she had to find out. If Nick was alive. She opened her car door and climbed out. The night air was cool and scented with fresh-cut hay from a nearby field. It struck her how remote this house was. The closest other residence had been up the road a good half mile.

If a person was to scream, no one would hear, Allie thought, then warned herself not to bother screaming. Belinda and the psychic were probably hoping for just such a reaction.

"I was surprised when you agreed to do this," Belinda said now, studying her as she joined Allie on the path to the house.

"I told you. I would do anything to make whatever is happening to me stop." Allie took a deep breath and let it out. "Let's get this over with."

They walked up the short sidewalk and Belinda knocked. Allie noticed that there weren't any other vehicles around except for an old station wagon parked in the open, equally old garage. If Nick was here he'd either been dropped off or he'd parked in the trees at the back of the property.

The door was opened by a small, unintimidating woman wearing a tie-dyed T-shirt and worn jeans. Her feet were bare. Allie had been expecting a woman in a bright caftan wearing some sort of headdress. She was a little disappointed.

"Please come in," the woman said in what sounded like a European accent. "I am Katrina," she said with a slight nod. "It is so nice to meet you, Allie. Please follow me. Your friend can stay here."

Belinda moved to a couch in what Allie assumed was the sparsely furnished living area.

Allie followed the woman down a dim hallway and through a door into a small room dominated by a table and two chairs. The table was bare.

Katrina closed the door, making the room feel even smaller. She took a seat behind the desk and motioned Allie into the chair on the opposite side.

This felt silly and it was all Allie could do not to laugh. She and a friend in the fifth grade had stopped at the fortune teller's booth at the fair one time—her friend Willow's idea, not hers.

"I want to know if I am going to marry Curt," her friend had said.

Allie could have told her that there was a good chance she wasn't going to marry some boy in her fifth grade class.

The fortune teller had told them they would have long, happy lives and marry their true loves. Five dollars each later they were standing outside the woman's booth. Willow had been so excited, believing what the fortune teller had said was that she would marry Curt. She'd clearly read what she wanted into the woman's words.

Willow didn't marry Curt but maybe she had found her true love since she'd moved away in sixth grade when her father was transferred. Allie hadn't had a happy life nor had she apparently married her true love and now here she was again sitting across from some woman who she feared really might know her future because she was about to control it.

"I understand you want me to try to reach your husband who has passed over," Katrina said. "I have to warn you that I am not always able to reach the other side, but I will try since your friend seems to think if I can reach…"

"Nick," Allie supplied.

"Yes, that it will give you some peace." The woman hesitated. "I hope that will be the case. It isn't always, I must warn you. Do you want to continue?"

Allie swallowed and nodded.

"Give me your hands. I need you to think of your husband." Katrina dimmed the lights and reached across the table to take Allie's hands in hers. "It helps if you will close your eyes and try to envision your husband."

That was about the last thing Allie wanted to do, but as Katrina closed hers, Allie did the same. She couldn't help but think of Nick and wonder if he was watching her at this very moment.

"WHILE WE'RE BREAKING the law, there is one other place I'd like to have a look before we head back," Jackson said to his brothers.

Hayes looked disapproving. "What part of breaking and entering don't you understand?"

"You can wait in the car."

Gallatin Canyon Specialty Construction was located on the outskirts of town next to a gravel pit. The industrial area was dark this time of the night as Jackson pulled in with his lights out and parked.

"Allie said the company hasn't been doing very well without Nick and wasn't doing that well even before Nick allegedly died," Jackson said. "I just want to take a look at the books."

"Good thing you brought me along," Laramie said. "You did mean, you want me to take a look, right?"

Jackson laughed. "Yeah, if you don't mind."

Hayes sighed and they all got out and walked toward the trailer that served as the office. Hayes unlocked the door then said, "I'll stand guard. Make it quick," before disappearing into the darkness.

"You do realize you might be jeopardizing everything by doing this," Laramie said. "Is this woman worth it?"

Jackson didn't answer as he pulled on the latex gloves Hayes had shoved at him in the car and handed his brother a pair before turning on a light and pointing at the file cabinets.

It wasn't until they were all three back in the car and headed south toward Cardwell Ranch that Jackson asked his brother what he'd found, if anything.

After Laramie tried to explain it in fiduciary terms, Hayes snapped, "The bottom line, please."

Laramie sighed. "It is clear why you all leave the business part of Texas Boys Barbecue up to me. All right, here it is. Drew Taylor is broke and has been siphoning off the money from the business before the sale."

"Sale?" Jackson said.

"While not of general knowledge, Drew has been trying to sell the business through a company in other states."

"That's suspicious," Hayes said.

"Is his mother involved in the construction business?" Jackson asked.

Laramie chuckled. "Excellent question. I believe she might have been a silent partner, which I take to mean she provided some of the money. Until recently, Drew was writing her a check each month."

"Think she knows what her son is up to?" Hayes asked.

"Doubtful. According to Allie, Mother Taylor rules the roost. Everyone is afraid of her."

"Sounds like our boy Drew is planning to escape in the dark of night," Hayes commented and Jackson agreed.

"As for the rest of the people you asked me to look at the finances of, Mildred Taylor is fine as long as her old, absentee husband sends her a check each month. She and her daughter live off the old man. Nick wasn't much of a breadwinner. Montana winters slow down construction, apparently. But he did okay. After his death, there wasn't much in his personal account."

"So the thirty-eight thousand Belinda just received wasn't from Nick, then," Hayes said.

Laramie continued, "Nick did, however, leave a hundred-thousand-dollar insurance policy, which is supposed to pay out any day once Nick has finally been ruled legally deceased."

"A hundred thousand?" Jackson exclaimed. "That doesn't seem like enough money to put Allie into the nuthouse for."

Laramie and Hayes agreed. "There could be other insurance policies I'm not aware of."

"What about Megan Knight?" Jackson asked.

"Just finished college, has thousands of dollars in student loans," Laramie said. "Majored in psychology so unless she goes to grad school…"

"What do you all make of this?" Jackson asked.

"Well," his brother Laramie said. "I've always said follow the money. That will usually take you to the source of the problem."

"SO WE HAVE Drew siphoning money from the business and Belinda coming into some money and Megan needing money to pay off her student loans," Jackson said. "So which of them has motive to want Allie in the nuthouse?"

"Your guess is as good as mine," Hayes said. "That photo you took from Belinda's apartment of her and Nick? The lovebirds didn't look like they were getting along."

"Wait a minute," Laramie said from the backseat. "Are you thinking with Nick gone, Drew and Belinda hooked up?"

"Good question," Jackson said.

"I've heard of stranger things happening," Hayes said.

"Or maybe it's blackmail money," Jackson said. "Maybe

Belinda has something on Drew and he's the source of the thirty-eight thousand."

"Or Drew is simply taking money from the business and giving it to Belinda to give to Nick," Hayes threw in.

"Which would mean that Drew knows Nick is alive," Jackson said.

"Or at least he has been led to believe his brother is alive according to Belinda," Hayes said.

"You two are making my head spin," Laramie cried and both brothers laughed. "No wonder I prefer facts and figures. They are so much less confusing."

"He's right," Hayes said. "It could be simple. Nick's dead, Belinda got her money from another source entirely and Drew is blowing his on beer."

As they reached Cardwell Ranch, Jackson glanced at the time. "Let's hope Allie gets some answers tonight," he said, unable to keep the worry out of his voice. "Who knows what horrors they have planned for her."

"ALLIE."

Nick's voice made Allie jump, but Katrina held tight to her hands. Goose bumps skittered over her skin as Nick spoke again.

"Allie?" His voice seemed to be coming from far away.

"We're here, Nick," Katrina said after she'd spent a good five minutes with her eyes closed, calling up Nick's spirit. "Is there something you want to say to Allie?"

She heard him groan. The sound sent her heart pounding even harder. Somehow it was more chilling than his saying her name.

"Please, Nick, do you have a message for Allie?"

Another groan, this one sounding farther away. Katrina seemed anxious as if she feared she was going to lose Nick before he said whatever it was he wanted to say.

Allie doubted that was going to happen, but maybe the

woman would try to drag this out, get more money from her by making her come back again.

She tried to pull away, but Katrina tightened her hold, pulling her forward so her elbows rested on the table.

"Nick, please, give your wife the peace she desperately needs."

Another groan. "Allie, *why?*" The last word was so ghostly that Allie felt her skin crawl. At that moment, she believed it was Nick calling to her from the grave.

"What are you asking?" Katrina called out to him.

Silence. It was so heavy that it pressed against Allie's chest until she thought she couldn't breathe.

Then a groan as forlorn as any she'd ever heard filled the small room. She shivered. "Allie," Nick said in a voice that broke. "Why did you kill me?"

Chapter Ten

Allie jerked her hands free and stumbled to her feet. She didn't realize she'd made a sound until she realized she was whimpering.

As the lights came up, she saw that Katrina was staring at her in shock as if whoever was behind this hadn't taken her into their confidence. Either that, or she was a good actress.

Allie rushed out of the room and down the hallway. Belinda wasn't in the living room where she'd been told to wait. Opening the door, Allie ran outside, stopping only when she reached Belinda's car.

None of that was real. But it had been Nick's voice; there was no doubt about that. He was either alive...or they'd somehow gotten a recording of Nick's voice. *That wasn't Nick speaking from his grave.* Intellectually, she knew that. But just hearing Nick's voice and those horrible groans...

Belinda came bursting out of the house. Allie turned to see Katrina standing at the doorway looking stunned. Or was that, too, an act?

"Allie?" Belinda ran to her looking scared. "What happened in there?"

She ignored the question. "Where were you?"

Belinda seemed taken aback by her tone, if not her question. "I had to go to the bathroom. I was just down the hall. Are you all right?"

"I want to go." Katrina was still standing in the doorway.

Allie reached for the door handle but the car was locked. "Belinda, I want to *go*."

"Okay, just a sec." She groped in her purse for her keys.

"Can't find them?" Allie taunted with a sneer. "Maybe you left them in the bathroom sink."

Belinda glanced up in surprise, frowning as if confused. "No, I have them. Honey, are you sure you're all right?"

Allie laughed. "How can you seriously ask that?"

Belinda stared at her for a moment before she opened the car doors and went around and slid behind the wheel.

They rode in silence for a few minutes before Belinda said, "I'm sorry. Clearly, you're upset. I thought—"

"What did you think?" Allie demanded.

Belinda shot her a glance before returning to her driving. "I seriously thought this might help."

"Really? Was it your idea or Nick's?"

"Nick's?" She shot her another quick look.

"I *know*, Belinda." Silence. "I know about you and Nick." Belinda started to deny it, but Allie cut her off. "You two had me going for a while, I'll give you that. I really did think I was losing my mind. But not anymore. How long have you and Nick been having an affair?"

"Allie—"

"I don't have to ask whose plan this was. It has Nick written all over it."

"Honey, I honestly don't know what you're talking about."

"No?" Allie reached into her pocket and pulled out the photo of Belinda and Nick standing next to the trailhead sign at Grouse Creek. "As you've often said, a picture is worth a thousand words."

Belinda groaned, not unlike Nick had back at the alleged psychic's. "It isn't what you think."

Allie laughed again as she put the photo back in her pocket. "It never is."

"I'm sorry." She sounded as if she were crying, but Allie could feel no compassion for her.

"What was the point of all that back there?" Allie demanded as they left the Gallatin Valley behind and entered the dark, narrow canyon.

"I swear I don't know what you're talking about. What happened in there that has you so angry and upset?"

"Don't play dumb, Belinda. It doesn't become you. But tell me, what's next?" Allie demanded. "You failed to make me crazy enough that you could take Natalie. Is it the insurance money? Is that what you're planning to use to open your own studio? But in order to get it, you're going to have to kill me. Is that the next part of your plot, Belinda?"

The woman gasped and shot her a wide-eyed look. "You sure you aren't crazy, because you are certainly talking that way. That photo of me and Nick? That was before he met and married you. I broke up with him. Why do you think he didn't like me? Why do you think he put up with me? Because I threatened to tell you about the two of us." She took a breath and let it out. "As for me trying to make you think you were crazy…" Belinda waved a hand through the air. "That's ridiculous. I'm the one who has been trying to help you. I should have told you about me and Nick, but it was water under the bridge. And Nick's insurance money? I don't need it. Remember I told you about my eccentric aunt Ethel? Well, it seems she'd been socking money away in her underwear drawer for years. Thirty-eight thousand of it was left to me, tax free. That's what I plan to use to start my own photo studio. Allie, no matter what you think, I'm your *friend*."

She had thought so, but now she didn't know what to believe. "How did you come up with the idea of me going to see Katrina?" she challenged.

Belinda drove in silence, the canyon highway a dark ribbon along the edge of the river. "I told you. I'd seen

Katrina a few times. But the idea for you to go see her so you could try to reach Nick and get closure? That was your sister *Megan*'s idea."

JACKSON FOUND HIMSELF walking the floor of his cabin until he couldn't take it anymore. Finally, he heard the sound of a vehicle, saw the headlights coming up the road and hurried down to the barn where Allie had left her van.

He waited in the shadows as both women got out of Belinda's car, neither speaking as they parted ways.

"Are you all right?" Jackson asked Allie as he stepped from the shadows. She jumped, surprised, and he mentally kicked himself for scaring her. "I'm sorry. I've been pacing the floor. I was so worried about you."

Her features softened. "I'm okay." She looked drained.

"If you don't want to talk about it tonight…"

Allie gave him a wane smile. "Natalie is staying with your family and I'm not going to be able to sleep, anyway."

"Do you mind coming up to my cabin?"

She shook her head and let him lead her up the mountainside through the pines. It was only a little after ten, but most everyone had turned in for the night so there was little light or sound on the ranch. Under the thick pine boughs, it was cool and dark and smelled of summer.

Jackson realized he was going to miss that smell when he returned to Texas. He didn't want to think about what else he might miss.

Once inside the cabin, they took a seat on the couch, turning to face each other. It was warm in the cabin away from the chill of the Montana summer night. Without prompting, Allie began to relate what had happened slowly as if she was exhausted. He didn't doubt she was.

He hated putting her through this. She told him about the ride to the psychic's and Belinda's apparent hesitancy to let her go through with it. Then she told him about Katrina and the small remote house.

"It all felt silly and like a waste of time, until I heard Nick's voice."

He looked at her and felt his heart drop. Hearing her husband's voice had clearly upset her. It surprised him that whoever was behind this had gone that far.

"You're sure it was Nick's voice."

She nodded. "It sounded as if it was far away and yet close."

"Could it have been a recording?"

"Possibly. His words were halting as if hard for him to speak and he…groaned." She shuddered. "It was an awful sound, unearthly."

"I'm so sorry. After you left, I regretted telling you to go." He sighed. "I was afraid it would just upset you and accomplish nothing."

"It gets worse. Nick…accused me of…killing him."

"*What?* That's ridiculous. I thought a grizzly killed him."

She shrugged. "The psychic believed it. You should have seen her face."

"Allie, the woman was in on it. This was just another ploy. You knew that going in."

"But I didn't know I would hear his voice. I didn't know he would ask me why I'd killed him. I didn't…" The tears came in a rush, dissolving the rest of whatever she was going to say.

Jackson pulled her to him. She buried her face into his chest. "None of this is real, Allie. Are you listening to me? None of it. They just want you to believe it is."

After a few moments, the sobs stopped. He handed her a tissue from the box by the couch and she got up and moved to the window. His cabin view was the rock cliff across the valley and a ribbon of Gallatin River below it.

As he got up, he moved to stand behind her. He could see starlight on that stretch of visible river. It shone like silver.

"If Nick is alive and I believe he is, then he has tried to do everything he can to make you think you're losing your mind. It hasn't worked. This isn't going to work, either. You're stronger than that."

"Am I?" she asked with a laugh. "I am when I'm with you, but…"

He turned her to face him. "You just needed someone to believe in you. I believe in you, Allie."

She looked up at him, her green eyes full of hope and trust and—

His gaze went to her mouth. Lowering his head, he kissed her.

A LOW MOAN escaped her lips. As he drew her closer, Allie closed her eyes, relishing in the feel of her body against his. It had been so long since a man had kissed her let alone held her. She couldn't remember the last time she'd made love. Nick had seemed to lose interest in her toward the end, which had been more than fine with her.

She banished all thoughts of Nick as she lost herself in Jackson's kiss. Her arms looped around his neck. She could feel her heart pounding next to his. Her breasts felt heavy, her nipples hard and aching as he deepened the kiss. A bolt of desire like none she'd ever known shot through her veins as he broke off the kiss to plant a trail of kisses down the column of her neck to the top of her breasts.

At her cry of arousal, Jackson pulled back to look into her eyes. "I've told myself all the reasons we shouldn't do this, but I want to make love to you."

"Yes," she said breathlessly, throwing caution to the wind. She wanted him, wanted to feel his bare skin against her own, to taste his mouth on hers again, to look up at him as he lowered himself onto her. She ached for his gentle touch, needed desperately to know the tenderness of love-making she'd never experienced with Nick but sensed in Jackson.

He swept her up in his arms and carried her to the bedroom, kicking the door closed before he carefully lowered her to the bed. She looked into his dark eyes as he lay down next to her. He touched her face with his fingertips, then slipped his hand around to the nape of her neck and drew her to him.

His kiss was slow and sensual. She could feel him fighting his own need as if determined to take it slow as he undid one button of her blouse, then another. She wanted to scream, unable to stand the barrier of their clothing between them. Grabbing his shirt, she pulled each side apart. The snaps sung as the Western shirt fell open exposing his tanned skin and the hard muscles under it.

She pressed her hands to his warm flesh as he undid the last button on her blouse. She heard his intake of breath an instant before she felt his fingertips skim across the tops of her breasts. Pushing her onto her back, he dropped his mouth to the hard points of her nipples, sucking gently through the thin, sheer fabric of her bra.

She arched against his mouth, felt him suck harder as his hand moved to the buttons of her jeans. With agonizing deliberate movements, he slowly undid the buttons of her jeans and slipped his hand beneath her panties. She cried out and fumbled at the zipper of his jeans.

"Please," she begged. "I need you."

"Not yet." His voice broke with the sound of his own need. "Not yet."

His hand dipped deeper into her panties. She arched against it, feeling the wet slickness of his fingers. He'd barely touched her when she felt the release.

"Oh, Allie," he said as if he, too, hadn't made love for a very long time. He shifted to the side to pull off her jeans and panties. She heard him shed the rest of his own clothing and then he was back, his body melding with hers in a rhythm as old as life itself.

THEY MADE LOVE twice more before the dawn. Jackson dozed off at some point, but woke to find Allie sleeping in his arms.

She looked more peaceful than she had since he'd met her. Like him, he suspected she hadn't made love with anyone for a very long time—much longer than her husband had allegedly been dead.

He cursed Nick Taylor. How could the fool not want this woman? How could the man mistreat someone so wonderful, not to mention ignore a child like Natalie? When he found the bastard...

When is it that you plan to find him?

The thought stopped him cold. There were only two more days until the wedding. He and Ford had tickets to fly out the following day.

He couldn't leave Allie now when she needed him the most. But how could he stay? He had Ford to think about. His son would be starting kindergarten next month. Jackson wasn't ready. He'd received a list from the school of the supplies his son would need, but he hadn't seen any reason to get them yet, thinking there was plenty of time. Same with the boy's new clothes.

He thought of his small ranch in Texas. Most of the land was leased, but he still had a house down there in the summer heat. He couldn't stay away indefinitely. What if he couldn't find Nick Taylor before Ford's school started?

His thoughts whirling, he looked down at Allie curled up next him and felt a pull so strong that it made him ache. What was he going to do?

Whatever it was, he couldn't think straight lying next to

this beautiful, naked woman. As he tried to pull free, she rolled away some, but didn't wake.

Slipping out of bed, he quickly dressed and stepped outside. The fresh Montana morning air helped a little. Earlier he'd heard voices down by the main house. He hoped to catch his brothers as he headed down the mountain. He needed desperately to talk to one of them, even though he had had a bad feeling what they were going to say to him. He'd been saying the same thing to himself since waking up next to Allie this morning.

ALLIE WOKE TO an empty bed. For a moment, she didn't know where she was. As last night came back to her with Jackson, she hugged herself. The lovemaking had been... amazing. This was what she'd been missing out on with Nick. Jackson had been so tender and yet so...passionate.

She lay back listening, thinking he must be in the bathroom or maybe the small kitchen. After a few minutes, she sat up. The cabin was too quiet. Surely Jackson hadn't left.

Slipping her feet over the side of the bed, she tiptoed out of the bedroom. The bathroom was empty. So was the living room and kitchen. Moving to the front window, she glanced out on the porch. No Jackson.

For a moment, she stood staring out at the view, trying to understand what this meant. Had he finally come to his senses? That was definitely one explanation.

Had he realized they had no future? That was another.

Hurrying into the bathroom, she showered, and, forced to put on the clothes she'd worn the night before, dressed. Fortunately, she'd been wearing jeans, a tank top and a blouse. She tucked the blouse into her large shoulder bag, pulled her wet hair up into a ponytail and looked at herself in the mirror.

Her cheeks were flushed from the lovemaking and the hot shower. Her skin still tingled at even the thought of

Jackson's touch. She swallowed. Hadn't she warned herself last night of all the reasons they shouldn't make love?

At a knock on the cabin door, she jumped. Her heart leaped to her throat as she saw a dark, large shadow move on the porch beyond the curtains. Jackson wouldn't knock. Maybe it was one of his brothers.

She held her breath, hoping he would go away. She didn't want to be caught here, even though she knew his brothers wouldn't tell anyone.

Another knock.

"Jackson?" Drew Taylor's voice made her cringe. She put her hand over her mouth to keep from crying out in surprise. "I need to check something in your cabin." She heard him try the door and felt her heart drop. What if Jackson had left the door open?

She was already backing up, frantically trying to decide where she could hide, when she heard Drew try the knob. Locked.

He swore, thumped around on the porch for a moment then retreated down the steps.

Allie finally had to let out the breath she'd been holding. If Drew had caught her here… What would he have done? Tell Nick. But what would a man who had faked his death do to stop his plan from working? She thought of Jackson and felt her heart drop. She'd put Jackson's life in danger, as well.

She waited until she was sure Drew had gone before she cautiously moved to the door, opened it and peered out. She could see nothing but pines as she slipped out and hurried across the mountainside, planning to slip into the barn as if she'd come to work early.

With luck, no one would be the wiser.

Allie didn't see Drew. But he saw her.

Chapter Eleven

Dana was sitting on the porch as Jackson approached the house. She motioned for him to join her.

"Where is everyone?" he asked, taking the rocker next to her.

"Early morning ride. Hud took everyone including the kids. Quiet, isn't it?" She glanced over at him. "How are you this morning?"

"Fine." He would have said great, but he had a bad feeling where Dana was headed with the conversation.

"I'm worried about Allie," she said, looking past him to the mountainside.

He glanced back toward the cabins in time to see Allie hurrying toward the barn from the direction of his cabin.

"Is she all right?"

In truth, he didn't know how she was. He regretted leaving before she'd awakened, but he'd needed to get out of there. "I—"

"She's been through so much. I would hate to see her get hurt. Wouldn't you?"

He felt as if she'd slapped him. He closed his eyes for a moment before he turned to look at her. "I told myself not to get involved, but..."

"So now you are involved?" Dana frowned. "She's in trouble, isn't she?"

Jackson nodded. "I have to help her." Even if it meant

staying in Montana longer, he couldn't abandon her. Isn't that what had scared the hell out of him when he'd awakened this morning? He was in deep, how deep, he didn't want to admit. "She's going through some things right now but she's working so hard on the wedding, it will be fine."

Dana studied him openly. "You care about her."

"I'm not going to hurt her."

"I hope not." She gave him a pat on the shoulder as she rose and went inside the house.

Jackson sat looking after his cousin, mentally kicking himself. *What the hell are you doing?*

"I was going to ask you the same thing." Laramie came walking up.

As he climbed the porch, Jackson said, "I thought you went riding with the others."

"I've been working," his brother said as he took a seat next to him. He shook his head. "I hope you know what you're doing, Jackson." He sighed and pulled out a sheet of paper. "Allie's mother spent the last seven years of her life in a mental institution. Paranoid schizophrenia."

As ALLIE SLIPPED into the barn, she was surprised to see Belinda setting up her gear for a shoot. She'd half expected Belinda to be gone after their argument last night. In fact, Allie had almost called several photographers she knew to see if they could possibly fill in at the last minute.

"So you're still here," she said as she approached Belinda.

"Where did you think I would be?"

"I wasn't sure. I thought you might have quit."

Belinda shook her head. "You really do have so little faith in me. I'm amazed. I'm the one who has stuck by you all these years. I'm sorry about…everything. But I'm here to do a job I love. Surely you understand that."

Allie did and said as much. "If I've underestimated you—"

Her friend laughed. "Or overestimated me given that you

think I'm capable of some diabolical plot to destroy you. And what? Steal your cabin on the river? Steal Nick's insurance money?" Her eyes widened. "Or was it steal Natalie?" Belinda looked aghast. "Oh, Allie, no wonder you're so upset. I get it now."

She felt tears rush her eyes as Belinda pulled her into a stiff, awkward hug.

"No matter what you believe, I'm still your friend," Belinda said as she broke the embrace and left the barn, passing Megan who looked bewildered as she came in.

Allie waited until she and Megan were alone before she spoke to her stepsister about what Belinda had told her. She didn't want to believe Megan had anything to do with the psychic or what had happened last night. Either Belinda was lying or there had to be another explanation.

"I need to ask you something."

"You sound so serious," Megan said. "What is it?"

"Was it your idea for me to see the psychic?"

Megan frowned. "I guess I was the one who suggested it. When Belinda told me about some of the things you'd been going through, I thought— Allie, why are you so upset?"

Allie had turned away, unable to look at her sister. Now she turned back, just as unable to hide her disappointment. "Why would you do that?"

"I just told you. I thought it would help."

"Trying to reach Nick on…the other side?" she demanded. "You can't be serious."

"A girl I knew at college lost her mother before the two of them could work some things out. She went to a psychic and was able to put some of the issues to rest. I thought…" Her gaze locked with her sister's. "I wanted to help you. I couldn't bear the things Belinda was telling me. It sounded as if you'd been going through hell. If I was wrong, I'm sorry."

Allie studied her for a moment. "You would never betray me, would you, Megan?"

"What a strange question to ask me."

"This past year since you came into my life and Natalie's… It's meant so much to both of us. Tell me you wouldn't betray that trust."

Megan frowned. "Does this have something to do with Jackson Cardwell? Is he the one putting these ideas in your head?"

"He has a theory about the so-called incidents I've been having," Allie confided. "He thinks someone is trying to make me think I'm crazy in order to take Natalie from me."

"That sounds…crazy in itself. Allie, I hate to say this, but you are starting to sound like your—"

"Don't say it," Allie cried. Wasn't that her real underlying fear, the one that had haunted her her whole life? That she was becoming sick like her mother? She rubbed a hand over the back of her neck. What was she sure of right now? She'd thought Jackson, but after this morning… "I know it sounds crazy, but if it's true, I have to find out who is behind it."

"And Jackson is *helping* you?" Megan said and frowned. "Or is he complicating things even more? You aren't…falling for him, are you?"

JACKSON WASN'T SURE what he was going to say to Allie. He felt like a heel for leaving her alone this morning. She must be furious with him. No, he thought, not Allie. She would be hurt, and that made him feel worse than if she was angry.

He headed for the barn to apologize to her. Once inside, though, he didn't see Allie.

"She said she had to run an errand," Megan told him with a shrug.

Glancing outside, he saw her van still parked where it had been last night. "Did she go on foot?"

"Her brother-in-law offered her a ride."

"Drew?" Jackson felt his heart race at the thought of Allie alone with that man. "Do you know where they went?"

Megan shook her head and kept working.

"You don't like me," he said, stepping farther into the barn. "Why is that?"

"I don't think you're good for my sister."

"Based on what?" he had to ask. "We have barely met."

"She told me about this crazy idea you have that someone is causing these incidents she's been having."

"You disagree?"

Megan gave him an impatient look. "I know the Taylors. The last thing they want is a five-year-old to raise."

"So you think what's been happening to Allie is all in her head?"

She put down what she'd been working on and gave him her full attention for the first time. "You just met her. You don't know anything about her. I love my stepsister, but I don't think she has been completely honest with you. Did you know that her mother spent her last years in a mental hospital? Or that she killed herself?"

"You aren't trying to tell me it runs in the family."

Megan raised a brow. "Allie's been through a lot. She has some issues she hasn't gotten past, including the fact that she wanted her husband gone. So she already told you about that, huh?" He nodded. "Did she also tell you that she bought a gun just before Nick went up into the mountains? That's right. I wonder what happened to it." She shrugged. "Like I said, I love Allie and Nat, but I also know that Allie hated her husband and would have done anything to escape him."

ALLIE HAD BEEN on her way to her van when Drew had suddenly appeared next to her.

"Where you off to?" he'd asked.

"I just have to pick up some ribbon at the store," she'd said, trying to act normal. What a joke. She hadn't felt *normal* in so long, she'd forgotten what it felt like. Worse, she feared that Drew would find out about last night. The Taylors wouldn't hesitate to use it against her, claiming it proved what a terrible mother she was.

Allie felt guilty enough. Her husband had been dead only months and here she was making love with another man. Did it matter that she hadn't loved Nick for years? She had a child to think about and Jackson Cardwell would be leaving in two days' time. Then what?

It would be just her and Nat and the Taylors.

"I'll give you a ride," Drew said. She started to argue but he stopped her. "It would be stupid to take your van when I'm going that way, anyway. You pick up your ribbon. I'll pick up the chalk I need next door at the hardware store. We'll be back here before you know it."

All her instincts warned her not to get into the pickup with him, but she couldn't think of a reason not to accept the ride without acting paranoid. Did she really think he would take her somewhere other than the store and what? Attack her?

She climbed into the passenger side of the pickup and remembered something Nick had said not long before he'd left to go hunting that day.

"You're so damned trusting, Allie. I worry about you. Don't you get tired of being so nice?" He'd laughed and pretended he was joking as he pulled her close and kissed the top of her head. "Don't change. It's refreshing."

It also had made it easier for him to control her.

"You want to know something crazy?" Drew said as he started the engine and drove down the road toward Big Sky. "When I got here this morning, your van was where you'd left it last night. There was dew on the window. I checked the motor. It hadn't been moved and even more interesting, you were nowhere to be found."

She didn't look at him as he roared down the road. Ahead

she could see the bridge that spanned the Gallatin River. Why hadn't she listened to her instincts and not gotten into the vehicle with Drew?

"It was like a mystery. I love mysteries. Did I ever tell you that?"

A recent rainstorm had washed out some of the road just before the bridge, leaving deep ruts that were to be filled this afternoon. Couldn't have the wedding guests being jarred by the ruts.

"I saw you come out of Jackson Cardwell's cabin this morning." Drew swore as he braked for the ruts. "You slut." He started to backhand her, but had to brake harder as he hit the first rut so his hand went back to the wheel before it reached its mark. "How could you screw—"

Allie unsnapped her seat belt and grabbed the door handle.

As the door swung open, Drew hit the brakes even harder, slamming her into the door as she jumped. She hit the soft earth at the side of the road, lost her footing and fell into the ditch.

Drew stopped the truck. She heard his door open and the shocks groan as he climbed out. By then she was on her feet and headed into the pines next to the road, running, even though her right ankle ached.

"Allie!" Drew yelled from the roadbed. "You could have killed yourself. You're crazy, you know that?"

She kept running through the pines. Her brother-in-law was right. She had been stupid. Stupid to get into the truck with him when all her instincts had been telling her not to, and crazy to jump out.

Behind her, she heard the truck engine rev, then the pickup rumble over the bridge. She slowed to catch her breath then limped the rest of the way back to the barn, telling herself she was through being naive and trusting.

JACKSON DIDN'T SEE Allie until that evening at the wedding rehearsal so he had no chance to get her alone. "We need to talk," he whispered in those few seconds he managed to get her somewhat alone.

She met his gaze. "Look, I think I already know what you're going to say."

"I doubt that." She wore a multicolored skirt and top that accentuated her lush body. "You look beautiful. That top brings out the green in your eyes."

"Thank you." Something glinted in those eyes for a moment. "Jackson—"

"I know. This isn't the place. But can we please talk later? It's important."

She nodded, though reluctantly.

He mentally kicked himself for running out on her this morning as he stood there, wanting to say more, but not able to find the right words.

Allie excused herself. He watched her head for the preacher as the rehearsal was about to begin. Was she limping?

All day he'd stewed over what Megan had told him. She was wrong about Allie, but he could understand why she felt the way she did. Maybe she really did love her sister. Or maybe not.

Belinda was busy behind her camera, shooting as they all went to their places. As one of the best men, Jackson was in a position to watch the others. He hadn't seen much of Sarah Taylor. But Sarah, her mother and brother would be at the rehearsal dinner tonight. He watched Sarah enter the barn and start up the aisle toward the steps to where the preacher was standing along with the best men and the groom.

An overweight woman with dull, brown hair pulled severely back from her face, Sarah seemed somewhere else, oblivious to what was happening. Either that or bored. Four more bridesmaids entered and took their places.

Harlan and Angus broke into "Here Comes the Bride" on their guitars and Lily came out of a small-framed building next to the meadow with her father and mother. Jackson hadn't met either of them yet but he wanted to laugh when he saw them looking as if in horror. Lily was smiling from ear to ear. So was her brother Ace from the sidelines. But clearly her parents hadn't expected this kind of wedding for their only daughter.

Jackson looked over at Allie. She really was beautiful. She glanced to the parking lot and quickly looked away as if she'd seen something that frightened her.

He followed her gaze. Drew Taylor stood lounging against his pickup, a malicious smirk on his face as if he was up to something.

THE REHEARSAL WENT off without a hitch. Allie tried to breathe a sigh of relief. Dana had booked an Italian restaurant in Bozeman for the night of the rehearsal dinner. "I know it's not the way things are normally done," she'd said with a laugh. But Lily and I discussed it."

Dana had insisted anyone involved in the wedding had to be there so that meant Allie and Natalie as well as Megan and Belinda.

They'd just gotten to the restaurant when Allie heard a strident voice behind her say, "There you are."

She bristled but didn't turn, putting off facing her mother-in-law as long as possible.

"Sarah thinks you're avoiding us," Mildred said. "But why would you do that?"

Allie turned, planting a smile on her face. "I wouldn't."

"Hmmm," her mother-in-law said. She gave Allie the once-over. "You look different."

Allie remembered that she was wearing one of two

outfits that she hadn't taken back to the store. This one was a multicolored top and skirt that Jackson had said brought out the green in her eyes. She loved it and while it was more expensive than she could really afford, she'd needed something to wear tonight.

"Where did you get that outfit?" Mildred asked, eyeing her with suspicion.

"I found it in my closet," Allie said honestly.

"Really?"

Allie felt a hand take hers and looked up to see Jackson.

"I saved you a spot down here," he said and led her to the other end of the table, away from the Taylors.

Dana had insisted that there be no prearranged seating. "Let everyone sit where they want. I like people to be comfortable." Lily had seemed relieved that she could sit by Tag, away from her parents.

Allie was grateful to Jackson for saving her. Dinner was served and the conversation around the table was light with lots of laughter and joking. She was glad Jackson didn't try to talk to her about last night.

It had been a mistake in so many ways. But tomorrow after the wedding, they would say goodbye and he and Ford would fly out the next day. She told herself that once the wedding was over, everything would be all right.

A part of her knew she was only kidding herself. There hadn't been any more incidents, no misplaced keys, no Nick sightings, no "black cat" scares and that almost worried her. What had changed? Or was Nick and whomever he had helping him just waiting to ambush her?

She had a feeling that the séance with the psychic hadn't produced the results they'd wanted. Now she, too, was waiting. Waiting for the other shoe to drop.

Just let it drop after the wedding, she prayed. Jackson and Ford would be back in Texas. Whatever was planned for her, she felt she could handle it once this job was over.

The one thing Jackson had done was made her feel stronger, more sure of herself. He'd also reminded her that she was a woman with needs that had long gone unmet until last night.

"Stop telling stories on me," Tag pleaded at the dinner table across from her. "Lily is going to change her mind about marrying me."

"Not a chance, cowboy," Lily said next to him before she'd kissed him to hoots and hollers.

Even Sarah seemed to be enjoying herself with the other bridesmaids since they had all worked together at Lily's brother's bar.

Allie avoided looking down the table to see how the Taylors were doing. She was so thankful to be sitting as far away from them as possible, especially Drew. To think that she'd trusted him and thought he'd really had her and Nat's best interest at heart. She'd felt his eyes on her all night. The few times she'd met his gaze, he'd scowled at her.

She glanced over at the children's table to see her daughter also enjoying herself. Dana's sister Stacy had the children at a separate table. Allie saw that her daughter was being on her best behavior. So ladylike, she was even using the manners Allie had taught her. She felt a swell of pride and told herself that she and Natalie were going to be all right no matter what happened after the wedding.

To her surprise, her eyes welled with tears and she quickly excused herself to go to the ladies' room. The bathroom was past an empty section of the restaurant, then down a long hallway. She was glad that no one had followed her. She needed a few minutes alone.

Inside the bathroom, she pulled herself together. Last night with Jackson had meant more to her than she'd admitted. It had hurt this morning when he hadn't been there, but she could understand why he'd panicked. Neither of them took that kind of intimacy lightly.

Feeling better, she left the bathroom. As she reached the

empty section of the restaurant, Drew stepped in front of her, startling her. She could smell the alcohol on him. The way he was standing... She recognized that stance after five years of being married to his brother.

Drew was looking for a fight. How had she thought the brothers were different? Because she hadn't seen this side of Drew. Until now.

"You *jumped* out of my truck. What the hell was that? Do I scare you, Allie?" he asked, slurring his words and blocking her way.

"Please, Drew, don't make a scene."

He laughed. "Oh, you don't want Dana to know that you slept with her cousin?"

"Drew—"

"Don't bother to lie to me," he said as he stepped toward her, shoving her back. "I *saw* you." His voice broke. "How can you do this to my brother?"

"Nick's...gone."

"And forgotten. Is that it?" He forced her back against the wall, caging her with one hand on each side of her.

"Please, Drew—"

"If Nick really was out of the picture..." He belched. "You have to know I've always wanted you," he said drunkenly. Before she could stop him, he bent down and tried to kiss her.

She turned her head to the side. He kissed her hair, then angrily grabbed her jaw in one hand. His fingers squeezed painfully as he turned her to face him.

"What? Am I not good enough for you?"

"Drew—"

Suddenly he was jerked away. Allie blinked as Jackson hauled back and swung. His fist connected with Drew's jaw and he went down hard, crashing into a table.

"Are you all right?" Jackson asked, stepping to her.

She nodded and glanced at her brother-in-law. He was

trying to get up, but he seemed to take one look at Jackson and decided to stay down.

"You'll pay for that!" he threatened as she and Jackson headed back toward their table. Allie knew he wasn't talking to Jackson. She would pay.

"If he bothers you again—" Jackson said as if reading her mind.

"Don't worry about me."

"How can I not?" he demanded. "That was about me, wasn't it?"

"Drew was just looking for a reason."

"And I provided it."

"He saw me leaving your cabin this morning," she said. "I don't think he's told anyone, but he will. I just wanted to warn you. I'm afraid what Nick might do to you."

"Allie, I don't give a damn about any of that. What I'm sorry about was leaving you this morning," he said, bringing her up short as he stopped and turned her to face him. "There is so much I want to say to you—"

"Oh, there you are," Mildred Taylor said as she approached. "I was just looking for Drew. I thought you might have seen him. Allie, you look terrible. I knew this job was going to be too much for you."

Natalie and Ford came running toward them. Mildred began to say something about giving Allie and Nat a ride home, but then Drew appeared, rubbing his jaw.

"Drew, whatever happened to you?" Mildred cried.

"I still need to talk to you," Jackson whispered to Allie, who was bending down to catch her daughter up into her arms.

"After the wedding," she said as she lifted Natalie, hugging her tightly. "Tonight I just need to take my daughter home."

Jackson wanted to stop her. But she was right. The wedding was the important thing right now. After that...

Chapter Twelve

Wedding Day. Allie woke at the crack of dawn. She couldn't help being nervous and excited. The wedding was to be held in a beautiful meadow near the house. Those attending had been told to wear Western attire as the seating at the wedding would be hay bales.

Drew had constructed an arch for the bride and groom to stand under with the preacher. Allie had walked through everything with the bride and groom, the caterer and the musicians. The barn was ready for the reception that would follow. But she still wanted to get to the ranch early to make sure she hadn't forgotten anything.

The last few days had felt like a roller-coaster ride. Today, she needed calm. Jackson hadn't tried to contact her after she and Natalie left the restaurant with Dana and family last night and she was glad. She needed time with her daughter.

Natalie hadn't slept in her own bed for several nights now. Allie made sure her daughter's window was locked as she put her to bed. She checked the other windows and the door. Then, realizing that any of the Taylors could have a key to her cabin, she pushed a straight-back chair under the doorknob.

She and Natalie hadn't been disturbed all night. At least not by intruders. In bed last night, Allie couldn't help but think about Jackson. And Nick.

"Please, just let me get through this wedding," she'd prayed and had finally fallen asleep.

Now as she drove into the ranch, she saw that Dana and the kids were waiting for Natalie.

"We have a fun morning planned," Dana said with a wink. "You don't have to worry about anything today."

Allie wished that was true. She looked down at the meadow to see that Megan was up early. She was sitting on a hay bale looking as if she were staring at the arch. Imagining her own wedding? Allie wondered as she approached.

"Good morning," she said and joined her sister on the bale.

"It's perfect. Drew really did do a good job," Megan said.

The arch had been made out of natural wood that blended in beautifully with its surroundings. Allie had asked Lily if she wanted it decorated with flowers.

"There will be enough wildflowers in the meadow and I will be carrying a bouquet. I think that is more than enough."

She had agreed and was happy that Lily preferred the more minimalist look.

"Have you been up to the barn?" Allie asked.

"Not yet." Megan finally looked over at her. "How are you?"

"Fine."

Her sister eyed her. "You can lean on me. I'm here for you and Natalie."

Allie hugged her, closing her eyes and praying it was true. She couldn't bear the thought of Megan betraying not only her but Natalie, as well.

Together they walked up to the barn. Allie turned on the lights and gasped.

JACKSON HAD TOSSED and turned all night—after he'd finally dropped off to sleep. He felt as if he'd let Allie down. Or maybe worse, gotten involved with her in the first place, knowing he would be leaving soon.

She wasn't out of the woods yet. She had to know that whoever was messing with her mind wasn't through. He still believed it had to be Nick. He had the most to gain. It scared Jackson to think that whoever was behind this might try to use Tag's wedding to put the last nail in Allie's coffin, so to speak.

His fear, since realizing what was going on, was that if they couldn't drive her crazy, they might actually try to kill her.

He was just getting dressed when he heard the knock at his cabin door. His mood instantly lifted as he thought it might be Allie. She'd said she would talk to him *after* the wedding. Maybe she had changed her mind. He sure hoped so.

Jackson couldn't hide his disappointment when he opened the door and saw his brothers standing there.

"I found something that I think might interest you," Laramie said and he stepped back to let them enter.

"Shouldn't you be getting ready for your wedding?" he asked Tag, who laughed and said, "I have been getting ready for months now. I just want this damned wedding over."

They took a seat while he remained standing. From the expressions on their faces, they hadn't brought good news.

"Nick and his brother, Drew, took out life insurance policies on each other through their construction business," Laramie said.

"That isn't unusual, right?" he asked.

"They purchased million-dollar policies and made each other the beneficiary, but Nick purchased another half million and made Allie the beneficiary."

Jackson let out a low whistle. "All Allie knew about was the hundred-thousand-dollar policy." He saw Hayes lift a brow. "She didn't kill her husband."

"Whether she knew or not about the policies, I believe it supports your theory that Nick is alive and trying to get that money," Laramie said.

"It hasn't paid out yet, right?"

"She should be getting the checks next week."

Jackson raked a hand through his hair. Allie was bound to have been notified. Maybe it had slipped her mind. "You're sure she is the beneficiary?"

Laramie nodded.

"Who gets the money if Allie is declared incompetent?"

"Her daughter, Natalie."

Jackson groaned. "Then this is why Nick is trying to have Allie committed. He, and whoever he is working with, would get the money and Natalie."

"Only if Nick is alive and *stays* dead," Hayes pointed out.

"If Nick stays dead the money would be used at the discretion of Natalie's *guardian.*"

Jackson looked at his brother, an ache starting at heart level. "Who is her guardian?"

"Megan Knight. The policy was changed eight months ago—just before Nick Taylor went up into the mountains hunting and a guardian was added."

ALLIE COULDN'T EVEN scream. Her voice had caught in her throat at the sight in the barn. Last night when she'd left, the barn had been ready for the reception except for putting out the fresh vases of flowers at each setting. The tables had been covered with the checked tablecloths and all the overhead lanterns had been in place along with the decorations on the walls and in the rafters.

"Oh, my word," Megan said next to her.

Allie still couldn't speak. Someone had ripped the tablecloths from the tables and piled them in the middle of the dance floor. The old boots that served as centerpieces that would hold the fresh flowers were arranged on the floor in a circle as if the invisible people in them were dancing.

Megan was the first one to move. She rushed to the table-cloths and, bending down, picked up the top one. "They've all been shredded." She turned to look at Allie, concern in her gaze.

"You can't think I did this."

Her sister looked at the tablecloth in her hand before returning her gaze to Allie. "This looks like a cry for help."

Allie shook her head. "It's someone who hates me."

"Hates you? Oh, Allie."

"What's happened?"

She swung around to see Jackson standing in the doorway. Tears filled her eyes. She wanted to run out the barn door and keep running, but he stepped to her and took one of her hands.

"I was afraid they weren't done with you," he said. "How bad is it?" he asked Megan.

"The tablecloths are ruined. Fortunately, whoever did this didn't do anything to the lanterns or the other decorations in the rafters. Probably couldn't reach them since the ladders have all been packed away." This last was directed at Allie, her meaning clear.

"Tag already ordered tablecloths for the restaurant," Jackson said, pulling out his cell phone. "I'll see if they've come in. We can have this fixed quickly if they have." He spoke into the phone for a moment. When he disconnected, he smiled at Allie and said, "Tag will bring up the red-checked cloths right away. With their help, we'll have it fixed before anyone else hears about it."

Allie went weak with relief as he quickly got rid of the ruined tablecloths and Tag showed up with new ones from the restaurant. With the Cardwell brothers' help, the problem was solved within minutes.

"I want at least two people here watching this barn until the wedding is over," Jackson said.

"I'll talk to Dana and see if there are a couple of ranch hands who can help," Laramie said.

"That really isn't necessary," Megan said. "I will stay here to make sure nothing else happens."

Jackson shook his head. "I'm not taking any chances. I'll feel better if you aren't left alone here. Whoever is doing this... Well, I think it might get dangerous before it's over."

"Why don't you just admit that you think I'm involved in this," Megan said and looked sadly at her sister. "Apparently, you aren't the only one who's paranoid." She sighed. "Whatever you need me to do. I don't want anything to spoil this wedding."

JACKSON HAD PLANNED to talk to Allie about the insurance policies, but he realized it could wait until after the wedding. Allie's spirit seemed buoyed once the barn was ready again and a ranch hand stayed behind with Megan to make sure nothing else went wrong.

He was having a hard time making sense of the insurance policy news. Why would Nick Taylor change the guardian from his brother to Allie's stepsister, Megan? The obvious answer would be if the two were in cahoots.

That would break Allie's heart, but a part of her had to know that her sister thought all of this was in her head. Megan had given him the impression that she was ready to step in as more than Natalie's guardian.

Jackson reminded himself that it was his brother's wedding day. As much as he didn't like weddings and hadn't attended one since his marriage had ended, he tried to concentrate on being there for Tag. He couldn't help being in awe as Allie went into wedding-planner mode. He admired the way she handled herself, even with all the stress she was under in her personal life. The day took on a feeling of celebration; after all it was the Fourth of July.

At the house, Allie made sure they were all ready, the men dressed in Western attire and boots, before she went to help the bride. Jackson had seen his father and uncle with their guitars heading for the meadow. They would be playing the "Wedding March" as well as accompanying several singers who would be performing. He just hoped everything went smoothly for Tag and Lily's sake, as well as Allie's.

"Look who's here," Laramie said, sounding too cheerful.

Jackson turned to see his mother on the arm of a nice-looking gray-haired Texas oilman. Franklin Wellington IV had oil written all over him. Jackson tried not to hold it against the man as he and his brothers took turns hugging their mother and wishing her well before shaking hands with Franklin.

His mother *did* look deliriously happy, Jackson had to admit, and Franklin was downright friendly and nice.

"Time to go," Allie said, sticking her head into the room where he and his brothers had been waiting.

Jackson introduced her to his mother and Franklin. He saw his mother lift a brow in the direction of Laramie and groaned inwardly. She would trust Laramie to tell her why she was being introduced to the wedding planner.

Allie didn't notice the interplay as she smiled at Tag. "Your bride looks absolutely beautiful and you don't look so bad yourself."

She was quite pretty, as well, in her navy dress with the white piping. She'd pulled her hair up. Silver earrings dangled at her lobes. She looked professional and yet as sexy as any woman he'd ever known. He felt a sense of pride in her, admiring her strength as well as her beauty. She'd been through so much.

Hell, he thought as he took his place, I *am* falling for her. That realization shook him to the soles of his boots.

In the meadow, his father and uncle began to play the "Wedding March" at Allie's nod. Compared to most, the wedding was small since Tag and Lily knew few people in Big Sky. But old canyon friends had come who had known the Cardwells, Savages and Justices for years.

As Lily appeared, Jackson agreed with Allie. She looked beautiful. He heard his brother's intake of breath and felt his heart soar at the look on Tag's face when he saw his bride-to-be. For a man who had sworn off weddings, Jackson had to admit, he was touched by this one.

The ceremony was wonderfully short, the music perfect and when Tag kissed the bride, Jackson felt his gaze searching for Allie. She was standing by a tree at the edge of the meadow. She was smiling, her expression one of happy contentment. She'd gotten them married.

Now if they could just get through the reception without any more trouble, he thought.

AT THE RECEPTION, Jackson watched the Taylor family sitting at a table away from the others. Mildred had a smile plastered on her face, but behind it he could see that she was sizing up everyone in the room. Her insecurities were showing as she leaned over and said something to her daughter.

Whatever her mother said to her, Sarah merely nodded. She didn't seem to have any interest in the guests, unlike her mother. Instead, she was watching Allie. What was it that Jackson caught in her gaze? Jealousy? Everyone at the wedding had been complimenting Allie on the job she'd done. Sarah couldn't have missed that.

Nor, according to Hud, had Sarah ever been married. She had to be in her late thirties. Was she thinking that it might never happen for her? Or was she content with living next to her mother and basically becoming her mother's caregiver?

Sarah reached for one of the boot-shaped cookies with Tag and Lily's wedding date on them. Her mother slapped her hand, making Sarah scowl at her before she took two cookies.

He wondered what grudges bubbled just below the surface in any family situation, let alone a wedding. Weddings, he thought, probably brought out the best and worst of people, depending how happy or unhappy you were in your own life.

As happy as he was for Tag, it still reminded him of his own sorry marriage. What did this wedding do to the Taylor clan? he wondered as he studied them. It certainly didn't seem to be bringing out any joy, that was for sure.

But his side of the family were having a wonderful time. He watched his brother Tag dancing with his bride. Their mother was dancing with her new husband, both women looking radiant. It really was a joyous day. Dana and Hud had all the kids out on the floor dancing.

Jackson thought the only thing that could make this day better would be if he could get the wedding planner to dance with him.

ALLIE TRIED TO breathe a little easier. The wedding had gone off without a hitch. Lily had been exquisite and Tag as handsome as any Cardwell, which was saying a lot. Allie had teared up like a lot of the guests when the two had exchanged their vows. She'd always loved weddings. This one would remain her favorite for years to come.

When the bride and groom kissed, she'd seen Jackson looking for her. Their eyes had locked for a long moment. She'd pulled away first, a lump in her throat, an ache in her heart. The wedding was over. There was nothing keeping Jackson and Ford in Montana.

Whoever had been trying to gaslight her, as Jackson had called it, hadn't succeeded. Maybe now they would give up trying. She certainly hoped so. If Nick was alive, then she should find out soon. The insurance check for the hundred thousand would be deposited into her account next week.

She'd already made plans for most of it to go into an interest-bearing account for Natalie's college.

Allie wondered what would happen then. If Nick was alive, would he just show up at her door? Or would the media be involved with reporters and photographers snapping photos of him outside the cabin as he returned from his ordeal?

All she knew was that the only way Nick could get his hands on the insurance money would be if he killed her. That thought unnerved her as she surveyed the reception. Belinda was busy shooting each event along with some candid shots of guests. Allie had to hand it to her, she appeared to be doing a great job.

Everything looked beautiful. Megan had taken care of the flowers in the boot vases, put the attendees' gifts on the tables and made sure the bar was open and serving. Appetizers were out. Allie checked to make sure the caterer was ready then looked around for her daughter. Nat was with the other kids and Dana. Allie had bought her a special dress for the wedding. Natalie looked beautiful and she knew it because she seemed to glow.

Her tomboy daughter loved getting dressed up. She smiled at the thought. She was thinking that they should dress up more when Mildred Taylor let out a scream at a table near the dance floor and stumbled to her feet.

Allie saw that she was clutching her cell phone, her other hand over her mouth.

"What is it?" Dana demanded, moving quickly to the Taylors' table.

"It's *my Nicky,*" Mildred cried, her gaze going to Allie, who froze thinking it was already happening. She was so sure she knew what her mother-in-law was about to say, that she thought she'd misunderstood.

"His body has been found," Mildred managed to say between sobs. She cried harder. "They say he was *murdered.*"

Chapter Thirteen

Pandemonium broke out with Mildred Taylor shrieking uncontrollably and everyone trying to calm her down.

Jackson looked over at Allie. All the color had bled from her face. He moved quickly to her. "Let's get you out of here," he said, taking her hand. "You look like you could use some fresh air."

"I'll see to Natalie," Dana said nearby as she motioned for Jackson and Allie to go.

Allie looked as if she were in shock. "It just won't end," she said in a breathless rush as he ushered her outside. "It just won't end."

"I'm so sorry," Jackson said, his mind reeling, as well.

"I was so sure he was *alive*." She met his gaze. "I thought…"

"We both thought he was alive. I'm as floored as you are." He realized that wasn't possible. Nick Taylor had been her husband, even if he had been a bad one, she would still be shocked and upset by this news. He was the father of her child.

"Nick was *murdered*? How is that possible? They found his backpack and his gun and the grizzly tracks."

"We need to wait until we have all the details," he said as his brothers Hayes and Laramie joined them.

"We're headed down to the police station now," Hayes said. "I'll let you know as soon as I have any information."

"Thank you." Jackson swallowed the lump in his throat. His brothers had been so great through his divorce and custody battle, and now this. He couldn't have been more grateful for them.

"The police will be looking for me," Allie said, her eyes widening.

He saw the fear in her eyes and at first had misunderstood it then he remembered what had happened at the psychic's. "No one believes you killed your husband."

"*Someone* already does."

"That's crazy. How could whoever was behind the séance know that Nick was even murdered unless they did the killing?"

She shook her head. "Mildred has blamed me for his death all along. Belinda thought I drove him to kill himself. Don't you see? They didn't have to know it was true. They just wanted me to feel responsible. Now that it *is* true... Even dead, he's going to ruin my life."

The last of the sun's rays slipped behind the mountains to the west, pitching the canyon in cool twilight. Inside the barn, the reception was continuing thanks to Megan and Dana, who had taken over.

"I need to go back in."

"No." Jackson stopped her with a hand on her arm. "You did a great job. No one expects you to do any more. You don't have to worry about any of that."

She met his gaze. "I don't understand what's going on."

"My brothers will find out. Allie, I'm sorry I left you the other morning. I...panicked. But I'm not leaving you now."

Allie shook her head and took a step back from him. "This isn't your problem. You should never have gotten involved because it's only going to get worse."

He remembered what Laramie had told him about the insurance policy and realized she was right. The money would definitely interest the police. He looked toward the barn. Some guests had come out into the evening air to admire the sunset.

"Please, come up to my cabin with me so we have some privacy. There's something important I need to tell you." He saw her expression and realized that she'd misunderstood.

She looked toward the barn, then up the mountain in the direction of his cabin.

"I just need to talk to you," he assured her.

"That wasn't what I…" She met his gaze. "Jackson, I've caused you enough grief as it is. If the Taylors come looking for me—"

"Let me worry about your in-laws. As for Drew, he won't be bothering you as long as I'm around."

She smiled at that. They both knew that once he left she would again be at the mercy of not just Drew but also the rest of the Taylor family.

He wanted to tell her he wouldn't leave her. But he couldn't make that promise, could he?

She was on her own and she knew it.

"Come on," he said and reached for her hand.

DARKNESS CAME ON quickly in the narrow canyon because of the steep mountains on each side. Allie could hear the fireworks vendors getting ready for the wedding grand finale and glanced at her watch. They were right on time. Maybe she wasn't as necessary as she'd thought since everything seemed to be going on schedule without her.

Overhead the pines swayed in the summer night's breeze. Jackson was so close she could smell his woodsy aftershave and remember his mouth on hers. The perfect summer night. Wasn't that what she'd been thinking earlier before her mother-in-law had started screaming?

Nick was dead. Murdered.

For days now she'd believed he was alive and behind all

the weird things that had been happening to her. Now how did she explain it?

Jackson stopped on the porch. "We can talk privately here, if you would be more comfortable not going inside." He must have seen the answer in her expression because he let go of her hand and moved to the edge of the porch.

Inside the cabin she would remember the two of them making love in his big, log-framed bed. Her skin ached at the memory of his touch.

"Allie, I hate to bring this up now, but the police will ask you…" He leaned against the porch railing, Allie just feet away. "Were you aware that your husband and brother-in-law took out life insurance policies on each other when they started their construction business?"

"No, but what does that have to do with me?"

"They purchased million-dollar policies and made the other brother the beneficiary, but Nick purchased another half million and made you beneficiary. He never mentioned it to you?"

She shook her head, shocked by the news and even more shocked by how it would look. "You think a million and a half dollars in insurance money gives me a motive for killing him."

"I don't, but I think the police might, given that just before your husband went up into the mountains on his hunting trip, he changed the beneficiary of his million-dollar insurance policy from Drew to you."

Allie didn't think anything else could surprise her. "Why would he do that?" Her eyes filled with tears as a reason came to her. She moved to the opposite railing and looked out across the darkening canyon. "Maybe he did go up there to kill himself," she said, her back to Jackson.

"Hayes will find out why they think he was murdered. In the meantime—"

All the ramifications of this news hit her like a battering ram. "What happens if I'm dead?" She had been looking out into the darkness, but now swung her gaze on him. "Who inherits the money?"

"Natalie. The money would be used for her care until she was twenty-one, at which time her guardian—"

"Her *guardian?*"

"Nick named a guardian in case of your…death or incarceration."

Allie's voice broke. *"Who?"*

"Originally Drew was listed as guardian on the policies, but Nick changed that, too, right before he headed for the mountains." He met her gaze. "Megan, as your next closest kin, even though she isn't a blood relative."

She staggered under the weight of it. She couldn't deal with this now. She had the wedding. "The fireworks show is about to start," she said. "I have to finish—"

"I'm sure Dana will see that the rest of the wedding goes off like it is supposed to," Jackson said, blocking her escape. "No one expects you to continue, given what's happened."

"I took the job. I want to finish it," Allie said, hugging herself against the evening chill. "I thought you would understand that."

"I do. But—" His cell phone rang. "It's Hayes." He took the call.

She had no choice but to wait. She had to know what he'd found out at the police station. As she waited, she watched the lights of Big Sky glitter in the growing darkness that fell over the canyon. A breeze seemed to grow in the shadowed pines. The boughs began to move as if with the music still playing down in the barn.

After a moment, Jackson thanked his brother and disconnected. She remained looking off into the distance, her back to him, as he said, "Nick Taylor's remains were found in a shallow grave. There was a .45 bullet lodged in his skull. The trajectory of the bullet based on where it entered and exited, along with the fact that it appears someone tried to hide the body… It's being investigated as a homicide."

She felt a jolt when he mentioned that the bullet was a .45 caliber and knew Jackson would have seen it. Still, she didn't turn.

"Megan told me you bought a gun and that it disappeared from the cabin," he said. She could feel his gaze on her, burning into her back. He thought he knew her. She could imagine what was going through his mind. He would desperately want to believe she had nothing to do with her husband's murder. "Was the gun you purchased a—"

"Forty-five?" She nodded as she turned to look at him. "Everyone will believe I killed him. You're not even sure anymore, are you?"

"Allie—" He took a step toward her, but she held up her hand to ward him off. It had grown dark enough that she couldn't make out his expression unless he came closer, which was a godsend. She couldn't bear to see the disappointment in his face.

Below them on the mountain everyone was coming out of the barn to gather in the meadow for the fireworks. She suddenly ached to see her daughter. Natalie had been all that had kept her sane for so long. Right now, she desperately needed to hold her.

What would happen to Natalie now? She was trembling with fear at the thought that came to her and would no doubt have already come to the police—and eventually Jackson. She didn't want to be around when that happened.

"With my husband dead, that is three insurance policies for more than a million and a half," she said. "Mother Taylor is convinced I've made up all the stories about someone gaslighting me, as you call it. She thinks I have some plot to make myself rich at her poor Nicky's expense. I'm sure she's shared all of that with the police by now. Maybe I did do it."

He stepped to her and took her shoulders in his hands.

"Don't. You didn't kill your husband and you *know* damned well that I believe you."

"Your ex-wife, she was a liar and con woman, right? Isn't that why you were so afraid to get involved with me? What makes you so sure I'm not just like her?"

"You can't push me away." He lifted her chin with his fingers so she couldn't avoid his gaze. Their faces were only a few inches apart. "You aren't like her."

"What if I'm crazy?" Her voice broke. "Crazy like a fox?" The first of the fireworks exploded, showering down a glittering red, white and blue light on the meadow below them. The boom echoed in her chest as another exploded to the oos and ahs of the wedding party. She felt scalding tears burn her throat. "What if Mother Taylor is right and all of this is some subconscious plot I have to not only free myself of Nick, but walk away with a million and a half dollars, as well?"

JACKSON COULDN'T BEAR to see Allie like this. He pulled her to him and, dropping his mouth to hers, kissed her. She leaned into him, letting him draw her even closer as the kiss deepened. Fireworks lit the night, booming in a blaze of glittering light before going dark again.

Desire ignited his blood. He wanted Allie like he'd never wanted anyone or anything before. She melted into him, warm and lush in his arms, a moan escaping her lips.

Then suddenly he felt her stiffen. She broke away. "I can't keep doing this," she cried and, tearing herself from his arms, took off down the steps and through the trees toward the barn.

He started after her, but a voice from the darkness stopped him.

"Let her go."

He turned to find his brother Laramie standing in the

nearby trees. More fireworks exploded below them. "What are you doing, little brother?"

"I'm in love with her." The words were out, more honest than he'd been with even himself—let alone Allie.

"Is that right?" Laramie moved to him in a burst of booming light from the meadow below. "So what are you going to do about it?"

Jackson shook his head. "I…I haven't gotten that far yet."

"Oh, I think you've gotten quite far already." Laramie sighed. "I don't want to see you jump into anything. Not again."

"She is nothing like Juliet."

His brother raised a brow. "I knew one day you would fall in love again. It was bound to happen, but Jackson, this is too fast. This woman has too many problems. Hayes and I just came from the police station. They are going to be questioning her about her husband's murder. It doesn't look good."

"She had nothing to do with his death."

"She owns a .45 pistol, the one they suspect is the murder weapon."

Jackson sighed and looked toward the meadow below. It was cast in darkness. Had the fireworks show already ended? "She did but whoever is trying to have her committed, took it to set her up. You know as well as I do that someone has been gaslighting her."

Laramie shook his head. "We only know what Allie has been telling you."

His first instinct was to get angry with his brother, but he understood what Laramie was saying. There was no proof. Instead, the evidence against her was stacking up.

"I believe her and I'm going to help her," he said as he stepped past his brother.

"I just hope you aren't making a mistake," Laramie said behind him as Jackson started down the mountainside.

He'd only taken a few steps when he saw people running all over and heard Allie screaming Natalie's name. He took off running toward her.

"What's wrong?" he demanded when he reached her.

"Nat's gone!" Allie cried.

Chapter Fourteen

"She *can't* be gone," Jackson said. "She was with Dana, right?"

"Dana said the kids were all together, but after one of the fireworks went off, she looked over and Nat wasn't with them. She asked Hank and he said she spilled her lemonade on her dress and went to the bathroom to try to wash it off. Dana ran up to the house and the barn, but she wasn't there." Allie began to cry. "She found this, though." She held up the tie that had been on Nat's dress. "Natalie might have gone looking for me. Or someone took her—"

"Allie," he said, taking her shoulders in his hands. "Even if she left the meadow to go to the house, she couldn't have gotten far. We'll find her."

The search of the ranch area began quickly with everyone from the wedding party out looking for the child.

"I turned my back for just a moment," Dana said, sounding as distraught as Allie when Jackson caught up with her.

"It's not your fault. If anyone is to blame, it's me. I've been trying to help Allie and have only made things worse. I need to know something," he said as he watched the searchers coming off the mountain from the cabins. No Natalie. "Did you see anyone go toward the house about the time you realized she was gone?"

She shook her head. "You mean Drew or his mother? They both left earlier to go talk to the police."

"What about his sister, Sarah? Have you seen her?"

Dana frowned. "She didn't leave with them, now that I think about it, and I haven't seen her since Nat went missing."

Jackson spotted Belinda trying to comfort Allie down by the main house. "How about Megan?"

She shook her head. "I haven't seen either of them." Dana looked worried. "You don't think—"

He did think. He ran down the slope toward the house and Allie. "Did either of you see Sarah or Megan?"

They looked at him in surprise.

"They left together not long after the fireworks started," Belinda said. "Sarah said she had a headache and asked Megan to give her a ride."

Jackson looked at Allie. "You know where Sarah lives, right?"

"You think they took Nat?" Allie looked even more frightened.

"Belinda, stay here and keep us informed if the searchers find Nat. Come on. Let's see if they have Natalie or might have seen her since they left about the time she went missing."

EACH BREATH WAS a labor as Allie stared out the windshield into the darkness ahead. She fought not to break down but it took all of her strength. She'd never been so frightened or felt so helpless. All she could do was pray that Natalie was safe.

"If they took her, then I'm sure they wouldn't hurt her," she said, needing desperately to believe that. "Sarah might have thought it was getting too late for Natalie to be out. Or maybe Nat's dress was so wet—"

"We're going to find her." Jackson sounded convinced of that.

She glanced over at him. His strong hands gripped the

wheel as he drove too fast. He was as scared as she was, she realized. Like her, he must be blaming himself. If the two of them hadn't left the wedding...

"Tell me where to turn. I don't know where they live."

"Take a left at the Big Sky resort turnoff. Mother Taylor... Mildred lives up the mountain."

"They don't have that much of a head start," he said, sounding as if he was trying to reassure himself as much as her.

"This is all my fault." She didn't realize she'd said the words aloud until he spoke.

"No, if anyone is to blame it's me," he said as he reached over and squeezed her hand. "You have been going through so much and all I did was complicate things for you."

She let out a nervous laugh. "Are you kidding? I would have been in a straitjacket by now if it wasn't for you. I still might end up there, but at least I had this time when there was someone who believed me."

"I *still* believe you. You're not crazy. Nor did you have anything to do with your husband's death. You're being set up and, if it is the last thing I do, I'm going to prove it."

Allie couldn't help but smile over at him. "Thank you but I can't ask you to keep—"

"You're not asking. There's something else I need to say." He glanced over at her before making the turn at Big Sky then turned back to his driving. "I hadn't been with another woman since my ex. I didn't *want* anyone. The mere thought of getting involved again... Then I met you," he said shooting her a quick look as they raced up the mountain toward Big Sky Resort.

"Turn at the next left when we reach the top of the mountain," she said, not sure she wanted to hear what he had to say.

"I hadn't felt anything like that in so long and then we made love and..."

She really didn't need him to let her down easy. Not right now. All she wanted to think about was Natalie. If he was just doing this to keep her from worrying… "You don't have to explain."

"I do. I panicked because making love with you was so amazing and meant so much and…" He shook his head. "I…I just needed time to digest it all. And, truthfully, I was scared. Ford's mom did a number on me. Admittedly, we were both young, too young to get married, let alone have a child together. I had this crazy idea that we wanted the same things. Turned out she wanted money, a big house, a good time. When she got pregnant with Ford…" He slowed to make the turn.

"It's up this road about a mile. Turn left when you see the sign for Elk Ridge."

He nodded. "Juliet didn't want the baby. I talked her into having Ford. She hated me for it, said it was going to ruin her figure." He shook his head at the memory. "I thought that after he was born, her mothering instincts would kick in. My mistake. She resented him even more than she did me. She basically handed him to me and went out with her friends."

"I can't imagine."

He glanced over at her. "No, *you* can't." He sighed. "After that, she started staying out all night, wouldn't come home for days. Fortunately, the barbecue businesses took off like crazy so I could stay home with Ford. I asked for a divorce only to find out that my wife liked being a Cardwell and didn't want to give up what she had, which was basically no responsibilities, but lots of money and freedom to do whatever she wanted."

"Keep going up this road," she told him. Then after a moment, said, "She didn't want a divorce."

"No. She said that if I pushed it, she would take Ford."

"How horrible," Allie cried. Hadn't that been her fear

with Nick? Hadn't she worried that he would be a bastard and try to hurt them both when she told him she was leaving him?

"After the battle I fought to keep my son, I was…broken."

"I understand. The last thing you wanted was to get involved with a woman who only reminded you of what you'd been through."

He glanced over at her. "That was part of it." He didn't say more as he reached the turnoff for Mildred Taylor's house and the guesthouse where her daughter, Sarah, lived. He turned down it and Mildred's house came into view.

JACKSON HAD ALMOST told Allie how he felt about her. That he loved her. But as he'd turned and seen Mildred Taylor's big house, he'd realized the timing was all wrong. First they had to find Natalie.

He prayed she would be here, safe. But if so, did the Taylors seriously think they could get away with this? Had they told someone they were taking Natalie and the person just forgot or couldn't find Allie and left? Was there a logical explanation for this?

He hoped it was just a misunderstanding. But in his heart, he didn't believe for a minute that Allie had imagined the things that had been happening to her. Someone was behind this and they weren't finished with Allie yet. What scared him was that one of them could have murdered Nick.

His heart began to pound harder as he pulled in front of the large stone-and-log house set back against the mountainside. There were two vehicles parked in front and the lights were on inside the massive house. He parked and opened his door, anxious to put Nat in her mother's arms. Allie was out her door the moment he stopped.

"Who all lives here?" Jackson asked as he caught up to her.

"Just Mildred in the main house. Sarah stays in the guesthouse behind it. Drew lives down in Gateway but he stays with his mother a lot up here. That's his pickup parked next to Mildred's SUV so he must be here."

As Jackson passed Mildred's SUV, he touched the hood. Still warm. They at least hadn't been here long.

"What does Sarah drive?" he asked, glancing toward the dark guesthouse.

"A pearl-white SUV. I don't see it."

At Allie's knock, he heard movement inside the house. If they were trying to hide Natalie, it wouldn't do them any good. He looked back down the mountainside telling himself that if Natalie was in this house, he'd find her.

Drew opened the door and looked surprised to see them standing there.

"Where is Natalie?" Allie cried as she pushed past him.

"Natalie?" Drew barely got the word out before Jackson pushed past him, as well. The two of them stormed into the main part of the house.

Mildred was seated on one of the large leather couches facing the window in the living room, a glass of wine in her hand. She looked up in surprise.

"Where is she?" Allie demanded. "I know you have my daughter."

"Natalie?" Mildred asked, frowning. "You can't *find* her?"

"They seem to think we have her," Drew said, closing the front door and joining them. "We've been at the police station. Why would you think we had Natalie?"

"Allie, stay here. I'll search the house," Jackson said.

"You most certainly will not," Mildred cried. "I'll call the cops."

"Call the cops, but I suspect the marshal is already on his way here," he told her and wasn't surprised when Drew stepped in front of him as if to block his way.

"You really want to do this now? Your niece is missing.

If you don't have her, then we need to be out looking for her, not seeing who is tougher between you and me."

"We don't have her," Drew said, "and you're not—"

Jackson hit him and didn't wait around to see if he got up.

He stormed through the house, calling Nat's name. There were a lot of rooms, a lot of closets, a lot of places to look. But it didn't take him long to realize she wasn't here. Whatever they might have done with her, she wasn't in this house.

"I'm going to have you arrested for trespassing and barging into our house and attacking my son," Mildred threatened but hadn't made the call when he returned. Drew had a package of frozen peas he was holding to his eye as he came out of the kitchen.

"Mildred swears she hasn't seen Sarah," Allie told him.

"Well, Natalie isn't here. I think we should still check the guesthouse."

"You planning to break in?" Drew asked. "Or would you like me to get the key?"

Mildred pushed to her feet. "Drew, you are most certainly not going to—"

"Shut up, Mother," he snapped. "Aren't you listening? Natalie is missing. If I can help find her, I will. What I'd like to know is why you aren't upset about it. If you know where Nat is, Mother, you'd better tell me right now."

Jackson felt his cell phone vibrate, checked it and said, "I just got a text that the marshal is on his way. Mrs. Taylor, you could be looking at felony kidnapping," he warned.

ALLIE STARED AT HER mother-in-law, seeing a pathetic, lonely woman who now looked trapped.

"She's not in the guesthouse," Mildred said. "She's *fine*. She's with Sarah and Megan."

"Where?" Allie demanded, her heart breaking at the

thought of Megan being involved in this. "Why would they take her?"

Mildred met her gaze. "Because you're an unfit mother. Megan told me all about your mother and her family. Crazy, all of them. And you? You see things and do things that prove you can't raise my Nicky's baby girl. She needs *family*. Natalie needs her *grandmother*," she said before bursting into tears.

"Call them and tell them to bring Natalie back," Jackson ordered.

"He's right, Mother. Natalie belongs with her mother."

"How can you say that?" Mildred cried, turning on her son. "I told you about all the crazy things she's been doing. Did you know she cut up all those lovely dresses my Nicky had bought her? She never liked them and with him gone—" Mildred stopped as if she felt Allie staring at her in shock. "She's *crazy*. Just look at her!"

"The dresses. I never told anyone other than Jackson about finding them cut up on my bed," Allie said, surprised by how normal her voice sounded. Even more surprised by the relief she felt. "It was the night Drew took Natalie and me to dinner. *You?* You bought the clothes in the closet that I found. No wonder you asked me about what I was wearing at the rehearsal dinner. You knew where I kept my checkbook in the desk drawer. Nick would have told you about the kind of clothes I liked. Forging my signature on a check wouldn't have been hard, not for a woman who has been forging her husband's signature on checks for years."

Mildred gasped. "Where would you get an idea like that?"

"*Your Nicky* told me. You've been stealing from the elderly man you married to keep up the lifestyle you believe you deserve. But you don't deserve my daughter."

"Is that true, Mother?" Drew asked with a groan.

"Never mind that cheap bastard. Men never stay so yes, I took advantage while it lasted and now he's divorcing me. Happy?" Mildred thrust her finger at Allie. "But you, you killed my Nicky!"

"How can you say that?" Allie demanded. "You can't really believe I followed him up into the mountains."

"You *paid* someone to kill him. I know you did," the older woman argued. "When I came over that weekend, you were packing up some of Nicky's belongings. You knew he was dead before we even heard."

"That was just some things he left out before he went hunting."

"She's lying," Mildred cried as she looked from Jackson to Drew. "She knew Nicky wasn't coming back. She was packing. I saw that she'd cleaned out the closet before she closed the bedroom door."

"I was packing my own things and Natalie's," Allie said. "I was planning to leave Nick. Ask Belinda. She'll tell you. I wanted a divorce."

Mildred looked shocked. "Why would you want to leave my Nicky? You must have found another man."

"No," Allie said, shaking her head. "I know how much you loved him but I didn't see the same man you did. Nick wasn't any happier than I was in the marriage."

"Oh, I have to sit down," Mildred cried. "Can't you see? She had every reason to want Nicky dead. She's admitted it."

"Make the call to your daughter, Mrs. Taylor," Jackson said, handing her his phone.

At the sound of a siren headed toward the house, Mildred took his phone.

"You'll get your daughter back, but only temporarily," her mother-in-law spat after making the call. "Once you go to prison for my Nicky's murder, you will get what you deserve and I will get my Nicky's baby."

"And all Nick's insurance money," Jackson said. "Isn't that what this is really about?"

Mildred didn't answer as Marshal Hud Savage pulled up out front.

Chapter Fifteen

Emotionally exhausted, all Allie could think about was holding her daughter. They'd all waited, the marshal included, until Megan and Sarah brought Natalie to the Taylor house.

Allie swept her daughter up into her arms, hugging her so tightly that Natalie cried, "Mama, you're squishing me!"

Hud took Mildred, Drew, Megan and Sarah down to the marshal's office to question them.

"Why don't you come stay at the ranch," Jackson suggested, but all Allie wanted to do was take her daughter home. "Okay, I'll drop you off there. I can give you a ride to the ranch in the morning to pick up your van."

She looked into his dark eyes and touched his arm. "Thank you."

They didn't talk on the drive to her cabin. Natalie fell asleep after complaining that she'd missed most of the fireworks. Apparently, Sarah and Megan had told her they were taking her to see her mama and that it was important.

As they drove, pockets of fireworks were going off around them. Allie had forgotten it was the Fourth of July. Even the wedding seemed like it had been a long time ago.

"If you need anything..." Jackson said after he'd insisted on carrying Natalie into her bed. He moved to the cabin door. "I'm here for you, Allie."

She could only nod, her emotions long spent.

"I'll see you tomorrow."

Allie doubted that. Jackson and Ford would be flying out. She told herself that she and Natalie were safe as she locked the front door, leaned against it and listened to Jackson drive away.

But in her heart she knew they wouldn't be safe until Nick's killer was caught.

"I RUINED TAG and Lily's wedding," Jackson said with a groan the next morning at breakfast.

"You did not," Dana said, patting his hand as she finished serving a huge ranch breakfast of elk steaks, biscuits and gravy, fried potatoes and eggs. She had invited them all down, saying that she knew it had been a rough night. Hud had left for his office first thing this morning.

The wedding couple had stayed at Big Sky Resort last night and flown out this morning to an undisclosed location for their two-week-long honeymoon.

"They loved everything about the wedding," Dana said. "They were just worried about Allie after Mildred's announcement and then concerned for Natalie. I'm just so thankful that she was found and is fine. I can't imagine what Sarah and Megan were thinking."

Jackson had filled everyone in on what had happened at the Taylors' and how apparently Mildred, Sarah and Megan had been gaslighting Allie.

"Oh, Allie must be heartbroken to find out her stepsister was in on it," Dana said.

"I'm sure Hud will sort it out," Jackson said as he watched his son eating breakfast with the Savage clan at the kid table. Ford, he noticed, had come out of his shell. Jackson couldn't believe the change in the boy from when they had arrived at the ranch. Montana had been good for his son.

"Natalie is safe and so is Allie, at least for the moment," he said. "The problem is Nick's murder," he said, dropping his voice, even though he doubted the kids could hear, given the amount of noise they were making at their table.

"They still don't know who killed him?" Dana asked.

Jackson shook his head. "Mildred is convinced Allie paid someone to do it. The police want to talk to her."

"You sound worried," Dana noted. "And your brothers haven't said a word," she said, looking from Hayes to Laramie and finally Jackson. "Why is that?"

"They've been helping me do some investigating," he admitted.

Dana rolled her eyes. "I should have known that was what was going on." She glanced at Hayes and Laramie. "You found something that makes her look guilty?"

"Someone is setting her up," Jackson said.

"The same people who tried to drive her crazy?" she asked.

"Maybe not. There could be more going on here than even we know." Jackson couldn't help sounding worried as he got to his feet. "Hayes and I are going to take her van to her. She called this morning. A homicide detective from Bozeman wants to see her."

ALLIE HAD AWAKENED in Natalie's bed to the sound of the phone. She'd expected it to be Jackson. That sent her heart lifting like helium. But as she reminded herself he was leaving today, her moment of euphoria evaporated.

Reaching for the receiver, she had a bad feeling it wasn't going to be good news. "We would like to ask you a few questions," the homicide detective told her. "When would be a good time?"

After she'd hung up, she'd called Jackson and told him the news.

"You knew this was coming. It's nothing to worry about," he'd told her, but she'd heard concern in his voice. "Do you want me to go with you?"

"No. This is something I have to do alone. Anyway, aren't you flying out today?"

Silence, then, "I canceled our flight."

"You shouldn't have done that," she said after a moment.

"Allie, I can't leave yet. I saw that the key is in the van. Hayes and I will bring it over."

"There is no hurry. I don't see the homicide detective until later."

Their conversation had felt awkward and ended just as badly. Allie told herself she couldn't keep leaning on Jackson. She knew now what Mildred and her daughter and Megan had done to her. She could understand Sarah going along with whatever her mother said, but Megan?

She'd felt like family. But then so had Drew.

Allie made Natalie her favorite pancakes when she woke up, then they went for a walk down by the river. Nat did love to throw rocks into the water. Allie watched the ripples they made, thinking about Jackson and the ripples he'd made in her life.

After a while, they walked back to the cabin. Dana had called saying she would love to take Natalie while Allie went to talk to the detective.

"If you trust me with her. I wouldn't blame you if you didn't. Just let me know."

Allie called Dana right back. "I would always trust you with Natalie and she would love to see the kids, not to mention Sugar, the horse."

Dana laughed and Allie could hear tears in her voice. "I was afraid you would never forgive me."

"There is nothing to forgive. Megan and Sarah took advantage of the fireworks show and the wedding."

"What were they thinking? Did they really believe they could get away with keeping her?"

"I suppose they thought I would come unglued, which

I did, proving that I was unbalanced. If it hadn't been for Jackson…" She really hadn't meant to go there.

"Is Natalie all right?"

"She didn't even realize anything was amiss. Apparently, they told her they were taking her to me, but when they reached Megan's motel room, they told her I was going to meet them there. Nat ended up falling asleep. So she had no idea what was going on."

"Thank goodness."

"I'll drop Nat off on my way, if that's okay."

"That's wonderful. We can't wait to see her. Tell her to wear her boots. We'll go for a ride."

"You NEED TO take the hint," Hayes said as he and Jackson drove away from Allie's cabin. They'd dropped off the van, Allie had thanked them and that was that, so Jackson knew what his brother was getting at. "Allie is handling all of this fine. I'm not sure there is anything you can do from here on out."

"You think she had him killed?" Jackson demanded.

Hayes shrugged. "I don't know her as well as you think you do. I don't think she paid anyone to do it. But if she gave Drew any kind of opening with her, I think he would have killed his brother for her—and the insurance money."

"She wasn't in cahoots with Drew. And stop doing that," he snapped as his brother shrugged again. "Do you realize how cynical you've become? Worse, does McKenzie?"

Hayes smiled. "Speaking of McKenzie… I'm opening a private investigator business here."

"You think that's a newsflash?" Jackson laughed. "We've all seen that coming for a mile. So when is the wedding?"

"I'm thinking we might elope. I'm not sure the family can live through another Cardwell Ranch wedding."

"Which reminds me, still no word from Austin?"

"You know our brother when he's on a case. But I am a little worried about him. I really thought he'd make Tag's wedding."

"Yeah, me too. Maybe I'll give a call down there. Knowing him, he probably didn't list any of us as emergency contacts."

ALLIE TRIED TO get comfortable in the chair the homicide detectives offered her. The room was like any office, no bare lightbulb shining into her eyes, no cops threatening her. But she still shifted in her chair.

On the drive here, she'd tried to concentrate on who might have killed Nick. Belinda had been up that trail with Nick when the two of them had been dating. Drew usually went hunting with his brother. Had Drew gone this time, as well, gotten in an argument with Nick and killed him?

She shuddered at the path her thoughts had taken. Did she really think someone in Nick's own family had killed him?

Better that than to think that her stepsister, Megan, had. Allie felt sick at the thought. Her sister had called this morning but Allie hadn't picked up.

"I need to explain," Megan had said on voice mail. "I did what I did for Natalie's sake. I love you and my niece. I really believed I was protecting you both. I had no idea Mildred and Sarah were doing those things to you, making you behave the way they told me you were. Please call me so we can talk about this."

The larger of the two homicide detectives cleared his voice. His name tag read Benson. "We need to know where you were the weekend your husband went up into the mountains."

"I was home that whole weekend."

"Did you talk to anyone? Anyone stop by?"

Allie tried to remember. Her mind was spinning. They

thought she'd had something to do with Nick's death? Of course they did, given the insurance policies and her mother-in-law's rantings and ravings.

Just yesterday, she'd been sure that Nick was alive. Jackson had been convinced, as well. She'd been even more convinced when she'd heard his voice at the séance. Nick's voice accusing her of killing him. She shivered at the memory.

"Mrs. Taylor?" the smaller of the two, whose name tag read Evans, asked.

She blinked. No one called her Mrs. Taylor. Mrs. Taylor was Nick's mother. "Please, call me Allie. I just need a moment to think." Had anyone stopped by that weekend?

Fighting all her conflicting thoughts, she tried to remember. Nick had left early, having packed the night before. He'd seemed excited about the prospect of going alone on this hunt. Why hadn't she noticed that something was wrong right there? It was the first red flag.

Had anyone stopped by? No. She frowned. She'd tried to call Belinda but hadn't been able to reach her, she recalled now. She'd wanted to tell her what Nick had said about making some changes when he returned from his hunting trip. She'd had misgivings about the trip even then and she'd needed to talk to someone. Had she worried that he might be thinking of killing himself?

"I don't remember anyone stopping by," she said, trying to keep her thoughts on the question. She ticked off everyone on her fingers. "I couldn't reach my friend Belinda." Had she tried Megan? "Or my stepsister, Megan. And my in-laws. I think that was the weekend that Mildred and Sarah went on a shopping trip to Billings. Drew… I don't know where he was. I didn't talk to him."

She looked up to see that both detectives were studying her. They were making her even more nervous.

"I was alone with my daughter that whole weekend." She

had no alibi. But they didn't really think she'd followed Nick up in the mountains and killed him, did they?

"Was it unusual for your husband to go hunting alone?"

"Very. I didn't think he had. I thought he was having an affair. I was surprised when I learned that he really had gone into the mountains."

The detectives shared a look before the lead one asked, "Did you have any reason to believe your husband was having an affair?"

"No. I guess it was wishful thinking. It would have made it easier for me."

The two shared another look. "Easier?"

She met the smaller detective's gaze. "I was going to leave Nick." Why not admit it? They probably already knew this after talking to her in-laws and Belinda and Megan. "But I didn't want him dead. You asked what I was doing that weekend? I didn't leave the house. I had my five-year-old daughter to take care of that weekend and I was busy packing."

"When were you planning to tell him?" Benson asked.

"As soon as he returned."

Evans picked up a sheet of paper from the desk. "Mrs. Tay— Excuse me, Allie, you own a .45 pistol?"

Chapter Sixteen

The gun. What had she been thinking when she'd bought it? Had she really thought that pulling it on Nick would be a good idea? She'd wanted something to protect herself for when she told him she was leaving.

Now she saw how ridiculous that was. Nick would have taken it away from her, knowing she couldn't shoot him and then he would have been so furious....

"Yes, I bought the gun for protection."

Benson raised a brow. "Protection? Against whom?"

"I was planning to leave my husband. My daughter and I would be alone—"

"But you hadn't left him yet," Evans pointed out. "So why buy a .45 pistol only days before your husband was to go on his hunting trip?"

"I...I...was afraid of how Nick was going to take it when he returned and I told him I was leaving him. Sometimes he scares me."

The two detectives exchanged another look.

"But it was impulsive and silly because Nick would have known I couldn't use it on him. He would have taken it away from me and..." She swallowed.

"You were afraid of your husband," Benson said.

"Sometimes."

"Where is the gun now?" Evans asked.

"I don't know. When I heard that Nick had been killed

with a .45, I looked for it, but it was gone." Allie could see the disbelief written all over their faces. Hadn't she known when she looked that it would be gone?

"I think someone is trying to set me up for his murder," she blurted out and instantly regretted it when she saw their expressions. Apparently, they'd heard this type of defense before.

"You're saying someone took the gun to frame you?" Benson asked. "Who knew you'd bought it?"

Allie met his gaze. "I didn't tell anyone, if that is what you're asking."

"Who had access to your house?" Evans asked.

"It's an old cabin. I don't know how many people might have a key. Nick was always going to change the locks…"

"Your in-laws? Did they have keys?" Benson asked.

"Yes."

"Friends?"

"Belinda and my stepsister, Megan, know where there's a key to get in."

"Where did you keep the gun that someone could have found it? You have a five-year-old. I assume you didn't just leave the gun lying around," Benson asked.

"Of course not. I put it on the top shelf of the closet. It wasn't loaded."

"But there were cartridges for it with the gun?"

She nodded.

"When was the last time you saw it?" Evans asked.

"The day I bought it. I put it on the shelf behind some shoe boxes… I'd forgotten all about it with Nick's…death… and all."

"So you were just going to leave him," Evans said. "This man who you said scared you sometimes, you were going to allow him to have joint custody of your child?"

"It hadn't gotten that far. I guess it would have been up to the court—"

"Oh, so you'd already seen a lawyer about a divorce?" Benson asked.

"Not yet. I couldn't afford to see one until I got a job and Nick wouldn't allow me to work."

The detectives exchanged looks.

"Was your husband abusive?" Benson asked not unkindly.

Allie hesitated. "He was…controlling."

"And he scared you," Evans said.

"Yes, sometimes. What is it you want me to say? He wasn't a good husband or father to our daughter. And yes, sometimes he scared me."

"Mrs. Taylor, did you kill your husband?" Evans asked.

"No. I told you. I could never—"

"Did you get your brother-in-law, Drew, or someone else close to you to do the killing for you?" Benson asked.

"*No!* I didn't want to be married to Nick anymore but I didn't want him dead."

Evans leaned forward. "But look how it turned out. Nick is no longer around to scare you, even sometimes. Your daughter is safe from him. And you are a wealthy woman thanks to his insurance money. Better than a divorce and a lengthy battle over your daughter, wouldn't you say?"

Allie felt as if the detectives had beaten her as she stumbled out of the police station. For a moment she forgot where she'd parked the van. Panic sent her blood pressure soaring before she spotted it. There it was, right where she'd left it. And there was…

"Jackson?"

He pushed off the van and moved quickly to her. "I had to see you before I left."

She frowned, still feeling off balance. "I thought you weren't flying out yet?"

"It's my brother Austin. He's a sheriff's deputy in Texas. He's been shot. He's critical. I have to fly out now. Franklin and Mom already left. Hayes, Laramie and I are taking the corporate jet as soon as I get to the airport."

"I'm so sorry, Jackson. Does Tag know?"

"We weren't able to reach him. He and Lily wanted their honeymoon to be a secret… Ford is staying with Dana until I get back. But I couldn't leave without seeing you. Are you all right?"

She started to say she was fine, but she couldn't get the lie past her lips. Her eyes filled with tears. "They think I killed Nick. Everyone does."

"Not me," he said and pulled her into his arms. "When I get back, we'll sort this out. I'm sorry I have to go."

She pulled back, brushed at her tears. "I'll say a prayer for your brother." As he ran to his rented SUV, she turned in time to see Detective Evans watching her from the front of the building. He looked like a man who'd just received a gift he hadn't expected. Jackson Cardwell. Another motive as to why she'd want her husband gone for good.

The jet owned by the corporation was waiting on the tarmac when Jackson arrived at the airport. He ran to climb aboard and Laramie alerted the captain that they were ready.

"Have you heard any more from Mom or the hospital?" Jackson asked as he buckled up.

"I just got off the phone with Mom," Hayes said. "Austin's still in surgery." His tone was sufficient for Jackson to know it didn't look good.

"Do we know what happened?" he asked as the plane began to taxi out to the runway.

"You know how hard it is to get anything out of the sheriff's department down there," Hayes said. "But I got the impression he was on one of the dangerous cases he seems to like so well." He raked a hand through his hair. "There was a woman involved. He'd apparently gone into a drug cartel to get her out."

"That sounds just like Austin," Jackson said with a sigh as the jet engine roared and the plane began to race down the runway. "Did he get her out?"

"Don't know. Doubtful, though, since some illegal immigrants found him after he'd been shot and got him to a gas station near the border."

Hayes shook his head. "Some of the same illegal immigrants his department is trying to catch and send back over the border. What a mess down there. I'm glad I'm done with it."

His brothers looked at him in surprise as the plane lifted off the ground.

"McKenzie and I signed the papers on a ranch in the canyon not far from Cardwell Ranch. When I get back, we're eloping. She's already looking for some office space for me at Big Sky to open a private investigation office up here."

"Congratulations," Laramie said.

"Have you told Mom?" Jackson asked. "I'm wondering how she is going to feel losing another son to Montana?" The plane fell silent as he realized she might be losing another son at this very moment, one that not even Montana got a chance to claim.

Speaking of Montana, he thought as he looked out the window at the mountains below them. He'd hated leaving Allie, especially as upset as she'd been. He promised himself he would return to the canyon just as soon as he knew his brother was going to be all right.

He said a prayer for Austin and one for Allie, as well.

DANA HAD CALLED to say she was taking the kids on a horseback ride and that Allie could pick Natalie up later, if that was all right. Ford apparently was very upset and worried about his uncle Austin, so Dana was trying to take their minds off everything for a while.

Not wanting to go back to an empty cabin, Allie had

busied herself with errands she'd put off since the wedding preparation. It was late afternoon by the time she got home. She'd called the ranch only to find out that Dana and the kids had gone to get ice cream and would be back soon.

Allie was carrying in groceries and her other purchases when she heard the vehicle pull up. She'd hoped to get everything put away before she went to pick up Natalie. She carried the bags into the cabin, dumping them on the kitchen counter, before she glanced out the window to see her mother-and sister-in-law pull up. She groaned as the two got out and came to the door.

For just an instant, she thought about not answering their knock, but they must have seen her carrying in her groceries. Mildred wasn't one to take the hint and go away.

"I just got back from the police station," she said as she opened the door. "I'm really not in the mood for visitors." She couldn't believe either of them would have the gall to show their faces around here after what they'd done. Well, they weren't coming in. Whatever they had to say, they could say it on the front step.

Allie had already talked to Hud this morning. He'd questioned all of them last night, but had had to let them all go. Maybe they had come by to apologize, but Allie doubted it.

"I just got a call from the police," Mildred said indignantly. "Why would you tell them that Sarah and I went to Billings the weekend my Nicky was killed?"

"I thought you had." She knew she shouldn't have been surprised. No apology for what they had tried to do to her.

"We'd planned to go, but Sarah was sick that whole weekend." She sniffed. "I was alone when I got the call about my Nicky." She glared at her daughter for a moment. "Sarah had taken my car down to the drugstore to get more medicine since her car was in the shop. I couldn't even leave the house to go to Drew." Mildred sighed.

"I'm sorry you were alone, Mother. I came right back. I

couldn't have been gone more than five minutes after you got the call," Sarah said.

"That was the longest five minutes of my life," Mildred said with another sniff.

"I guess I had forgotten the two of you hadn't gone to Billings, but I'm sure you straightened it out with the police," Allie said. "And Sarah couldn't have known that would be the time you would get the call about Nick," Allie pointed out.

Sarah gave her a grateful smile, then added, "I hate to ask, but do you happen to have a cola in your fridge?"

"Oh, for crying out loud, Sarah, how many times have I told you that stuff is horrible for you?" her mother demanded.

"Help yourself," Allie said, moving to the side of the doorway to let her pass. She saw that the sun had disappeared behind Lone Mountain, casting the canyon in a cool darkness. Where had this day gone? "I hate to run you off, but I have to go pick up Natalie."

"Once this foolishness is over, I hope you'll forgive me and let me spend some time with my granddaughter," Mildred said.

As Sarah came out with a can of cola, Allie moved aside again to let her pass, hoping they would now leave.

Mildred looked in the yard at Nick's pickup, where it had been parked since someone from the forest service had found it at the trailhead and had it dropped off. "Why are you driving that awful van of yours? You should either drive Nicky's pickup or sell it. Terrible waste to just let it sit."

Allie planned to sell the pickup but she'd been waiting, hoping in time Mildred wouldn't get so upset about it.

"I'd like to buy it," Sarah said, making them both turn to look at her in surprise.

"What in the world do you need with Nicky's pickup?"

Mildred demanded. "I'm not giving you the money for it and I couldn't bear looking at it every day."

"It was just a thought," Sarah said as she started toward her SUV. The young woman took so much grief from her mother.

Her gaze went to Nick's pickup. The keys were probably still in it, she realized. As Sarah climbed behind the wheel and waited for her mother to get into the passenger side of the SUV, Allie walked out to the pickup, opened the door and reached inside to pull the keys.

The pickup smelled like Nick's aftershave and made her a little sick to her stomach. She pocketed the keys as she hurriedly closed the door. The truck was Nick's baby. He loved it more than he did either her or Natalie. That's why she was surprised as she started to step away to see that the right rear panel near the back was dented. She moved to the dent and ran her fingers over it. That would have to be fixed before she could sell it since the rest of the truck was in mint condition.

Just something else to take care of, she thought as she dusted what looked like chalky white flakes off her fingers. She looked up and saw that her in-laws hadn't left. Mildred was going on about something. Sarah was bent toward the passenger seat apparently helping her mother buckle up. Mildred was probably giving her hell, Allie thought.

When Sarah straightened, she looked up from behind the wheel and seemed surprised to see Allie standing by Nick's truck. Her surprise gave way to sadness as she looked past Allie to her brother's pickup.

Was it possible Sarah really did want Nick's pickup for sentimental reasons? Maybe she should have it. Allie had never thought Sarah and her brother were that close. Well, at least Nick hadn't been that crazy about his sister. He'd been even more disparaging than his mother toward Sarah.

Allie met her sister-in-law's dark gaze for a moment,

feeling again sorry for her. Maybe she would just give her the pickup. She waved as Sarah began to pull away, relieved they were finally leaving.

Her cell phone rang. She hoped it was Jackson with news of his brother. She said a silent prayer for Austin before she saw that it was Dana.

"Is everything all right?" Allie asked, instantly afraid.

"Ford is still upset about his uncle. Natalie told him that you were picking her up soon…"

Allie knew what was coming. She couldn't bear the thought. She wanted Natalie home with her. The way things were going, she feared she might soon be under arrest for Nick's murder. She didn't know how much time she and Nat had together.

"Natalie wishes to speak with you," Dana said before Allie could say no.

"Mama?" Just the sound of her daughter's voice made her smile. "Please say I can stay. Ford is very sad about his uncle. Please let me stay."

"Maybe Ford could come stay with you—"

"We're all going to sleep in the living room in front of the fire. Mrs. Savage said we could. She is going to make popcorn. It is Mary and Hank's favorite."

Allie closed her eyes, picturing how perfect it would be in front of Dana's fireplace in that big living room with the smell of popcorn and the sound of children's laughter. She wanted to sleep right in the middle of all of them.

"Of course you need to stay for your new friend," she heard herself say as tears burned her eyes. "Tell Mrs. Savage that I will pick you up first thing in the morning. I love you."

"I love you, too, Mama." And Natalie was gone, the phone passed to Dana who said, "I'm sorry. This was the kids' idea."

"It's fine."

"What about you? How did it go with the police?"

"As expected. They think I killed Nick. Or at least got someone to do it for me."

"That's ridiculous. Allie, listen, you shouldn't be alone. Why don't you come stay here tonight? I think you need your daughter. Do you like butter on your popcorn? Come whenever you want. Or take a little time for yourself. If you're like me, when was the last time you got a nice leisurely bath without being interrupted? Whatever you need, but bring your pjs. We're having a pajama party. Right now the kids all want to go help feed the animals. See you later."

As THE JET touched down just outside of Houston, Hayes got the call from their mother. Jackson watched his expression, waiting for the news. Relief flooded his brother's face. He gave thumbs up and disconnected.

"Mom says Austin is out of surgery. The doctor says he should make it."

Jackson let out the breath he'd been holding. As the plane taxied toward the private plan terminal, he put in a call to Allie. It went straight to voice mail.

He left a message, telling her the good news, then asking her to call when she got the message. "I'm worried about you." As he disconnected, he realized he'd been worried the entire flight about both his brother and Allie.

"I can't reach Allie."

His brothers looked at him in concern as the plane neared the small brightly lit terminal. It was already dark here, but it would still be light in Montana.

"Call Dana," Hayes said. "She's probably over there."

He called. "No answer."

"They probably went for a horseback ride," Laramie said. "Wasn't that what Ford told you they were going to do the last time you talked to him?"

Jackson nodded, telling himself his brother was probably

right. He glanced at Hayes. He understood what Laramie couldn't really grasp. Laramie was a businessman. Hayes was a former sheriff's deputy, a private investigation. He understood Jackson's concern. There was a killer still loose in Montana.

The plane came to a stop. Jackson tried Allie again. The call again went straight to voice mail. He got Mildred Taylor's number and called her.

"Have you seen Allie?" he asked. He couldn't explain his fear, just a feeling in the pit of his stomach that was growing with each passing minute.

"Earlier. She wouldn't even let me in her house." She sniffed. "She was on her way to Cardwell Ranch to pick up Natalie the last I saw of her. Driving that old van. Why she doesn't drive Nickie's pickup I will never—"

He disconnected and tried Dana. Still no answer. He tried Allie again. Then he called the marshal's office in Big Sky.

"Marshal Savage is unavailable," the dispatcher told him.

"Is there anyone there who can do a welfare check?"

"Not at the moment. Do you want me to have the marshal call you when he comes in?"

Jackson started to give the dispatcher his number but Hayes stopped him.

"Take the plane," Hayes said. "Mother said it would be hours before we could even see Austin. I'll keep you informed of his progress."

"Are you kidding?" Laramie demanded. "What is it with you and this woman? Have you forgotten that she's the number one suspect in her husband's murder?"

"She didn't kill him," Jackson and Hayes said in unison.

"Let us know as soon as you hear something," Hayes said.

Jackson hugged his brother, relieved that he understood. He moved to cockpit and asked the pilot how long before they could get the plane back in the air. As Hayes and Laramie disembarked, he sat down again and buckled his seatbelt, trying to remain calm.

He had no reason to believe anything had happened. And yet…that bad feeling he'd gotten when her phone had gone to voice mail had only increased with each passing second. His every instinct told him that Allie was in real trouble.

Chapter Seventeen

Allie had taken a hot bath, but had kept it short. She was too anxious to see her daughter. She changed her clothes, relieved she was going to Dana's. She really didn't want to be alone tonight. She'd heard Natalie's happy chatter in the background and couldn't wait to reach the ranch.

In fact, she had started out the door when she realized she didn't have her purse or her van keys. Leaving the door open, she turned back remembering that she'd left them on the small table between the living room and kitchen when she brought in her groceries earlier.

She was sure she'd left her purse on the table, but it wasn't there. As she started to search for it, she began to have that awful feeling again. Her mind reeled. Mildred wasn't still fooling with her, was she? No Mildred hadn't come into the cabin. But Sarah had. Why would Sarah hide her purse? It made no sense.

Racking her brain, she moved through the small cabin. The purse wasn't anywhere. On her way back through, she realized she must have left it in the van. She was so used to leaving her purse on that small table, she'd thought she remembered doing it again.

She started toward the open door when a dark figure suddenly filled the doorway. The scream that rose in her throat came out a sharp cry before she could stop it.

"Drew, you scared me. I didn't hear you drive up."

"My truck's down the river a ways. I was fishing...."

The lie was so obvious that he didn't bother finishing it. He wasn't dressed for fishing nor was he carrying a rod.

"The truth is, I wanted to talk to you and after everything that's happened, I thought you'd chase me off before I could have my say."

"Drew, this isn't a good time. I was just leaving."

He laughed. "That's exactly why I didn't drive up in your yard. I figured you'd say something just like that."

"Well, in this case, it's true. Natalie is waiting for me. I'm staying at Cardwell Ranch tonight. Dana is going to be wondering where I am if I don't—"

"This won't take long." He took a breath. "I'm so sorry for everything."

Allie felt her blood heat to boiling. No one in this family ever listened to her. How dare he insist she hear him out when she just told him she was leaving? "You and your mother tried to drive me insane."

"I didn't know anything about that, I swear," Drew cried. "Mother told me that you had already forgotten about Nick. It was breaking her heart. She said you needed to be reminded and if you saw someone who looked like Nick..."

"You expect me to believe that?"

He shrugged. "It's true. I did it just to shut her up. You know how Mother is."

She did. She also knew arguing about this now was a waste of time and breath. She glanced at the clock on the mantel. "I really need to go."

"Just give me another minute, please. Also I wanted to apologize for the other night. I had too much to drink." He shook his head. "I don't know what I was thinking. But you have to know, I've always liked you." He looked at her shyly. "I would have done anything for you and now the cops think I killed Nick for you."

Her pulse jumped, her heart a thunder in her chest. "That's ridiculous."

"That's what I told them. I could never hurt my brother. I loved Nick. But I have to tell you, I was jealous of him when he married you."

"Drew, I really don't have time to get into this right—"

"Don't get me wrong," he said as if she hadn't spoken. "If I thought there was chance with you…"

A ripple of panic ran up her spine. "There isn't, Drew."

"Right. Jackson Cardwell."

"That isn't the reason."

"Right," he said sarcastically. His jaw tightened, his expression going dark. She'd been married to his brother long enough to know the signs. Nick could go from charming to furious and frightening in seconds. Apparently so could his brother.

"Drew—"

"What if I did kill him for you, Allie?" He stepped toward her. "What if I knew where he would be up that trail? What if I wanted to save you from him? You think I don't know how he was with you?" He let out a laugh. "Jackson Cardwell isn't the only knight in shining armor who wants to come to your rescue."

She didn't want to hear his confession and feared that was exactly what she was hearing. "Drew, I would never want you to hurt your brother for any reason, especially for me."

"Oh yea? But what if I did, Allie? Wouldn't you owe me something?"

He took another a step toward her.

She tried to hold her ground but Drew was much stronger, much larger, much scarier. With Nick, she'd learned that standing up to him only made things worse. But she was determined that this man wasn't going to touch her. She'd backed down too many times with Nick.

"This isn't happening, Drew." She stepped to the side

and picked up the poker from the fireplace. "It's time for you to go."

She could almost read his mind. He was pretty sure he could get the poker away from her before she did much bodily harm to him. She lifted it, ready to swing, when she heard a vehicle come into the yard.

Drew heard it to. "Jackson Cardwell to the rescue again?"

But it couldn't be Jackson. He was in Texas by now.

Allie was relieved to see his sister Sarah stick her head in the door. "I hope I'm not interrupting anything," she said into the tense silence.

"Not at all," Allie assured her sister-in-law. Her voice sounded more normal than she'd thought it would. Had Drew just confessed to killing Nick? "Drew was just leaving."

"We're not through talking about this," he said as he started for the door.

"Oh, I think we already covered the subject. Goodbye Drew."

"Is everything all right?" Sarah asked as Allie returned the poker to its spot next to the fireplace. She stepped in and closed the door behind her.

"Fine. You didn't happen to see my purse when you were here earlier, did you? Dana is expecting me and I can't seem to find it."

"No. You still haven't picked up Natalie?"

"No, Dana invited me for a sleepover with the kids. I was just heading there when Drew arrived."

"I didn't see his truck," Sarah said glancing toward the window.

"He said he parked it down river where he was fishing." She glanced around the living room one more time. "I need to find my purse and get going."

"Your purse? Oh, that explains why you didn't answer

your cell phone. I tried to call you," Sarah said. "Do you want me to help you look?"

"No, maybe I'll just take Nick's truck." The idea repulsed her, but she was anxious to get to the ranch. "I'm sure my purse will turn up. Oh, that's right, I was going out to check the van and see if I left it there when Drew showed up."

"So you're off to a kids sleepover?"

Allie knew she should be more upset with Sarah for taking Natalie last night, but Sarah had always done her mother's bidding. Allie couldn't help but feel sorry for the woman.

"Nat wanted to spend the night over there for Ford. He's upset about his uncle Austin who was shot down in Texas. His brothers should be at the hospital by now. No wonder I haven't heard anything with my cell phone missing."

"Natalie and Ford sure hit it off, didn't they? It's too bad Nat doesn't have a sibling. I always thought you and Nick would have another child."

Allie found Nick's truck keys in her jacket pocket and held them up. "If you still want Nick's truck, you can have it. I was planning to sell it. But the back side panel is dented." She frowned. "It's odd that Nick didn't mention it. You know how he was about truck…"

Her thoughts tumbled over each other in a matter of an instant as her gaze went to her fingers and she remembered the white flakes she'd brushed off the dent. It hadn't registered at the time. The dent. The white paint from the vehicle that had hit it. Pearl white on Nick's black pickup.

Nick would have been out of his mind if someone had hit his pickup. So it couldn't have happened before his hunting trip, which meant it happened where? At the trailhead?

ANOTHER VEHICLE MUST have hit the pickup. Allie's thoughts fell into a straight, heart-stopping line. A pearl-white vehicle like the one Sarah was having repaired the day the call came about Nick's death.

Allie felt the hair rise on the back of her neck as she looked up and saw Sarah's expression.

"I knew you would figure it out the minute I saw you standing next to the dent in Nick's pickup. Nick was so particular about his truck. One little scratch and he would have been losing his mind. Isn't that what you were realizing?"

"Oh Sarah," she said, her heart breaking.

"That's all you have to say to the woman who killed your husband?" she asked as she pulled Allie's .45 out of her pocket and pointed the barrel at Allie's heart.

JACKSON HAD LEFT his rental car at the Bozeman airport. The moment the jet landed he ran to it and headed up the canyon. He tried Allie again. Still no answer. He left a message just in case there was a good reason she wasn't taking calls.

The only reason he could come up with was that she was at Dana's with the kids and didn't want to be disturbed. But she would have taken his calls. She would have wanted to know how Austin was doing.

He tried Dana and was relieved when at least she answered. "I'm looking for Allie. Have you seen her?"

"Not yet. I talked to her earlier. I told her to take a nice hot, long bath and relax, then come over for a sleepover." He could hear Dana let out a surprised sound. "I didn't realize it was so late. She should have been here by now."

"Her calls are going straight to voice mail."

"I'm sure she's just running late…" Dana sounded worried. "How is Austin?"

"He's out of surgery. The doctor said he should make it. I left Hayes and Laramie in Houston."

"Where are you now?"

"On my way to Allie's cabin. If you hear from her, will you please call me?"

He disconnected and drove as fast as he could through the winding narrow canyon. Something was wrong. Dana felt it, too. He prayed that Allie was all right. But feared she wasn't.

Realizing his greatest fear, he called Drew's number. When he'd heard the part Allie's brother-in-law had played in gaslighting her, he'd wanted to punch Drew again. He didn't trust the man, sensed he was a lot like Nick had been; another reason to hate the bastard.

But Jackson also worried that Drew might have killed Nick. The problem was motive. He wouldn't benefit from his brother's death since Nick had changed his beneficiaries on his insurance policy. Or was there something else Drew wanted more than money?

It came to him in a flash. Allie. If he had her, he would also have Nick's money and Nick's life.

Drew answered on the third ring. "What?" He sounded drunk.

Jackson's pulse jumped. "Have you seen Allie?"

"Who the hell is this?"

"Jackson Cardwell." He heard Drew's sneer even on the phone.

"What do *you* want? Just call to rub it in? Well, you haven't got Allie yet so I wouldn't go counting your chickens—"

His heart was pounding like a war drum. "Is she with you?"

Drew laughed. "She's having a sleepover but not with me. Not yet."

"She isn't at the sleepover. When did you see her?"

Finally picking up on Jackson's concern, he said, "She was with my sister at the cabin."

Jackson frowned. "Your sister?"

"They both think I killed Nick. But Sarah had more of a motive than I do. She hated Nick, especially since he'd been trying to get Mother to kick her out. Sarah might look sweet, but I have a scar from when we were kids. She hit me with a tire iron. A tire iron! Can you believe that?"

Jackson saw the turnoff ahead. As he took it, his headlights flashed on the cabin down the road. There were three vehicles parked out front. Nick's black pickup. Allie's van. Sarah's pearl-white SUV.

Chapter Eighteen

"I don't understand," Allie said. "Why would you kill your brother?"

Sarah smiled. "Sweet, lovable *Nickie*? You of all people know what he was like. You had to know the way he talked about me."

Allie couldn't deny it. "He was cruel and insensitive, but—"

"He was trying to get Mother to kick me out without a cent!" Her face reddened with anger. "I gave up my life to take care of her and Nickie is in her ear telling her I am nothing but a parasite and that if she ever wants to see me get married, she has to kick me out and force me to make it on my own. Can you believe that?"

She could. Nick was often worried about any money that would be coming to him via his mother. He was afraid Sarah would get the lion's share because his mother felt sorry for her.

"He was jealous," Allie said. "He was afraid you were becoming her favorite just because she depends on you so much."

Sarah laughed. "Her *favorite?* She can't stand the sight of me. She'd marry me off in a heartbeat if she could find someone to take me off her hands."

"That isn't true. You know she would be lost without you." With a start, Allie realized that Mildred was going to get a chance to see what life was like without Sarah once Sarah went to prison. That is, unless she got away with murdering Nick. With Allie out of the way, Sarah just might.

"I still can't believe you killed him," Allie said as she searched her mind for anything within reach of where she was standing that she could use to defend herself. Something dawned on her. "How did you get my gun?"

"Mother had sent me to your cabin to see if you still had that pink sweater she gave you for Christmas. You never wore it and it was driving her crazy. I told her pink didn't look good on you, but she got it on sale… You know how she is."

Oh yes, she knew. That ugly pink sweater. Allie had put the gun under it behind the shoe boxes.

"When I found the gun, I took it. I was thinking I would try to scare Nick. After all, we have the same genes. He should have known I could be as heartless as him. But Nick had always underestimated me. I tried to talk to him, but he went off on women, you in particular."

Allie blinked in surprise. *"Me?"*

"He said some women needed to be kept in their place and that you thought you were going to leave him and take his child. He had news for you. He laughed, saying how you'd been stealing small amounts of his money thinking he wouldn't notice but he was on to you. He'd given you a few days to think about what you were doing, but when he came back there were going to be big changes. He was going to take you in hand. He said, 'I'll kill her before I'll let her leave me.' Then he told me to get out of his way and took off up the trail."

So Nick hadn't been promising to change, she thought. He was going to change her when he got back. Allie felt sick to her stomach, imagining what Nick would have been like if he had ever returned home to find her packing to leave him.

"His parting shot was to yell back at me. 'You big fat ugly pig. Go home to your mommy because when I get back your butt is out of that guesthouse.' Then he laughed and disappeared into the trees."

"Oh, Sarah, I'm so sorry. Nick was horrible. If you tell the police all of this—and I will back you up—I'm sure they will—"

"Will what? Let me go? You can't be that naive. I'll go to prison."

Allie had a crazy thought that prison would be preferable to living with Mildred Taylor.

"No, Allie, there is another way. You are the only one who knows what I did."

"If you kill me, they'll eventually catch you and since this will be cold-blooded murder, you will never get out of prison. Don't throw your life away because of Nick."

"I'm going to make you a deal," Sarah said. "I will spare your daughter if you do what I say."

"What? You would hurt Natalie?" Allie's terror ramped up as she realized this was a woman who felt no remorse for killing her own brother. Nor would she feel any for killing her sister-in-law now. That she could even think of hurting Natalie...

"Do you know why I look like I do?" Sarah asked. "I made myself fat after my mother's first divorce when I was just a little older than Natalie." She stepped closer, making Allie take a step back. "My stepfather thought I was adorable and couldn't keep his hands off me. My other stepfathers were just as bad until I gained enough weight that, like my mother, they only had contempt for me."

Allie couldn't hold back the tears. "I'm so sorry. I had no idea."

"No one did. My mother knew, though." Her eyebrow

shot up. "That surprises you?" She laughed. "You really have no idea what *Mother Taylor* is capable of doing or why she dotes on her granddaughter. This latest husband is divorcing her, but there will be another husband, one who will think your little Natalie is adorable. Think about that. You do what I say and I will make sure what happened to me doesn't happen to Nat."

Allie was too stunned almost to breathe. What was Sarah saying?

"That's right, Mother Taylor *needs* Natalie," her sister-in-law said. "Now you can either take this gun and shoot yourself or I will shoot you. But if I have to do it, I will probably get caught as you say and go to prison. Imagine what will happen to Natalie without me here to protect her. Oh, and don't even think about turning the gun on me because trust me I will take you with me and Natalie will have a new grandpa, one who will adore her."

Allie couldn't bear the choice Sarah was demanding she make. "Natalie needs me," she pleaded as she looked at the .45 her sister-in-law held out to her.

"She needs me more. Just imagine the danger Natalie would have been in if I hadn't warned you."

"Don't you think I suspected something was wrong at that house? I didn't like Natalie going there. I didn't trust your family."

"With good reason as it turns out. You have good mothering instincts. I wonder what my life would have been like if I'd had a good mother?"

Allie's heart went out to her even though the woman was determined she would die tonight. "I'm so sorry, Sarah, but we don't have to do this. I won't tell the police about the dent in the pickup."

"You're too honest. Every time you saw me, we would both know." She shook her head. "One day you would have to clear your conscience. You know what would happen to me if I went to prison. No, this is the best way. Think of your daughter."

How could she think of anything else? That's when she heard the vehicle approaching.

Sarah got a strange look on her face as she cocked her head at the sound of the motor roaring up into the yard. "This has to end now," she said.

Allie couldn't imagine who had just driven up. Dana and the kids? She couldn't take the chance that someone else would walk into this.

She grabbed for the gun.

JACKSON HIT THE door running. He told himself he was going to look like a damned fool barging in like this. But all his instincts told him something was very wrong.

As he burst through the door, he saw Allie and Sarah. Then he saw the gun they were struggling over.

The sound of the report in the tiny cabin was deafening. Jackson jumped between them going for the gun that Sarah still gripped in her hands. The silence after the gunshot was shattered as Allie began to scream.

Jackson fought to get the gun out of Sarah's hands. She was stronger than she looked. Her eyes were wide. She smiled at him as she managed to pull the trigger a second time.

The second silence after the gunshot was much louder.

"Allie, are you hit?" Jackson cried as he wrenched the gun from Sarah's hand.

She looked at him, tears in her eyes, and shook her head.

For a moment all three of them stood there, then Sarah fell to her knees, Allie dropping to the floor with her, to take the woman in her arms.

"She killed herself," Allie said to Jackson. "She could have killed me, but she turned the gun on herself." Still holding Sarah, Allie began to cry.

Jackson pulled out the phone, tapped in 911 and asked for an ambulance and the marshal, but one look at Sarah and he also asked for the coroner.

Epilogue

Be careful who you marry—including the family you marry into. That had been Jackson's mother's advice when he'd married Juliet. He hadn't listened. But Allie's in-laws made Juliet's look like a dream family.

"If you want to file charges," Marshal Hud Savage was saying. "You can get your mother-in-law for trespassing, vandalism, criminal mischief…but as far as the gaslighting…"

"I don't want to file charges," Allie said. "The real harm she's done… Well, there isn't a law against it, at least not for Mildred. And like you said, no way to prove it. How is Mildred?"

After what Allie had told him, Jackson hoped the woman was going through her own private hell. She deserved much worse.

"She's shocked, devastated, but knowing Mildred, she'll bounce back," Hud said. "How are you doing?"

"I'm okay. I'm just glad it's over."

Jackson could see the weight of all this on her. He wanted to scoop her and Natalie up and take them far away from this mess. But he knew the timing was all wrong. Allie had to deal with this before she would be free of Nick and his family.

"I did talk to the psychic Belinda took you to," Hud said. "She claims she didn't know what was planned. Mildred had given her a recording of Nick's voice that had been digitally altered with Drew helping with any extra words that were needed. She alleges she was as shocked as anyone when Nick said what he did."

"I believe her," Allie said.

"As for who shot your horse up in the mountains…" Hud rubbed a hand over his face. "I've arrested Drew for that. I can't hold him for long without evidence, but he does own a .22 caliber rifle and he did have access to the ranch."

"So that whole family gets off scot-free?" Jackson demanded.

Hud raised a brow. "I wouldn't say scot-free. I'd love to throw the book at Mildred and Drew, believe me. But neither will see jail time I'm afraid. Their justice will have to come when they meet their maker." Hud shook his head and turned to Jackson. "I heard Austin is recovering fine."

"It was touch and go for a while, but he's tough. The doctor said he will be released from the hospital in a week or so, but he is looking at weeks if not months before he can go back to work. He might actually get up to Montana to see the Texas Boys Barbecue joint before the grand opening."

"I suppose you're headed back to Texas then?" Hud asked. "Dana said Ford will be starting kindergarten his year?"

Jackson nodded. "I suppose I need to get a few things sorted out fairly soon."

ALLIE COULDN'T FACE the cabin. She had nothing but bad memories there. So she'd been so relieved when Dana had insisted she and Natalie stay in one of the cabins. All but one of them was now free since Laramie had gone back to Texas, and Hayes and McKenzie had bought a ranch down the highway with a large house that they were remodeling. Only Jackson and Ford were still in their cabin, not that

Ford spent much time there since he was having so much fun with his cousins.

The same with Natalie. Allie hardly saw her over the next few days. She'd gotten through the funerals of Sarah and a second one for Nick. Mildred had tried to make her feel guilty about Sarah's death. But when Mildred started insisting that Natalie come stay with her, Allie had finally had to explain to her mother-in-law that she wouldn't be seeing Nat and why.

Of course Mildred denied everything, insisting Sarah had been a liar and blamed everything on her poor mother.

"We're done," Allie said. "No matter what I decide to do in the future, you're not going to be a part of my life or Natalie's."

"I'll take you to court, I'll…" Mildred had burst into tears. "How can you be so cruel to me? It's because you have all my Nickie's money now. I can't hold my head up in this canyon anymore, my husband is divorcing me, Drew is selling out and leaving… Where am I supposed to go?"

"I don't care as long as I never have to see you." Allie had walked away from her and hadn't looked back.

"I don't want Nick's insurance money," she'd told Dana the day she and Natalie had moved into one of the ranch cabins.

"Use just what you need and put the rest away for Natalie. Who knows what a good education will cost by the time Nat goes to college? Then put that family behind you."

But it was her own family that Allie was struggling to put behind her, she thought as she saw Megan drive up in the ranch yard. Megan had been calling her almost every day. She hadn't wanted to talk to her. She didn't want to now, but she knew she had to deal with it, no matter how painful it was.

Stepping out on the porch, she watched her half sister get out of the car. Natalie, who'd been playing with the kids, saw her aunt and ran to her. Allie watched Megan hug Natalie to her and felt a lump form in her throat.

"We can talk out here," she told Megan as Natalie went to join her friends.

Allie took a seat on the porch swing. Megan remained standing. Allie saw that she'd been crying.

"I used to ask about you when I was little," Megan said. "I'd seen photographs of you and you were so pretty." She let out a chuckle. "I was so jealous of your green eyes and your dimples. I remember asking Dad why I got brown eyes and no holes in my cheeks."

Allie said nothing, just letting her talk, but her heart ached as she listened.

"I always wanted to be you," Megan said. "Dad wouldn't talk about your mother, so that made me all the more curious about what had happened to her. When I found out… I was half afraid when I met you, but then you were so sweet. And Natalie—" she waved a hand through the air, her face splitting into a huge smile "—I fell in love with her the moment I saw her. But I guess I was looking for cracks in your sanity even before Nick was killed and Mildred began telling me things. I'm sorry. Can you ever forgive me?"

Allie had thought that what she couldn't do was ever trust Megan again, especially with Natalie. But as she looked at her stepsister, she knew she had to for Natalie's sake. She rose from the chair and stepped to her sister to pull her into her arms.

They both began to cry, hugging each other tightly. There was something to this family thing, Allie thought. They might not be related by blood, but Allie couldn't cut Megan out of their lives, no matter where the future led them.

ALLIE WATCHED HER sister with Natalie and the kids. Megan, at twenty-three, was still a kid herself, she thought as she watched her playing tag with them. She knew she'd made the right decision and felt good about it.

She felt freer than she had in years. She'd also made up with Belinda. They would never be as close, not after her friend had kept her relationship with Nick from her. But they would remain friends and Allie was glad of it.

Belinda said she wanted her to meet the man in her life. Maybe Allie would, since it seemed that this time the relationship was serious.

Drew had tried to talk to her at the funeral, but she'd told him what she'd told his mother. She never wanted to see either of them again and with both of them leaving the canyon, she probably never would.

Beyond that, she didn't know. She would sell the cabin, Nick's pickup, everything she owned and start over. She just didn't know where yet, she thought as she saw Jackson coming up the mountainside.

He took off his Stetson as he approached the steps to her cabin and looked up at her. "Allie," he said. "I was hoping we could talk."

She motioned him up onto the porch. He looked so bashful. She smiled at the sight of his handsome face. The cowboy had saved her more times than she could count. He'd coming riding in on his white horse like something out of a fairytale and stolen her heart like an old-time outlaw.

"What did you want to talk about?" she asked. He seemed as tongue tied as Ford had been when he'd met Natalie.

"I…I…" He swallowed. "I love you."

Her eyes filled with tears. Those were the three little words she had ached to hear. Her heart pounded as she stepped to him. "I love you, Jackson."

He let out a whoop and picking her up, spun her around. As he set her down, he was still laughing. "Run away with me?"

"Anywhere."

"Texas?"

"If that's where you want to go."

"Well, here is the problem. You know my father, Harlan? I think he might just make a better grandfather than he ever did a father. I want Ford to have that."

She smiled. "Montana?"

"This is where I was born. I guess it is calling back my whole family. Did I tell you that my mother's new husband, Franklin, owns some land in the state? They're going to be spending half the year here. Hayes and McKenzie bought a place up the road and Tag and Lily will be living close by, as well. Dana said we can stay on the ranch until we find a place. The only thing we have to do is make sure our kids are in school next month."

"Montana it is then."

"Wait a minute." He looked shy again as he dropped to one knee. She noticed he had on new jeans and a nice Western dress shirt. Reaching into his pocket, he pulled out a ring box. "You're going to think I'm nuts. I bought this the day Tag and I went to pick up his rings for the wedding. I saw it and I thought, 'It's the same color as Allie's eyes.' Damned if I knew what I was going to do with it. Until now." He took a breath and let it out. "Would you marry me, Allie?"

She stared down at the beautiful emerald-green engagement ring set between two sparkling diamonds and felt her eyes widen. "It's the most beautiful thing I have ever seen."

He laughed. "No, honey, that would be you," he said as he put the ring on her finger, then drew her close and kissed her. "I can't wait to tell the kids. I have a feeling Ford and Natalie are going to like living in Montana on their very own ranch, with their very own horses and lots of family around them."

Allie felt like pinching herself. She'd been through so much, but in the end she'd gotten something she'd never dreamed of, a loving man she could depend on and love with all her heart. For so long, she'd been afraid to hope that dreams could come true.

She smiled as Jackson took her hand and they went to tell the kids the news.

* * * * *

LET'S TALK
Romance

For exclusive extracts, competitions
and special offers, find us online:

f facebook.com/millsandboon

🐦 @MillsandBoon

📷 @MillsandBoonUK

Get in touch on 01413 063232

MILLS & BOON

THE HEART OF ROMANCE

A ROMANCE FOR EVERY READER

MODERN

Prepare to be swept off your feet by sophisticated, sexy and seductive heroes, in some of the world's most glamourous and romantic locations, where power and passion collide.

HISTORICAL

Escape with historical heroes from time gone by. Whether your passion is for wicked Regency Rakes, muscled Vikings or rugged Highlanders, awaken the romance of the past.

MEDICAL

Set your pulse racing with dedicated, delectable doctors in the high-pressure world of medicine, where emotions run high and passion, comfort and love are the best medicine.

True Love

Celebrate true love with tender stories of heartfelt romance, from the rush of falling in love to the joy a new baby can bring, and a focus on the emotional heart of a relationship.

Desire

Indulge in secrets and scandal, intense drama and plenty of sizzling hot action with powerful and passionate heroes who have it all: wealth, status, good looks…everything but the right woman.

HEROES

Experience all the excitement of a gripping thriller, with an intense romance at its heart. Resourceful, true-to-life women and strong, fearless men face danger and desire - a killer combination!

To see which titles are coming soon, please visit

millsandboon.co.uk/nextmonth

JOIN US ON SOCIAL MEDIA!

Stay up to date with our latest releases, author news and gossip, special offers and discounts, and all the behind-the-scenes action from Mills & Boon...

 @millsandboon

 @millsandboonuk

 facebook.com/millsandboon

 @millsandboonuk

It might just be true love...

GET YOUR ROMANCE FIX!

Get the latest romance news,
exclusive author interviews, story
extracts and much more!

MILLS & BOON

MODERN

Power and Passion

Prepare to be swept off your feet by sophisticated, sexy and seductive heroes, in some of the world's most glamourous and romantic locations, where power and passion collide.